Outstanding P

"Dang captures the surface cynicis[...] would adopt to mask the flameo[...] simmering rage against multiple [...] a class variety. . . . But Dang smartly pivots the nov[...] reflection of savior complexes and the ways we can be blinded by projected images rather than remaining true to ourselves."
—*New York Times Book Review*

"A thriller that offers a tongue-in-cheek take on the idea of 'Minnesota nice,' this story is about a girl who moves back to her Midwestern hometown and finds herself wrapped up in the murder of a local social media star." —*Entertainment Weekly*

"If you're a total true crime addict, Catherine Dang's debut novel will have you hooked *real* fast. It follows a nice girl turned cynical failure who mysteriously got kicked out of college her senior year. When she meddles in the cases of two missing girls, she ends up facing a devastating truth." —*Cosmopolitan*

"Complex characters, questionable choices, and conflicted feelings about who we are and the people we leave behind combine in a compelling thriller that will have you flipping pages to discover how it all fits together."
—Darby Kane, #1 internationally bestselling author of *Pretty Little Wife*

"Catherine Dang's darkly delicious debut, *Nice Girls*, is about the girlhood we never really leave behind, and what happens when we dare to confront our past demons. A pulsating mystery with a narrator you won't soon forget." —Laura Dave, #1 *New York Times* bestselling author of *The Last Thing He Told Me*

"A refreshingly original and intriguingly written mystery with a flawed yet relatable protagonist at its heart. *Nice Girls* drew me in and I found it hard to put down as the tension rose to its I-didn't-see-that-coming end. A highly recommended and brilliant read."
—Karen Hamilton, internationally bestselling author of *The Last Wife*

"Nice girls don't get kicked out of college in their senior year, they don't move back to the hometown they swore to escape from, and they definitely don't get involved in the disappearance of their childhood frenemy. But that's exactly what Mary does in this engrossing and sharp debut that true crime fans will devour faster than an episode of *My Favorite Murder*." —E! Online

"True crime fans, this one is for you." —PopSugar

"Catherine Dang is an asset to the woman's suspense genre. She layers the story so it builds and slowly lets the reader in. . . . It was hard to put down. . . . *Nice Girls* talks about anxiety, depression, and the importance of mental health. It points out racism in the police force and the media, and inequality in the way crimes are investigated. It brought up many important points while also being an exciting and mysterious read. I recommend this debut to lovers of *All the Missing Girls* and *Luckiest Girl Alive*." —*Mystery & Suspense Magazine*

"Mary isn't always a sympathetic narrator . . . adding to the edginess as readers are gripped by the story's provocative twists and turns. . . . Compelling." —*Booklist*

"Dang has created a thriller that is gripping both in the sense of its genre but also due to its cultural relevance. . . . Both woke and riveting, *Nice Girls* finds itself among the most haunting of mysteries, those that resonate with our current affairs, like Alyssa Cole's *When No One Is Watching* and Rumaan Alam's *Leave the World Behind*. Perfect for the millennial armchair detective, *Nice Girls* will satisfy your true crime addiction and intensify your desire for justice." —Paperback Paris

"Jessica Knoll's *Luckiest Girl Alive* meets *Cruel Summer* in this engaging thriller. . . . A page-turning, multifaceted mystery with emotional depth and a thrilling conclusion." —*School Library Journal*

"*Nice Girls* by Catherine Dang is a pulse-pounding thriller debut that resonates with current affairs, exploring the hungry, angry, and dark side of girlhood. . . . Add this novel to the list of thought-provoking thrillers that question what it means to matter in twenty-first-century America." —Criminal Element

"Missing girls, overlooked girls, smart girls, ambitious girls emerge in Catherine Dang's scintillating debut novel. . . . Expertly character-driven, *Nice Girls* shows Dang is a talent to watch." —Shelf Awareness

"The suspense builds as the uncomfortable secrets of the well-drawn and varied characters gradually emerge. Dang provides a full complement of thrills and suspense while addressing status inequities based on looks, race, and wealth. Readers will eagerly await her next." —*Publishers Weekly*

"Engaging, edgy, and packed with suspense, Dang's debut is sure to appeal to any fans of true crime." —Book Riot

Nice Girls

a novel

CATHERINE DANG

wm

WILLIAM MORROW

An Imprint of HarperCollinsPublishers

P.S.™ is a trademark of HarperCollins Publishers.

NICE GIRLS. Copyright © 2021 by Catherine Dang. All rights reserved. Printed in the United States of America. No part of this book may be used or reproduced in any manner whatsoever without written permission except in the case of brief quotations embodied in critical articles and reviews. For information, address HarperCollins Publishers, 195 Broadway, New York, NY 10007.

HarperCollins books may be purchased for educational, business, or sales promotional use. For information, please email the Special Markets Department at SPsales@harpercollins.com.

A hardcover edition of this book was published in 2021 by William Morrow, an imprint of HarperCollins Publishers.

FIRST WILLIAM MORROW PAPERBACK EDITION PUBLISHED 2022.

Library of Congress Cataloging-in-Publication Data has been applied for.

ISBN 978-0-06-302756-5

22 23 24 25 26 LSC 10 9 8 7 6 5 4 3 2 1

To Mom, Dad & Teresa

Behold the beast, for which I have turned back; Do thou protect me from her, famous Sage. For she doth make my veins and pulses tremble.

THE DIVINE COMEDY OF DANTE ALIGHIERI,
TRANSLATED BY HENRY WADSWORTH LONGFELLOW

1

My father was growing bald. All my life, his hair had been thick and black, darker than the pieces of charcoal that I'd use in elementary school art class. But as he hunched over his toolbox, I couldn't seem to look away from the bald spot. It was slightly bigger than a quarter.

He pulled out a screwdriver and stared back at my desk lying on the floor. It was nicer than anything the school had offered. Now its legs stood straight in the air like a dead animal's.

"You need me to help with anything?" I asked.

Dad said nothing. He began unscrewing a leg from one corner of the desk. When it was out, he chucked it on the floor and unscrewed another one.

He'd driven to the dorm in less than twenty-four hours. Coming from the Midwest, it was a seventeen-hour drive, nonstop. Dad had probably slept in the rental van during his breaks. And when he finally made it to my dorm, Dad had only handed me a box of black garbage bags. Told me to pack up everything as fast as I could. He had nothing to say to me in person—he'd barely even spoken over the phone.

My room was now mostly packed, except for my backpack, my suitcase, and the desk. The black garbage bags were piled in the moving cart. I used that to block the door—I didn't want one of the other RAs barging in.

Throughout the morning, I kept hearing voices out in the hallway. The walls in the dorm were paper thin. You could hear everything here—freshmen urging each other to take a shot in their rooms or a poor freshman girl awkwardly moaning as some boy jackhammered her. After three years, you got used to the noises. You blocked it all out like the wind.

But I kept hearing my name in every loud conversation or hushed tone, in the laughter as a pair of girls walked by.

I didn't know if that was better or worse than the text messages. I currently had forty-three of them, unopened, burning on my phone. They came from friends, acquaintances, coworkers, but nearly half of them had come from numbers that I didn't recognize. It was as if they all smelled blood and came for the carnage.

The texts were straightforward: You're a fucking bitch, Mary. You deserve worse.

And what could I say to that? I didn't disagree. It was my own hands that had reached out, my own fists that had flown. The damage that I'd done to her—only a bitch could do it. Even my own father was stunned.

He'd finished dismantling the desk. He left the legs on the floor and laid the desk on top of the moving cart. It looked like it would slip off any second. But Dad was already opening the door, gesturing to my suitcase, backpack, and desk legs.

"You carry those," he said, wheeling the cart past the door. I scooped up my things and took one last look at the room. For the past two years, I'd lived in a small off-white box with a window and a tiny nook of a closet. I didn't mind the faulty thermostat and the muggy heat in the winters. Over the summer, I'd kept my things here, even as I'd bounced far away from one sublet to another—a perk of being a resident adviser.

The room hadn't been glamorous, but it had been home enough for me.

Now it was over.

I followed Dad as he wheeled the cart down the hallway. He wasn't moving fast enough. I stared straight ahead as we passed by the dorm rooms, then the common area.

There was a group of freshmen sitting around the couches, their laptops and coffees spread out in front of them. Like sheep, they all looked over as soon as the cart squeaked by.

Carly was one of them.

And I felt it again—that burst of white-hot rage in my veins.

Carly smirked, then turned to whisper to a boy sitting next to her. And I saw it, my stomach flipping over.

She was wearing a thick pair of glasses today. Her red hair was piled up into a bun over her head, pulled away from her face. Her lips were swollen. There was a large, black bruise that covered the top of her right cheek, just below her eye.

The bruise shouldn't have been that dark—it hadn't been that dark yesterday.

As Dad and I waited for the elevator, we could hear loud laughter from the common room, where Carly and the others sat. My phone was vibrating now—more texts pouring in. The news was spreading throughout campus. I could feel it.

On our way to the front desk, Dad and I passed by more freshmen, all flocking in for lunch. They seemed to rush out of our way. Two freshman boys slipped past us, snickering, their arms raised in surrender, as if I were putting a gun to their heads.

I hated them all. At least now I could be fully honest about it. They were so bright-eyed and ambitious. Every freshman thought they were going to make something of themselves, like working for the UN, running a Fortune 500 company, or writing a future *New York Times* bestseller. Some of them were awfully cocky about it.

I wanted to tell them that it wasn't worth it. That it wouldn't happen. That the world didn't give a shit about most of us.

At the front desk, I handed my work polo and my badge over to Mohamed, the RA who lived two floors above me. He studied economics. I once gave him a joint that I'd confiscated from the women's bathroom. He once shared some of his Adderall with me during finals week. The two of us got along pretty well.

But as he worked on the computer, Mohamed didn't say much. He almost acted like I wasn't there.

"One final thing," he said. "I need your master key, Mary."

Mohamed was uneasy, his face taut. He looked at me as if horns had sprung out of my head. In reality, he might have been looking for a bruise or a scar on my face, some sign that I had gotten into a fight with a freshman girl. Yet somehow my face had been spared. Carly had terrible aim.

I felt my cheeks start to burn, that rush as I contemplated running out of the office, away from campus and Mohamed and Carly and everyone else who knew. Everyone who would know.

I fumbled in my backpack. Dug past the laptop and the wires and the wallet. I yanked out the master key to the dorm and chucked it on the desk. Mohamed stared at it.

"Well, that was the last thing," he said, unsmiling. "You can go."

The drive back home was slow. Soul-crushing. Dad and I were cramped together in the cargo van that he'd rented. We listened to whatever Dad could find on the radio—usually any station that played classic rock from the seventies and eighties.

We wove past large red oaks and birches. In the third week of October, their leaves were now fiery red and deep orange. They were a staple in Ithaca. Later, we reached miles of flat plains. The roads and highways started to blend together: impatient drivers speeding by, a stranded car, ugly soundproof barriers that flanked the sides of the road, little highway shrines for victims of roadside violence. Or it was more grass, endless stretches of grass. I offered to take over the driving, but Dad shook his head.

"You can barely keep your hands to yourself," he said dully.

I felt a lump in my throat. I knew Dad was angry, bitter, but I realized there was something else. He didn't trust me anymore. I hadn't kept my hands to myself. I hadn't behaved like he'd known me to be. I was a liability now.

Everyone else I'd left behind—my peers, my professors, my co-workers at the dorm, the boys I'd slept with—what did they now think of me? Was I unhinged to them, frightening? Were they even shocked? Maybe they'd sensed it all along. Maybe that was why few of them ever got close.

And the friends I'd made, the people I'd found throughout college—we'd connected so quickly, like kids in a sandbox. Our past three years together had flown by: crying over finals, only to laugh in hysterics at two in the morning; going out and getting drunk, or staying in and getting high; making out with guys right after puking at a party. We even shared alcohol that I'd confiscated from the freshmen. We'd been through all of it. In college, it was shared mayhem.

But this was a different mess that I'd gotten into. Something darker, more convoluted. I couldn't justify myself to anyone. Any friends I'd had at school were gone.

Any way you looked at the situation—I looked like a monster.

Around eight, Dad and I stopped for the night in Holiday City. Despite the cheery name, the place was run-down, mostly a cluster of seedy gas stations and motels that served the truck drivers who passed through. Dad booked us a motel room with double beds. We had dinner there, dry hamburgers and stale french fries. Dad watched the news, then fell asleep soon after.

I stayed up in my bed, looking at the new texts on my phone. I'd finally opened all of them, but I hadn't sent a single reply. I felt like I'd been ripped open.

I was "trash" to people. I was a "fucking bitch" for terrorizing a weak freshman. I needed to "eat shit." The news had spread—it always did on a college campus.

Next, they would pry for gossip. They would ask Mohamed about my move-out. They would discuss my time at the dorm, my behavior over the fall. Since I was no longer there, the only explanation would come from Carly.

Then they'd go online. They would search for me, deciphering my pictures, my comments, my posts for any hint of what I would do. Of what I was.

I knew this because I had done the same. I had watched other people burn before. Like the sorority girl from last year, who had been photographed making a Hitler salute at a G.I. Joes and Army Hoes party. By the time I saw the photos online, she'd already been suspended and stripped of her Fortune 500 internship. It was a mesmerizing train wreck. There was satisfaction in watching someone else suffer for their sins.

But now I was the one being watched. And if they prodded, I was afraid of what they would find.

I went through my social media—Facebook, Instagram, Twitter, Tinder. I deactivated everything and scrubbed myself off the Internet. After a cursory search, I no longer appeared online, no posts nor pictures. No one needed to know anything about me.

My reputation might've been over at school, but I would protect it everywhere else. After I was done, I turned off my phone. Placed it on the nightstand.

I gulped down a glass of water and my escitalopram and tried to fall asleep. Instead, I kept thinking about the lovely old buildings at school, the first hint of snow coming in the next few weeks, and the smell of coffee as I walked to class with a friend, musing about theses and grad school. Madison and I had talked of backpacking through Europe after graduation. But now I had no reason to go.

When I woke up the next day, my eyes were sticky with dried salt.

2

After an early breakfast, Dad and I hit the road. We drove past more small towns in the middle of nowhere, more empty hovels, more stretches of highways. Dad refused to let me drive, so I plugged in my earbuds and listened to podcasts on my phone.

I learned about the invention of the dishwasher, the chopstick, the radio, and even the history of the wheelie office chair. I listened as one podcaster complained about how one of her ex-boyfriends was, "like, definitely gay." By the time they broke up, he'd given her chlamydia. The other podcaster laughed.

At one point, I dozed off. When Dad tapped me on the shoulder, I was slumped against the passenger's-side window, a small stream of drool sliding down my chin. The car display said it was just a little past four in the afternoon.

"We're home," Dad said, his eyes glued to the road.

We'd already passed Liberty Lake. We were in the northwestern region of the city, now entering our subdivision of homes, the Castles of Cordoba. The green wooden sign at the entrance to the neighborhood had been replaced—we'd upgraded to a large block of stone that sat on the street divider, etched in dark medieval script.

Some of the homes in the area had been renovated, but they all looked the same: each house two stories high with sprawling yard space, a basement, and a deck. There were still the same broad fences that wrapped around each property, protecting the pools and the patio areas inside. Still the same elm, basswood, and pine trees that dotted the area.

A line of kids biked past us on the sidewalk—they were heading toward the park tucked away in the neighborhood. Their mother was behind them, holding a leash in one hand. Their dog, a fluffy Samoyed mix, watched us as we drove by. I nearly expected to see Mormon missionaries behind them, proselytizing two by two.

It seemed like nothing had changed in the past three years. The neighborhood was still bland and sleepy and steady, full of families with even steadier lives. The Castles of Cordoba was not as uppity as some of the other neighborhoods, but the stench of money was still here. We were middle class and unrepentant.

Dad circled us around the cul-de-sac, our house standing near the exit. Back in high school I'd always been anxious about backing out of the driveway—I imagined someone rear-ending me as they turned the corner.

To the right of our house, a little boy was dribbling a basketball in one hand, holding a candy ring in the other. As we pulled into the driveway the boy watched us, sucking on his candy. I looked him straight in the eyes, waiting for him to blink. But he raced away. When I'd last seen the neighbor's kid, he was waddling in diapers.

Dad had updated the house. He'd repaired the siding, so you could no longer see the hail damage that had accumulated over the years. The hedges in front had been trimmed, the lawn mowed. Dad had also replaced our entire asphalt driveway with white concrete. He had mentioned it over a year ago—one of the few times he'd sounded genuinely excited about something. It looked nice enough.

In an hour, Dad and I had moved everything from the cargo

van to my bedroom. We piled the black garbage bags and suitcase around my bed. They looked eerie against the pale purple walls. In the space next to the closet, Dad dumped the fragments of my desk and my chair.

I sat there on the bed, looking at the scattered pieces of my life.

"You'll get this sorted," said Dad as he shut the door.

Now that he'd successfully moved me back home, Dad was at ease again. He normally preferred our conversations to revolve around needs—what food I wanted to eat, where I wanted to go, how much money I had to "borrow." In return, I spared him details about my personal life.

Through the window, I could see some of the Halloween lights glowing orange down the street. A man was nailing a plastic skeleton to a tree. A mechanical witch stood hunched behind him, her broomstick pointing menacingly at the road. The neighborhood was quiet, sleepy. It felt like I'd never left. I was a sullen teenager again, hiding in my room from the rest of the world, daydreaming about better days.

Except instead of clinging onto those dreams, I had lost them completely.

An hour passed. Then another. I lay in bed, drifting in a half sleep. When it got dark, I finally shuffled downstairs. I passed by Dad's room. The door was closed, but I could hear the roar of college football on his TV.

On the kitchen table, he'd left a stack of job applications. Ten in total, for local coffee shops and restaurants. Customer service work, where the odds of running into a familiar face were high.

I was supposed to be a thousand miles away at school. But to be home in the middle of fall semester, working in retail? It looked suspicious. People would talk. They would know that something had happened, and they would gloat to themselves that my life had ended up as shitty as their own.

Worse, I would run into someone like Olivia Willand. She'd walk in with her blond hair and perfect smile, and she would take one look at me behind the counter and smirk. I would see the contempt in her eyes. She'd tell me that I hadn't changed at all, and I would know that she was right—I was the same fat, forgettable Mary from childhood.

My face was burning. I wanted to hide, not work.

But I could hear Dad's voice again over the phone, how gruff he got when I told him I'd been expelled. He'd been furious, crushed. I hadn't come home for years because of school—my one crowning achievement in life—and I'd screwed it up.

I made a cup of tea and looked through the applications, a knot in my stomach. The longer I stared at the forms, the more I stopped focusing on the words. I couldn't fill out a single one. A few days ago, I was reading Derrida for a thesis—now I could barely write my name.

The house was too quiet. I couldn't hear any sound outside my own thoughts. I preferred the silence—the whole family did, even when Mom had been alive. But the silence was deafening now.

I needed some air.

In the garage, I climbed into Mom's old black sedan. Dad rarely used it, but the car had a full tank of gas, ready to go. I felt the guilt gnaw at me as I backed out of the driveway.

At night, our corner of Liberty Lake looked like it always had—the same blocks of houses, parks, and retail areas where the housewives would congregate. I passed by the old elementary school and the sports field next to it, no children in sight.

Jittery, I started driving eastward to the lake. I had missed the water and the sprawling trees, the calm beaches, and the fresh smell of lake water in the air. It reminded me of Madison Nguyen.

When we needed a break in high school, Madison and I would go for long drives around the lake, listening to the radio. Sometimes we picked up pop and french fries. On the highway next to Liberty Lake, we would roll down the windows, letting the wind rough up our hair. Madison's long black hair would snake around the driver's seat as she cackled, the two of us screaming out the window. Venting our frustration, our fears, our fatigue.

Sometimes we parked by the lake. We stayed in the car, and we would sit there and watch the gray-green surface of the water and the people who walked in the sand. We liked to count all the plaid shirts we saw, the sports jerseys, and the odd deerskin jacket.

We talked about everything: school, grades, the latest boy that we liked. We ranted about the people around us and how we were destined for bigger, better things.

"I hate it," Madison once said. "They take one look and think, That's it, that's how you are."

I stayed silent in her car.

"After that one look, it's over. You don't get another shot," she murmured. "That's the worst part."

I knew what she meant. We were both thinking about it—that *look* that happened on the first day of junior high school. It defined us for years in Liberty Lake. The irony was that it started our friendship.

That day, as the other seventh graders flocked to each other, I hid in the corner of first-period math. My summer had been lonely, friendless. After one look, the other kids seemed to stay away.

Madison was the last to enter the classroom. By then, the seats had filled up except for the one near mine. She stopped short when she saw me. I saw the disdain in her eyes, and I felt my own.

It was a look of mutual recognition: two girls who realized that they were the least attractive people in the room. I was the fat one with a rash of pimples across her face and a silence around her that was neither cute nor charming. She was the gawky Asian one. Her hair was greasy, draped over a dull hoodie that swallowed her body.

Two utterly unappealing girls, now trapped at the same desk. Madison sighed as she sat down next to me.

I wanted to melt into my seat.

In class, we were given a comprehension quiz. A few minutes in, I heard the sound of pencil puncturing paper, scraping against desk. It was a loud, relentless sound.

Madison was flying through her quiz, already flipping to the next page. Other heads turned back, staring at her as she worked. She was showing off.

When class was over, I clambered up from my seat, but Madison suddenly held down my arm. She was surprisingly strong.

"You wanna borrow my hoodie?" she asked.

I shook my head. But Madison kept holding my arm, leaning in with a whisper: "Maybe you should check your seat."

I turned around, slowly squatting off the chair. There was a splash of blood at the center. I suddenly noticed the wetness between my legs.

I had just gotten my first period.

Madison handed me her hoodie. I stood up unsteadily, holding it around my waist to cover the back of my jeans. We said nothing to the teacher and walked out of the classroom.

"He can deal with it," she said, as if reading my thoughts. "But you should clean up before someone calls you 'Bloody Mary.'"

I grinned as we ducked into a bathroom.

We stuck together after that. We were not pretty or well liked, but we were smart. Unlike everyone else, we were discontent with the milieu around us. The other kids were lazy, complacent, mediocre. We were better. We would get out.

In college, we did just that—she went to the West Coast and I went east. We grew busy with college, but still texted frequently. Last summer, I'd even gone to L.A. to see her. Madison was thriving in California. She glowed now, claiming it was all the kale, kombucha, and vitamin D. Madison was set to graduate summa cum laude.

A few nights ago, she'd texted me about her ex.

I hadn't replied back. It was hard to care when I was getting kicked out of school.

And I had no plans of telling her. Everyone else hated me. Madison was the last friend I had left. Why would I risk losing her, too?

I found myself tearing up at a stoplight, my nose runny. I was winded. Everything had happened so quickly in the past few days. I was at school, and then I wasn't. I was a student, and then I wasn't. Now I was here, and I could barely comprehend why.

As the stoplight turned green, I saw a church steeple in the sky, only a few blocks away. The black steeple had a white cross at the top and a large bronze bell that rang twice a day.

Instead of going straight, I suddenly turned right—the car behind me honked angrily, but I kept turning. I was going to St. Rita's.

3

The parking lot at St. Rita's Catholic Church was empty. Sunday services were over for the day. After I shut off the engine, I stayed put, staring at the brick building. At night, it looked like a hulking beast in the dark.

I entered the church through a side entrance. The front office was vacant. I found myself hovering near an old computer.

Mom used to always hang around St. Rita's. She'd often volunteered for the parish. She helped care for the flower gardens and supervised the food and clothing drives, often taking me with her.

There was a revolving roster of elderly women who manned the front desk, and they adored Mom.

"Your hat is lovely," one of them told her. "I love the yellow knit. It looks good on you."

"I made it myself," she said cheerfully.

It was the same routine. The women always complimented Mom on her hats—everything from the baseball caps to the turbans to the head wraps. They would mention everything except her hair loss. I just stood in the background as the adults gawked at me.

"Mary's a real healthy girl," said one to my mother. "She's got a big appetite, doesn't she?"

"Big fan of the hot dish, this one," said another.

They laughed.

"Don't worry, Mary," said the first woman. She winked at me, as if we were sharing a secret. "It's what's on the inside that counts. You're very nice, just like your mother."

Mom was beaming, but I only felt embarrassed.

The door opened and startled me out of my thoughts. A priest hobbled in, leaning on a dark wooden cane. He wore a long black cassock, his face mottled and weather-beaten. He carried a cardboard box under one arm. I didn't recognize him.

"Uff da," he muttered as he set down the box. He turned to me. "Can I help you?"

"I—I wanted to do a quick confession."

The priest pulled out his watch, squinting at it.

"I probably should've set up an appointment—" I started. He waved the thought off.

"If you give me a few minutes to prepare, I can meet you in the confession room closest to the baptistery. Is that all right?"

I nodded, strangely relieved, and headed inside.

The confession room was white and sterile. A lamp glowed in one corner. There was a tissue box and a prayer book on the table beside me, but I kept my hands clasped together on the pew. A white curtain separated me from the priest. I could see his shadow as he struggled to lower himself onto his knees.

We performed the sign of the cross.

"You've had the sacrament of reconciliation before?" he asked.

"Yes, Father."

"And how long has it been since your last confession?"

"A couple of years, I think?"

Over a decade, to be precise. The last confession I could remember

had been fourteen years earlier. I was eight. It was my very first confession. I'd rattled off my sins face-to-face to a young priest. I told
him about how I'd yelled at Mom and Dad for always bringing me to
the hospital with them when I wanted to stay home; how Mom and I
had argued when she told me I'd have to miss Olivia's birthday party;
how I sometimes wished I'd had different parents.

After the prayers were said, the priest had assigned me five Hail
Marys to pray as penance. And I prayed those Hail Marys eagerly—
it was quick, painless. I felt like I'd been scrubbed clean from the
inside out.

I wanted that magic again. My soul dusted and cleaned.

There was an uncomfortable moment of silence.

"You're welcome to recount your sins whenever you're ready,"
said the priest.

My mind had been whirling and suddenly I had nothing. I closed
my eyes, lowered my forehead over my clasped hands. I saw only
darkness.

So much had accumulated over the years. So many sins. Was I
supposed to list them all, or only the most recent ones?

"I guess I haven't been the best daughter," I said lamely. During
college, I hadn't come home to celebrate Easter or Christmas with
Dad. I'd stayed at school or spent the holidays with friends. It was
better than sitting in front of the TV with him.

When Mom died, he didn't offer much consolation. At the hos-
pice, we spent an hour waiting for the undertaker to arrive. Mom
had passed away in her sleep.

Her corpse scared me. Her skin had yellowed, and it barely
seemed to cover her bones. Her cheeks were hollow, as if the air had
been sucked out of them. She was tiny.

Dad and I stood next to her, unmoving.

At eight years old, I was too shocked to cry. It seemed like somebody else had died in my mother's bed.

Still, Dad held the corpse's hand. I dared myself to touch her wrist
with my thumb. She was cold.

"Bye, Mom," I murmured. That was all I could say.

"She's in heaven, I think," Dad said.

But I could hear the doubt in his voice. He had no idea if it was true. He didn't know where her soul had gone after death. My father, the man who could fix anything and everything, had doubts.

It seemed like a betrayal. An adult was supposed to know things. They were supposed to reassure their kids. But when Mom died, Dad was at a loss, like me.

Later, we scattered half of Mom's ashes in the backyard. We gave the other half to my grandparents.

Without her, the house grew quieter. We went to church less and less. We barely spoke beyond the usual. Our lives had orbited around my mother—the warmth she'd brought—but without her, we drifted apart.

The one thing that connected us now was my schooling. I was good at it, and I only seemed to get better with each passing year. All the high marks and accolades and glowing report cards piled up. Dad was proud of me.

But now I couldn't even finish my degree. I'd lost it completely.

All I had was grief. It permeated me, filling me up like air. I'd already lost my mother. Now I'd lost my school, my friends, and the life that I'd built.

Instead, I was stuck back home with Dad in an empty house, groveling for a job that I didn't want. Wondering if I had any more to lose.

"I'm still listening," said the priest. I opened my eyes. Behind the curtain, his shadow was scratching its nose.

"I'm thinking, sorry," I stammered. "It's been a while."

I closed my eyes again, my stomach suddenly gurgling. I hadn't eaten since breakfast. The sound was unpleasant, but the sensation afterward was nice—the airiness in my belly. I could feel small again.

Back at Cornell I had been small. In college, I learned how to walk more, eat less. I skipped meals and snacked just enough to function. I preferred salads in the dining hall, and I subsisted on water and coffee. Calories were wasted on booze, not pizza. I learned to embrace my hunger. It kept me sharp, awake, and focused. It kept me thin, and it kept me pretty.

Not beautiful or gorgeous or hot, but *pretty*. It was a petite word compared to the others, not fiery or elegant or definite. But for so many people, it was enough. To be pretty was enough.

Clothing stores were kinder to you. Strangers opened the door for you. A teaching assistant raised a grade for you, provided that you were a bit flirty. And there was no better feeling than to catch the eyes of a handsome man and to see that brief flicker of lust there for you. That was all worth it.

The world was less forgiving of its fat, ugly women. I knew that from firsthand experience. At best, people ignored you. At worst, they insulted you. Your existence was barely tolerated. By virtue of your looks, you had nothing to offer. It didn't matter if you were smart, thoughtful, or funny—no one listened. No one cared.

I learned that the hard way through high school—quiet, fat Mary who kept her head down in her textbooks and dreaded the mandatory gym class. In college, I changed myself for the better. I had no intention of losing that.

Until Carly came along.

"I've been angry, Father," I said softly. "Not your regular kind of anger. But a deeper one."

I pictured Carly's long red hair that seemed to shine under the shitty dorm lights. It looked so soft that I wanted to run my fingers through it. Then I would yank it out until I'd ripped it off her skull.

I would never forget her smug expression and the way my life had crumbled right after. Carly had the next four years ahead of her at school—her future ahead of her—while I had been kicked home. All my hard work flushed down the drain.

Carly hadn't fought her way to be there. She hadn't gambled on loans to pay for tuition. She hadn't molded herself into someone better. No, Carly knew very little about struggle. She had no fear that she would lose it all in an instant.

Because she knew that if she failed, the world would save her, again and again and again.

I wanted vengeance, not forgiveness.

"I didn't act for the best, Father," I said. "I did something that I shouldn't have. It was my own fault."

But I didn't believe that—I was telling him what he wanted to hear.

The things I wanted to say, he wouldn't understand. He wouldn't know how crucial it was to be pretty—he would say I was being *vain*. He would tell me to forgive Carly, that forgiveness was a *strength,* that my grief was temporary, and that everything happened for a *reason.*

God is there in the end, he would say, his eyes glazing over. *Pray the rosary three times as penance.*

A trite penance for a trite sin.

But my sins were messy, and I wasn't sure that I wanted forgiveness. Maybe it would've been easier if I'd killed someone. Maybe then I would've sought true penance.

But in the confession room, I only felt heavy.

"And I'm sorry for being that way," I said softly.

Through the curtain, the priest nodded.

"Nothing else to add?"

"Nothing," I whispered.

4

The next morning, Dad slammed my door open. I woke up startled from the noise.

"You'll feel better if you work," he said, handing me the job applications. "Sallie Mae is waiting."

I was dazed as he left the room. Throughout my life, Dad had often griped about "freeloaders"—and now he thought I was becoming one.

But he was right. My student loans were due. I owed over twenty-five thousand dollars, interest not included. And since I had never gotten my degree, none of that money had paid for shit. I was in debt for nothing.

I buried my head in my hands.

An hour later, I finished scribbling through the applications. The idea of working in town, running into people—none of that appealed to me. But I needed the money more. I put on jeans and a sweater and hit the road.

As I passed the elementary school, I heard the wail of sirens. Two police cars appeared far behind me, their lights flashing red and blue. I quickly pulled over. The police sped by so quickly that the car shook.

A few minutes later, I saw two more speeding by. Madison used to joke about the secret meth labs in the suburbs. With the amount of police I'd seen, she might have been right.

I stopped first at Goodhue Groceries. It was a popular supermarket in Minnesota. People liked the organic groceries and the soothing green interior. Dad hated the pricing.

On a Monday morning, Goodhue Groceries was surprisingly busy. There were long lines of harried shoppers and only two open registers. The store was decorated for Halloween—fake cobwebs over the shelves, orange streamers, and displays of candy everywhere. I flagged down a tall teenager in a green polo. His face was pimply.

"Hi, where do I drop off a job application?"

The teenager stared at me, as if I'd spoken in Dutch. The badge on his shirt said his name was Ron.

I handed him the form.

"Can you just give this to your supervisor?"

Ron's ears glowed pink as he spoke into a walkie-talkie: "Hey, what am I supposed to do with a paper application? Can you handle this? I'm near checkout nine."

As we waited, Ron skimmed through the form. He looked like he was barely out of high school. The longer he looked at my information, the more uncomfortable I got.

"You interested in working for us?" asked a voice.

I wanted to shrivel up immediately—I recognized him. Even in a green polo shirt and a pair of khakis, he looked the same as ever: Dwayne Turner, former high school football star. Tall, handsome. He'd made history as the first Black prom king at our high school. That same year, he helped carry the Liberty Lake Patriots to the state football championship. Other than one semester of eleventh-grade AP English, we'd never interacted.

"What am I supposed to do with a paper application?" Ron asked. With Dwayne now towering over him, Ron had straightened up.

"Most people apply online," said Dwayne, addressing me. "But since you're here already, we can do a quick interview."

I could only nod.

We left Ron out on the floor and headed through a large back room. Down a hallway we passed by the break room and entered a small assistant manager's office. Dwayne sat down at the computer. On a lone shelf above the desk, there was a row of small trophies and medals. They were awards for wrestling and track-and-field—sports that Dwayne had played during the off-season. But his football memorabilia were nowhere to be found.

"I'll talk to my supervisor Jim about you," said Dwayne, typing on the computer. "With the holidays, we wanted to hire more people anyway."

"Okay."

"I'll just send him a quick reminder email about you . . . Mary," said Dwayne, glancing at the form. He paused, doing a double take. "Ivy League Mary?"

As stupid as it was, I found myself nodding.

Ivy League Mary, resident whiz kid and overachiever. Perennial honor roll student. AP scholar with distinction. Midwest Regionals Quiz Bowl champion. National Honor Society secretary. School newspaper copy desk chief. Drama club stagehand. Prominent community volunteer, total logged hours in twelfth grade: 372. ACT score: 35. SAT score: 2320. Liberty Lake's Academic Patriot Scholarship winner. Cumulative GPA: 4.09. High school class of 2012 salutatorian, second only to Madison.

Ivy League Mary, the girl with the big stomach and the baggy clothes and the quiet voice. Ivy League Mary, who had been ignored and called a teacher's pet during all of high school. Until college acceptances came in the spring of 2012.

Instead of attending a state school or a no-name private school, I had managed to ditch the entire Midwest for one of the most elite universities in the world: Cornell. I'd made it big.

I was featured in the local newspaper as "Liberty Lake's 'Ivy League Mary.'" The city had produced other Ivy League students before, but none of them had a dead mother like mine and an equally sad appearance to boot. I was a feel-good story, a memorable one. And the nickname stuck. During those last few months of high school, I *reveled* in it. Suddenly people were speaking to me at school, wishing me congratulations. Even when Olivia Willand and Sydney Bello had sniped that I'd gotten into the *easiest Ivy,* it didn't matter.

Ivy League Mary was going to do big things.

Ivy League Mary was never going to come back.

"Sorry if I sounded shocked," said Dwayne, his eyes on the screen. "I didn't recognize you."

"It's fine," I said. The last time anyone had seen me in town, I'd been about fifty pounds heavier.

"Not to be rude," he said gently, still typing away, "but aren't you supposed to be at school?"

I felt my face growing hot, the conversation heading somewhere that I didn't want to go.

"Why exactly is Ivy League Mary back home?"

"Why aren't you playing college football?" I said.

Dwayne's eyes snapped onto mine. We stared at each other blankly. I couldn't read him.

It was the middle of college football season. As Liberty Lake's star quarterback, Dwayne had signed on to play for one of the state schools. He was supposed to be living the high life at some sprawling university campus. Not working at his hometown grocery store.

My stomach was growing queasy.

Dwayne suddenly looked away, a large dimple appearing on one cheek. I realized he was grinning.

"I guess we all have things we don't want to talk about, Mary," he said lightly. "And I need to learn to shut the hell up sometimes."

"Maybe a little," I said, but I felt a small smile growing on my face.

"Anyways, you're free to go."

"I'm not getting the job then?"

"Nah, you're starting tomorrow," said Dwayne, winking.

At home, I ate half of a Caesar salad for brunch. I even added some croutons as a treat.

I sat in the kitchen, facing the glass doors to the deck. Outside, a squirrel was gliding across the fence. Then it sprang onto the orange branch of an elm tree. The weather was mild, the sky a nice cool blue.

It was my first solitary meal without a phone. I kept it shut off in my purse. I had no one to talk to, no social media to peruse, no people to text. Even the angry messages had slowed. I was disconnected from everyone.

But it was bearable. No one was here to hate me. Dad was bitter, but he left me alone. And if Dwayne hadn't recognized me at first, then maybe no one would. I could work in peace. I could pay off my loans. I could disappear.

Carly would have wanted me to suffer. But I would set things straight, day by day.

And her black eye would take weeks to heal.

As I washed the dishes, there was a low rumble outside—the garage door was opening. Dad was home early.

He barged in from the garage.

"I got a job," I said loudly.

Dad stopped, his face stricken. He hadn't heard me.

I shut off the water.

"What's wrong?" I asked.

He looked from me to the TV on the kitchen counter. He seemed unsure of what to do.

"What is it?"

"Your friend Olivia's gone missing."

5

We're not friends," I said quickly. "It's been years."

Dad shook his head, frowning.

"Why the hell does that matter?" he asked, snatching the remote off the table. "She's missing."

"How do you know?"

"Her dad told me. I was working on a house in their neighborhood, then Mr. Willand came by to talk to the homeowner."

My head was spinning.

Olivia Willand.

I hadn't seen her since high school. It was even longer since we'd spoken.

In college, I didn't dwell on the people back home. They were specks meant to be forgotten. Why think of the past when the present was better?

Still, the temptation was there.

Last summer in L.A., Madison and I were drunk one night at a taco joint. The conversation drifted back to high school. How are they, we wondered, those people we ditched? We found out through

Snapchat, Facebook, Twitter, Instagram. To our delight, a few people had gained weight. Another two girls had gotten knocked up. One boy had dropped out of the army. Somebody else had a mug shot.

But to our dismay, Olivia Willand was thriving. Beautiful, popular, successful Olivia. She had gotten big on social media—twelve thousand Instagram followers and counting. None of the extra weight like we'd hoped. There were endless sorority photos, vacation photos, cabin photos.

That was when Madison and I called it a night.

"It's supposed to be live," Dad said, flipping through each TV channel.

Then he stopped.

On screen, there was a male news anchor. Next to him, an old photo of Olivia.

It was her high school senior year portrait. She would have been eighteen. Olivia had posed in front of a white hydrangea bush, her blond hair coiffed in an updo. She wore a lacy white dress that matched the flower in her hands. She was stunning, but it was the eyes that caught you—there was a glint to them, a sharpness, as if she were taunting you. Olivia knew she stood out.

"Authorities are seeking help in the search for a missing Liberty Lake resident, Olivia Willand," said the news anchor. "The twenty-two-year-old college student was visiting her parents' home Sunday when she disappeared."

The screen cut to a pink-faced man with light blond hair. Olivia's father, Martin Willand, was trying to rub the tears off his face. He had a giant Rolex on his wrist.

"It was supposed to be a weekend visit," said Mr. Willand, his jowls quivering. "Everything was fine. Then yesterday afternoon she went biking to run some errands. Her mom and I were using the cars, so we thought nothing of it. But she never came back. She didn't answer her phone. We couldn't even track it."

The news anchor returned.

"Ms. Willand is a graduate of Liberty Lake High School and currently a fourth-year marketing major at the University of Minnesota. But to many people online, Willand is a rising social media star, with an Instagram following of around fifty thousand users. Willand is also said to have received a few sponsorships from clothing and beauty brands."

My jaw dropped.

Since last summer, Olivia had more than quadrupled her Instagram following. Fifty thousand was a modest number on the Internet—big celebrities had six-figure, seven-figure followings all the time. But for a girl living in the Midwest, fifty thousand was huge. She had gotten bigger than all of us.

The screen panned down her Instagram page as Mr. Willand's voice narrated: "Olivia is a star. Her disappearance hurts not only me and her mom but also her followers."

The news anchor returned.

"Willand was last seen biking Sunday afternoon around four P.M. She was wearing a black coat, a maroon college sweater, black leggings, and white tennis shoes. Any information on her whereabouts can be directed to the Liberty Lake Police Department at 911.

"Ms. Willand's father also requests additional help from the public."

The screen cut to Mr. Willand again.

"I'd like to thank the Liberty Lake police force for being so quick in their search efforts. They've been at it since last night, but we need more manpower. We are searching throughout Littlewood Park Reserve today from noon until eight P.M. Any additional volunteers can help canvass nearby areas. The police will provide instructions onsite."

The screen lingered on Mr. Willand, who took a deep breath. "And if you're listening, Olivia, please come home," he implored, his pink eyes staring directly at us. "We love you, honey!"

The news anchor spoke again, but Dad lowered the volume.

"You should change into something warm," he said. "I don't know how long we're gonna be out there."

I didn't move.

"Mary?"

"It's been less than twenty-four hours."

"She's *missing*."

I crossed my arms.

"Have they tried calling her friends?" I asked. "Maybe her parents are freaking out over nothing."

Dad stared at me.

"At school we had a girl who went 'missing' two years ago. It turned out she was just high at her new boyfriend's place. Everyone freaked out for no reason."

Dad said nothing.

"It's a true story," I added. "People went searching for her during finals. When they found her, the administration was pissed."

"Why don't you want to go?" Dad pressed.

"I don't think it's worth it," I said.

"You trying to avoid people?"

I shook my head.

"You grew up with her."

"Why does that matter?"

"Human decency, Mary."

"That's easy for you to say," I said loudly. "You don't know her like I did."

Dad said nothing and shook his head. He turned off the TV and grabbed two plastic bottles of water from the fridge. He scrounged through the kitchen for a bag of chips and a flashlight.

"I still see them at St. Rita's, you know," he murmured. "We talk."

I shrugged, as if it didn't bother me.

Finally, he left the kitchen.

"I got a job," I called out, but Dad had already slammed the door shut.

▶ ▶ ▶

I watched a livestream of the search. It was a mess of people around Littlewood Park Reserve. Hundreds of volunteers had shown up in the middle of the day. People in peacoats and down vests, others with dogs, who searched the woods near Olivia's home. Dad was among them.

I realized that was why I'd seen so many police earlier. They were everywhere. They blocked off the playground. They redirected traffic around the parking lots. The police brought canine units and even two helicopters that flew overhead.

Littlewood Park Reserve had over twenty-seven hundred acres of land. With dense trees, walking trails, and streams weaving through it, the reserve stretched nearly two miles. The area was easily big enough to conceal a body.

But I had faith in Olivia.

She'd lived next to the reserve all her life, only fifteen minutes away. As children, the two of us had biked there by ourselves. We had no parents to watch us. We knew the woods and the different trails. Olivia was many things, but she wasn't stupid.

After an hour of watching the livestream, I went outside. I took a walk to the park tucked away in our neighborhood. The weather was brisk. Kids scurried off a school bus.

At the park, I sat down on an empty swing. I turned on my cell phone.

I scrolled through Olivia's Instagram page. She had over four hundred photos. Her last picture had been posted three days ago. Olivia was sitting on a bench. She held a slice of cheese pizza in front of her, an oversized college sweatshirt draping off one shoulder.

You've stolen a pizza my heart! #ad #RaffaelesPizza, read the caption.

She made the photo look effortless. That was key. The perfect hair and makeup, the size zero figure, the impish smirk, and the caption were all carefully planned.

Most of her photos followed the same formula: gorgeous girl lives gorgeous life, like lounging on a beach in the Bahamas, cuddling a chow chow in Berlin, or posing with a baby kangaroo in Australia. Olivia had been all over the world since she was a teenager. She had more money, photos, and fame than most people could hope for. With fifty thousand followers, there was more to come.

I put the phone away and began to swing.

For a moment, I pictured myself with Dad and the volunteers. Given the situation, I would bump into Olivia's parents, an old classmate, a former teacher.

My presence posed too many questions.

How have you been, Mary?

Why aren't you in New York?

Aren't you supposed to be in school?

Even in a tragedy, people were nosy.

I had nothing to say. I was too raw.

Olivia just complicated things. She'd gone missing the night that I had come home. And I was home because of an act of violence at school . . .

The swing groaned as I kicked harder.

The incident with Carly, my arrival back home, my history with Olivia—all of that tainted me. I looked suspicious. And I'd had enough havoc in the last few days. I didn't need to be poked and prodded about Olivia's disappearance. I'd already had enough misery from her. I owed her nothing.

Dad thought I was callous, but I was just being smart.

He didn't know who she was.

A high school teacher once sent me to check on her. Olivia had been gone in the restroom for over twenty minutes. I found her kneeling in front of a toilet in a back stall. She was clutching her blond hair as she retched. It sounded like she was hissing.

"Are you okay?"

The noises stopped. Olivia turned around slowly, a stream of orange bile dripping down her mouth. She didn't respond, just stared at me coldly, her eyes wet and hard. We were the only two people in the bathroom.

With a piece of toilet paper, Olivia wiped her lips and walked back to class. She didn't bother flushing the toilet. Olivia later told the teacher that she'd been having a panic attack over our math test. The teacher gave her a redo.

My father, her parents, the police, the volunteers—none of them knew her.

Olivia did whatever she wanted. Nothing fazed her. Maybe she'd run off with a secret boyfriend. Maybe she was high on someone's couch. Maybe it was a publicity stunt.

With Olivia, it was hard to know.

6

A *fist smashed into my eye.*

I cried out, the world going black. Light suddenly drilled into my other eye, and I saw Carly above my left, her red hair covering her eyes. To my right, I saw Olivia's blond locks. I couldn't move at all—I was being pelted in the face, their fists raining down on me, smashing my skull, my teeth, my brain—

I woke up sweaty beneath the bedsheets. I was alone in my bedroom.

On my phone, I had one new text: Rot in hell you stupid bitch. There were no updates about Olivia, but her story had been shared on CNN, MSNBC, Fox. Barely a day, and she'd hit cable news.

Downstairs, Dad was already packing his lunch box. During the fall, his contracting schedule was hectic as clients pushed for their projects to be completed before the winter.

He'd come home early last night. He'd spent hours searching in the cold. Dad said most of the volunteers stayed as long as he did. They found a kid's broken sandal, beer bottles, a box of condoms, but nothing of interest. He went to bed right after dinner.

This morning, he had heavy bags under his eyes.

"Are you searching today?" I asked.

"Can't. I have to make up the work I missed yesterday."

I poured myself a cup of coffee.

Dad checked his phone, then took his thermos and lunch box.

"You joining the search?" he asked.

"No. I have training today."

"Good. Don't go searching by yourself," he said.

At the grocery store, I met with Jim, Dwayne's boss and the manager of Goodhue Groceries. Jim was thin, white-haired, and somewhere in his sixties. He carried a handkerchief in one pocket.

I was given a green polo shirt like Dwayne's and a walking tour of the store.

"Dwayne speaks highly of you," Jim said. He reached out and tapped a bag of chips as we passed by.

"Thanks," I said awkwardly.

"I trust him. Dwayne's the best assistant manager I have. Real sharp and reliable. Very popular with the ladies."

I couldn't help but smirk—I imagined a whole checkout line of women who swooned as Dwayne walked by.

"Real good guy," said Jim, growing quiet. "Shame about the championship, though."

"Wasn't that four years ago?"

"It still hurts, Mary. I lost money on that game," he said, sighing. "We never get anywhere in football, so that year was wild. Dwayne was a miracle. Maybe that was too much pressure for him, you know?"

I nodded.

Dwayne had carried the Patriots to the state football championship in our last year of high school. He even made the front page of the newspaper—there was a large picture of him in uniform, all muddied from the dirt and rain, triumphantly raising a fist to the sky. Dwayne Turner, number twenty-four, Liberty Lake's star quarterback and hometown hero.

We were the seventh-biggest city in Minnesota, with a good school system and a well-funded athletic program. In theory, we should've had a good football team—we had the money for it. But the city never got anywhere in sports. We won bronze medals and consolation prizes, but nothing *worthwhile*.

Until Dwayne Turner brought us to the state football championship.

Madison and I had watched the game together at her house: Liberty Lake versus North Hamilton. Neither of us gave a shit about sports, but even we could sense that history was being made. The Liberty Lake Patriots dominated the first quarter, scoring 6–0. The blue-and-red faces in the crowd went wild, screaming and chanting in the stands.

Then, in the second quarter, the Patriots crumbled. It was a drastic change. Suddenly they were fumbling, getting blitzed. But Dwayne had it the worst. He was slowing down, bulldozing right into North Hamilton's defense. The football slipped through his arms. The broadcast zoomed in on him as he got tackled over and over again, Liberty Lake's dreams getting crushed along with him.

When Madison's father called her from work, even he had been disappointed.

That day, the city lost its chance at football glory. But there was still hope that the star quarterback, number twenty-four, would make it professionally one day.

"Do you know why Dwayne's not playing college football?" I asked Jim.

He shrugged, leading us down the pet food aisle.

"You can ask him tomorrow. Poor kid's out sick today."

"He's sick?"

Jim nodded.

A toddler began to wail from a shopping cart. Jim beelined for the mother, leaving my question in the air.

▶ ▶ ▶

In one day, I learned how to use the cash register, how to properly bag items, and how to restock products. I memorized a rough layout of the store. The work was physical, monotonous. But it made the time pass. It was a luxury to not think—just do.

I ran into no one, except Ron. We finished our shifts at the same time. At the locker bank, Ron took out his backpack and an orange skateboard. They clashed against his green polo shirt. Ron was very pale.

He murmured something.

"What did you say?"

"How was your day?" he murmured louder.

"It was fine."

Ron nodded. He lingered, as if he had more to say, but then he quickly walked out.

I shut my locker and checked my phone. No texts from school, nor updates on Olivia.

In the hallway, I passed by Dwayne's office. He was the one person I wanted to see at work. We might have talked about Olivia. Back in high school, they'd been friends. They'd dated briefly. They still might have kept in touch.

It was strange to see an old friend on the news. But for Dwayne, it might have been surreal to see a close one.

At home, I sat in the living room and watched the search on TV. The police and volunteers were still canvassing Littlewood Park Reserve. This time, some of them wore neon safety vests.

Neither of Olivia's parents seemed to be in attendance. Instead, the reporters interviewed a few of the volunteers.

"Just a beautiful girl, beautiful family," said one woman. "And the weather's nice, so that's a sign that we have to keep looking."

"I pray it's not the lake," said another man.

The volunteers were earnest. The concern on each face, as if they had known Olivia personally, as if they thought she would have cared for them just the same. I pitied them.

When Dad came home, he sank into his armchair. He opened a beer.

"I ordered pho for dinner," he said.

"Sounds good."

"It should be ready when you get there."

I turned to look at him.

"Where'd you order?"

"Same as always."

I felt a flicker of panic.

"I can't go."

Dad frowned. The lines showed on his forehead.

"Quit being so dramatic, Mary. Just say hi to her dad and pick up the food."

"I can't, I haven't—"

Dad watched as I faltered.

"You haven't told her?"

"It's not the right time."

"The sooner you tell her, the less it'll hurt," he said. "If you run into her dad, she's gonna have questions. Might as well beat her to it."

When I shook my head, Dad raised his beer. He took a long, slow chug.

Instead of taking the highway by the lake, I cut through residential roads. Pho Village sat in the center of the city, in a humdrum strip mall. The area was surrounded by industrial buildings and gray woods. It was a dull place, centered on blue-collar work.

"You should move the restaurant, Ba," Madison had once complained. "You'd have more business in a nicer place."

"But rent is cheap here," he'd replied, shrugging.

Pho Village did well. Madison once told me that the best Vietnamese restaurants were the smallest and dinkiest ones, and that seemed to be true for Mr. Nguyen's. The restaurant had been ranked as one of Minnesota's top-five "Diamonds in the Rough." Local politicians had a fondness for taking pictures there.

It was crowded for the dinner rush. Servers had to squeeze their way between the tables.

At the cash register, Mr. Nguyen was handing out takeout orders. He took off his baseball cap and wiped his forehead. There was a cross on the wall behind him and a laughing gold Buddha on the counter. The Nguyens were Catholic, but Mr. Nguyen said his customers liked the gold décor. They tipped less without it.

After a minute, he waved me over.

"Hello. Dine in or takeout?"

"Takeout," I said.

"Under what name?"

He didn't seem to recognize me. I could have lied if the food wasn't under Dad's name.

"It's me—Mary," I said quickly. "Madison's friend?"

Mr. Nguyen blinked. Then he broke into a smile.

"Wow, is that you?" he asked. "You look so different. Tall and professional."

I grinned. It was his way of saying that I'd lost weight.

"What are you doing here?" he asked. "You're at Cornell, right?"

My mind went blank. I remembered Carly's red hair and the way my nails had dug into my palms, trying to puncture the skin. The way my hands had moved on their own.

"I'm home for a school project," I said casually, my heart pounding. "Doing research for my thesis."

"Exciting. What's it about?"

"It's very difficult to explain," I said quickly. "The research and the readings—it's very complicated."

Mr. Nguyen nodded, his gaze flashing to a patron who walked by.

"Well, it's good that you're back. Madison is finishing her senior year at school. I guess it works different in the Ivy League," he said, shrugging. "Go get your degree, Mary. Many people don't have the chance like you do."

His daughter had been one of those people. Yale was Madison's dream school.

Years ago, we'd sat at the library, waiting for college decisions. It was spring break. Instead of doing homework, we kept refreshing the online university portals. I stared mindlessly at the web page. In a blink, it changed. I burst out screaming. The people around us glared. Across from me, Madison's face fell.

At school, I was discreet—I told only a few teachers and acquaintances. I knew that was how news would spread the fastest. After that, the city newspaper interviewed me, then the district bulletin. But around Madison, I kept quiet. She was disinterested when I mentioned college, and she would suddenly get distracted by other things, other people. We never talked about Yale again.

I was one of the lucky few. It didn't matter what I did afterward— my university degree would impress most people. An Ivy League degree was gold.

And I'd lost it. Ripped right out of my hands. Four years of high school, three years of college, now gone. I had nothing but debt.

In the end, Ivy League Mary couldn't live up to her name.

"How's Madison been?" I croaked.

"She's happy. She'll probably stay in Los Angeles after graduation. You've seen her—she really likes the weather over there."

He sounded sad. With Madison gone in California, he was probably alone most of the time outside of the restaurant. His wife had left him years ago.

"Madison will be back for Christmas, though," said Mr. Nguyen. "Maybe you two can get together at our house."

"We will," I said. But I didn't plan on it. Madison was flying back to L.A. the day after Christmas. She'd purchased the flight last summer when I came to see her.

"When I'm home, I just lose momentum," she'd said. "There's

nothing for me in Liberty Lake. Maybe snow on Christmas. But that's it."

A server brought Mr. Nguyen two paper bags of orders.

"The chicken pho and pork eggrolls?" he asked, checking one of them.

"Yes, how much—"

Mr. Nguyen waved it off.

"Don't worry about it."

"Are you sure?"

"You need the energy for all that studying," he said. In one hand he gave me the food and in the other, a white flyer.

I nearly dropped the bag.

I was staring at Olivia's face.

"What's this?"

"Flyer for the missing girl," said Mr. Nguyen. He leaned in across the counter, his voice lowered. "The search committee gave me a stack of three hundred to give away. They said flyers work better than signs. But I don't want to upset the customers while they're eating."

The flyer showed Olivia's senior-year portrait from the news. Beneath it, in bold red letters, the flyer promised a reward for information on her disappearance.

"Twenty-five grand?" I balked.

"If I had that kind of money, I would spend it to find my kid, too. But you know how many people would lie for that?" said Mr. Nguyen, shaking his head.

I imagined Mr. Willand and his wife sitting at their dining room table, surrounded by dozens of rotary phones. The noise would be deafening as the phones rang, the crystals on the chandelier vibrating above them. At the center of the table, there would be a silver briefcase with a mountain of cash on top of it, a scene out of a movie.

But the reality was starker—the Willands were panicking. And Olivia was missing.

7

Dwayne was out sick for the next two days, so I continued to train with Jim. He stopped by once to check on my work, but after that, he simply liked to talk. He told me about his college baseball days and the scholarship he received. Before he could elaborate, he began to cough violently into his handkerchief.

To the customers, Jim was a sunny presence. He was flirty with the women, friendly with the men. But once in a while, he would say something unsettling.

"One day you're twenty, smoking on the beach with your frat brothers, and the next, you're rotting with lung cancer," Jim said to me.

I couldn't tell if he was serious, but Jim just laughed and walked away.

I ran into Ron more frequently. He often passed by my cash register or the shelves where I restocked. At lunch, he hovered near my seat as if he wanted to join. To my relief, he sat somewhere else.

I began to recognize some of my other coworkers—they were people I'd seen in high school, whose faces I remembered but whose names I'd never known. None of them had made it out of Liberty Lake. They were here, and they would never leave. The thought depressed me, and it repulsed me. I kept my distance. I preferred the loneliness over the shame.

At home, Dad and I watched the news over dinner, waiting for updates on Olivia's case. Each day the volunteers and the police returned to Littlewood Park Reserve. The crowds shrank, but there was talk of the FBI coming in.

The police reportedly received hundreds of tips about Olivia, but the twenty-five-thousand-dollar reward remained undisbursed. It seemed as if the investigation was going nowhere.

On Friday morning, I arrived early at work. The light was turned on in Dwayne's office. Through the glass, Jim was laughing, and he put a hand on Dwayne's shoulder.

I spent the morning with a box cart, restocking chips and snacks. At the candy display, I heard Dwayne's voice. Down the aisle, he was speaking to a tiny old woman. He handed her a bag of chocolates from the top shelf.

"I'm shocked, Pam. I thought you were prepared for Halloween. But the week before?"

"Oh, shush," she said, tapping his arm. "I'm busy."

"I'm sure you are," Dwayne teased.

The woman giggled. After she wheeled her cart away, Dwayne came over.

"How's it going, Ivy League?" he asked, grinning, a dimple in his cheek.

I straightened up.

"Things are going."

"How's your first week? Jim treating you okay?"

"It's been fine," I said, but I sounded insincere. "Still getting used to it. It's not like—"

"School?" Dwayne finished, his voice soft. "Yeah, you get used to that."

I found myself nodding. He understood. We were in the same predicament. Dwayne and I were meant to be somewhere else—him on the football field, me in Ithaca. We had tests to take and parties to attend and people to meet. Things to achieve. But here we were, two workers at a grocery store.

"Are you feeling better?" I asked.

"Yeah. I had a bout of the stomach flu. Not contagious anymore," he said, raising his hands.

I wrinkled my nose.

"Glad you're alive," I joked, then stopped. The words seemed to hang heavy in the air. I went back to stocking some veggie straws. Dwayne helped me.

"Olivia's gone missing," he said softly. "It's scary, isn't it?"

"It's strange. We knew her. And she was your friend, so that must be even scarier."

"We used to be friends," Dwayne said. He sounded wistful. "Olivia was cool. We used to party a lot in high school. But after graduation, we didn't talk as much, you know? We got busy. She had Instagram, college. I had . . . this." He gestured around him.

"That's kind of sad."

"It was a mutual thing," he said, shrugging. "Happens a lot. Your high school friends were people who just happened to be there. Not really people you liked that much."

I had a feeling that he was no longer talking about Olivia.

"But I would've gone looking for her if I could," he added. "Did you go?"

I shook my head.

"My dad said they had too many people," I said quickly. "I didn't want to get in the way."

"Makes sense. I just hope she's okay."

"You never know. Maybe she's on a beach out there," I said.

Dwayne gave me an odd look, but he nodded.

We fell quiet after that.

▶ ▶ ▶

After my shift, I collected my things from the locker bank. Dwayne joined me. He had a black duffel bag slung over one shoulder. He pulled out a crumpled receipt from his pants pocket and launched it over my head. Without turning, I heard it land in the trash behind me.

"Show-off."

"Come on, Mary, it's the weekend," said Dwayne, grinning. "Speaking of which—"

The door opened. Ron stalked in. He looked at Dwayne, then me, his eyes roving between us. Ron silently went to his locker and took out his skateboard, headphones, backpack, and coat. After an eternity, he left.

"I always get the feeling that Ron doesn't like me," Dwayne said after the door shut.

"I wish he'd feel that way about me."

Dwayne raised an eyebrow, but I shrugged. Ron made me uncomfortable. He hadn't done anything wrong—but there was a tension around him. He would hover, but he wouldn't speak. It bothered me.

"You have plans tonight?"

"No. Why? Are you joining the search?" I asked quickly.

Dwayne looked confused.

"I'm going later this weekend. I know the situation with Olivia looks serious, but I really can't tonight. It's my cousin's birthday party. I promised him we'd celebrate. You're welcome to join us," he added.

I perked up immediately.

"Where's the party?"

"My cousin's friend's place here in Liberty Lake. I can give you a ride."

I nodded. I hadn't relaxed once since I'd been home. Every day it was either work or despair.

But a party was better. I needed booze, music, dancing. I needed to lose myself in a crowd. I needed to be normal again, like every other twenty-two-year-old who went out. I could pretend at least.

Dwayne and I exchanged cell phone numbers. He said he'd pick me up at half past ten.

As he headed out, Dwayne called after me.

"Mary?"

"Yes?"

"My cousin Jayden and his friends can be a little messy."

I was grinning.

"I like messy."

At home, I took a nap. I showered, had dinner, and got ready. I dug through the trash bags for a decent outfit and settled on a pair of white jeans, a glittery top, and a leather jacket. I plastered on some makeup. I nearly gawked at myself in the mirror—somehow, even after everything, I looked good.

By the time I came downstairs, it was already half past ten.

"Are you going out tonight?" Dad asked from his armchair. He was watching a boxing match on TV and drinking a beer.

"Am I not allowed to go out?"

"You do whatever you want, Mary. I just want you to be careful," he said, his gaze on the TV. "Who are you going out with?"

"A friend."

"Which friend? Where you guys heading?"

He wanted me to elaborate, but I said nothing. I felt like I was six-teen again, a petulant teenager who needed supervision. It was as if he'd forgotten the past three years that I'd been away.

A beam of headlights flashed through the window. Dwayne was outside.

"Be safe," Dad called after me. I didn't respond.

Outside, there was a beat-up tan car in the driveway. Dwayne was holding the passenger door open. When he saw me, his eye-brows rose in surprise.

"I almost didn't recognize you," he said as I slipped in my seat.

"It's because I don't have the work polo," I said.

Dwayne grinned as he closed the door shut. He looked different, too—it was jarring to see him outside of his work uniform. He slipped into the driver's seat. There was a moment of silence as Dwayne started the car, the awkwardness creeping around us.

"You clean up good, Ivy League," he said suddenly. "You look nice."

"Thanks. You do, too," I said. I tried not to sound too pleased.

As Dwayne pulled out of the driveway, I expected to see Dad watching us through the window blinds. But there was nobody there.

I was jittery in the car, the reality sinking in—formerly fat Ivy League Mary was going to a party with the high school quarterback. It was a stupid, trivial thing. But it was something that high school Mary could never have imagined. She was pretty, she was cool, and she seemed successful. She was worth something.

If only they could've all seen.

Dwayne took us on the highway and turned on the radio. A breezy male DJ was speaking.

"—more prayers for Olivia Willand," he said. "Just a huge story right now in the state. A lot of people think that there was foul play involved. It's such a sad story. I look at her picture, and I'm like, this is horrifying to think—"

"Can you turn it off?" I asked.

"Yeah," Dwayne said. The car fell silent again. "It's kind of eerie."

I couldn't escape Olivia. She already had enough attention from the world and the people who looked for her, prayed for her. What was one less person? I'd dealt with Olivia my whole life. I wanted just one short night away from her, one fleeting moment.

We zipped past the lake, wide and never-ending, the water darker than the sky overhead. I could see the thickets of trees that surrounded the lake, blocking out the city lights from behind it.

But there was something that glowed out of the darkness. It was brighter than anything nearby—a giant beacon of light at the edge of the water. A tower of glass. It was beautiful, mesmerizing.

"Jayden's a bit of a character," Dwayne said softly. "A little blunt, but he's a good guy. He's grumpy about turning twenty-three, though."

"Why?"

"He's afraid of getting old."

A few minutes later, Dwayne took the exit ramp. We were past the lake, entering the southern division of the city. I recognized it from the fast food restaurants and run-down homes. I could feel the streets beneath us, uneven and potholed. We passed by a defunct auto shop, a furniture store with a shattered front window, and an empty shack of a restaurant.

I was nervous. Dad told me that decades ago, the area had been the city's landfill. Once Liberty Lake found another trash site, they decided to build over the area. The south side of the city became home to cheap one-story houses and quaint shops. It became a neighborhood of young midwestern families.

Then, a few decades later, came white flight. Minorities began to move in from other cities. Property values went down. It became a fast game of self-preservation. Anyone with money moved farther north in the city or left it altogether. Crime went up—petty robberies and domestic violence and shootings. People griped about the area like it was Compton or Newark, crime-infested areas plagued with gang violence. I didn't know if it was true or not, but I'd avoided the area my whole life.

In elementary school, the older kids taught us that the shit from the lake was filtered down to the south side of the city. We called it the Sewers of Liberty Lake.

As if reading my thoughts, Dwayne cleared his throat.

"It's not the nicest part of town, but it's not as bad as people say it is."

I could only nod, looking out the window.

Dwayne eventually turned onto a street of ramshackle homes. At the end of it, an apartment building loomed off to our right. It was ugly and covered in clapboard siding. The curtains were closed in most of the apartments. Dwayne parked us in a tight corner of the parking lot, next to the curb and a minivan with plastic over the driver's window.

"You ready, Ivy League?" Dwayne asked as he sent a quick text.

"Can't wait," I murmured.

As soon as we left the car, I smelled weed in the air. The scent was pungent and heavy, as if someone was smoking right behind us. I turned back and checked the parking lot, but there was no one there. I clutched my purse tighter, staying behind Dwayne as we hurried into the apartment building. The heavy bass of a song was pulsing through the floors above us.

Dwayne laughed after he checked his phone.

"Man, they sound hyped to see us," he said.

We followed the bright orange carpet up to the third floor. At the end of the hallway, loud music was pouring out from an apartment.

I followed Dwayne. My pulse seemed to climb with the music. I had to remind myself that we were fine. Everything I'd heard about the Sewers—the violence, the crime—was overblown. They were rumors meant to scare kids from the north side of the city, nothing else.

A door suddenly slammed open. The noise was hitting us at full blast, as if an earplug had been yanked out.

There was movement, the blur of a white T-shirt and dark skin stumbling out. It was a guy who reeled a few steps back. In the next moment, another blur shot out of the apartment: a guy with a bun made of dreadlocks. With one hand, he grabbed at the white shirt; with the other, he formed a fist, drawing it back like an arrow.

White Shirt screamed.

The second guy swung. His fist slammed into the other's cheek.

White Shirt staggered backward—for a moment, he seemed stunned.

Then he collapsed onto the orange carpet.

He didn't move.

8

Dwayne immediately rushed forward. But instead of helping White Shirt on the ground, he shoved the other guy away.

"Get off me," grunted Man Bun. He angrily shoved back until Dwayne let go.

"The fuck are you doing?" asked Dwayne. The two of them were the same height, staring each other down.

"Get your goody-two-shoes ass out of my face!"

"What the hell are you doing?"

A few people had rushed out of the apartment. They hovered over White Shirt, chattering in excitement.

"Damn, not much of a fight," someone murmured. Someone else laughed.

One guy bent down. He reached out and shook White Shirt's shoulder.

"Come on, man, wake up. Go home," he said. He shook White Shirt again with a little more force, but nothing happened. The alarm now seeped into his voice. "Hey, he's not waking up."

"Actually?" a girl asked.

"Yeah, he's actually not moving."

"Oh, shit. Is he——?"

I pulled out my cell phone, not knowing what else to do. It was a knee-jerk reaction.

The group sounded panicked. One of them raced back into the apartment.

Out of the corner of my eye, I saw a head poke out of a door nearby. It was an elderly woman in a fuzzy pink bathrobe. She took one look at the hallway and shook her head in disgust.

As she closed the door, the woman looked me over, the disapproval written all over her face.

I heard the click of a dead bolt.

In the background, Dwayne and Man Bun had calmed down slightly, their voices no longer audible. Dwayne turned back, looking perturbed at White Shirt.

The pungent mix of weed and booze slammed into me. The back of my head was throbbing from it all—the noise, the smells, the fight I'd just seen. I wanted to be somewhere dark and quiet, a glass of wine in one hand and a modest joint in the other. I was too sober for the present.

All of a sudden, there was a hush. Someone had shut off the music.

"Everyone get out!" shouted a girl's voice. "Cops are coming. They're on Hyde Street."

Everyone froze.

"Aw, shit," said the guy near White Shirt. He bolted for the stairs. Someone else booked it, too.

The apartment had suddenly been uncorked. People poured out. One burly guy shuffled out with a bong, smoke still rolling from the glass pipe. Another one came out with a tequila bottle tucked under his arm. Girls hobbled out with half-empty water bottles—they reminded me of the freshmen residents at school, who all thought they were so clever for sneaking vodka that way. As if reading my thoughts, the girls glared at me. I skirted out of the way as two other guys lumbered in my direction.

"Damn, she looks scared as hell," said one of them, looking me over. "Thinks we'll mug her or something."

"Bitch probably called the cops," said his friend, disgusted.

My face was burning as I squeezed the phone in my hand. I hadn't even set foot in the party, yet people could still sense who I was—the same fat, straitlaced girl from high school.

The hallway was now empty except for Dwayne, Man Bun, and a petite girl with long curly hair and hoop earrings. The girl squatted down next to the body.

"Hey, you don't have to touch him," said Man Bun.

But the girl reached out and checked the pulse on White Shirt's wrist. No one moved until she got back up.

"He's fine," she said. "Pulse is normal, he's breathing, no blood. Probably has a slight concussion."

Man Bun turned to Dwayne, relief on his face.

"Told you," he said. "I was right—"

"We need to leave, Jayden," said the girl.

"I know, but—"

"You guys can crash at my place," said Dwayne. "My birthday gift to you, man."

Jayden nodded. But even as the girl tugged at his arm, he squatted down next to White Shirt's body. He gently patted the guy's cheek.

"Just a cute little warning," muttered Jayden. "Don't try that shit again."

Dwayne made me drive. As soon as we stepped outside, he tossed me the keys. He told me that if I drove, we wouldn't be pulled over.

My hands were shaking on the wheel as I pulled us out of the parking lot, Dwayne in the passenger's seat while Jayden and the girl, Charice, hid in the back. Through the rearview mirror, I could see Jayden curled down in his seat, as if he were trying to melt off it. Charice held his hand, staring out the window.

No one said anything in the car. We were too afraid to even turn on the radio, as if the noise would jinx us. I could hear the wailing of sirens nearby in the neighborhood.

"Mary," said Dwayne calmly, "you're driving a little slow. Just drive like you usually do."

I gripped my shaking hands even tighter on the wheel and focused on the road, trying to keep the car centered in the lane. I pretended that we were on a roller coaster track. Blue and red lights flashed down the road. A cop car was driving toward us in the other lane. Heading for the apartment.

"No one fucking look," hissed Jayden.

I was driving thirty on a residential road, my foot straining against the accelerator. We were passing the police car now, its interior light glowing yellow. As we passed each other, I looked out my window at the cop car—I couldn't help it, with the adrenaline running through me. The officer was staring back through his open window, his face stony.

We were so close that I could see a light blond buzz cut and a pair of watery blue eyes.

I recognized that police officer. We'd grown up together, trapped in the same classes each year from childhood to adolescence. I still hated him.

Kevin Obermueller.

I shuddered when the police car disappeared behind us. Then another one sped by, followed by an ambulance. When their lights had all but disappeared in the distance, I felt myself gulping for air.

"Well, thank God," murmured Jayden.

"You got lucky tonight, baby," said Charice.

"If it's my damn birthday, I better be," said Jayden. He chuckled, his voice warm like coffee. It was jarring to know that he'd knocked someone out only a few minutes ago.

"You okay, Mary?" asked Dwayne. He lightly touched my arm. I nodded, but my hands still trembled at the wheel.

"Did you see the cop that passed by us?" I asked quietly.

"The dude in the first car?"

"It was Kevin Obermueller," I said, glancing over. I couldn't see Dwayne's face, but I could hear the pause that lingered between us.

Kevin had been Dwayne's friend in high school. They sat at the same lunch table and hung out in the mornings together. I saw them messing around all the time. Kevin was a wrestler, but he was an unofficial member of the football team. I remembered their prom pictures online—Dwayne and Kevin in the back of a limo, grinning in their tuxedos. Olivia had been there, too, as everyone posed for a group picture.

But from a distance, the two of them had seemed mismatched, unbalanced. Dwayne was the star athlete. Kevin was simply there. People preferred the handsome, gifted football player, but to reach him, you first had to deal with his unpleasant friend. It was always Kevin who clung onto Dwayne, never the other way around. He was part of a narrative that didn't need him.

"Yeah, Kevin's a cop now," said Dwayne.

"You've got a contact with the police, too?" asked Charice.

"Not exactly. We were in the same high school class together."

Dwayne said nothing else. He made it sound as if they barely knew each other.

"Oh, well," said Charice. "Maybe my brother knows him. They might have been cadets together or something."

"Why the hell do we care about any of this?" asked Jayden, snorting. "You guys get too excited for cops and shit. That Kevin dude was after us."

"He didn't stop us," said Dwayne.

"Only because the driver wasn't Black," said Jayden. "If she'd looked like any of us, we would've been stopped and our asses beat."

My face burned, the anger making me light-headed. I could hear the bitterness in Jayden's voice. He made it sound as if I had done something wrong. As if I had given someone a concussion.

But that wasn't me. I was merely a getaway driver who had been roped into the mess. I hadn't done anything wrong. Jayden could only blame himself. He was the one who'd started the fight. He was the one who lacked self-control. And whatever was coming, he deserved it. It was inevitable.

"I'm not interested in cops," said Jayden darkly. "I don't care if that cop is my cousin's friend or my girlfriend's brother. A pig still eats shit."

"Jayden," warned Charice, her voice low. Jayden didn't reply. "Don't you talk about my brother like that. Felix was the one who warned us about the cops coming. He saved us—you should be kissing his ass."

Jayden stayed silent.

"And you know who's been dealing with a male rape victim downtown? Felix. He's trying to fucking help people. What do you do?"

There was a long, uncomfortable silence. Then Jayden muttered something, and Charice sighed, whispering back.

"Where do you want me to go, Dwayne?" I asked.

I was aimlessly taking us northward, back to the safety of the northern suburbs, where life was quiet and uneventful. I was done with the Sewers.

"I live by the lake," said Dwayne, scrolling through his phone.

"Could you be a little more specific?" I asked, an edge in my voice.

"The Jewel of Liberty Lake. The big apartment building next to the lake."

He was talking about the tower of glass.

Dwayne turned in his seat, addressing Jayden in the back.

"I love you, man, but you need to keep a low profile. Someday this shit's gonna come back to bite you in the ass."

Jayden snorted.

"I believe in biblical justice. You hear me, Dwayne? I don't go around picking fights. But if someone tries me and I bust their shit . . . that's on them. They've got no one to blame but themselves."

I felt a shiver down my back. I remembered the flow of red hair, my hands reaching out on their own, that rush of anger burning in my veins.

I glanced up at the rearview mirror. Under a streetlight, I saw Jayden's eyes looking into mine.

9

At twelve stories high, the Jewel of Liberty Lake towered over the rest of the city. It was a high-end apartment complex. I'd seen those glossy buildings before in Los Angeles and New York City. They had sprung up everywhere, even near college campuses.

But against the backdrop of the lake and the suburban sprawl, the Jewel was a novelty. There was something unsettling about it—it was too bright, too pristine. The lights were nearly blinding. Through the large glass windows, I could see everything inside the apartments—the sleek countertops, flat-screen TVs, houseplants. I looked up and saw a couple lounging on their black leather couch.

It seemed wrong to see inside so clearly. Even the closed curtains couldn't block out the sliver of a kitchen, a bedroom. They were exposed to everyone, a diorama come to life.

I parked Dwayne's car in the parking garage. Inside, the lobby was empty, except for a security guard who stared at his phone.

"That dude didn't even look at us," said Jayden, laughing in the elevator.

"They're here for show," Dwayne said, shrugging. "Cheaper than cameras, I guess."

He lived on the eleventh floor. Unlike the previous apartment, the hallways at Dwayne's place were cool and monochrome. I felt a hush fall over us as we crept down the hallway, aware of the wealth that we passed.

We entered a small studio. Dwayne's bed was only a few feet away from his couch. But the apartment looked no different from the other units I'd seen. His place had the same appliances and sophisticated design, including the mounted flat-screen TV and a leather couch. Dwayne even had a shoe rack with several pairs of Jordans near the front door.

But I found myself drawn to the window. It sat at the end of Dwayne's studio. It covered one wall, reaching from floor to ceiling. Dwayne had a full view of the lake. During the day, he could see the lake water and the beaches below, all the boats and canoes that traveled down into the distant horizon. Dwayne had pushed his king-size bed against the window, so that each day the lake would be the first and final thing he saw. And the view would be breathtaking, rain, shine, or snow.

I didn't know how Dwayne could afford it. The Jewel of Liberty Lake was expensive, especially because of its prime spot on the lake. A white-collar worker would have blown a lot of money on it. I wasn't sure how Dwayne's grocery store salary could keep up.

Charice looked out the window while Jayden searched through the kitchen cabinets. Dwayne watched him warily.

"Do your neighbors ever spy on you?" asked Charice. She leaned against the window, trying to peer into the apartment window next door.

"The neighbor saw me butt naked once," said Dwayne, grinning. "Since then, he always keeps the blinds down."

"I guess no one paid to see your naked ass."

"You got any blow?" Jayden asked.

"Nah, man, I don't do that anymore."

Jayden snickered.

I stayed near the front door, looking up a car service online. I balked at the surge prices—the cheapest ride home was thirty-six dollars.

"You're allowed to sit down, you know," said Dwayne as he came over.

"I think I'm gonna Uber home," I said. "I've had too much excitement for one night."

"I thought you said you liked a mess."

"I said I liked messy things. Not be in the middle of a mess . . . And it's Jayden's birthday, right? You should celebrate with him."

"You can join us, Mary. I'm not stingy about my booze."

"I don't think Jayden wants me here," I said softly. Jayden had made it clear in the car. He distrusted me, and I was wary of him right back.

At the kitchen counter, Jayden suddenly whooped as he poured some booze into a coffee mug.

"Damn, I love cognac. Next thing you know, I'll be playing golf in Hawaii." He passed the coffee mug to Charice, who was giggling.

"Jayden's a bit of a character, but he's a good guy," said Dwayne.

"Of course you think he is—he's your cousin," I muttered. "But I just saw him knock someone out. It's fucked up."

"That guy tried to assault Charice," said Dwayne.

My stomach dropped.

"Jayden said Charice went into a bedroom to grab a box of tissues for someone, and the guy—Van—he tried to corner her in there. It's his apartment. Charice got out of there, and Jayden . . . you saw what he did." Dwayne paused. "In his defense, though, Jayden could've done worse."

My eyes drifted over to him. He was scrolling through his phone in the kitchen. Charice leaned into him, tightly holding on to his arm with both hands. Jayden was cackling at a loud video.

"Why not go to the police?" I asked.

"They wouldn't help us, Mary." Dwayne's voice was flat. "Even if they wanted to, the police are slow. Too much red tape. Charice knows that, and she doesn't want to bring her brother into it. But Jayden was pissed. No one hurts his girl. He took things into his own hands."

I pictured Van lying unconscious on the ground, monstrous and pathetic.

"And what if Van rats Jayden out?" I asked.

"He wouldn't do that. Van's a piece of shit, but he wouldn't do that. No one wants to be a snitch."

Jayden coughed loudly. His arms were stretched out in the air. "Can I have my birthday toast?" he heckled at us.

I caught Dwayne's eye. He smirked.

Time was slipping by. One second, I had rum and coke in my coffee mug, and in the next, I was sneaking sips of cognac. On the TV we were watching music videos of hits from our childhood—videos with pianos being played in the middle of nowhere, people crooning in the rain, dollar bills flying in the air, and clubs pulsing with life. Jayden and Charice were dancing and suddenly I was dancing, too, with Dwayne, my limbs unwinding, my brain melting.

And Charice and I were somehow at the sink, chugging water out of our mugs. She was telling me that she was nineteen and studying to be a nurse, but she was struggling in community college. She and Jayden had been dating for over two years. Charice avoided talking about the party entirely—I couldn't blame her. She only said that Jayden could be stressful sometimes.

"If he feels strongly about something, then he just does it," she said. "He doesn't really take it sitting down, you know?"

I nodded politely.

"That's why I want a family with him," she said dreamily, her eyes closed. "He'd always protect us, but he's a big teddy bear, too. I'd stay at home, and I'd raise the kids right, cook for them, make them read the Bible. And then I'd go to some PTA meetings just to piss off the hoity-toity soccer moms."

The two of us were cackling, breathless. The lights seemed to halo around Charice's hair. The night had been chaotic, but Charice's eyeliner had stayed pristine in two sharp lines. And I remembered that I'd had this conversation before at other parties with girls with nice eyeliner. This had been a normal occurrence once. It seemed like a lifetime ago.

"This eyeliner doesn't take skill, Mary," said Charice, waving off the compliment. "Like maybe ten percent skill. But most of the time? It's luck."

"Maybe it brought us good luck tonight," I said. I could hear Jayden's trash talk in the background. The two boys had started racing video game cars on the TV.

Charice glanced at Jayden.

"Yeah, Jayden pulled through for me. But I'm glad Felix saved everyone else," she said softly. "My brother's always been like that. Felix was a pushover when we were kids. He'd give me his cookie, his juice, the TV remote. But he was smarter than I was. And when he said he wanted to be a cop, no one stopped him. Felix was always going to go places, you know? Just one of those people." There was a tinge of sadness in her voice.

I thought of Olivia, Dwayne, me. In our separate ways, we were supposed to go places. Our trajectories had looked so clear, as if destiny had guided us. But who knew if it was destiny or sheer luck? Because in the next moment, our lives had veered off course. I was no longer in school. Dwayne no longer played football. Olivia had vanished.

But Carly would keep going. Carly, who was either drunk or asleep in Ithaca, her future unscathed. She would go places. That much was certain.

I teared up, blubbering through my words. Charice and I were drunk, and I didn't care if she cared about what I said. The words poured out—about school, Carly. I wanted to feel better, but instead I only grew tired.

Charice patted me on the back. She didn't know how else to help me, and I said that it was fine. At least she listened. At least the kitchen was warm.

And as fast as it started, we were all in front of the TV again, listening to Kendrick Lamar and Adele and Simon & Garfunkel, all of them crooning mournfully in the background, everyone quiet and worn out. Charice was crying now, whispering to Jayden. He wrapped his arms around her and kissed her on the forehead.

I was sleepy. I popped an escitalopram and felt the world starting to turn. I stumbled over to the warm bed by the window. The gray comforter was soft. I crawled under it and closed my eyes, only for a bit.

The apartment had gone dark, the lights all shut off. My eyes slowly adjusted, everything just out of focus. The window blinds had been lowered halfway down, but I could still see the slight ripples on the lake. I was freezing by the window. As I rolled away, I bumped into something firm.

It stirred, and I realized that I'd bumped into Dwayne. He turned around and faced me, his face sleepy.

"Hi," I whispered.

"Hi," he murmured.

"I'm cold."

"Do you want the whole blanket?" he asked, moving the comforter toward me.

I shook my head. Instead my hand reached out and grabbed his, the movement slow and gauzy, as if I were wading in water. I wrapped his arm around me. Moved closer. Neither of us spoke as I buried my face into his chest, the soft fabric of a pajama shirt against my cheek. I could feel his chest heave as he breathed, his other arm closing around me.

And I fell back asleep in Dwayne's arms, feeling warm and steady.

10

I woke up to the smell of coffee. I heard voices in the kitchen, the sound of a fridge door getting shut. The chill of the window burned into my forehead. I'd slept against it overnight, having extricated myself from Dwayne's arms. I was alone in the bed.

Far below me, Liberty Lake seemed to stretch on forever into the distance, an opaque mass of slate. Not a boat in sight, though the public docks were hidden somewhere to the west. Outside, the wind was blowing briskly, sending choppy waves along the water's surface. It sounded like a woman's voice moaning in the air, morose and heartbroken. Even the trees—fiery red and gold and orange—looked dull today under the clouds. Rain was coming. It was the type of weather where people locked themselves inside all day.

When I craned my neck, I could see the beachfront at the bottom of the window. Spots of neon blues, yellows, and pinks were moving across the sand—runners training in their weatherproof jackets.

I realized Jayden was standing a few feet away from the foot of the bed, sipping a mug of coffee. He was also looking outside. He'd untied his hair, his dreadlocks now hanging over his shoulders. He seemed mesmerized by the view.

I finally sat up in bed, smiling awkwardly as he glanced over.

"Morning," I said.

Jayden only nodded and turned back to the window.

Over in the kitchen area, Dwayne and Charice were cooking—stirring pancake mix, ripping open a package of bacon, and heating up a pan. Charice waved when they saw me.

There were blankets and pillows strewn about on the leather couch and on the floor beside it—presumably where Charice and Jayden had slept last night.

I realized they'd seen Dwayne and me in bed together. For some reason, I felt embarrassed, as if they could sense what a mismatch it was—Ivy League Mary hanging out with the school football star, forcing her way into his bed.

I wanted to hide under the sheets again.

"Sleep good?" Jayden asked as he came over.

"Yeah. I knocked out pretty quick last night."

"I know." Jayden handed me his mug, and for a second, I thought he was offering me a sip. But Jayden promptly sat down next to me, facing the window.

"I'm on your bed, man!" hollered Jayden to the kitchen. "You better be cool with that shit."

Dwayne laughed.

Jayden shifted, getting onto his knees now, pressing his forehead to the window. I tried to give him room, but I felt awkward, taking up space next to him.

"That's a damn pretty view," said Jayden, his eyes glued outside. "Even if it's all gray and shit."

"I agree."

Everyone in the city visited the lake, but it was rare to get a view of it from above. The water was vast, impenetrable, its surface rippling as the wind picked up. Liberty Lake was small compared to Lake Michigan, but it was big enough to be the lifeblood of our city.

"You know what my mama used to tell me about the lake?" Jayden asked softly, not looking at me.

"What did she tell you?"

"She told me the lake was full of shit. Poop water. 'You don't need that shit water up there. You don't need to go to that lake too much. It's full of shit, son.' I believed her for years until someone told me otherwise."

"That's horrible," I murmured, not knowing what else to say.

"She was trying to protect me, I guess. Doing a piss-poor job, though. And now Dwayne's living right here, next to the lake."

I swallowed, my mouth feeling dry all of a sudden. Over in the kitchen, Dwayne was frying some bacon, the hiss of oil filling up the room.

"'Your cousin Dwayne is so good at sports, Jayden. He's so polite. He gets good grades. He's a star. Why can't you do that?'" Jayden's voice got even quieter. "Even when Dwayne fucks up, he still gets to live next to the lake. Dude's on some lucky shit."

"How did Dwayne fuck up?" I whispered.

Jayden didn't say anything. His gaze was on the lake, but he was tilting his head now, craning to get a better look.

"What happened with Dwayne?" I pressed again.

But Jayden wasn't listening. He was staring intently down below.

"They found something," he said loudly.

"Who did, baby?" asked Charice from the kitchen.

"They found something in the lake. There's a group of people out there." Jayden hopped out of bed, wrapping himself in a blanket from the floor.

"We just made breakfast!"

But Jayden was already out the front door, heading down the hallway. I looked out the window again. There was a small cluster of people on the beachfront. Others were moving across the sand toward them.

"I guess we're joining him?" asked Dwayne, looking bewildered.

"I guess we are."

▶ ▶ ▶

The Jewel of Liberty Lake had a posh stone patio in the back. It also had an expensive grill, hot tub, bar, and furniture for its tenants to use. Dwayne, Charice, and I rushed past all of it, following Jayden's trail as he sped down a stone path that led to the lakefront. It was freezing outside, the cold air cutting at me beneath my leather jacket.

There was a small group of people gathered on the sand about a yard away from the water. They surrounded something unseen. Jayden disappeared into the crowd first, sidestepping past an older couple and a blond woman who held her pug.

We sped up, passing by two runners who stood separate from the others. One was hunched over, his hands on his knees, taking deep breaths. Suddenly he gagged onto the sand, long strands of saliva dripping out of his mouth. The other runner stood by, patting him on the back.

"Excuse us," Dwayne said politely to the older couple. They stepped aside without turning.

At first, I wasn't sure what we were looking at. It looked like a mottled tree branch in the sand, slightly damp from the water. It split off into individual nubs. At the other end, there were ragged pieces of bark where the branch had separated from the tree. A small chunk of white protruded past it, and it glowed brighter than the sand.

It was a human forearm.

The fingers were spread out, the palm facing downward as if splayed over a piano. Fish had already eaten away at chunks of the forearm, leaving wide gaps within the gray flesh. A pale bone stuck out from where the forearm had once been connected to the rest of the body. It had been completely severed.

I could feel the bile rising up my throat. I was almost afraid to swallow, as if I'd been contaminated.

I thought of Olivia's house, where I often played as a child. The two of us adored the neighbor's dog behind the white picket fence.

If you stepped on a rung, you could stick your hand over it and pet the dog's head. One time, Olivia whipped her arm back too quickly, and the picket sliced through the tender flesh of her underarm. The blood had flowed out in one long, steady stream. She bled so badly that she'd needed stitches.

Olivia hadn't run away.

She had been murdered here in Liberty Lake, her body ripped apart and dumped in the water.

The crowd was quiet, staring at the arm, almost too afraid to speak.

"Did anyone call the police?" Dwayne asked quietly.

"I called them a few minutes ago. They'll be here soon," said the pug owner.

A man nearby was taking pictures on his phone. Jayden noticed it, and he looked enraged.

"Damn, have some respect," said Jayden. The man looked up, livid, his mustache slightly curling.

"You should mind your own business," said the man.

"You're taking pictures of a murder scene."

"They're for the police and the news people. First Amendment rights. Again, mind your own business."

"You're being distasteful," said Jayden.

"*I'm* distasteful?" The man's lip curled as he gave Jayden a once-over, the contempt radiating off him.

Charice held on to Jayden's arm. She looked over at Dwayne for help. If Jayden picked a fight on the beach, there would be no winning outcome for him. And with the police coming, things would only go downhill.

Jayden sensed this, too, and he glared back down at the sand. The man kept taking photos.

"It's Olivia Willand, isn't it?" asked one of the runners.

"Most likely," said the man with the cell phone.

The older woman shook her head.

"That poor girl," she said. I realized that she was crying, her shoulders shaking in her husband's arms. "That beautiful girl. God rest her soul."

We were all thinking of the picture that had circulated on the news: Olivia in high school, radiant in her white dress. Young, beautiful, promising. Now hacked apart.

We hadn't been friends for about a decade now. It had been years since we'd spoken to each other. Even longer since we'd been amicable. But there was a history between us. A childhood. I had loved her once. Now she was gone.

And what had I done in the last few days?

I hadn't looked for her. I hadn't worried. I hadn't cared.

I had brushed her off like a fly.

All while she'd been murdered here in town.

I felt Dwayne's hand on my back as I wept.

By the time the police arrived at the beach, Dwayne was already driving us away from the Jewel. Jayden didn't want to stay for the police. He was anxious about it, no doubt thinking about the party and wondering if Van had, in fact, snitched.

After what we saw on the beach, none of us were hungry anymore. We left the food untouched back in Dwayne's apartment.

By the time he dropped me off at my house, I was already tired again, my eyes heavy and wet. I wanted to be alone in my room, curled under the sheets in a deep sleep.

"See you Monday," said Dwayne as I climbed out of the car.

"Bye, Mary." Charice was half waving out the window.

"Happy birthday, Jayden," I said.

He nodded glumly from the back seat, and then they left.

Inside the house, I went upstairs to my room and crawled into bed. I heard Dad come out of his room. He was hovering outside my door, straining to hear that I'd come home safely. Once the news spread in town, other parents would do the same.

I turned over in bed and closed my eyes.

▶ ▶ ▶

I could remember Olivia in sixth grade.

She was still blond and tiny. She wore a bright pink hoodie. The two of us sat in the back of our math class. We were taking a test. And I was doing well, jotting down answers that I'd long practiced.

The math teacher quietly slipped out of the room for a bathroom break.

Olivia was suddenly tapping me on the arm. She looked at me expectantly, her hand held out. I was supposed to pass her my test.

My stomach sank when I thought about the grade she would get. She had put in no effort. She hadn't studied. She had piggybacked off me, the chubby sixth grader who at least fucking tried.

But I passed over my test anyway. I watched her blond hair cover the paper as she copied my answers. My stomach sank, my fingers digging into my chewed pencil.

That was when I first realized that maybe I hated Olivia after all.

11

I slept on and off through most of Saturday. In my sleep, I kept seeing Olivia's arm in the sand, the pale bone sticking out, almost radiant against the rotted flesh.

When I woke up, I kept waiting for the image to go away, but it never did.

At around dinnertime, Dad finally opened my door.

"You need to eat, Mary," he said, turning on the light.

I crawled out of bed in the same clothes that I'd worn to the party.

In the kitchen, I watched as Dad piled a small helping of spaghetti onto a plate for me. I wasn't hungry at all. The two of us had dinner in silence, the kitchen TV airing a college football game in the background. I moved the spaghetti around my plate until I could leave.

Dad offered to make me tea, muttering that I needed to hydrate more if I was going to drink myself into a damn hangover. I said nothing and left him in the kitchen.

In the shower, I stood there, letting the water spill over me. My mind was blank. I couldn't process anything except for a single thought:

Olivia was dead.

The next morning, I heard Dad open the door to my room. He tried to stir me awake to go to Sunday Mass with him. But I kept my eyes shut tight, pretending to be asleep.

I stayed like that until he eventually gave up and left for church by himself. Then I was alone.

I grabbed the phone off my nightstand. Zero text messages.

I searched for Olivia's name on the Internet and the recent news about the arm. But I only found the same repeating articles—the announcement that rising social media star Olivia Willand had gone missing.

The police had yet to release the information. They'd inform the Willands first and extend their deepest sympathies. Knowing Mr. Willand, he would demand to know where the rest of Olivia's body lay. There would be red-and-white rescue boats skimming over the lake, searching for the rest of her. The police, maybe even the FBI, would scour the city.

Afterward, if anything else was found, Mr. Willand would demand to know who had killed her and why. And the police wouldn't have an answer. Olivia's killer would go free.

It was all so bleak.

I put my phone back on the nightstand and buried myself under the sheets.

For dinner, Dad made me join him again. He'd bought a fried chicken meal and made mashed potatoes. He tried to get me to eat, but my stomach was so empty that I felt bloated.

"Did anything happen at St. Rita's today?" I asked.

"Not much. We prayed for Olivia during the petitions."

"Were her parents there?"

Dad shook his head.

He turned on the kitchen TV, switching it to the news. The news anchors talked about a discrimination case between a lesbian couple and a bakery owner. Both parties were hoping that the matter would go to the Supreme Court. Then the anchors talked about a fire in North Hamilton.

I peeled off a piece of fried chicken skin and nibbled on it. One of the anchors paused, squinting at the screen.

"On Saturday morning," the anchor began, straight-faced, "a group of residents discovered an arm that washed up on the shore of Liberty Lake."

I sucked in my breath. The screen flashed to a pale-faced runner. It was the same one who had been gagging in the sand.

"Uh, so our running group was just passing through the area. For the lake views, you know?" said the runner, blinking rapidly. "But as we ran, I noticed something weird in the sand. I thought it was a stick or something. But up close, we couldn't believe it—it was a whole . . . arm."

"Police say the arm was found on the northwestern shoreline," continued the news anchor. "Since this morning, rescue boats have continued to drag the lake for further evidence. Investigators have already retrieved several other unspecified human remains from the lake. Though forensic evidence is still being processed, investigators believe that the remains belonged to nineteen-year-old DeMaria Jackson."

My head was spinning now, as if I had whiplash.

The news channel showed a picture of a pretty teenage girl. She had long black plaits and full eyebrows, and she was darker than Dwayne and Charice. In the photo, she was smiling on a cracked brown couch, her knees held tight to her chest.

"Ms. Jackson was reported missing from Liberty Lake this past July. Authorities believe that she was a runaway at the time. Ms. Jackson's family has declined to comment on the situation. We'll keep you updated as more details come in."

The news cut to a commercial.

My mouth was open from shock. When I looked at Dad, he only shook his head and went back to his food.

"Scary stuff," he said. "At least it's not Olivia."

Other people seemed to feel the same way.

When I looked up an online article about DeMaria Jackson, thirty-four people had already left comments. Most of them didn't mention her:

Loading my shotgun tonight. Keep your kids safe, folks.

Thoughts and prayers for Olivia Willand!!! She might be ok!!

LL police better be doing their goddamn jobs and keep the community safe

Hope the killer didn't get Olivia Willand

Olivia was still possibly alive. The forearm from the beach had belonged to someone else. There was no proof that Olivia had been kidnapped or killed.

But DeMaria Jackson's death was worrying. It was too much of a coincidence—two young women who disappeared from the same midwestern town in the span of a few months. Within a week of one going missing, the other had been found dead.

Only one comment seemed suspicious about it:

Two missing women in LL is NOT NORMAL—serial killer at play?

I felt a chill run through me.

Serial killer. The concept had always been there. It flickered in the news, in films, in books. A serial killer was as exotic as a suicide bomber—they lurked in other places, bringing pain to other people.

But not us. Here in Liberty Lake, we were too boring, too quiet to attract any attention. We were immune to danger.

But now the concept had taken flesh, a faceless being who slinked around the city. A real serial killer. There was somebody in Liberty Lake who had taken DeMaria Jackson. They'd hacked her apart and tossed her into a lake. They might have done worse to her. And Olivia was out there, possibly suffering the same fate.

I refreshed the article again. No updates. I was looking at the same photo of DeMaria. She looked like she could've been one of my freshmen residents at school—pretty and young enough to be dumb, reckless, free. She was young enough to do anything, really.

Now she was dead, her body mutilated. People couldn't even spare a few seconds to think about her, not even on her own news report. Her death seemed to matter to very few. There was something unbearably sad about it.

I skimmed through the article again. DeMaria had gone missing back in July. She was declared a runaway. Yet online, there was no previous mention of her anywhere. No news articles, no press releases. The police had kept her disappearance to themselves. I couldn't even find any of her social media accounts. She'd kept herself private online.

My eyes were straining in the dark. I closed them for a second, rubbing them gently. When I blinked the sparks from my eyes, I suddenly saw DeMaria's name at the bottom of my search results—someone had made a public Facebook post about her.

It was a short post written by a woman named Leticia Jackson. She claimed to be DeMaria's mother:

Liberty Lake police is full of shit!! My daughter did not run away, she was kidnapped and I'm tired of the news pulling this BS on my child. Police did not take action when I reported her missing this summer. Said she was a runaway, told me to wait. Now my daughter was butchered like some ANIMAL. And LL police has the nerve to slander her in death. There is no justice. DeMaria, I love you! You deserved better than this earth.

At the bottom of the post, Leticia Jackson had already received several replies. More comments appeared in quick succession:

Now don't blame the police, they're doing all they can

I'm sorry for your loss

i'm sorry, ma'am, but maybe this would have been avoided had your daughter not run away. If LL police say she ran away, then she probably did. Don't blame the people who try to help you

Play stupid games, win stupid prizes.

I closed my laptop.

There was something unsettling about all of it: the hacked body of DeMaria Jackson, her mother's claims about the police force, the response from the city. Now some people assumed that she'd brought her death on herself: *Play stupid games, win stupid prizes.*

But DeMaria was important. There was more to her story. Perhaps she wasn't a runaway. If Leticia Jackson was right, then her daughter had vanished in town just like Olivia had. And DeMaria had washed up a week after Olivia went missing.

Two disappearances, one town, a few months. There was a connection between the two of them—I could feel it. The coincidence was too great.

And to help Olivia, you needed to investigate DeMaria.

Leticia Jackson said that the police had failed to act for her daughter, but perhaps things had changed. With a confirmed death, there was more pressure. The police had to be moving in the right direction, and if they weren't, then they needed to be pushed.

And I only knew one person in the Liberty Lake police force.

Kevin Obermueller.

12

I was bleary-eyed at work on Monday. I kept glancing at the clocks on the walls, counting down the hours, then the minutes until lunch. At my cash register, I had a stream of customers who moved even slower.

"Smile, Mary! Start off the week on a positive note!" said Jim, passing by. The light was bouncing off his white hair. I smiled at him so hard that my cheeks hurt.

I saw Dwayne once during the morning. He came by to refill the change drawer with new rolled coins. Dwayne wasn't smiling much, either. He looked pale, as if he'd fallen sick.

"You okay, Ivy League?" he asked quietly, not looking at me.

"I've been better."

"Did you hear about what happened at the lake? Like after we left?"

"The arm wasn't Olivia's."

"Nope," said Dwayne glumly. "It was a whole other girl."

"It's horrible, and I hate to say it, but at least it wasn't—"

"Olivia?" Dwayne finished, shaking his head. "That's one hell of a silver lining."

He was thinking about it, too—the mottled, gray forearm in the sand. The way that the bone had been hacked off from the rest of the body. The fact that there was a murderer out there who'd killed DeMaria Jackson. The fact that Olivia was still unaccounted for. It haunted him, too.

After Dwayne left, I scanned more grocery items until it was finally lunch. As I sped past the customer service desk, I heard a woman's angry voice.

"Goddammit, how dare you people try to sell me spoiled food— you really think someone wouldn't notice?"

I recognized that voice—Mrs. Willand, Olivia's mother. Svelte, blond Mrs. Willand who looked like she'd just stepped out of yoga class. Beneath her jacket, she wore Lululemon leggings and bright orange tennis shoes. Her hair was in a bob cut. A stocky brunet man stood next to her, also in athletic wear. It wasn't her blond husband.

They both had their backs turned to me.

"I'm sorry, ma'am, for the inconvenience. But this Greek yogurt isn't spoiled," said Sara, the overweight woman who worked at the desk.

"This yogurt is expiring in less than a week," ranted Mrs. Willand, leaning on the counter. "This should've been off the shelves a week ago."

"I can give you a refund, ma'am—"

"Why do you people keep *testing* me," fumed Mrs. Willand, burying her head in her hands. "I'm so tired. I can't deal with this, too."

Her back was heaving—Mrs. Willand was crying now. The brunet man tenderly put a hand on her back. He said something to Sara, his voice low like gravel.

Sara nodded, her face growing pale. She suddenly saw me over Mrs. Willand's shoulder.

Sara's eyes looked desperate, begging for me to come help her. But I backed away, beelining for the back room.

"I think my mom's having an affair," Olivia once told me. We were ten or eleven years old, lying on a mess of blankets and pillows on the floor of Olivia's pink bedroom. It was a sleepover for the two of us.

"Do you have any proof?" I asked.

"Mom's pretty. Men all look at her," said Olivia, shrugging. "That stuff always happens in the movies."

I couldn't understand how one parent could cheat on the other. Mom had been dead for a couple of years, but I doubted that she would have cheated. She was too religious, too kind to do that. And Dad was too lazy—even too loyal—to hurt Mom. Our family preferred to keep things the way they were. We were steady.

"What about your dad?" I asked.

Olivia giggled, turning to me on her pillow.

"Ew, why would he cheat? Who wants to cheat with him?" she asked, wrinkling her nose. "That's why he uses the Internet. And the magazines at the cabin."

"That's—ew. Ew!"

The two of us cackled with laughter. Olivia was right—who would cheat with Mr. Willand? He had a pink face and a growing potbelly.

Soon after, Olivia fell asleep, her hair messy over her pillow and her mouth slightly agape.

I always knew that the Willands had a nicer house, nicer clothes, and more money than my family. The Willands were prettier than us, better liked. But that night I felt smug to know that at least my parents weren't bad people.

In the lunchroom, I sat at the far end of a table by myself. I nibbled through a salad, scrolling through the Internet on my phone.

It only took me a minute to find Kevin's Facebook account. His profile picture was basic—Kevin holding a gargantuan fish that he'd caught on a boat. His face was covered beneath a pair of sports sunglasses.

We were Facebook friends. I'd spent years hating him, only for us to add each other in high school. It happened all the time on the Internet—people despised each other in person, but online, they were happy enough to add one another as a "friend" or "follower." The numbers were more important. The clout was everything.

Kevin's Facebook listed his cell phone number. I spent a long time drafting a text message. I kept deleting, then rewriting the entire thing.

After most of my lunch break had passed, I sent it, my heart pounding: Hey Kevin! This is Mary from high school. I'm back in LL right now. Things seem really crazy here, and I was hoping to catch up with you. Would you want to grab coffee sometime?

I was embarrassed by my own text. It was too casual. There was no guarantee that Kevin would respond. For all he knew, I was still the same fat girl from high school. I wasn't worth the time or the attention.

We weren't even classmates anymore. We were strangers.

My phone vibrated—I'd gotten a text. It was a reply from Kevin: LOL, how'd you get my number?

I typed back quickly: I've had it since high school, I don't remember, haha.

As the seconds passed, I felt my pulse racing faster. I was groveling, he could sense it, he was ignoring me, I was humiliating myself—

My phone buzzed. Kevin had replied back: Let's get coffee then! I have Tuesdays off if you want to meet up tomorrow morning. Espresso Haus?

I let out a shaky breath, my fingers flying over the phone screen.

13

"You're sick?" Jim asked. He sounded incredulous over the phone. I cleared my throat again, sniffling through my morning allergies.

"I think I caught something at work yesterday," I said weakly. "But it's such short notice . . . I can still come into work today."

"No. No need, Mary," said Jim. "Take the next two days off. You get better, okay? We'll see where you're at on Thursday, okay?"

"Thanks, Jim," I murmured.

After I hung up, I went into the bathroom, primping myself for the day. Dad had already left for work. I moisturized my face and flossed. I drew on some eyeliner and curled my eyelashes. I spent another half hour digging through my trash bags for my best push-up bra.

By the time I finished zipping up my boots, it was already nine thirty. I would be late to the coffee shop, but I didn't care. I liked the idea of making Kevin wait. It was crucial that Ivy League Mary looked good.

As a teenager, I told myself I was above it all—beauty, clothes, makeup. They showed too much effort on a woman. They showed her vanity, her desperation, her lack of confidence. If she was secure in herself, then why did she care so much? Why try so hard?

Meanwhile, I hated myself. I was too big, and if I couldn't make my body smaller, I could certainly hide most of it.

But I knew better now. I understood why some girls at school dressed up for every class. Makeup was a placebo, clothes a disguise. They allowed us to embody our ideal selves. A pair of heels gave us height, a sense of power, authority. A red lip made us sexy. A French manicure made us classy.

If I was going to talk to Kevin Obermueller, I needed to be charming, persuasive. Kevin was simple—he loved blondes, but he also liked pretty women who looked fuckable. In his world, they were the only ones worth meeting.

As I parked in front of Espresso Haus, I saw Olivia's face again. It was a flyer plastered in the window. An old couple sat at a table beneath the sign.

Inside, the coffee shop was snug. The log cabin walls were decked with witchy decals and a chalkboard that showed the countdown until Halloween: *4 DAYS!!!* I scanned the rest of the shop. I couldn't find Kevin in any of the seats.

The asshole had stood me up.

"Mary!"

I turned around. Kevin peered out from behind a wooden pole, one hand languidly in the air. As I came over, he got up from his seat. His face was boxier up close, and it matched his bulky frame. He wore a fleece vest over a plaid button-up.

Kevin looked like a business student, not a cop. I wouldn't have recognized him. Back in high school, he wore exclusively hoodies and his letterman jacket.

"Sorry for being late, Kevin."

He reached out and hugged me warmly. I fought the urge to pull away.

We sat down across from each other. Kevin's eyes lingered on my face, as if he were trying to figure out where fat Mary ended and skinny Mary began. I was embarrassed.

"You gonna order anything?" he asked as he sipped his coffee.

"I don't really need the caffeine," I said. My legs were already shaky beneath the table.

"Friday night, I thought I was going crazy. Seeing Ivy League Mary around in the Sewers." Kevin smiled. "You were one of the last people I thought I'd run into down there."

"I was driving up from the south metro. Visiting a cousin," I said, my mind racing.

"Just be careful when you're down in the Sewers. That area's a shithole."

I nodded. I waited for Kevin to mention Dwayne or the other people in the car that night. But he just sipped his coffee. The conversation seemed to end there, the awkwardness seeping in.

"What are you doing here in town?" he asked.

"I'm doing some local research here for my thesis."

"Funny. I didn't know colleges let you do that."

"I got special permission for it," I said lamely. "And you . . . you're like an actual police officer now?"

"I am," said Kevin. He was beaming. "It's weird, isn't it? I never thought I'd be someone to join law enforcement."

"Why's it weird?"

"I mean, I was a huge shit when I was younger. Always being a dick to the other kids in our class. Picking on people for no reason."

"Kids are awful."

"But I was a different breed of it, Mary," he said, his voice growing quiet. His blue eyes reminded me of toilet bowl cleaner. "Look at what I did to you when we were younger."

I felt my face grow hot, the anger rising like steam.

We were eight years old and on a school field trip to a farm. It was autumn, only a few months after Mom had passed away. The class roamed inside of a large pen with baby goats. I followed a small brown one with Olivia.

Back then, Kevin was short—one of the smallest boys in our class. As we passed him, Olivia snatched the baseball cap off of his head. Kevin scrambled after her as Olivia waved it in the air. Her blond hair was flying around her face, her arms somewhat impeded by her bright pink jacket. Even then, she glowed. Kevin was laughing, too, his hands half reaching toward her. He wasn't putting much effort in the chase.

"Here, Mary!" said Olivia. She chucked the baseball cap toward me. I caught it, backing away.

Kevin turned, and as soon as he saw me, his face curled up in disgust. All of the mirth had gone from his eyes.

He approached me slowly. A baby goat fled out of the way. I was taller than him, but Kevin wasn't fazed at all.

"Don't touch my hat, you fat-ass!" he roared.

There came a flurry of fists—Kevin's fists smashing into my doughy stomach, one after the other. I felt the wind knocked out of me, my stomach squelching in pain, my lunch threatening to burst out of my body. I cried—I didn't know how else to react.

It finally stopped when a farmer grabbed Kevin and took him away to our teacher.

Olivia looked at me from the other side of the pen. She was unscathed. As the rest of the class watched, I threw Kevin's baseball cap on the ground. I stomped on it, over and over and over again.

For the rest of the week, Kevin was absent from school. I was relieved to not see him. There were rumors that he'd gotten kicked out. I prayed that he'd somehow died.

But then the next week, Kevin was back in class, as if nothing had happened. During our lunch break, I was pulled into a meeting with him. The two of us sat side by side as our teacher explained that Kevin had been punished and that this type of "violent event" would never happen again.

"Mary wants an apology from you, Kevin," said the teacher. "Right, Mary?"

She gave me a stern look. I knew the answer I was supposed to give. There was no other option.

So I nodded, and I watched as Kevin quickly apologized to my shoulder.

But I didn't want a damn apology. It wasn't good enough. I wanted to hit him right back with as much fury as he'd hit me. I wanted him to cry like I had, the wind knocked out of him. I wanted him in pain.

As the years passed, we continued to end up in the same class throughout elementary school, middle school, high school. Kevin had learned his lesson—he stayed far away from me. He pretended that I didn't exist. As for me, I carried a lifelong aversion toward him. Other people grew to like Kevin, long forgetting what he'd done to me. But I would always remember the rage in his eyes.

Now here we were, the two of us in our twenties, sitting across from each other at a coffee shop. We pretended like we were friends.

"Mary? I'm sorry about what I did to you when we were younger," Kevin repeated. His eyes looked watery.

I was speechless. I felt like the rest of the coffee shop was watching me. There was only one answer to give, and I didn't want to give it.

"Thanks, but I honestly don't even remember it that much," I croaked.

"I'm not trying to make you uncomfortable, Mary. I'm just trying to do the right thing nowadays. Life's too short," he said, looking into his coffee cup. "Especially with what's happened to Olivia."

My pulse began to race.

"Do you know what's going on? Have the search parties found anything?"

"Her case is supposed to be confidential. But there's not even anything to hide," Kevin said slowly. "We haven't found Olivia's bike or clothes. No footage of her anywhere in the city. We can't even find her cell phone. We only know that its last recorded location was at Littlewood Park Reserve."

The news had reported daily searches for Olivia. Though the crowds shrank, people still scoured the area. But if they hadn't found anything in over a week, then the situation was grim.

"I hope she's okay," I murmured.

He nodded, looking glum.

"After what happened with DeMaria Jackson . . . do you think Olivia might be connected to her in some way?" I asked.

Kevin blinked. He grinned slightly.

"The DeMaria Jackson news is crazy, isn't it? I can barely imagine a forty-pound trout in the lake, but body parts in it? It's wild."

"What else did they find?"

"The rescue boats picked up the girl's left and right legs after a three-hour sweep of the water. They were surprisingly intact, too. Like from thigh to foot."

My mouth dropped, the arm flashing in my head.

"Don't you think there's too much of a coincidence?" I stammered. "DeMaria's remains showed up shortly after Olivia disappeared, right? What if the killer was done with one girl and then moved on to the other? You know, like a . . . serial killer."

Kevin stared at me.

"That's a lot of what-ifs. We don't operate on assumptions, Mary."

He waited for me to continue, but I'd run out of things to say.

"It was just a theory I heard somewhere," I faltered.

"Well, whoever said that was an idiot," said Kevin, leaning back in his seat. "Just because two women disappear from the same town, it doesn't mean that there's a serial killer. Serial killers follow a pattern and an MO, and they have a preferred victim that they go after. They're not politically correct, Mary. They don't believe in being all-inclusive when they kill people."

My eyes followed a woman who sat down at a table nearby.

"DeMaria and Olivia are both young women from Liberty Lake," I said carefully. "They're the same demographic of victim."

"Hardly," said Kevin. He sounded as if he would start wagging his finger. "Aside from what you said, Olivia and DeMaria are almost complete opposites. One is white, the other's Black. One is upper middle class, the other is poor. You've got a college student versus high school dropout. They lived on opposite ends of the city. And Olivia doesn't have a criminal record. Meanwhile, DeMaria's criminal history is a fucking headache—a school suspension, a DWI."

My mind was racing. I was overwhelmed, trying to make sense of everything he'd said. Admittedly, Kevin had a point.

"So what happened to DeMaria Jackson then? Why was she cut up and dumped in the lake?"

"Some people in the force think it was gang violence that went haywire. And to clean up their mess, they just cut her up and threw the evidence away."

"She was in a gang?" I asked.

Kevin shrugged and downed the rest of his coffee.

"It's confidential," he finished. "Personally, I think DeMaria ran away from her family. Just couldn't deal with her life anymore, but then a gang caught up to her, you know? Everyone's gonna have a theory on the DeMaria girl's body. It's fascinating. But right now, I think she's a time suck. She's dead. It's sad, but it's over. Meanwhile, you've got Olivia still missing out there."

We both turned to look at the flyer in the window. Olivia had been a presence in both of our lives, but for Kevin, her disappearance was more personal. His friendship with her had lasted longer than mine—where Olivia and I had ended, she and Kevin began. The two of them were more similar than they knew.

In high school, they had looked so carefree together—Kevin, Dwayne, Olivia, their whole circle of friends. They looked as if things would always stay that way.

"Did you two still talk?" I asked quietly.

Kevin nodded, not looking at me.

"We talked less when she went away to college. She got busy with Instagram and sorority stuff. But whenever Olivia came back home for break, it was like nothing had changed. We still saw movies and hit up bars and everything. She was cool like that," he said wistfully. "I just wish this shit had never happened."

I didn't know what else to add to that. Kevin glanced at his watch.

"You okay if I cut this short, Mary? I have lunch plans downtown."

"That's fine," I said, relieved.

"I feel bad that we never even got to talk about you," he said, standing up. "I want to hear more about your research."

Despite the queasiness in my stomach, I smiled, the apples of my cheeks rising on their own.

"It's complicated," I said.

"Hopefully we can do this again then."

"Sounds good."

"And Mary?"

"Yeah?"

"Tell Dwayne I said hi," said Kevin, disappearing out the door.

14

I couldn't sleep.

Each time I started to drift off, I kept picturing a cold metal gurney. There was a head lying at one end. And below that, there was one full, rotted forearm and two long legs positioned in their proper spots.

But the limbs weren't attached. The rest of her body was missing: no abdomen, no other arm. There were only open spaces of air.

She was a dismembered doll come to life—her limbs yanked apart by something more brutal than a rough child. Eventually, her brown eyes would flutter open, widening in shock as she realized what had happened . . .

I shivered, tightening my comforter around me. I lay awake in bed, staring at the moonlight that filtered through the window blinds.

One night, a girl had been asleep in Liberty Lake. The next night, she was gone.

DeMaria Jackson was a mystery. There was nothing about her on the Internet, only a single Facebook post left by her mother. Kevin said that DeMaria had a criminal history and gang involvement.

None of it was related to Olivia.

Still, two disappearances in this city was unusual. It wasn't hard to imagine that someone had snatched one girl off the street. Then a few months later, they'd decided to snatch another. They both could have been at the wrong place at the wrong time.

No one even mentioned the circumstances around DeMaria's disappearance: where she'd last been seen, what she'd been doing. The police had one story, Leticia Jackson had another. Somewhere, the communication had failed between them. Leticia Jackson might have failed to mention a crucial lead, or the police could have misinterpreted her. With how upset she'd been in her post, it might have been the latter.

Someone else needed to talk to DeMaria's mother. I could even do it. It was easy enough to find her in the city.

I hadn't done much else for Olivia. I hadn't joined the search efforts. I'd tried to ignore all of it. Even now, as she was missing, I couldn't shake off the old bitterness. It seeped out of me like sweat. Olivia was possibly dead, and I still couldn't let it go.

I owed it to her to try.

I could talk to Leticia Jackson, pick up anything that the police had missed.

If it helped Olivia somehow, then I would have done my part.

If nothing came out of it, then I could be at peace. I had tried, I was done.

Olivia would have nothing over me.

Early the next morning, I crept downstairs to the kitchen. Dad was already there, sitting at the kitchen table, a cup of coffee and his cell phone in front of him. He cradled his head against his hands, his eyes covered, elbows on the table.

I turned back in the hallway, but the floor creaked.

"Morning," Dad called. "There's some extra coffee for you."

"Thanks."

As I passed by him, Dad straightened up in his seat. I poured my-self a cup and sat down across from him.

"Are you okay? You seem stressed."

Dad nodded as he rubbed his eyes.

"There's always things to be stressed about. But Jesus, there's been a lot of it lately . . ."

Dad wouldn't look at me, but I knew what he was thinking.

I was the stress. My expulsion from school, the incident with Carly, my student loans. The fact that I now made minimum wage at a grocery store, my education shat down the drain. He was worn out by all of it.

"Just a rough client. That's all," Dad muttered. He wouldn't look at me.

"What happened?"

"We're doing a roofing project, but the homeowner keeps check-ing up on the work we do. I don't mind if he does it once in a while, but he watches us every half hour now. He even scheduled to work from home for this project."

"He sounds anal," I said.

"That's giving him too much credit. Man acts like some mentally ill dipshit." He stopped then, realizing what he'd said. He remembered he was sitting across the table from one. "He's a . . . dumbass."

Dad didn't believe in coddling. He wanted people to pull them-selves up by their bootstraps. His philosophy was one of direct-ness: you faced your problem directly, and you either fixed it or you didn't. It was how he handled his contracting work. If there was hail damage on a rooftop, Dad and his crew would get to work and fix it, buffer it up for the next storm. If there was a fly in the house, Dad would kill it.

But I posed a different problem.

How the hell did you fix anxiety, depression? I'd carried them with me as a teenager. The overwhelming sense of dread at school, as if each test would determine the rest of my life. The way my body trembled before a presentation and the fatigue afterward, where I felt so tired I wanted to sleep. The days when I held all of it in, until I was ready to burst out screaming on the highway in Madison's car. The nights where I would eat until I felt better.

Dad said I was overdramatic. He thought I wasn't trying hard enough to deal with it.

Then after high school, when I was a thousand miles away, I finally sought medication. I wanted Ivy League Mary to be different in college. She would change for the better, both physically and mentally. The medication dulled the dread in my body. It kept the dark thoughts away. It made life manageable.

Dad didn't understand it, but he didn't complain, either. Medication didn't bother him, so long as it fixed the problem.

But the problem wasn't fully fixed. That much was clear. Carly had brought it all back. Afterward, when I told Dad that I'd gotten expelled, his voice had gotten low and gruff. His first words to me in response: "I thought you were on medication, Mary."

I was.

But the problem would always be with me, like a virus hidden in my cells. It was dormant until it wasn't. Then it would flare up.

I couldn't fix it like a roof.

The irony was that Dad had his own neuroses. He was a perfectionist running on anxiety. He couldn't handle it when people watched him work.

As a child, I noticed how Dad would only mow the lawn in the evenings. The sun would be setting, and I would be doing homework in my room with the lights turned on. All of a sudden, I would hear the lawn mower engine revving outside. Dad would cut the grass in the dark, a shadow moving in front of our house. In the mornings, there would be long strips of overgrown grass that he'd completely missed. But Dad didn't mind, so long as people didn't watch him. He didn't want someone to see him fail.

Like father, like daughter.

▶ ▶ ▶

I waited for Dad to leave for work. I sat alone in the living room, still in my pajamas. Dwayne had sent me a text: Hope you're feeling better today!

I replied back, a small smile on my face.

As soon as Dad's truck left the cul-de-sac, I went to the wooden TV cabinet. In the far-right shelf, Dad had dumped most of our miscellaneous books and pamphlets: an old cable TV guide, a thesaurus, an instruction manual for the Blu-ray player, personal finance guides.

And an old phone book for the City of Liberty Lake, dated a little over a decade ago.

I pulled it out, dust flying around me. I flipped through the pages, scanning the columns of names.

And then I found it near the bottom of a page. Leticia Jackson's address.

15

Mrs. Leticia Jackson lived down in the Sewers, about five minutes away from the apartment where I'd first met Jayden and Charice. After circling the neighborhood once, I pulled up to a small one-story house. It sat on a busy street, just a block away from a gas station and a strip mall. In the driveway, I could hear the roar as cars rushed past.

The front yard hadn't been raked in some time. There were plastic bags and pop cans littered about, probably blown in from the strip mall nearby. The asphalt in the driveway was cracked. Beneath a front window, there was a small white wooden cross planted in the grass.

Before I left the car, I double-checked Mrs. Jackson's address online, on the phone book's updated website. Then I checked my makeup in the rearview mirror—the concealer still smudged beneath my eyes and my lips covered with balm. I made sure the collar on my trench coat was straightened out, my school bag clasped shut.

I looked like Ivy League Mary again.

As soon as I reached the front door, I heard a heavy thud from inside the house. The door jerked slightly open. Through the crack, I saw an eye peer out at me.

"What do you want?" a voice asked. It was soft, barely more than a whisper.

"Hello," I squeaked, the script in my head vanishing. "I—I'm Maddie Johnson. I was wondering if I could—"

"No."

The door slammed shut.

I took a deep breath. With a shaky hand, I knocked.

"Hi, Mrs. Jackson. My name is Maddie Johnson, and I wanted to interview you about your daughter, DeMaria. It's for an Ivy League school newspaper. We're focused on social justice."

The door opened again, just a tiny crack.

"I—I saw the post you made online about DeMaria. You reported her missing, but the police said she was a runaway, right? I'm trying to tell your version of events since DeMaria's story was underreported."

The eye blinked, said nothing.

"And I'm sorry for your loss, Mrs. Jackson. My condolences to you and your family. What DeMaria went through was . . . awful," I faltered.

"It's not 'deh-*mare*-ee-ah,'" the voice said. "It's pronounced 'deh-*mahr*-ee-ah.' Get her name right."

"I—I'm sorry," I said, my stomach in my throat. The crack in the door widened.

"Come in."

"Thank you, Mrs.—"

"I prefer Leticia."

I followed Mrs. Jackson into the house, a shadow moving into the foyer. I made sure to close the door behind me. But when I tried to lock it, the thumb turn wouldn't move. It was jammed in place.

"Door doesn't lock," said Mrs. Jackson, her voice already in another room. "Just make sure the barricade is in place."

"Okay," I said. I looked around and saw the plank of wood that leaned against the wall nearby. It was a makeshift barricade, propped up by a small row of nails on each side of the door. I slid the plank of wood across the door, unsure if I'd done it correctly. It was flimsy protection, a thin piece of wood meant to protect an even bigger one.

The interior of Mrs. Jackson's house was dim with dark wooden walls. The carpeting was an old mustard yellow. Past the foyer, the living room and kitchen sat across from each other.

Not knowing what else to do, I wandered into the living room. I heard Mrs. Jackson shuffling around in the kitchen, but I couldn't catch a glimpse of her. The blinds were drawn over the lone window. I sat down on a large brown sofa propped against one wall, next to a TV set, a lamp, and a TV tray. Above the sofa, there hung a large painting of a forest. A gray playpen sat at the other end of the room.

"You can sit in this one." I looked up, startled.

Mrs. Jackson was larger and shorter than I expected. She was draped in a baggy sweatsuit, a pair of furry slippers on her feet. She made no sound as she moved, ghostlike, and set up a metal folding chair between the TV and the sofa. I immediately moved into the metal seat, taking the plastic water bottle that she handed me.

"Thank you, Mrs.—Leticia," I said, quickly. Mrs. Jackson said nothing and floated over to the couch across from me. Her short black hair was spiky. Mrs. Jackson looked like she was either in her late thirties or early forties.

I could feel the weight of her eyes as I struggled to pull my laptop and notebook out of my bag. My legs were jittering. I wanted small talk to fill the silence, but Mrs. Jackson only stared. She was subdued in person—there was none of the fervor that she'd showed online.

My laptop wouldn't turn on fast enough. I started flipping through my notebook, listening to the rustle as the pages turned. The silence grew heavier. My hands were shaky. Mrs. Jackson was becoming suspicious—I could feel it. The longer the silence dragged on, the more she'd sense that Maddie Johnson was not, in fact, a journalist. That Maddie Johnson needed to be kicked out, the police called on her.

And this would be a repeat of what happened with Carly, wouldn't it—me, the crazy bitch who got involved when she shouldn't have.

I heard a giggle. A baby waddled in from the hallway. He looked to be around a year old. He wore a light yellow onesie, a pacifier in hand. The boy's eyes were big and brown. He had dimples and a dopey smile on his face, the kind that babies seemed to have when they discovered something new. He waved to us with a flailing hand, giddy. I waved back as he wobbled over to Mrs. Jackson, his arms outstretched.

"What do you want, Demetrius?" she asked as she scooped him up. Demetrius let out a delighted squeal.

"Cute kid."

Mrs. Jackson didn't respond, placing the pacifier in Demetrius's mouth. He set to work sucking on it and turned to stare at me.

"Is he—?"

"Yes, he is," she said quietly.

The news had never mentioned anything about DeMaria Jackson's child. Kevin had alluded to it, something about DeMaria running away from her family, not being able to "deal" with them anymore. I thought he'd meant her mother, but Kevin was talking about the baby, Demetrius. Her son.

Demetrius seemed to lighten the mood. Mrs. Jackson had someone to occupy her, and I could focus again. I turned on the audio recorder on my laptop.

"I'm here interviewing Leticia Jackson, mother of DeMaria Jackson," I said out loud, checking that the recording app was on. "Leticia, if you could just give me your age, your occupation, and the city where you reside?"

Leticia leaned forward. "My name is Leticia Hughes Jackson. I am forty-one, and I live in south Liberty Lake. I work as a legal secretary."

Her voice was so soft that I could barely see the sound waves on the app.

"Uh, could you speak a little louder for the laptop?" I asked.

She nodded, bouncing Demetrius on one jittery knee.

"Can you tell me about the last time you saw DeMaria?"

Mrs. Jackson took a deep breath, her eyes fixed on the ground. She was scrambling through the details, carefully setting them all together.

"It was a Friday, July tenth. My day off. I was sitting in here, watching TV and taking care of Demetrius," said Mrs. Jackson, her eyes fixed on the ground. "DeMaria comes in to say goodbye to her baby boy . . . Always gives him a little kiss on his belly. She was wearing her black restaurant shoes, black pants, black shirt, and a white apron from the restaurant. Had her cell phone and wallet with her. Then she left. Someone gave her a ride."

I felt the hair rise on my neck.

"Did you see—"

"No," said Mrs. Jackson promptly, not looking up. "I didn't see the damn driver. And I didn't see the damn car. DeMaria often borrowed rides from other people. I never thought anything strange of it. I thought she was carpooling with someone to work."

I said nothing. DeMaria had potentially walked right into the killer's car. If Mrs. Jackson had only looked out the front window, then she could've seen the driver. She could've at least seen the car. And Mrs. Jackson had blown that chance.

"Where did she work?" I asked.

"A French restaurant called La Rue. I thought she was a server there."

"You thought?"

Mrs. Jackson sighed.

"DeMaria wasn't working there anymore. She quit her job months ago. That was all the manager told me. She was working someplace else, but I didn't know where."

I jotted the name of La Rue down in my notebook, circling it.

"And was she acting strange before she left?"

Mrs. Jackson shook her head.

"Did you two say anything to each other?"

"Nothing. DeMaria was in a hurry," said Mrs. Jackson. She moved Demetrius to her other knee. He leaned against her, his arms outstretched around the curve of her stomach.

"So the real reason why I'm here . . . I saw your Facebook post about the discovery of DeMaria's . . . body."

"Yes."

"You said the police didn't take you seriously when you reported that DeMaria was missing."

"The Liberty Lake police were useless," said Mrs. Jackson. Her voice was still soft, but there was an edge to it. "I called them the next morning when DeMaria didn't come home. The police told me something about how 'adults can go anywhere they please.' De-Maria was nineteen and young, so they thought she ran away. Just ditched her mama and her baby boy . . . Two days later I call them back. She's still not home. A police officer finally comes by, some pasty white cadet kid who looks like he's barely fifteen. He looks around her room for a few minutes and then leaves. No sign of foul play, so DeMaria can't possibly be missing. He was acting like I was a fool. The nerve of that little rat-faced shit."

I imagined Kevin. Not the guy I'd met at Espresso Haus, but the cop that I'd driven past in the Sewers. Kevin had a farmer's tan, and he looked older than his age. It was a different cop who'd stopped by, but more than likely, it was someone that Kevin knew.

"Leticia, you said that DeMaria had been kidnapped. What made you so convinced?"

"You'll think I'm stupid for saying this," murmured Mrs. Jackson.

"You're not stupid for worrying about your daughter."

"Well . . . I had a gut feeling that she'd been kidnapped," said Mrs. Jackson. My heart sank, and I could already hear Kevin's snort. "I mean, why would she leave? She had a son to take care of. This past year was so good for her after Demetrius was born. She'd been through some shit, but this little man right here was like sunshine.

"All of a sudden DeMaria was trying again, you know? All of a sudden, she was waking up early to take care of Demetrius. Talking to me again, going to church with me. A few months after Demetrius was born, she even went back to school for her GED. And then later she tells me, 'Mama, I'm gonna go to college. I'm gonna be a youth counselor for all the other kids out there who need help. And I'm gonna pay for it on my own, you don't need to worry.'"

"That's amazing," I said. Mrs. Jackson nodded, not looking at me.

"Demetrius was a miracle. He changed her life for the better," said Mrs. Jackson. Her voice was hoarse. She cleared her throat. "When DeMaria got pregnant, it seemed like the end of the world for us. She was moody, upset all the time. Picking nasty fights. She complained that her life was worth shit . . . not worth living.

"But the day after DeMaria gave birth, I knew something had happened to her. She was glowing in the hospital, all calm with Demetrius in her arms. I knew she'd be more responsible as a mother."

"I guess having a baby forces you to grow up," I said. Demetrius was falling asleep in his grandmother's arms.

"I guess it does," said Mrs. Jackson, sounding doubtful. "But DeMaria's change was drastic. She was like a different person. One day she was pregnant and suicidal, and the next? Like a saint. All calm. Even when her dumb ex-boyfriend came around, DeMaria ignored him. She had goals now, you know?"

"Is her ex still in the picture?"

Mrs. Jackson shook her head, scoffing.

"Her ex is a dumbass. Charles was arrested in a drug bust right after Demetrius was born. Caught dealing marijuana. That was when things ended. But the dumbass was still in prison when DeMaria disappeared," added Mrs. Jackson. "Otherwise, he would've been my first suspect."

I nodded. The angry ex seemed obvious—someone bitter over being rejected by his girlfriend and stressed over the responsibilities of a new child. But if the ex was locked away, then he couldn't have killed her.

Mrs. Jackson moved Demetrius off her lap, cradling him in her arms. She sat in the middle of the sofa, the orange light glowing softly to her right. Over her head, the painting showed a landscape of trees, all soft gray and brown, the sky a gentle white. There was no grass in the painting, only dark brown earth. It was a ghostly image, faint and surreal. Mrs. Jackson sat poised beneath it, as if she, too, were part of the painting. I realized that if Mrs. Jackson had never moved, she could have disappeared into the background. I wouldn't have noticed.

Our eyes met. I turned back to my notebook, skimming through my list of questions.

"You probably heard DeMaria was a hood rat," said Mrs. Jackson suddenly. "A troublemaker with a criminal record, right? Like she deserved it?"

I swallowed, unsure of what to say.

"DeMaria had a DWI. She was driving home drunk from some boy's party. That was two years ago. But this all started in high school," said Mrs. Jackson, staring at the ground. "I don't know what happened to her. She was a sweet kid. Very, very shy. And then high school . . . I didn't recognize her. One second, she'd be angry; the next, just so sad. Couldn't get out of bed sometimes. These weren't normal feelings, either. Everything was so extreme with her. Almost life or death.

"She was acting out, skipping school, sneaking out. She stopped trying anymore in class. But I thought she was with the wrong crowd, you know? The kids who smoke weed all day and think they're destined to be some famous rapper or entertainer. Half of them are delusional. The rest are desperate."

"That sounds . . . rough."

"Yeah. But there was one incident in her junior year." Mrs. Jackson's voice was growing faint, almost a whisper now. "Apparently, she'd been getting bullied by another girl. She never did anything about it. Until lunch that day. I don't know what happened, but DeMaria slapped her."

"What?"

"Just one slap," she murmured. "The administration stepped in immediately. She was suspended for two weeks."

I stiffened, the blood draining out of my face. I could picture the scene without much effort: the anger seething in her hand as she swung, the relief that she'd finally done it.

"Violence is not appropriate on a girl," murmured Mrs. Jackson, "but DeMaria was boiling."

I remembered the flash of red hair and my hands digging into Carly's scalp.

"Was DeMaria ever in a gang?" I croaked.

Mrs. Jackson frowned.

"My daughter was no gangbanger, if that's what you're implying. She had a rough streak, and she was stupid when she was young. But DeMaria was a good mother."

"I—I know that, Leticia, I was just—"

"And it's not bad enough that some monster takes my daughter and chops her up like some . . . meat." Mrs. Jackson practically spat out the word. "Then it's the news and the police. They didn't give a shit about DeMaria for three months. She was just some hood rat on the run to them. Now they find her body parts, and they still don't care. Just call her names."

"I'm sorry, Leticia," I said softly.

"I tried putting up signs for DeMaria, but almost no stores would let me. I kept calling the police. Every. Single. Damn. Day. And they stopped taking my calls. I tried telling the news about DeMaria, and they said thank you and never aired it. The only thing I could do was pray. And even that felt useless." Mrs. Jackson shook her head, her gaze on the floor. "I just wanted *something* for her. But nothing happened. And when that Olivia girl disappeared . . . I knew it was over for DeMaria."

Mrs. Jackson's shoulders were shaking. She sniffed, bending her head over the baby in her arms, her face hidden. I realized that she was crying.

Someone else might have reached out and hugged her. Or told her that things would be all right.

But I was glued to my seat, afraid to move. A hug was too personal. Anything I said would've felt like a lie—I didn't know if things would be all right. I didn't know if she would find closure over DeMaria's death.

"Is there a bathroom here?" I murmured.

"Down the hall, far right," said Mrs. Jackson, sniffing.

I left the living room and followed the mustard-yellow carpet to the bathroom at the end of the hallway. The bathroom was small, the tiles a sterile yellow. I grabbed a wad of toilet paper and rushed back to the living room. Mrs. Jackson buried her face in it.

"Is there anything else you need, Leticia?"

"I'm fine," she said, her voice muffled. "I'm just . . . tired. I need to wrap this up."

"I get it," I said. I felt tired, too, drained from the interview. "But before I go, could I just do one more thing?"

16

DeMaria's bedroom was messy. It was as if she'd disappeared yesterday in a rush, her clothes strewn about on the floor and plastic water bottles littered on the desk. Her bed was unmade, the sheets crumpled in a ball. In her closet, a plastic dresser peeked out beneath a pile of shirts and a bikini top.

Mrs. Jackson hadn't cleaned up DeMaria's room since July. She said she'd been afraid of contaminating the evidence. But aside from the policeman who'd stopped by, no one else came.

"The police are sending an investigator later this week, so this is the only time to look around," said Mrs. Jackson before she left.

For a while, I stayed near the door. I was unsure of where to start.

The wall next to DeMaria's bed was covered in posters and pictures. She had magazine cutouts of celebrities and musicians. Other cutouts showed glamorous destinations: a tropical beach, a desert, a quaint café in Paris. And she had a corkboard with photos pinned to it. They showed different occasions throughout her life: an elementary school Halloween party in one photo; a group of friends posing in a restaurant booth; DeMaria sitting in a delivery room with a baby in her arms.

There was one family picture taken in the Jacksons' living room. Mrs. Jackson looked younger in the photo, her face slimmer, her lips painted bright red. She was sitting on the same sofa where I'd interviewed her. In the photo, she was leaning into a large man with a thick mustache: Mr. Jackson. Sitting on his other side was a little girl in cornrows. She was pointing her finger at Mr. Jackson's open mouth. I could almost hear the excited squeals, the warm laughter as Mr. Jackson pretended to gobble up DeMaria's finger. They looked happy.

In all of the photos, DeMaria Jackson was the one constant. She resembled her father mostly—the same sharp cheekbones and dark complexion. But she had her mother's eyes. They had the same wary look to them.

Most of the room was messy, except for two places: her nightstand and a large indentation on the floor where Demetrius's crib had once been. He'd slept in DeMaria's room since birth, but after she'd disappeared, Mrs. Jackson had moved his crib over to her room.

I went over to the nightstand. There was a cheap desk lamp on top and a wooden picture frame. The picture was a selfie of DeMaria and Demetrius, the camera pointed up close to both of their faces. Demetrius was drooling, barely a few months old, and DeMaria was smiling at him, her forehead leaning against his.

I spent the next few minutes looking at DeMaria's things. I looked under the piles of clothes on the floor, searching through the pockets of her jeans and hoodies. I looked in her closet and dug through her drawers of shirts, underwear, pajamas. I moved her knickknacks and empty water bottles around her desk. In the desk drawers, I found a mess of school supplies and half-used notebooks, nail polish, a makeup bag, chargers, and some pads and tampons. I flipped through her GED materials on the floor. I even checked her wastebasket, but I found only snack wrappers and crumpled papers.

I found nothing strange. Her room was innocuous.

Mrs. Jackson was convinced that DeMaria had changed after becoming a mother. She'd put her entire history behind her—the truancy in school, the arguments, the shitty ex-boyfriend, the DWI. DeMaria had changed completely.

But what did Mrs. Jackson actually know about her daughter?

What did any of our parents know about us?

Olivia's parents, Madison's dad, my own father—they had comfortable ideas about their children. They thought we were virgins. They thought we didn't do drugs. They thought we drank responsibly. We were nice and good in their eyes.

We made it look that way. We stowed away the unsavory bits of our lives, the things that would disappoint them and break their hearts. We hid those parts of us until we couldn't anymore. And we did it to protect them. We did it out of love.

Most nineteen-year-olds were the same. They always had something to hide.

But there was no contraband in DeMaria's room, not even a relic from the past. No cigarettes, vapes, or prescription bottles full of weed. No condoms or birth control pills. No gun or pepper spray. No booze or vibrator hidden deep within a drawer. I couldn't even find a journal or diary.

DeMaria had been discreet.

I sat down on the floor, leaning against the bed. I rubbed my eyes for a moment. In the hallway, Mrs. Jackson seemed to float back and forth from her bedroom to the bathroom to the kitchen. She'd tucked in Demetrius for a nap. I couldn't hear her footsteps, but I could feel her presence drift past the door, like a soft breeze.

Maybe life had always been like this for DeMaria, her mother floating around her. She couldn't hide anything without Mrs. Jackson hovering nearby.

Except online, I realized.

Sometimes we hid things that weren't physical.

But DeMaria's cell phone had vanished with her. She'd left a chunky gray laptop on her desk, but Mrs. Jackson had been unable to log in. She was saving it for law enforcement to analyze. DeMaria had taken her password with her to the grave.

After another minute, I stood up. I did one last spin around the room.

And I stopped at the nightstand. My eyes fell on the framed photo of DeMaria and Demetrius, Mrs. Jackson's words ringing in my ears. Demetrius had been the sunshine in DeMaria's life. If there was anything important in the room, then it would have been him.

I unsnapped the back of the picture frame and opened it up. There was nothing behind the photo.

As I set it back down, I noticed a Bible on the nightstand. The tome was cream-colored, nearly blending into the table. DeMaria had used it as a platform for the picture frame.

With a finger, I traced the soft green vines running around the cream-colored cover, the tiny pink flowers and cherubs woven among them. On the inside cover, there was a little box for DeMaria's contact information in case she lost it. The handwriting was large and scraggly, written with glittery pink ink. A child's handwriting. De-Maria had received the Bible years ago.

But the pages looked brand-new. It looked as if she'd barely used it.

There was a slight rattle when I picked up the Bible. I shook it again, listening to the sound.

I checked behind me.

My back turned to the door, I started flipping through the pages, skipping through chunks of the Old Testament. No pages were missing or marked. I flipped through it even faster into the New Testament. And suddenly the pages flipped over a worn crease.

There was a small rectangle carved deep within the bottom of the pages. The rectangle had been roughly cut with either scissors or a knife, the frayed edges of the paper still curling inward. It was a makeshift compartment.

Inside it, DeMaria had stored an orange prescription bottle. The tiny white pills inside looked familiar. By the time I pulled out the bottle, I already knew what it was.

A prescription for escitalopram, a drug meant to balance the serotonin levels in one's brain. The pharmacy had refilled DeMaria's prescription on July 5, only a few days before she'd gone missing. Her dosage was forty milligrams per day. It was heavy, about four times higher than my own prescription.

DeMaria Jackson had suffered from major depression and anxiety.

I checked over my shoulder, my hands shaking. Then I quickly put the pills back and closed the Bible. I rearranged the nightstand back to normal.

In the kitchen, Mrs. Jackson was staring out the window, drinking a cup of water. She seemed dazed, turning slowly as I stepped in.

"Thanks for letting me check out her room, Mrs. Jackson," I mumbled. "I'll be heading out now."

"Did you find anything?"

I shook my head.

Mrs. Jackson didn't react—she'd sensed it already. She led me to the front door. Just as I was stepping out, Mrs. Jackson handed me a scrap of paper.

"You'll send me a link to the article, right, Maddie?" she asked. "I want to see her story told to the public."

Maddie Johnson just nodded. It was scary how easy it was to nod and tell her goodbye. I could hear the hard click as Leticia barricaded her door again with the plank of wood.

I slowly walked back to the car. I didn't know what was worse—that I'd lied to her about being a journalist or that I hadn't told her about what I'd found.

DeMaria Jackson had changed after her son's birth. But her son had only been one factor in it. The other was the medication.

And I realized that DeMaria Jackson had been a lot like me. Another sad, angry girl trapped in Liberty Lake.

17

I was winded after the interview. It seemed like the lethargy from Mrs. Jackson's home had clung onto me. I sped on the highway back up north, my head spinning.

DeMaria Jackson with her messy past.

Demetrius in his little onesie.

Leticia with her light footsteps.

Kevin in his police uniform.

The Bible and the prescription bottle inside.

As soon as I got home, I raced up to my room and closed the blinds shut. Then I curled up in bed and slept.

Dinner was quiet. Dad and I ate in silence as the TV blared in the background. Our days around other people had left us exhausted—Dad, from work; me, from the interview.

I debated having a second helping of mashed potatoes, my mind blank.

Then I heard DeMaria's name.

I turned to the TV, the dread heavy in my stomach.

The news channel showed a press conference from earlier in the day. Police Chief Todd Johnson spoke at the podium. He was a stout man with brown hair and a peppery mustache.

"We do not believe that Ms. Jackson's death is in any way connected to the disappearance of Olivia Willand," said the chief as the cameras flashed. "We have received a few tips concerning both women, but we have cause to believe that these are two isolated incidents. Our investigators are working on Ms. Jackson's case, but currently the disappearance of Olivia Willand takes full precedence."

I thought of DeMaria's messy bedroom, untouched since July. No detective had yet to investigate it.

"We are nearing the two-week mark since Ms. Willand disappeared. And I can speak for both Martin Willand and Heather Willand when I say that there is a real sense of urgency in this case. We are mounting a full-scale search operation this Saturday in coordination with the 'Find Olivia Willand' search committee. Please visit their website and sign up to volunteer. We have twenty-seven hundred acres of land to cover again at Littlewood Park Reserve, so we need all hands on deck for this operation."

The big search was on Halloween.

Dad exhaled and went back to his food. He would go—the Willands would expect it. He didn't bother to ask me if I would.

Before I went to bed, I looked up the "Find Olivia Willand" website. The layout was simple, but the Willands had posted several photos of Olivia on the site. They showed her as a toddler on a blue tricycle, posing in her high school graduation robe, and grinning beneath a white veil at her First Communion.

I had a lump in my throat, looking at each photo, one after the other.

On Halloween, the volunteers would flood Littlewood Park Reserve once again. I now had a chance to go back, to revisit the place where Olivia and I had spent our childhood together. I owed it to her, after all the other chances I'd skipped.

But I hated the idea. The park reserve had too many memories. It seemed wrong to go, as if I would be encroaching on her park, on her neighborhood, on her life, even after she'd made it clear long ago that I wasn't welcome. We had moved on from each other, hadn't we?

After a long moment, I clicked on the Volunteer link.

It led to an online form.

I entered my name, cell phone number, email address. I submitted the form before I could stop myself. Then I closed the laptop and settled into bed.

I had a couple of days to figure out what I would do on Halloween.

But first, I had my own lead to focus on: La Rue, the restaurant where DeMaria had once worked.

I had no idea if DeMaria Jackson and Olivia Willand were connected. I hadn't found anything that remotely linked them.

But after the stunt I had pulled on Leticia Jackson, I owed her something out of our interview, even if she would never find out about it.

On Thursday morning, I showed up at Goodhue Groceries, miraculously healed.

"Look happy, Mary," Jim chided, patting me on the shoulder. "You're not sick anymore, and you're at work again. That's something to be happy about."

I smiled blandly as Jim left my checkout lane.

The morning passed by in an anxious blur. I had four different customers who griped at me in the checkout lane, arguing over coupons and weekly deals. One customer asked me why I was "overcharging" on candy even though Halloween was only a couple of days away.

"I'm not paying over five dollars for this bag of chocolate," said a man, chucking the candy off the conveyor belt. "No one should waste their hard-earned money on this."

I gritted my teeth, smiling back politely.

At lunch, I waited to see if Dwayne would come in. But after twenty minutes had passed, it seemed like he would eat later. He had been too busy on the floor to even say hi.

I shoved in my earbuds and skimmed through the news on my phone.

Ron suddenly joined me. He said nothing as he plopped down with a steaming container of ravioli in his hands, his gaze intensely focused on it.

I went back to scrolling through the news. A minute later, I felt Ron lean toward me. I pulled out an earbud.

"Ivy League Mary . . . how's it going?" Ron asked. His voice was monotone.

The nickname sounded odd from his lips, as if he were struggling to climb through the syllables. He'd probably heard it from Dwayne or Jim in passing.

"I'm fine. How are you?"

"I'm okay. I have a lot of comp sci homework," said Ron, shrugging. He was chewing through his food, barely looking at me. Up close, his arms looked thin beneath his green work polo.

"So . . ." he continued. "Are you doing anything for Halloween?"

"I'm working the closing shift."

"You're not hanging out with anyone?"

"I am," I blurted out. "I made plans to go out with friends."

It wasn't a lie. Back at school, I was supposed to go out on Halloween. My friends and I had three parties to attend and then we agreed to wing the rest of the night. I had even arranged my work schedule there around it.

Halloween was an institution in college, the time of year when students got sluttier, more monstrous. They wandered in one drunken haze from the bars to the house parties to whatever place was still open at 4:00 A.M. It was the messiest event of the entire school year.

I loved the complete lack of inhibition, as if putting one mask on stripped another mask off. I loved the camaraderie and the decorations.

It was supposed to be my last Halloween of college, the end of an era.

Now those plans had vanished completely.

"You and your friends are free to stop at my place. I'm having a small party on Halloween night. There'll be booze," Ron added, as if it were contraband.

I could smell his hot ravioli breath. My stomach lurched.

"Our plans are pretty tight. Sorry," I said.

Ron finally looked at me, his blue eyes beady, and he leaned in.

"I know a guy who can score us some weed," he whispered.

I leaned away, shaking my head.

"I'm not interested—"

"It'll be fun, Mary."

"I'm really not interested."

"You would be if Dwayne asked you," he said quietly. It was an accusation.

My patience was gone. I felt a flash of rage in my chest, the words spilling out.

"What does he have to do with it? I'm not interested. I won't be interested. Ever. That's the truth."

Ron blinked, his mouth slightly agape. I almost felt sorry for him. Then he leaned in.

"I wouldn't think so highly of myself," he muttered.

"I'm not—"

"You're not hot like that Olivia chick. Nowhere fucking close. And you see what happened to her?" he hissed. "That slut went missing."

My jaw dropped.

Ron bolted up from his seat. He grabbed his lunch and hurried out of the room at lightning speed, the back of his neck turning bright red.

A pair of employees turned in my direction, their interest piqued. One of them shook his head.

I left the break room fuming. The conversation with Ron had escalated so quickly. He thought I fawned over Dwayne. He'd attacked me personally. And while the city—even the country—was panicking over Olivia, he'd called her a slut. I heard no empathy in his voice, only disgust.

You see what happened to her? he'd asked me.

It almost sounded like a threat.

After work, I hurried out to Mom's car. I avoided Ron on the way out. I didn't think I could look at him without getting enraged all over again.

I followed my phone's directions to La Rue. The restaurant had opened only a couple of years before, in the upper north side of Liberty Lake. It was about twenty minutes away from where the Willands lived.

From the outside, it looked like a typical upscale modern restaurant. The interior had dark purple lights and an indoor water fountain. It could have served anything—sushi, steak, seafood, gambling.

At the hostess stand, a young woman was stacking a pile of black menus together. Her hair was red, flowing down her chest. My heart suddenly started pounding, until she looked in my direction.

"How many seats?" she asked, then stopped. "Ivy League Mary!"

"Hi, Liz," I said limply.

Liz was a high school classmate. Back then, she'd been one of the stars of our school's musical theater department, playing Sandy in *Grease* and then Kim MacAfee in *Bye Bye Birdie*. Liz had been nice to me and the other stagehands. She'd also been stick thin. But since then, her chest had gotten significantly bigger. She'd either gotten breast implants or a better push-up bra.

"How've you been?" Liz asked.

I shrugged.

"Could I talk to the manager here?"

"If you're looking for a job application—"

"I'm not," I said firmly. "I wanted to talk about DeMaria Jackson. She used to work here, apparently?"

Liz froze, glancing behind her at the white tables and the servers who glided by.

"Could you get me the manager?" I asked again.

Liz suddenly walked around the hostess stand, her heels clicking on the wooden floor. She grabbed me by the wrist, yanking me with her. Liz was surprisingly strong, her red hair swaying in front of me.

For a second, I was back in the dorms with Carly, my hands flying out in front of me.

We were in the back of the parking lot when Liz finally let go.

"What the hell was that for?"

"I don't want my boss getting pissed again," said Liz, her arms folded together. "She already told the police everything she knows. My boss is, like, this close to having a meltdown over DeMaria. And I am not going to let her bitch at me during my shift."

Out in the daylight, I could see the smudges of liner beneath Liz's eyes, the black clumps on her eyelashes.

"I'm not trying to piss off your boss," I said, trying to sound calm. "But do you know anything about DeMaria Jackson?"

Liz took a deep breath.

"I didn't talk to her much. DeMaria seemed sweet, kind of shy. But I just got the sense that she didn't belong, you know?"

I waited for Liz to elaborate. But she just stared back.

"She didn't belong?"

"The vibe was off," said Liz, shrugging. "DeMaria just seemed uncomfortable at the restaurant. She quit here about a year ago."

"Do you know where she worked after that?" I asked.

Liz shivered in the cold.

"I'm pretty sure she went to work at a Vietnamese place in town," said Liz. "Pho Village."

18

On Friday morning, Jim came by my lane with a plastic box of headbands. I watched as he tried to pull one out.

"Uff da," he muttered, struggling. He then handed me a black headband with two small pumpkins on top. He waited until I put it on my head.

"We have to be festive against the competition, Mary. If we bring in customers for Halloween weekend, then we've got them for Thanksgiving and Christmas," said Jim. He was serious, eyeing the black and orange streamers that decked the checkout lanes.

When lunch came around, I yanked off my headband and sat alone at a table in the break room. I put in my earbuds and scarfed down a hummus wrap.

Out of the corner of my eye, a green polo shirt joined me. I stiffened, but it was only Dwayne. He sat down opposite me. He looked like he hadn't slept in the past few nights. He seemed flimsy, like he would topple over any second.

"I haven't seen you in forever."

"Yeah, the holidays get busy as hell around here," Dwayne said sheepishly. He carried a club sandwich from the store's deli section.

"How've you been?"

"You tell me, Ivy League," he said, unwrapping his food. "You're the one who's been out sick."

I hadn't seen Dwayne in a couple of days. It was less than a week since we'd discovered DeMaria Jackson's arm. But it felt longer—like years had passed. There was too much information to process, too many conversations to keep straight. One of them involved Dwayne.

"Kevin Obermueller says hi."

"Oh, yeah?" Dwayne asked, straightening up. "Why were you talking to Kevin?"

I swallowed. He stared at me, his eyes flashing.

"I thought he'd know something about the disappearances since he's in the police force, like updates on Olivia. Maybe the two women are connected."

"You find out anything useful?" Dwayne asked, shaking his head. "I bet I already know the answer."

"What did I do?" I whispered.

"I wouldn't trust anything he says. He's a pig, Mary. I thought that was fucking obvious."

"What happened?" I asked. But Dwayne was already climbing out of his seat, leaving the break room.

I was floored. Whatever friendship Kevin and Dwayne had shared hadn't faded away—it had erupted completely.

At a different table, a man snorted. He was one of the same men who'd seen me talk to Ron.

"Bit of a drama queen, aren't we?" he asked.

I didn't see Dwayne for the rest of my shift—I didn't know if he was busy or if he was avoiding me. It was probably both.

It stung.

I thought Dwayne would have listened. He'd been there at the beach. He'd known Olivia. If there was one person who would have cared about both cases, it was him.

Instead, I had pissed him off.

I was on my own.

In the car, I waited for the heat to turn on. I nearly ducked down as Ron left the store on his skateboard. But he didn't see me. He was bundled up, speeding into the cold chill.

I had a plan to visit Pho Village, where DeMaria had worked after quitting La Rue. It was supposed to be a simple conversation with Mr. Nguyen. The police might have interviewed him already.

Yet I was stalling in the car.

Mr. Nguyen was my best friend's father. He'd given me free meals at his restaurant, given me rides with Madison when we'd needed them. At sleepovers, Mr. Nguyen brought snacks or nail polish when he came home from the restaurant. He cared about our education, and he did anything to help us study.

Mr. Nguyen had been good to me—he didn't deserve to be bothered.

And after what had happened with Dwayne, I didn't want to upset anyone else.

I looked up Madison's number on my cell phone.

She could pry without raising any suspicion. Madison might not have liked Olivia back in high school, but she would have felt bad for DeMaria Jackson. She would understand how crucial it was to talk to her father.

I called Madison. Los Angeles was running two hours behind, but she would most likely be out of class or work.

After several rings, she picked up her cell phone.

"Mary?" There was the hum of a crowd from her end.

"Hey, how are you?" I squeaked.

"Hang on a sec. I'll get somewhere quieter," she said. A few seconds later, the voices had dulled down completely. "I'm at a networking event right now."

"That sounds cool."

"I wish," she said, sighing. "You know how stressful it is to graduate soon? Everyone's trying to land a job. Meanwhile I'm just trying to find something that lets me stay in L.A. Is that too much to ask?"

"No," I croaked. I could hear the heavy thud of a door closing in the background, the faint echo of shoe heels against tile. I pictured Madison in full business wear, pacing back and forth in an empty hallway of a glass corporate building.

"And have you looked at the GRE?" she asked.

"Not really."

"It's awful. It's like the SAT all over again, except this time you've burnt most of your brain cells in undergrad."

I tried to laugh, but it came out as a weak titter.

There was a pause after that. I could hear Madison's heels clicking on the other end of the phone. She was tunneling full speed toward graduation, the workforce, then grad school. Only four years ago, we'd been stuck in the same humdrum city. We'd both dreamt of escaping it, even if it meant that one went east and the other went west.

But now our lives had diverged completely from each other, one of us heading up, the other one tumbling down.

"My dad told me you're back in LL," said Madison. "Why would you go home for research?"

My mouth felt dry. I had forgotten about my early visit to Pho Village. I'd come home without telling her—and her father had known about it first. It looked suspicious.

"I'm back for my thesis," I said quickly. "The research requires a lot of materials here. I can't exactly transfer them to school."

"What's the project about?"

"It's complicated," I said. "I don't want to waste your time. You're supposed to be networking, right?"

"Right . . ." she said, trailing off. "Well, whatever's happening, it'll be okay, Mary. The Ivy League can really wear people down—

it's normal. But if you need to shit-talk, I'm here for you," she added brightly. "And you can come to L.A. for a bit."

"Thanks."

"But I should be heading back," she said, sighing. "Why'd you call me?"

I had a brief glimpse of Mr. Nguyen, the restaurant, DeMaria, but my mind couldn't connect them anymore. I felt like I could barely talk, the words all stuck in my mouth.

"Nothing serious. I just felt like calling you."

"Did you get my text?" she asked innocently. I realized I hadn't replied back to her in two weeks.

"The one about your ex?"

"Yeah. You'll be proud of me—I avoided Jake like the plague at karaoke night."

"That's great," I said. There was a long pause. I waited for Madison to elaborate, but she said nothing. She was waiting for me to explain why I'd ignored her. It seemed like neither of us was willing to budge.

"I should be heading back. Miss you, Mary," said Madison. "We'll talk soon. See you in December."

"Sure. Love you," I said, hanging up.

On the drive home, I could hear her voice. She sounded optimistic, breezy. Madison had a future. She was moving on with her life away from Liberty Lake, while I was sinking deeper into it. Ivy League Mary was now wasting away at a grocery store.

Before dinner, I carried a box of cookies up to my room. I ate them alone in bed, my trash bags still unemptied, my desk still unassembled in a corner of my room. While Madison was finishing her senior year, I was living alone in a pigsty.

Through the window, the street glowed with Halloween decorations. One of the neighbors had turned on a mechanical witch. It cranked its arm up and down, broomstick in hand, as a car drove past.

It was Friday, the night before Halloween. People would be running wild on campus, in Liberty Lake, everywhere else. It was an early celebration to start off Halloween weekend.

And the morning after, it would be the day of the search for Olivia.

19

I was in the lake. The water was warm and calm, but the rest of the city was cold, blanketed in snow. I was floating faceup in the water, my body warmed up from the sunlight that peeked through the clouds.

Something brushed against my leg. Nearby, another body was floating in the water. It was DeMaria Jackson, her eyes closed and her face shining under the sunlight. I slowly looked to my right, and I saw Olivia floating in the water, too, her eyes closed. We were all floating together, despite the snow.

I woke up just after dawn. There was a dread in my stomach. It made me nauseous as I lay in bed. I knew what I feared—that I would find another arm in the woods, rotting on a pile of leaves. This time it would be Olivia's.

But I crawled out of bed anyway. I bundled up for the day ahead, and I beat Dad to the kitchen. When he arrived, I had already brewed some coffee.

"You're going?" he asked.

I nodded and poured myself a second cup.

We left the house at half past eight. On Halloween morning, there were kids already dressed up in their costumes. Three of them raced around the cul-de-sac on their bikes: two monsters chased down by a fairy. One of the neighbors was setting up a small chalkboard on her lawn, beneath a scarecrow. The sign read: WE'RE OPEN AT 6 PM!

In the truck, Dad drove us past homes with trees covered in toilet paper. We passed by a pair of twin princesses who waved from a bike trailer.

The sun was out, the sky a wholesome blue. It was perfect weather for a Saturday Halloween: warm enough for activities in the day, then revelry at night. It boded well for a search.

By the time we reached Littlewood Park Reserve, cars had already spilled out from the parking lot into the streets. Police cars were stationed at the entrance, monitoring the crowds of people who clustered in the grass. The curbside parking stretched on for at least five blocks from the main park entrance. Around the corner, we saw more cars parked in front of looming two-story homes, their rears sticking out into the street.

"Why does nobody know how to park in the damn suburbs," Dad muttered.

He eventually parked us at the corner of a residential street about four blocks away. As we left the car, a middle-aged couple came out of the house nearby. They wore matching plaid tan scarves. Dad froze, his hand still on the door handle.

"Howdy!" said the man, waving at us.

"Are you going to the search, too?" asked the wife.

"Yeah. We didn't know that there'd be this many people, though," said Dad.

"The Willands are like family to us. We're not a community if we don't help each other out," said the wife.

"And don't worry about the parking," said the husband, winking at me. "Today is an important occasion."

As Dad and I hurried away, I heard a yap from the house. A Chihuahua had dashed out of the garage, followed by a sullen teenage boy, dressed all in black. The plaid couple stopped smiling as their son joined them.

Dad and I signed in at a check-in booth. The volunteer was perky as she checked our IDs.

"Thanks for coming," she said. "You're good people."

A crowd had gathered in front of the pavilion next to the playground, hundreds of people in fall coats. There were a few dogs present, including a snowy-white poodle who sat patiently in the grass. But I lost count of all the children and toddlers at the event—little superheroes, monsters, and witches who stood beside their parents, looking bored.

The police officers stalked around the edge of the crowd, their dogs sniffing the air. They kept the two news crews sequestered near the park entrance, away from the searchers.

Dad and I weaved our way to the front. I tried looking for Dwayne, but the crowd was too dense.

Olivia's parents, both blond and well dressed, waited in front of the pavilion. Kevin Obermueller was with them, dressed in the same fleece vest as before. He spoke into a walkie-talkie in his hand. And off to the side, there was his father, Ronald Obermueller, the would-be mayor who'd killed two teenagers.

I was in junior high school when it happened. Kevin, Madison, and I were in the same class. That year, Kevin's father ran for mayor. He was a successful businessman, one of Liberty Lake's biggest real estate developers. His campaign had invested in numerous radio and television ads that railroaded his opponent, an unknown retired teacher.

Less than a month before the election, Mr. Obermueller drove home late from a campaign event. Reports said that he'd been drinking heavily before he left. As a car waited at a stoplight just off the freeway, Mr. Obermueller's luxury SUV rammed right into it.

The impact had sent the first car smashing into the traffic pole.

The teenage couple inside had died instantly. Neither of them had worn a seat belt.

The traffic cameras later showed Mr. Obermueller's car backing away from the mess, its front bumper scratched but mostly intact. The SUV plowed away on the freeway.

Mr. Obermueller's political career had died as instantly as his victims. The local news went ballistic over the story, and he lost his race. He was later charged with two counts of felony hit-and-run. The prosecution had pushed for a fifteen-year jail sentence, but he'd dodged it. Somehow, Mr. Obermueller had gotten his sentence reduced to six hundred hours of community service and undisclosed payments to the families of the teenage victims.

Before the court proceedings were over, his wife quietly filed for divorce. She later moved up north, but Kevin stayed behind in Liberty Lake.

I could remember the whispers circulating around the lunchroom and the girls' bathroom, the email chains and instant messages that people sent each other. The fact that Kevin's father had killed two people and gotten away with it.

"Like father, like son?" people asked. Others made bets about how many people Kevin would kill.

But Kevin seemed oblivious at school. He clung to his group of friends, and he acted like the same prick that he'd always been. Some of us even wondered if his parents had hidden the news from him. But of course, he'd known. He just bore it all.

In person, Ronald Obermueller was an older version of his son. He was bald and goateed. He was relaxed as he spoke to another man among them. The other man was short and stocky, and he had dark hair and square, wire-rimmed glasses. He wore a deerskin jacket. It was the same man who'd accompanied Mrs. Willand at Goodhue Groceries.

"Jay!" shouted Mr. Willand, waving to us. The group all turned to look as Dad and I joined them.

"Thank you both for coming here," said Mr. Willand, his arms outstretched toward Dad. He squeezed him in a half hug while Dad stiffly patted his back. Mr. Willand was wearing a camo hunting jacket, a megaphone in one hand.

"Mary, is that you?" asked Mrs. Willand. Before I could answer, she wrapped me in a hug, the scent of her lilac perfume filling the air. Olivia's mother felt bony, as if she'd stopped eating entirely since the disappearance.

"I'm sorry about Olivia—"

"I know, honey, thank you," said Mrs. Willand, patting me on the cheek. She smiled at me tightly, the crow's-feet stretching around her eyes. "But look at you, our town's little Ivy League graduate. You've blossomed so much, Mary—you look so good!"

"Thank you, Mrs. Willand," I said. To my relief, she hadn't asked about school.

"I know that Olivia appreciates you being here," she said, squeezing my hand. "I've missed seeing you around the house."

I could only nod. I hadn't set foot in their house for nearly a decade now.

Nearby, Dad was awkwardly in a conversation with the men. They had formed a half circle to talk, but there was a large space between Dad and the man in the deerskin jacket.

Mr. Willand suddenly handed the megaphone to Kevin's dad, who nodded, rolling back his sleeves. The three of them, including Mrs. Willand, approached the large crowd.

"Hiya, folks!" blared Mr. Obermueller into the megaphone. "Wait, is the volume on?"

The crowd laughed, Mr. Obermueller chuckling along with them. Then he put out a hand to quiet the crowd.

"Ronald Obermueller here. I just want to take the time to say thank you for showing up and helping us find one of our revered community members. We wouldn't be able to do any of this without help from the fine people of Liberty Lake!"

The crowd cheered. A few men even punched the air with their fists.

"As your city council president, I do not tolerate any kind of pain or suffering in this fine city. Liberty Lake is a city of good people, and good people take care of their own. We're all family over here."

The crowd broke out into applause and cheering. Mr. Obermueller beamed, the top of his head glinting with sunlight. The faces in the crowd adored him. A decade ago, these same people had been outraged against him. They'd called him a child killer, an alcoholic murderer. They'd cheered over his election loss.

But Mr. Obermueller's political career had never ended after all. He might not have become mayor, but he'd wormed his way into something just as reputable—city council president. Mr. Obermueller hadn't just saved his career—he'd made people forget.

He handed Olivia's father the megaphone, the two of them patting each other on the back. Mr. Willand cleared his throat.

"I couldn't have said it better myself, Ron, thank you. And thank you all for being here. Everyone's support and love mean so much to us. Olivia would be just . . . Thank you." Mr. Willand cleared his throat again, once, twice, the sound of wetness reverberating in the park.

His face had turned bright pink. He handed the megaphone back to Mr. Obermueller and suddenly walked into the pavilion, his shoulders shaking.

Mr. Obermueller quickly took the megaphone again in one hand, his other hand gesturing deliberately as he spoke.

"We will help Olivia Willand today. But we can only do that if we're cooperative and observant, folks. A few ground rules for our search in Littlewood Park: No one explores by themselves. Always be in a group of two or more. No minors are allowed by themselves, so, parents, please watch out. We'll be meeting back at the entrance at noon for a break, free lunch for all the volunteers, and a prayer. If anyone wants to stay after, we'll do another two-hour sweep of the park. Any questions, folks?"

A man in a hunting jacket raised his hand, a sleepy bloodhound sitting still at his feet. "Can we use our dogs to sniff for Olivia?" he asked.

Mr. Obermueller scratched his head.

"That's a good question, sir. I have no idea. But lucky for us, we're in the presence here of a Liberty Lake police officer: my son, Kevin."

Kevin slowly stepped forward. Mr. Obermueller was beaming as he gave him the megaphone, but Kevin looked like he wanted to melt into the ground.

"Hi, everyone," said Kevin, stammering. "Uh, usually we don't want animals to contaminate the crime scene or anything. And police dogs are trained for this type of—"

"Baxter here is the best hunting dog in the state, better than those German shepherds you got there," said the man in the hunting jacket.

"I'm sure he is, sir, but—"

"My pugs are just as well behaved, and they're very patient with their work," said an elderly woman.

"I appreciate the enthusiasm, but we, uh, don't have anything with Olivia's scent on it."

Mrs. Willand waved a hand at Kevin.

"I brought some of Olivia's old clothes and the perfume she always wore," said Mrs. Willand loudly. "The other dogs can help, too."

Kevin looked like he was getting a headache from all the suggestions. Mr. Obermueller noticed it, too. He swooped the megaphone out of his son's hands.

"If any of you folks have a dog interested in helping us out, please wait here as we check with the police. Are we all clear, folks?"

The crowd nodded, slightly impatient.

"And one other thing," said Mr. Obermueller, a hand stretching out to temper the crowd. "If you find anything of interest in the park, please contact the police. We have a special tip line with them, so please report any items or things or—" Mr. Obermueller paused, the word "bodies" hanging in front of all of us. "*Anything* of interest, please call the police first."

As the crowd flooded the trails, Mrs. Willand reached for my arm.

"Mary, you and Olivia played at the reserve a lot, remember? Maybe you could help them retrace those spots that Olivia liked most?" She looked so downtrodden that I nodded. I didn't mention that Olivia had been restless and wandered everywhere around the park.

Mrs. Willand disappeared into the pavilion, where her husband was still inside.

Dad and I were stuck with the Obermuellers and the man in the deerskin jacket.

"Are you Jay's daughter?" the man asked me, his voice uncomfortably deep. "I'm John Stack, a client of your father's."

"I'm Mary," I said as we shook hands.

"I've been working on his roofing project, Mary," said Dad softly.

I was meeting the client who made Dad anxious, the one who monitored his progress at work.

"Okay," said Mr. Obermueller to the rest of us. "I think the kids can get a head start in the woods. You okay with that, Kevin?"

He nodded, not looking at me.

"Good. The rest of us old folks will join you after I'm done with the puppy patrol. And don't worry, hon," said Mr. Obermueller, winking at me, "I won't let John harass your father about the roof."

John Stack shrugged.

"I think Olivia takes precedence today," he said. His voice was like gravel.

I followed Kevin onto the trail. Dad was trapped behind with the others. As Kevin passed the entrance sign, I stopped, my heart beginning to race. The trees loomed over us, the woods stretching interminably ahead.

The thought seemed to hit me—I was stuck with the boy who'd

pummeled me as a child. He was a man now, and I was going to be alone with him in the woods for hours, searching for a missing woman.

Kevin turned around to look at me.

"What? Are you afraid of me, Mary?" he joked.

I said nothing as I joined him, my stomach already churning.

20

Sunlight dappled through the trees above us. I could hear birds chirping nearby, the autumn air growing sharper and cooler now in the woods. There were groups of people scattered in the distance, their heads bent toward the ground as they searched. What for, nobody knew.

I followed Kevin's lead. He made his way down a slight slope off the left of the trail, the brown and orange leaves crunching beneath our feet. At the bottom of the slope, there was a small creek, only a few feet wide. The water was shallow.

Without hesitation, we followed the creek. We heard the squawk of geese flying over the trees, the occasional scream of a child in the distance. At one point, there was loud barking—it sounded as if two dogs had gotten aggressive with each other. As we walked, there were always other people within our line of sight.

Neither of us spoke for a while. Kevin was continually scanning the area, his neck craning from left to right and back again. He was more attentive than I was. Kevin stopped a few times to turn over a rock or to examine a dense pile of leaves. But his diligence slowed us down. In half an hour, we'd only surveyed a few hundred feet of the stream.

"What exactly are you looking for?"

Kevin was squatting on the ground, prodding at some leaves with a branch he'd picked up.

"Just use your common sense, Mary. If you find scraps of clothing, a phone, or a bloodstain, that's probably important. Anything that seems like a disturbance here is important."

"People have been searching the area already. Everything's a disturbance."

"You'll figure it out, Mary."

"How do we know the area hasn't already been contaminated?"

"If you're going to whine the whole time, you can leave," said Kevin, standing up again. "Meanwhile some of us are actually invested in helping Olivia."

When his back turned, I flipped him a middle finger. I kept my eyes peeled throughout the area, but I saw nothing strange. There were too many dense leaves, branches, mounds of dirt everywhere. Too many people had wandered the park. Unless Olivia had dropped a giant neon sign, it didn't seem likely that we'd find anything.

As the wind picked up, I was reminded of the scene at the beach. The day was just as cold, but grayer, cloudier. The crowd there had gawked at DeMaria Jackson's forearm. I would always remember what it looked like—the bone peering through the raw, gray flesh. The decay of a murder victim.

And I wondered if, by some twist of fate, I would stumble onto Olivia's body, too. I was marked now, dirty. I'd left school dirty and reckless, and now I'd lied and forced my way into the lives of two missing women. Deep down, I was tainted—things would only get worse. Whether through God or karma or mere coincidence, I was stuck in the narrative.

I didn't want to find Olivia with my own two eyes. I couldn't stomach the idea of it.

"You okay, Mary?" Kevin stared at me, the stick still in his hand.

I realized I was standing close to the creek, the water only a couple of inches away from my boots.

"I'm fine. Just . . . winded."

"If it's about what I said earlier—"

"That was nothing."

"Yeah, well . . . I'm sorry if I sounded like a dick," said Kevin, not looking at me. "I'm on edge, Mary."

"I think we all are."

Kevin stared off in the direction of the main trail. A puppy was yapping in the distance.

"Did you know that it's nearly been two weeks since she went missing?" he asked quietly.

I nodded.

"Every day that she doesn't come home, things look worse. You know that?" Kevin looked like he was about to spit on the ground, but he didn't. "And I think it's kind of screwed up that everyone keeps hoping that she's *only* been kidnapped and not murdered. We think that Olivia being taken hostage by some asshole is a good thing."

"This whole situation is fucked up."

"Yeah, it is. And if I find the son of a bitch who did it, I'm gonna bash a hole in his head. And that's before I even get my hunting gear," said Kevin darkly. I could tell he meant it, too. Kevin had always had a disposition for violence, but it was odd to see it now justified. He'd cared for Olivia since childhood. She might have even been the unrequited love of his life.

"Did you and Olivia ever get together?" I asked suddenly.

Kevin's face reddened.

"I can't answer that."

"Why not?"

He didn't answer.

"Why not, Kevin?"

"Because I don't know."

"What's that supposed to mean?"

Kevin shook his head like a dog trying to shake off a flea.

"It means I don't know. Olivia was always . . . hard to read. I was never sure if she was flirting with me or making fun of me. It's been that way since forever, you know?"

She'd been that way all her life. Olivia seemed to know her presence, how much people wanted her to simply like them. She didn't have to keep sweet to anybody. It was easy for her, since she was surrounded by people like me and Kevin—outsiders who were desperate to be liked.

That was why Olivia always chose what games we played, what roles we took when we played with our Barbies. That was why she took charge whenever we were in the woods, heading in whatever direction she chose. And that was why, years later, in high school, Olivia didn't balk when I found out she was bulimic. She knew I would cover for her.

And she treated Kevin like a toy. When we were kids, Olivia once dared him to lick a frozen pole on the school playground. Kevin had obliged. But his tongue was glued to the swing set for half an hour. When a gym teacher finally melted Kevin's tongue off of the metal, he was in tears. He later said that his tongue was on fire, as if knives had cut through it.

People adored Olivia.

But it bored her, didn't it? There was no challenge when other people keeled over. She was reckless with others, and she could keep pushing them, taunting them to lick that frozen pole. They would do it. But maybe she wanted a different outcome once in a while. She wanted someone to stand up to her, to tell her no. No one ever did.

"One weekend in August, Olivia and I were at a movie theater. One of those discount movie nights for some shitty comedy," said Kevin, his voice getting lower. "We were like two of the five people there, we're just sitting together in the back row. I'm just chilling, eating my popcorn, and then I feel Olivia coming closer to me. And then out of nowhere, she kisses me."

"What?"

"Yeah. It never happened like that before."

"It happened before?"

"A few times," said Kevin, his eyes firmly planted on some spot in the distance. "Usually some high school party or a bar night downtown. But we'd always be drunk, and Olivia would be super wasted. It just happened sometimes, you know? We'd kiss each other. Like a quick peck on the lips.

"But this time was different. Olivia was kissing me, and it . . . escalated."

The discomfort wafted around us like an odor, but I kept my mouth shut.

"Her tongue is down my throat, and her hands are all over me. She starts . . . caressing me. I thought I was in the middle of some dream, it was that unreal," said Kevin, shaking his head. "But it was real, and I was holding Olivia. And even with three people around us in the theater, Olivia . . . went down on me."

I flinched. Kevin's face reddened. He avoided my gaze. None of it made sense: Why him? For years, he'd reeked of desperation around her. As Liberty Lake's social media star, Olivia did not lack for men. She had been in a sorority in college, surrounded by hundreds of fraternity brothers. She knew guys with job prospects in finance. She knew rugby players and future doctors. Why would she settle for someone who was little more than a Podunk police officer?

I wasn't sure. It was something only she knew, and the explanation could have been anything from boredom to recklessness. Perhaps in some way, she genuinely liked him.

"And then what happened?" I finally asked.

"I . . . I came." Kevin was almost whispering now, as if he were in a confessional. "And after the movie, I dropped Olivia off at her house."

"Did you guys—?"

"No. We didn't." He paused, dwelling on what hadn't happened that day. "We never did, actually."

"Okay."

"And we never talked about what happened that night at the movie theater. Olivia never brought it up, so I didn't, either. We just . . . hung out more, you know? We got coffee, went out for dinner, watched more movies together. You know."

"It sounds like you guys were almost a couple."

"Yeah, I thought so, too. Everything was going great for the two of us. We even talked about a ski trip together during her winter break. But then she went back to school. I didn't even know she was home when . . ." Kevin trailed off, his eyes blinking rapidly. He turned away, lifting a sleeve to his face.

In a way, I felt sorry for him. Kevin had done what very few people ever did—get together with their unrequited love. Olivia might have truly liked him back, and for that brief period of time, his dream had become reality.

He sniffled and turned around. His eyes were slightly pink.

"You have any ideas of where to go?" he asked. "Anything big in the park?"

I looked around, trying to remember.

Olivia and I would swing for hours or dig large holes in the sandboxes at the park. Other times we caught bugs. Sometimes we pretended we were spies who stalked the older kids. We wondered why they ran from us whenever we tried to join them.

By the time we were ten, Olivia and I were old enough to bike to the reserve on our own. We would spend the rest of the day there. Olivia was given a flip phone and a whistle from her parents in case anything happened. But nothing ever did.

Olivia had loved to bike on the trails, but she especially loved to roam off course. We found graffiti painted on rocks, in caverns. We brought snacks and picnicked in the dirt, carefully collecting the trash in our backpacks. Other times we followed a tiny creek that crept up out of the earth, wondering where it led, what lived near it. We didn't talk so much as explore, and we had multiple sites that we revisited.

But there was one image that I could see clearly in my mind:

Olivia's back had been turned to me. She was peering down at the drop below.

"There's a cliff," I said softly.

Kevin looked confused.

"Most of the park is pretty flat, Mary."

"It wasn't a big cliff. I just know there's one in the park."

"Jesus," Kevin muttered. "Do you know where it would be?"

I hadn't set foot in the park reserve in years. I hadn't gone back since my days with Olivia. I could remember the moment at the cliff, but I couldn't recall how to get there. The woods looked familiar and unfamiliar at the same time. Slowly, I shook my head.

Kevin sighed and checked his watch.

"It's a quarter to noon. We should be heading back for break."

"Yeah."

Kevin bent over and pushed his branch into the ground, a couple of feet between a tree and the stream. It was a marker for later, when Kevin would inevitably return to sweep the area.

As we joined the other searchers on the trail, I tried to rack my brain for the location of the cliff.

"You still shocked about me and Olivia?" Kevin asked.

"Kind of," I said. "Did anyone know about you guys?"

"Olivia wanted to take it slow, I think. After the shit her exes pulled, she had a lot of trust issues." Kevin sounded sad. "I guess with me, she was waiting for us to be serious before announcing it to anyone. And I was patient. I didn't care how long it would take for her to trust me."

With Olivia, it was hard to tell what her motives were. But she never struck me as the type who was slow in a relationship. If anything, she would have moved too quickly, then gotten bored. She would have thrived on the uncertainty, the passion, the drama around love.

Kevin provided something different—he would have been devoted, obsequious, and kind to her. He was different from her type, and I had no idea if that was a good or bad thing.

"I guess in hindsight, I was lucky that Olivia was quiet about us," Kevin said.

"Why's that?"

"Because most violent crimes against women are committed by a significant other. Looking at the statistics, who do you think the police would've suspected first?"

I felt the skin on my neck go cold. Kevin was staring straight ahead on the trail. I looked around, relieved by the people and dogs who surrounded us.

"If people had known about me and Olivia, I'd be prime suspect number one," said Kevin. "They would have suspended me from the force. Hell, they probably wouldn't even let me be here right now."

"I believe you," I said. But I was being polite, as always.

"If I had killed Olivia, I wouldn't be telling you this, Ivy League."

"Sure."

"And I trust you, Mary. You're smart. You don't follow things blindly."

"Course not," I replied.

A couple of dogs barked in the distance. The main trail grew more crowded as the search groups returned for break. The couple in front of us talked about a cabin rental they were considering. The kids behind us complained about their sweaty costumes. People were so close by that Kevin and I stayed quiet.

As we approached the exit, I smelled charcoal smoke and grilled meat in the air. Out in front of the park's pavilion, there were some plastic tables set up in a long serving line, stacked with plastic utensils, plates, and tinfoil platters full of sandwich buns, tater tots, coleslaw, and cookies. There was a stack of water bottles and a cooler at the end of the line. Mr. Willand and a volunteer were cooking on two separate charcoal grills while Mrs. Willand was ushering people into a line with a tight smile. The crowd seemed to speed over, eager for lunch.

The event was strange. After we'd gone looking for a missing woman, we were having a picnic. It seemed morbid. But if the

Willands wanted people to keep searching in the cold, then they needed to entice them with food. They had the resources to do it.

Dad, Mr. Obermueller, and John were already eating near the park map. Kevin's dad was gulping down his hamburger. As we followed the crowd, Mr. Obermueller picked up his megaphone.

"Hi, folks!" he boomed. "The Willands and the rest of the search committee want to thank you all for coming today and helping us out. We know it's cold, but we hope this free lunch shows our gratitude to you all."

There was some clapping and a few cheers.

"I also think now might be a good time to pray and reflect as we're all together. My best friend from college, Mr. John Stack, has offered to lead us in prayer."

John Stack went up to take the megaphone. He looked less than thrilled to be standing in front of a crowd, but he extended a hand toward all of us.

"Please bow your heads," said John. His voice was reminiscent of thunder crashing upon us. I didn't need to look up to know that everyone obeyed. "Blessed Father, thank you for bringing each soul out here to the park reserve. In this time of great need, you have shown us your love and compassion by bringing your flock together—"

My phone vibrated in my pocket. Suddenly there was a cacophony of sound as ringtones blasted from different cell phones—there was George Michael's upbeat voice, croons from Etta James, and riffs from Britney. I heard a country twang escape out of Kevin's vest, waxing poetic about a summer night by the lake. John continued on, the annoyance plain on his face.

"We ask for your guidance, oh Lord. I beseech you to help us."

The ringtones didn't stop. The noise continued to fill the park as John droned on. My phone continued to vibrate, as if it were itching for me to answer.

"Heavenly Father above us, please help us to find and reunite a member of your flock. Please keep her safe for us and help show us the way to her, wherever she may be."

As quickly as it began, my phone stopped vibrating. The cell phones all stopped ringing. It was quiet in the park again, aside from the rumble of John's deep voice.

"Please, oh Lord, help us find Olivia Willand."

For a moment, it seemed as if an electric current was rushing through all of us. I could sense it as I closed my eyes and kept my head bent. Everyone in the park wanted Olivia to be safe. She was one of us, a citizen of Liberty Lake, our daughter and our sister, our neighbor and our friend. She deserved better.

My phone started jolting again in my pocket. As if on cue, music blasted throughout the park again, Beyoncé and Eminem squaring off against Kevin's country ringtone. The couple ahead of us looked at their phones sheepishly.

"Amen," said John finally. With his heavy eyebrows and wire-rimmed glasses, John looked severe, like a preacher about to berate his congregation. I understood why he made Dad anxious. "If we could all just turn off our cell phones, please, to show a moment of silence and respect."

I pulled out my phone. An unknown number was trying to reach me.

"Hello?" I answered.

There was a pause, then a single word: "Email."

"Who is this?"

There was a click as the call ended. The voice on the other end had been artificial, robotic.

Outside in the park, among the line of searchers, I felt like I was being watched. I could feel it on me, as if someone's breath was on the back of my neck. But no one was watching me. Everyone was either listening to John or looking at their phones.

My fingers chilled, I slowly swiped through my phone's email. I hadn't checked it in days. But as thirty-two new emails loaded, I noticed the newest one that I'd received about three minutes ago.

The email sender was someone named E69Ch3aT896. The email's subject heading: "olivia willand."

For a second, I was back at the lake, staring down at DeMaria Jackson's arm in the sand.

I clicked it.

The image loaded on my screen slowly, a blurred box of colors. Suddenly it went crisp.

On my phone, Olivia Willand was sitting on a bed, her legs slightly spread apart. A lacy purple bra was slung off her shoulders, one of her breasts exposed in the dim light. She was leaning back, her arms propping her up. Her lips were curled into a sly grin. She was taunting the viewer—you could only look but not touch. Aside from the bra, she wore nothing else. At the bottom of the image was a single emoji: a kissy face.

I could hear the blood pumping in my ears. My heart was speeding in my chest, the shock and shame hitting me all at once.

I reached for Kevin instinctively.

But he was already running out of the lunch line, frantically waving his arms at John Stack.

"John! Shut it down!"

John frowned as Kevin's father joined him, his mouth drawn into a tight smile. "What are you saying?" Mr. Obermueller called out.

"Dad, please, shut it down!" Kevin shouted.

The couple ahead of me stared at their phones. The woman's mouth was half-open in shock. Her husband quickly shoved his phone back into his pocket. His face was burning red.

I suddenly realized what was happening. Up near the park entrance, Kevin yanked the megaphone from John and started shouting into it.

"If you've received the email with Olivia Willand's name, do not open it. I repeat: Do. Not. Open. It." Kevin was gesturing wildly at the crowd, his voice trembling. "Please report it to me, report it to the Liberty Lake police. We can get this sorted out, but please for the love of God, don't open it."

But it was too late. I could already see the heads bending toward their phones and the sharp turns as they saw the email.

There was a howl from the front of the lunch line. It sounded enraged and hysterical and in pain, as if an animal were being ripped apart in front of us. I didn't need to see it to know that it was Mr. Willand crying out. His missing daughter's nude photo had been exposed to the whole world.

21

There was a mass exodus as people abandoned the lunch line for their cars, the street, anywhere else. Mr. Willand—big, potbellied Mr. Willand—quickly bolted for the pavilion, his face bright red. He left the hot dogs burning on the grill. I'd never seen him run before in my life. Mrs. Willand just stared at the scene in front of her, unmoving. John put a hand on her back, whispering to her. She squeezed his other hand. It was a tender gesture.

By the time I made my way over to Dad, Mr. Obermueller was already trying to do damage control.

"Again, I can't thank you all enough for coming, folks," boomed Mr. Obermueller into the megaphone. His words seemed to fall on deaf, fleeing ears. "Please, everyone, don't hesitate to take your evidence to the police."

It was clear that Olivia's nude photo was evidence, but no one knew what it meant. The photo could have implied anything—that she'd been kidnapped, trafficked. The photo could have been a sick prank. It might have been fake. And it said nothing about whether she was dead or alive.

But I couldn't forget the expression on Olivia's face—seduction. She'd taken the nude photo for her personal use. She hadn't been coerced into it. The photo was meant for a boyfriend or a hookup.

Like Kevin.

While most of the crowd was dispersing, a few stragglers stayed behind. They were clustered around Officer Kevin Obermueller, bombarding him with questions. Kevin looked sickly pale, his eyes darting from one face to another.

"Will we be prosecuted if we received the photo?" asked a man. "I never asked for this."

"No one is getting charged for the photo if they received it," Kevin said quickly to the crowd. "If you want to file a report, there are other officers here who can assist you."

"I want this lewd picture off my phone now," said a blocky man, one reassuring hand on his wife's back.

"Believe me, I wish no one had seen the picture, either," said Kevin. He looked like he was on the verge of fainting. "This is the last thing any of us wants."

"I agree," said the man's wife. "This kind of thing is disgusting."

"It's a stupid stunt. That's what's happening here," said her husband.

There were other voices who now joined in, asking about the state of Olivia's case and whether their private information had been hacked. Kevin kept shaking his head at each question and comment that pelted him. He didn't know what to do.

Then he caught my eye. Kevin shook his head firmly, deliberately. He knew what I was thinking, and his message was clear: he hadn't leaked the photo.

"We should head out," Dad said quietly.

Without saying any goodbyes, Dad and I left the park together in a hurry. It seemed like we were holding our breaths until we escaped back into the truck, away from the chaos.

As Dad drove, I watched the other cars on the road, wondering which of the drivers had seen Olivia's photo. They would all learn about it soon enough. Some of them would even masturbate to it—it didn't matter if the woman was missing or potentially dead. The thought made me nauseous.

The photo had most likely originated from Olivia's phone. When she disappeared, someone else had gotten access to both. Then this person had leaked the photo during the search, when hundreds of people had gathered together in one setting, their cell phones on them. This person had called everyone, then sent them the email.

Someone had access to everyone's contact information—that was how they knew who the searchers were, what time people would assemble. It was someone close to the search committee.

Instinctively, my first thought was Kevin, but he'd been next to me the entire time. I'd followed him in the woods, and all we did was talk. I thought of the rest of the people from the search committee: Mr. and Mrs. Willand, John Stack, Mr. Obermueller, the other members who might not have shown up. There was the woman from the check-in table and the dozens of volunteers who had access to everyone's contact information. The search committee also worked in conjunction with the Liberty Lake Police Department, which had access, too.

There had been hundreds of people at the park reserve. Any of us could have sent out the photo unnoticed.

And what was the purpose in leaking her nude? There was no ransom note attached, no threat sent.

I couldn't think of any reason why, except that they were playing games with the searchers. Taunting us.

A couple of hours later, I was back at Goodhue Groceries—it felt like whiplash after the grim morning at the park. At work, I wore my pumpkin headband and plastered on my Goodhue smile, and I worked until close. The night was busy, and I liked being preoccupied. Otherwise, I would have thought about the park.

"Have you seen Dwayne?" I asked Jim as he passed by. Jim shook his head.

"Dwayne's visiting family this weekend," he said.

It explained why I hadn't seen Dwayne at the park reserve. I thought he would have gone looking for Olivia, but I realized I knew very little about him. If Dwayne and Kevin were no longer on good terms, then he might have fallen out with Olivia, too.

After we closed for the night, I walked back to Mom's car. The parking lot was empty except for a few employee vehicles.

I shivered, remembering the phone call at the park. It felt like somebody had watched us.

Halfway to the car, I heard the crunch of wheels behind me, speeding up, barreling toward me.

I swiveled around.

Ron was skateboarding into me like a bullet.

I braced for impact, my heart pounding.

But nothing happened—the wheels crunched around me. When I looked up, Ron was skateboarding past the car, his head turned to look at me, his middle fingers flicked in the air.

My heart was rattling in my chest. I was frozen in place. But I pictured the skateboard in my hands, striking up and down as I battered it over Ron's head. The smirk would be smashed off his face, the way it had disappeared off Carly's.

By the time I got home, most of the trick-or-treaters had already left the neighborhood. Most of the lights were shut off in the cul-de-sac. But the night was only starting for Madison in L.A. and my friends back at school. Carly would be celebrating her first Halloween in college—she would have a blast, not a care in the world. People my age were going out in their costumes, drinking and dancing and hooking up.

But not me. I only crawled into bed, angry and exhausted.

Dad woke me up early on Sunday morning. He turned on the lights in my room and gently shook my shoulder. I kept my eyes closed. After the past two weeks, I craved sleep more than anything else.

"C'mon, Mary, we're gonna be late for Mass. It's All Saints Day."

I didn't move.

Dad shook my shoulder again.

"I think we need it," he murmured.

Fifteen minutes later, we were both in the truck. I didn't bother to dress up—I wore jeans and a hoodie beneath my coat.

The neighborhood was covered in mist. The string lights had been shut off. The mechanical witch no longer moved. The chalkboard had collapsed onto the ground. They were shadows, and by the end of the day, they would disappear.

I thought of Olivia in her nude photo, and I rubbed my eyes, trying to clear it away. Dad and I had never discussed it. But I knew he had received one, too. He'd seen the photo of his daughter's childhood friend.

"You think we should report the emails to the police?" I asked quietly.

"No." Dad kept his eyes on the road. "The police were there. I think they know everyone got it."

The rest of the car ride was silent.

At St. Rita's, we sat in the back pew. It was where we used to sit with Mom, on the periphery. We could watch everyone else without being watched.

The church was unchanged except for one new addition: a large crucifix suspended in the air above the altar. The crucifix was held up by a series of thin black wires. The limbs on the body were contorted in agony, the blood splashed like inkblots on the carved flesh. I had to look away.

The priest from my confession led the Mass. The church bulletin said his name was Father Greg. As he shuffled up to the altar, he passed by a blond bob of hair. It was Mrs. Willand. She sat on the other side of the church. John Stack was next to her, his gaze following the priest.

But Mr. Willand was nowhere to be seen. He'd skipped Mass.

After his outburst in the park, it was clear that he didn't want to be around other people. He'd been horrified, humiliated by Olivia's photo. He knew that soon enough, everyone would know about it—including the members of his own church.

He'd seen a part of his daughter's life that he had never considered. He didn't want to know. It wounded him.

And that was why she'd kept it hidden. That was why we all did.

For most of Mass, my mind was blank. I didn't have to think or do anything. I simply followed what the others did. I didn't even listen until I heard the petitions.

"For the victims of unjust murders, may God bring them peace in his embrace," said the reader.

"Lord, hear our prayer," said the parish.

"And for Olivia Willand, our fellow parishioner here at St. Rita's, may God protect her and guide her back to us in safety."

"Lord, hear our prayer."

Far away, Mrs. Willand turned to John. He leaned in toward her, whispering. Then he squeezed her hand. It was similar to the scene at the park: John comforting Mrs. Willand with a tender, intimate gesture.

I had never seen the Willands reach for each other like that. They were hardly ever home together when I'd been around. And when they were, they never seemed to meet, like two lines running parallel to each other. They talked of shopping, family trips, and activities for Olivia, but they showed no intimacy.

Even Olivia had mused about her mother's affairs. She expected the worst from her parents. She might have been right after all.

During Communion, I saw Mr. Nguyen waiting in line. He was bundled in a winter jacket, no hat on his head. He didn't notice me, but I remembered the conversation that we needed to have. He was connected to DeMaria's case.

And DeMaria's case was connected to Olivia's.

I couldn't be convinced otherwise. DeMaria's body parts had

washed up so quickly after Olivia disappeared. There was at least one other person online who agreed—the women were connected. There was a potential serial killer involved.

The Liberty Lake Police Department said that the two cases were unrelated. But there wasn't enough information to prove anything. They had neglected DeMaria's case since July. Olivia's case had mostly turned up nothing.

I didn't know what other information the police had: the things the searchers might have found, the investigation that they were doing on the nude photo, the list of suspects they had made.

Kevin would have access to all of it. He would have broken a few rules for Olivia.

But at the park, he'd been useless. He had the badge, but none of the authority. He couldn't calm down a few angry suburbanites. I doubted he was sly enough to not get caught. He wasn't even bothered by DeMaria's case, so he saw no reason to investigate it.

There had to be someone else in the police force who knew what was going on. In turn, the police department needed more pressure to connect the women. Otherwise, they were ignoring a crucial lead.

I reached the front of the Communion line.

"The Body of Christ," said the woman. She held the Communion wafer in front of me.

"Amen," I said, bowing slightly.

She put the wafer in my hand, and as my fingers reached for it, it fell onto the ground. Embarrassed, I quickly picked it up and shoved it in my mouth. I hurried back to the pew, my mind starting to race.

And I realized that I did know someone.

22

It was easy enough to find Charice online. She was one of Dwayne's Facebook friends. Her profile page was public, and it showed pictures of her clubbing and going out with friends—she had over two thousand of them on Facebook. She'd also listed her phone number.

I called her instead of texting. It was more direct that way.

"Hello?"

"Hey, Charice. It's Mary. We met on Jayden's birthday?"

"Yeah, what's up?" She coughed, her voice faint and scratchy.

"Is this not a good time to talk?"

"It's fine. I think I got sick last night," croaked Charice. She and everyone else our age had stayed up until dawn, partying. "I've been sleeping in. What's going on?"

"Do you remember the morning at the beach?" I asked.

Charice cleared her throat, but she said nothing.

"I read somewhere that the police were mishandling DeMaria's investigation. A lot of people think more needs to be done for her."

"The cops don't give a shit," said Charice.

"Exactly. But some people think that she's connected to—"

"The Olivia girl," Charice finished. "I know—the serial killer theory. I've seen it online. No one's looking into it, though."

"We could change that," I said softly. "If the details of DeMaria's case were to be leaked online, then maybe the police would be forced to investigate it. There'd be more eyes on them, you know? They'd have to be held accountable for DeMaria."

"Maybe . . ."

"And your brother Felix is a cop, right? You guys mentioned him."

There was a long pause. Charice was thinking, weighing her options.

"It's just an idea," I said carefully. I didn't want to push it.

"Are you free tomorrow or Tuesday?" she finally asked.

Monday was my day off, but I spent most of it waiting for Charice to get out of class. At two thirty, I drove straight to the Isles Mall, located northeast of the city.

I found Charice at the food court. She was texting and dressed in a puffy gray jacket and a pair of black joggers. Her fingers moved furiously. Jayden sat beside her, watching a video on his phone.

"Hi, guys."

Charice flashed a smile while Jayden just nodded.

She'd never mentioned that he was coming along. Normally, I would've been annoyed if a friend's boyfriend showed up unannounced to our meeting.

But the current situation wasn't normal. We were doing something dangerous and illegal, and it put me, Charice, and her brother at risk.

Worse, she most likely had told her boyfriend everything. Jayden's presence compounded the situation—the more people involved, the greater the risk. I regretted calling her, but I had no other options.

"I was thinking of stopping at a store while we're here?" asked Charice. She flashed us a winning smile.

We stopped at Macy's. Charice was looking for a pair of warm and chunky high-heeled boots. While she was trying some on, I drifted toward the sale aisle. Jayden followed me, his hands in his jean pockets. He seemed tense, his eyes darting around the rest of the store. I realized that he was eyeing the cameras, the employees, the other customers nearby. He was watching them to see if they were watching him. I realized that was why he followed me—to avoid being stopped and checked. It seemed exhausting.

"So how's Dwayne?" I asked. We had nothing else to talk about.

"I don't know. Don't you two work together or something?"

"We do. Dwayne's just been . . . off lately. Like he's a little preoccupied."

"Damn," said Jayden. He sounded concerned. "I haven't seen my cousin since the lake thing."

"What?"

"Yeah. I've tried to hang out and shit, but he's been turning me down. Thought he was busy." Jayden sighed. "Dwayne's probably freaked out by what happened."

"You think so?"

"Yeah." Jayden stared at me. "Aren't you?"

The morning at Dwayne's apartment had shaken us all. One week ago, none of us had been prepared to find a hacked limb in the sand. You could read about cruelty and murder, you could see it depicted on screen and through art. But it was different to witness it with your own two eyes. The experience became a part of you. And the distance was gone. You realized that the violence was out there, a town, a mile, a block away from you.

No one was ever truly safe.

I glanced back at Charice. She was checking the bottom of her shoe.

"I thought we were supposed to talk about DeMaria here," I said quietly.

Jayden let out a loud cackle, so loud that some of the store employees turned to look at us. He clapped his hands together, amused.

"That's the funniest shit I've heard all day," he said.

▶ ▶ ▶

"You thought we'd talk about this at the mall?" Charice sounded incredulous.

We sat in Jayden's beat-up black car. After buying a pair of thigh-high black boots with a stiletto heel, Charice picked up a large pop from the food court. We went straight to Jayden's car right after.

"I thought that's what we planned."

"Nah. It's the mall parking lot that's safe. High traffic, lots of cars moving around. I figured I might as well buy something since we're here. But I planned for all this."

Charice unclasped her bag and handed me a unicorn folder. It was the kind I'd had back in elementary school.

"Not mine," she added. "It's my niece's."

There was a thin stack of paper inside. When I opened it, I felt my breath catch in my throat.

"Are these copies?" I whispered. Each sheet was in black and white, but the images were grainy and slightly off-kilter.

"I wish," said Charice. "My brother was paranoid about being tracked, so he just took photos of everything. They were real shitty photos, too."

"When did your brother do this?"

"For a while now . . . after I told him about what we saw," said Charice, her voice faint. "Felix has been working on it unofficially, but he can't really do much. He knows the people in the police department. They're not like the kind you see on *Law & Order*. A few of them are smart, but a lot of them are dumb as rocks. And they don't give a shit. No one thought a missing Black girl was someone to worry about."

"Not surprised," Jayden muttered. "Racist pigs."

"But they're okay with Felix."

Jayden snorted.

"Of course they are. He's one of them," Jayden shot back. "He does what they want him to do. Felix doesn't even care that much

about DeMaria—he just wants to be a police hero, right? Get pro-
moted to lieutenant or captain next year? Maybe get a cute medal or
some shit?"

Charice glared at him, unmoving.

"Babe, you don't have to be here with us," she said, her voice ee-
rily calm. "Mary and I can talk somewhere else."

Jayden said nothing. He stared out his window instead.

"Anyway, Mary," said Charice, turning back to me, "I cleaned up
the photos as much as I could. It's all readable."

I skimmed through the first three documents. It was the filed police report on DeMaria Jackson's forearm. It was less detailed than
I expected—only a few sentences and descriptions about everything
I'd witnessed at the beach. Next, there were the police reports for the
subsequent rescue boat operations that day. Charice had organized
the documents in order of relevance.

"I put the photos in the back. Just a warning, Mary. It's . . . rough."

I stopped flipping through the pages.

"Thanks," I said. I meant it for both the warning and the documents. "You really didn't have to do all this."

Charice shrugged, but she looked sad.

"We wouldn't have to do anything if people gave a shit," she said
softly.

I nodded.

"Me and Jayden skimmed through all of it, too," she added. "We
just wanted to see what was up."

"That's fine. If we plan to leak all of this, then it doesn't matter
who reads it," I said quietly. "We're all screwed if something happens."

Jayden said nothing.

"A lot of the info is like red-tape legal mumbo jumbo," said Charice. She lowered her voice. "Nothing about DeMaria being connected to Olivia. No mention of a serial killer. But the DeMaria
Jackson case is messy on its own."

"What do you mean?"

Charice shifted in the passenger's seat so that she faced both me and the back window.

"Okay, so she disappeared on Friday, July tenth. Her mom said she was going to work at a bougie restaurant called La Rue. De-Maria left her house at three thirty and never came back. But you know what the cops found out? She hadn't worked at La Rue for *months*. She'd lied to her mom. She was working at an Asian restaurant."

I nodded, pretending to be surprised.

"A few days later," continued Charice, "the police sent some rookie cop to look at DeMaria Jackson's room. The cop said he saw nothing strange, except that her wallet, phone, and some IDs were missing. Which makes sense."

"And then?"

"That's it," said Charice, looking glum. "There were no signs of foul play. Since she was over eighteen, DeMaria wasn't considered to be a missing person. It seemed like she just abandoned her family. She had a baby boy—did you know that?"

I shook my head. I thought about Demetrius waddling around their living room.

"The whole story is so sad. And DeMaria's mama kept calling the police, saying she was afraid that DeMaria had been kidnapped and placed in some sex trafficking ring."

"That's dark," Jayden murmured.

I remembered the crime documentaries I'd seen, where women were shuttled throughout the country in semitrucks and passed from hand to hand like a cigarette. They were drugged, raped, and beaten. I didn't want to think of DeMaria or Olivia being one of them.

"But that's only what her mama said," continued Charice. "Of-ficially, the police think she ran away—DeMaria was stuck raising a baby on her own, and her medical records show she'd been di-agnosed with depression. And before she disappeared, she'd gotten into a fight with her mama."

"What fight?" I asked. My voice was so loud that even Jayden turned around.

"It was over money. DeMaria never asked for child support. Her mama kept giving her shit for it. But that day, DeMaria told her to fuck off and disappeared."

My head began to ache.

During my interview with her, Leticia Jackson had never mentioned a fight. She made it seem like DeMaria had gone missing one random day. If there was no child support, then DeMaria was struggling on her own. Her ex, Charles, was in prison, so she couldn't have asked him for money. And if she'd had a depressive episode, then she could have spiraled. The entire situation looked grim—it almost seemed as if she'd run away because of financial problems.

There was a reason why Mrs. Jackson had hidden the fight—she couldn't afford the negative slant. She knew that the money situation would taint DeMaria's story. It was hard enough to get the public to care about her, so why share the unpleasant details? It was easier to shape her daughter in simpler terms: a young single mother who had disappeared one day.

In hiding the fight, Mrs. Jackson didn't implicate herself. She didn't look as if she'd pushed her daughter away after the fight.

The car ignition suddenly roared. Jayden was pulling us out of the parking lot.

"Why are we leaving?" asked Charice, annoyed.

"We look suspicious if we park here too long. And I do not want to get caught whistleblowing," said Jayden. Through the rearview mirror, he was looking at the unicorn envelope in my hands. "I'm just driving us around."

"Thanks for watching out." Charice and I quickly put our seat belts on.

"You should tell Mary about the medical shit, though. It's important."

Charice turned back, her eyes wide.

"The autopsy reports were hard to read. Not gonna lie—it was some horrible shit. Some rescue boats found DeMaria Jackson's legs in the lake. Like . . . her entire legs."

It corroborated with what Kevin had said at Espresso Haus. The legs would have floated along the lake current, about as indistinguishable as the tree branches that fell in.

"And you remember how the skin at the end of the arm looked ratty?"

I nodded. The splintered skin had looked like the frayed edges of a worn rope.

"The coroner said that her cuts might've been made with a splitting maul. They're used for splitting down wood logs."

"Okay," I said slowly.

"The coroner said that the splitting maul is sharp enough for precise, clean cuts. But the marks on DeMaria's legs were messy. There were like multiple marks, too, that barely scratched the skin. That's not supposed to happen with a maul. The coroner suggested that whoever did the chopping was moving fast. Like they were angry. There might've been a struggle . . ."

"She was cut while she was alive?" I asked.

Neither of them wanted to respond. The unicorn envelope was sitting in my lap, both of my hands planted firmly over it. I was afraid the papers would suddenly disappear.

Outside the sky had grown cloudy, an eerie mix of white and gray blanketing over us. It was a sky that promised an early November snow.

"Do they know when it happened?" I murmured. "Her death?"

"The coroner said that the arm was frozen on the inside. But the exterior had already started thawing in the lake water. Coroner thinks she could've been frozen for a while. Potentially up to three and a half months."

I swallowed.

"What an evil motherfucker," muttered Jayden.

"Agreed."

We were silent as he drove.

"Other issue here: How the fuck are we gonna leak all this?" he asked.

I took a deep breath.

"We send it to the online tip lines at the *New York Times, Washington Post, Boston Globe,* the big ones. They have programs that encrypt the information we send them, so there's no online paper trail that leads to us. In theory, we don't get tracked."

"'In theory,'" repeated Jayden. "I don't like those odds."

"We can also mail paper copies."

"Won't they catch our fingerprints on the envelope?" he pressed.

"Not if we're careful."

"If we get caught, I'm getting my ass beat. You understand that? Charice's brother loses his job, we all go to jail. You might not—"

"No, I get it."

"I don't think you do."

"How about we buy somebody's used tablet?" asked Charice loudly. Jayden and I fell silent. "We use a coffee shop's Wi-Fi and send the file to a bunch of newspapers through their encrypted system. Then we break the tablet and dump it somewhere else. They can't really track us then. It's almost foolproof."

After a moment, Jayden whistled.

"Damn, that actually sounds good."

When we returned to the Isles Mall parking lot, I dug into my purse and handed Charice thirty dollars.

"This is my share for the tablet. I'm not sure how expensive they are."

Charice handed me back a ten-dollar bill.

"I'll find some shitty tablet on Craigslist for less than fifty, don't worry," she said. "We'll cover the rest in cash, too."

"And what are you gonna do?" Jayden asked as he turned around. He gave me a hard look. "We're leaking DeMaria's police file to the big newspapers, and you are . . . ?"

"I'm gonna target the local newspapers," I said quickly. I had to look away from Jayden's gaze. "It's harder to reach out to them un-detected. But they might be more likely to talk about DeMaria's case if the *NYT* doesn't. And I might check with a few journalist friends to see what they can do."

"Okay," said Charice. "We all do this quick then."

I unbuckled my seat belt. Before I left, I had one last question.

"Did your brother ever have access to Olivia Willand's file?"

Charice shook her head.

"It was too risky. There's a lot of eyes on her case," she said. "Fe-lix said they interviewed a ton of people, including her sorority, but not much of it was useful. She just vanished in the park reserve."

"And her nude photo?"

"They're still investigating it."

I sighed. Even in death, Olivia was hard to read. I realized that I now knew more about a stranger than I did my childhood friend. I wasn't sure if I'd ever known her.

"The whole damn universe is looking for the Olivia girl," mut-tered Jayden. "I wouldn't give two shits if it didn't involve DeMaria."

I ignored him. Jayden's actions were more crucial than his words—and I needed him to cooperate.

"Thanks for everything, Charice," I croaked. I meant it.

"Stay safe," she said. She took a sip of her pop—a large Dr Pepper—and scanned the parking lot through her window. "If we're right, then there's a serial killer out here somewhere. That's scary as hell."

"Evil-ass creep," muttered Jayden.

As soon as I got back into Mom's car, I slammed on the lock, peering behind at the back of the car. I hid the unicorn folder under my seat, the back of my neck crawling. And before I left, I looked back one final time.

23

At home, I locked myself in my room and opened the folder that Charice had given me. But the words seemed to slip right before my eyes. I couldn't concentrate.

I turned to the back of the documents, where Charice had placed the photos. I braced myself for the gore. But the pictures were grainy—a photo of another photo on a computer screen. DeMaria's legs and forearm had been photographed at multiple angles. In one image, DeMaria's left leg looked ghostly. It was speckled with craters where the fish had eaten away at her flesh.

At the bottom of the stack, there was a close-up image of De-Maria's hand. Someone had stretched out her fingers so that they were far apart from each other. Her thumb and forefinger made the letter "L." In the small web of skin between her two fingers, there was a tiny black heart. A tattoo.

I turned to the initial autopsy report that Charice had summarized. The coroner had found multiple incisions in the radius and ulna in her forearm, some of which had gone completely through the bone. The coroner suggested that the wounds had been made with a sharp common outdoor tool, likely a splitter maul.

On DeMaria's right leg, the coroner also noted multiple incised wounds through the femur, but they were too numerous and detailed to count, as Charice had mentioned. On DeMaria's left leg, there was a similar set of fewer wounds. The killer had most likely dismembered her right leg first, gotten tired, and then worked on her left leg.

But there was an inconsistency to the killer's work. The coroner noted that the incised wounds on the legs had all been relatively contained to the same area. The wounds on DeMaria's forearm, however, were scattered. There were shallower cuts that grazed farther down. The coroner believed that DeMaria's arms had been moving—she had been struggling before she died.

And there was one detail that Charice had forgotten to mention: there were deep rope indentations on DeMaria's wrist and ankles. She'd been restrained while she struggled.

The coroner's overall conclusion was that DeMaria had been dismembered alive.

I put the photos away. The more I knew about what had happened, the less I could stomach looking at them.

I skimmed through the last of the police reports. There was a jolt in my stomach when I saw Mr. Nguyen's name. A police officer had interviewed him a few days ago.

The officer wrote a single paragraph: *Mr. Nguyen was cooperative and is eager to help with future inquiries. Mr. Nguyen verified that DeMaria Jackson had worked for him as a server between February–July. He claims that DeMaria was scheduled to work on July 10, the day of disappearance. DeMaria showed up late and then promptly quit. Mr. Nguyen saw her leave and noted nothing strange about her behavior. I left him a card with contact information.*

I closed the folder and slid it under my bed.

▶ ▶ ▶

Pho Village was quiet during the lull between lunch and dinner. Mr. Nguyen was tapping through his phone at the cash register, a Vikings baseball cap on his head.

"Hi, Mr. Nguyen," I said loudly. I sounded chipper.

"Mary," he said, glancing back at his phone. "Are you eating here today, or—"

"I just wanted to talk to you about something important," I said lightly, as if we were discussing a day at the cabin. "It's about De-Maria Jackson."

Mr. Nguyen suddenly looked up, stone-faced. His eyes seemed to dart back and forth between mine. It was a trait that Madison shared. The few times that we'd argued, Madison would remain passive as her eyes roved back and forth. They were scoping out some weakness, some flaw. I was always uncomfortable when it happened, as if I were being studied under a microscope.

"If you need more information, you can talk to the police."

"They won't tell me anything."

"Then you shouldn't ask me."

"I think it's important."

Mr. Nguyen shook his head. His gaze shifted over to the lone group of customers sitting at a booth.

"I think you should go back to studying," he said. "You're giving yourself a headache here."

I leaned forward, keeping my voice as pleasant as possible.

"I know DeMaria worked at Pho Village for a little while. And you said you saw her on the day she disappeared."

"How would you know that?" he asked. His eyes were hard and dark. He was frowning, the wrinkle lines drawn near his mouth.

I ignored him.

"I just need to know about the last time you saw her. Like what did she say and where was she going afterward? Did you notice any-thing strange about her on that day?"

Mr. Nguyen suddenly headed for the front door of the restaurant. I followed him outside into the cold, the door slamming behind me.

"Mr. Nguyen, I know you don't want to talk about this, but it's important. There might be a killer here in the city who went after DeMaria, then Olivia Willand. And that killer might go after some-one else, too, unless—"

"Please leave, Mary," said Mr. Nguyen, his eyes flashing. "I al-ready talked to the police about this. I'm just trying to work."

"DeMaria quit here on the day she disappeared. Don't you think you might have noticed something important?"

"Why would I know anything?"

"Your employee's body was found ripped apart in a lake. Now another girl is missing. Doesn't that concern you?"

Mr. Nguyen said nothing.

"And if someone else dies, wouldn't part of that be your fault?" I blurted.

He glared, his jaw set. I had never seen Mr. Nguyen look so angry before. The contempt radiated off him. He typed a number into his cell phone and put it against his ear.

"There are other people's lives at stake."

"Hello? Hi, I'm requesting police," he said into the phone.

A shiver ran through me.

"Yes, I'd like to report a harasser here at my restaurant . . . Yes, she's still here . . . No violence so far, but harasser refuses to leave my property. I'd like someone to remove her."

My eyes were growing wet, watching as Mr. Nguyen described my clothes and my features to the police dispatcher. He was treating me as if I were a stranger, a criminal.

"Should I give her one last warning?" asked Mr. Nguyen.

But I was backing away, already beelining for Mom's car. When I was out of the parking lot, Mr. Nguyen was still on the phone.

▶ ▶ ▶

I lay on the couch, staring aimlessly at a law drama on TV. I never even got up to make dinner for Dad, who was coming home late. Instead, I dug my hands into a bag of barbecue-flavored potato chips.

But no matter how hard I tried, I kept looking at my cell phone on the coffee table. I kept watching it, waiting for an angry phone call from Mr. Nguyen. Or the police.

After my incident with Carly, there had been a phone call. An RA named Vince had spoken on the phone. And I had watched him, my stomach growling in the hallway. I was nearly giddy—I knew he was talking about me. But I should have known that it was the beginning of the end.

There was a buzz from the coffee table—my cell phone was vibrating. I stared at it, unmoving. It was either Mr. Nguyen or the police. Whoever it was, it didn't bode well.

Slowly, I reached for the phone. It was an incoming call from Madison. I began to tremble.

"Madison?"

"Did you harass my dad at work?"

I could hear my own breathing in the phone.

"I was asking him about a missing girl who once worked at the restaurant."

"He had nothing to do with her death," Madison said. Her words were cold, clipped. It was almost worse that way.

"I never said that I suspected him."

"You told my dad that it was his fault if another girl died. You know how fucking insane you sound?"

My mouth felt dry.

"I just think your dad knows something about DeMaria Jackson. And if there's a serial killer out there—"

"What serial killer?"

"The same person who went after Olivia—"

"I don't fucking care about Olivia," said Madison, her voice rising. I realized that the memory still haunted her.

Madison was euphoric when our high school made her the valedictorian. Her GPA had beaten mine by a hundredth of a decimal. Madison thought it would help her with college applications. She thought Yale would appreciate it.

Then in calculus class, one of Olivia's friends mentioned the news. Olivia sighed. She sat only a few rows behind us.

"Why's the valedictorian always Asian?" asked Olivia. "Can't the rest of America get a chance?"

"Right?" someone else agreed. "It's kind of annoying."

"We should have two of them. One Asian, one normal," said Olivia. Her friends snickered. Other people agreed.

Meanwhile Madison said nothing. We sat in the front row, and Madison kept working in her notebook. With me, she was outspoken and blunt. But in class, she couldn't say anything to Olivia or our classmates. I couldn't defend her, either. No one would take our side.

Later, in private, Madison was fuming.

"Sorry I can't fuck my way to the top," she ranted in the car. "It's not my fault I'm not a lazy, stupid bitch."

I did my best to comfort her. I had never seen Madison so upset before. But the day was supposed to be hers—we were meant to celebrate her hard work, the hours she'd put in. Instead, Olivia had shat on it in less than a minute. The moment had stuck with her.

"I don't care about Olivia," Madison repeated. "I don't even care about the other girl. The police and the FBI are handling it. They're supposed to be talking to my dad, not you."

I swallowed, but I couldn't think of anything to say.

"What are you trying to prove with this?" she asked.

I leaned against the couch cushion, words spinning in my head.

I imagined Madison standing outside a corporate office building. She might have just left an internship, dressed in a nice skirt, blazer, and heels. To a stranger, she probably looked like she was in the middle of a fierce business deal.

"Look," said Madison. She sighed, as if our talk had lasted longer than she preferred. "I know you're bored at home, and I know you're sad about flunking out of Cornell. But there is no need for you to go around harassing people."

"I didn't flunk out," I blurted loudly. The thought pained me. "I didn't harass your dad. But if he knows something about a murdered girl, he should be talking about it."

"You think he's hiding something?"

I hesitated. I knew how badly the conversation would go. It was inevitable, like a car dashing off the side of a cliff. It was too late to stop.

"I think your dad knows more than he's letting on," I murmured.

Through the living room window, I watched a tree branch shifting in the wind.

"I thought you'd changed, Mary," said Madison, her voice soft. "But you are still so pretentious. It's disgusting."

"I'm just trying to help," I whispered.

"Of course you are, Mary. You're a saint who does things out of the kindness of her heart."

I shook my head, but Madison couldn't see. She kept talking.

"You think you're so smart and special and misunderstood that you don't belong back home. You thought Cornell made you better than everyone else. And you thought you were gonna be some chic city girl who everyone was gonna talk about. But what happens? You still end up back home anyway. Now you're using *murders* to make yourself feel better?"

"That's not—"

"Stop with the morality bullshit. Please. You said that Olivia was gonna end up a pregnant white trash bitch. Don't you remember? Because I do." Madison paused, the anger seeping into her words. "Don't pretend you're any better, Mary. You are as fake and irrelevant as the people back home."

I shook my head. My face was burning. And I realized my eyes were wet.

Madison and I had wanted more than Liberty Lake—that was what brought us together. We were smart and hardworking and unloved. We were the underdogs. And as the underdogs, we were due for more than the other people in our school, our class, our city.

But how cruel we could be about the others: the boys who we hoped were locked up by high school graduation; the girls who we assumed would get knocked up afterward; the comments I'd make about girls who would one day be dead.

As teenagers, Madison and I were jealous and vindictive. We recognized it, too, that rage and that spite in each other. But we left it unsaid. We never directed it at each other.

But now Madison had said the unspoken. It hurt, as if she'd reached up under my rib cage and throttled my lungs. I heard no lies.

"Don't talk to my dad again," Madison said quietly. "All he does is work at the restaurant. He doesn't get involved in anything outside of it. I thought you knew that."

I put a hand to my mouth, trying to cover the watery hiccup that was coming out.

"And whatever kind of shit you're trying to do, stop it."

There was a click and then silence.

24

S mile, Mary," said Jim. "You look so glum."

He passed by my aisle early in the morning, giving me a thumbs-up. But I only stared back. Jim's smile quickly disappeared.

"If you feel the urge to upchuck, you go home, okay?" said Jim, half-jokingly. "Whole store keeps getting sick. We don't want our customers getting puked on, do we?"

"No, we don't," I murmured.

The day at Goodhue Groceries was long and mindless—one customer after the other. They each paid too much for their organic peppers and kale and oat milk. I was mechanical. I punched in the proper codes, returned the exact change, and rescanned someone's entire order because they had forgotten to give me their coupons. At work, I barely existed.

But it was better than the alternative—being trapped at home, alone. The house was too quiet.

When I'd woken up, I could already hear Madison's voice in my ears. It was like a chain that held me down, yanking at my shoulders and my throat. It left me immobile in bed.

Madison wasn't wrong about me. Everything that I had tried to bury and forget—it washed over me, drowning me. I hated high school and I liked college, but none of it mattered anymore. They were all in the past.

Ivy League Mary was gone.

Now only Mary was left, and she only had herself to blame.

I could deal with the grocery store lights and the shitty customers. But I couldn't be left alone with Madison. Not like that.

I slogged through the day until lunch. When I entered the break room, Dwayne was picking up a bag of chips from the vending machine. He saw me before I could leave.

"Hey," he said sheepishly. "Mind if I join you?"

I nodded without thinking.

Neither of us spoke as we ate. I felt better when the volume rose and more people trickled in for lunch. The last time I'd spoken to Dwayne, he'd snapped at me over Kevin.

I wasn't in the mood to talk.

Dwayne seemed to realize this, too. He said nothing, scrolling through his phone. Up close his green polo shirt was wrinkled, as if he'd left it too long in the dryer.

Past his shoulder, I noticed Ron's dark hair. He was heating up his lunch at the office microwave, his back turned to us. I remembered the scene in the parking lot, and the anger stung all over again. I had let him scare me. I had let him call Olivia a missing slut. I had let him assume things about me and Dwayne. And Ron thought he could get away untouched—

"How have things been?" Dwayne asked.

"I've been fine."

"Did you hear about what happened on Saturday? The thing about Olivia?"

"Someone leaked her nude at the park," I said. "Apparently emailed a shit-ton of people."

Dwayne shook his head.

"I couldn't make the search, but honestly," he said, his voice getting lower, "I'm kind of glad I didn't go. You know how many people are talking about it?"

I shook my head, but I could guess. I assumed it was everyone. Olivia was being discussed everywhere—national news, cable news, Internet publications, gossip sites, forum threads, word of mouth. But the conversation had moved on from her disappearance. It was focused on her nude photo. It would inspire editorials and debates about sexual freedom, slutty behavior, purity culture. There would be discussions about what Olivia meant and what her nude photo represented in the current sociological landscape.

But there was less talk about how to find her.

"I just hope she's okay," I murmured.

Dwayne turned his bag of chips in my direction. It was an offering.

"This is my apology for last week," said Dwayne, pushing the chips toward me. "I'm sorry for being a dick."

"That's a weak apology," I said, but I felt a grin sprouting on my face. I reached out and took one chip. "I won't talk about Kevin again."

Dwayne scoffed, but he said nothing. He reached over the table and took my sandwich wrapper and his and crumpled them together into a ball. He reminded me of a little boy—he was distracting himself because he didn't know what else to do.

"But is there a reason why you two aren't cool anymore?" I asked softly. Dwayne shrugged, rolling the trash ball in his hands.

"I don't know. I liked Kevin in high school. He used to pick up the tab for me whenever we got tacos or pizza. And he knew how to throw a good party. Never afraid to share his hot tub or his dad's liquor cabinet."

Back in high school, Kevin had lived in a McMansion on the border of North Hamilton. The house had a pool and a fancy grill in the backyard, along with a hot tub. After losing the election and his wife, Mr. Obermueller put more time into working. He traveled more, and Kevin often had the place to himself.

People made out at Kevin's parties, threw up in Kevin's yard, and hooked up in Kevin's pool. His friendship came with many perks. It was why people like Dwayne and Olivia had tolerated him.

But everything I knew about Kevin's parties was hearsay. In all four years of high school, Madison and I had never received a single invitation. I made up for lost time in college—the frat parties, the drugs, the booze, the sex. But by then, those things had lost the appeal, the *taboo,* that they seemed to carry in Liberty Lake. It was never as exciting.

Dwayne seemed to miss all of it. Why wouldn't he, when high school had been so good to him?

"I thought you guys drifted apart," I murmured.

"That's one way to put it," said Dwayne. He wasn't looking at me. "I liked Kevin in high school. Yeah, he said some weird shit sometimes, but I let a lot of it slide back then. But then after graduation, Kevin went off to police school or whatever you call it."

"Police academy?" I offered.

"Yeah. *Police academy.* He became a cop." Dwayne hesitated, as if he were carefully picking his words. "I dunno. The vibe changed. Now he had a Taser and a gun. And it felt like he was on some sort of . . . power trip. He got bold. These weren't the same old jokes anymore. He'd say some really fucked-up things . . . Shit, I didn't want to talk about politics or any of that stuff with him. But he kept pushing it. And it felt like he was egging me on, you know? He wanted to piss me off. Like he wanted me to start something.

"And I couldn't." I watched as Dwayne took apart the wrappers in his hands. "I was supposed to just take it. One wrong move, and I was fucked. He could really do anything to me. Like I could piss him off, and he could arrest me, you know? He could literally start beating my ass, and he could make it seem okay. And if he killed me . . . not much would have happened."

I couldn't think of anything to say back.

"But . . . would he do that?" I asked finally. "He's a cop. He could do that stuff to anybody."

"Some people more than others . . ." Dwayne said, trailing off.

He seemed lost in thought. For some reason, I thought of Jayden and his aversion toward Charice's brother.

But Kevin confused me. He was thorny, and he came off as more vindictive than he meant to be. He'd hurt me as a child, and he was rude to people he didn't care for. Kevin had lurked in Dwayne's shadow for years, but things had changed. Kevin had power as a police officer, and he liked that he now had it over Dwayne. He would have relished it, and Dwayne would have taken things the wrong way.

But Kevin cared about Olivia. I believed it fully. He'd loved her since childhood. At the park, he'd diligently searched for her. When her nude photo had been leaked, Kevin had tried to stop the situation, even though he'd been flustered. I knew that no matter how badly he treated other people, he would make Olivia the exception. I had to trust him.

Dwayne cleared his throat. He had a tired grin on his face.

"I don't want you to feel bad for me, Mary. Things change after high school. Some people drift apart, others just cut it off. Kevin and I happen to be very different people," he said mirthlessly. "It would've always ended up like this. Outside of the partying, we didn't have much in common anyway. It was all convenience."

I thought about Madison. Maybe our friendship had been like that—one of convenience. Maybe we stuck together because instinctively we knew it was better to have someone than no one. Perhaps we'd never liked each other—it was all contempt, masked by high school desperation.

"Who'd have thought things would turn out the way they did?" Dwayne asked. I heard the unmistakable pang in his voice.

"You sound like an old man when you say that."

"I do feel old," he said.

"That makes two of us."

By the time my shift was over, it was already dark outside. In the break room, I put on my winter jacket and grabbed my purse.

Dwayne suddenly came in, a black duffel bag slung around his shoulder.

"You heading to the gym?" I asked.

"Mm-hm."

The two of us left the break room together, walking down the hallway.

"You got plans tonight, Ivy League?"

"Probably dinner with my dad and some TV."

"Sounds exciting."

"That's me. Always exciting."

But more than likely, I would be holed up in my room.

I had no idea how to leak DeMaria's investigation to the local press. Their websites couldn't protect their anonymous sources—there were no encryption programs in place. Even a fake email account could be tracked. I could only think of sending paper copies through the mail, but there was more room for human error.

Meanwhile I had to hope that Charice and Jayden were doing their work. I couldn't risk texting them for updates.

Dwayne stopped at the exit doors, an arm out on the handle. He turned toward me, smiling sheepishly.

"If you're not busy tonight, would you want to come over to my place and hang out?"

There was a pause as we looked at each other. My face grew warm, and I thought about how my hair stuck out from under my wool hat and how my scarf was unkempt around my neck. My pulse was racing. It was strange how this exact moment had occurred other times before, with other people. Yet I still never knew how to react when it did.

A door slammed down the hallway—the two of us nearly jumped. Ron skulked by, a skateboard under his arm. He squinted at us, suspicious.

Dwayne raised a hand to greet him. Ron just looked from me to Dwayne, his expression sour, as if the guilt were apparent on both of our faces. Ron left without a word.

When it was just the two of us, I felt my face burn again.

"I'll see you tonight after dinner then," I said.

Dwayne nodded, his smile still sheepish.

By the time I made it to my car, the cold air had blasted across my face and seeped onto my fingertips. But I could only focus on the small knot of warmth that had built up in my chest.

After dinner, I showered. When it got late, I told Dad I was going to see a movie with my friend Charice. I would be sleeping over at her place for the night.

Dad said nothing as he watched TV. He told me to drive safe. He could tell that I was lying to him, and he probably suspected that there was no Charice for the night and no wholesome girls' movie to watch. But what else could he do except play along?

At the Jewel of Liberty Lake, I parked in the only open guest spot, beneath a light pole. Dwayne buzzed me through the front doors, and I waited as the elevator propelled me upward.

It was quiet in the hallway when I knocked. I fought the urge to turn back. I was past high school, I was older now, I was better—

And then the door opened. Dwayne peered down at me in a gray T-shirt. The apartment was dark. I could hear my heart pounding in my ears, feel the air ripple with heat. And I liked that rush as the thoughts went away and pure feeling remained.

"Hey."

"Hey."

As soon as he shut the door, I felt his fingers dig into my waist. And his lips were falling onto mine and my arms were wrapping around his shoulders. He lifted me through the dark of the apartment, tossing me onto the bed as our hands peeled off each other's layers. We were greedy and hungry and desperate. We were frenzied, as if we'd been deprived our whole lives.

And as moonlight spilled through the window, the two of us were rocking and clinging onto each other until we'd worn ourselves out. And I saw his eyes peering up at me from the pillow, watching as I rocked.

He didn't love me, and I didn't love him. But for those brief moments, we were enough.

25

I woke up shivering. I was curled up against the window. Dwayne's comforter barely covered my waist. The rest of it was on top of him, his back turned to me. He was snoring as I slipped out of bed, naked.

It was still dark outside, but I could no longer see the moon. The lake and the sky seemed to blend together as one.

I found my oversized sweater on the floor and slipped it on before using the toilet.

Dwayne's bathroom was clean, the tiles and the sink all immaculate, as if they had just been washed. Even after I flushed, the toilet reeked of mild bleach. At the sink, I rinsed out my mouth and washed my face.

In the mirror, my cheeks were still flushed from before—I looked like I was sick with a mild fever. My hair was messy around my face. But I looked alive. I looked more alive than I had back in high school, when my hair was limp and my body was doughy. Time, for the moment, had taken mercy on me.

At eighteen, I never dreamt of kissing the school football star. I never even thought that he'd look at me in that kind of way. But four years later, I had somehow done it and then some. In a way, it was poetic justice—I was making up for all those lost years in high school. I had proven them wrong.

Madison would have been proud of me. She would have understood the achievement, and she would've been screaming over the phone, asking me for the details. We'd cackle giddily, as if I'd just lost my virginity all over again. Then we would reminisce about the past and how those painful years had paid off.

But Madison had moved on, both from the city and me.

As I tiptoed back to bed, I heard a slight buzz. The sound was muffled on the other side of the apartment. In the dark, I saw a tiny sliver of light on the floor next to the kitchen counter. It was Dwayne's phone, whirring in a pocket of his jeans.

Dwayne didn't stir.

The vibrations stopped as soon as I pulled out the phone. It was abrupt, like the phone call at Littlewood Park had been.

But Dwayne had only received two texts. They were from Jayden, who was still apparently awake. His phone only showed a few snippets of each text:

69,000 days later . . . You good???

And youre dealing with shit . . .

Before I could help it, my thumb tapped on the first text. A screen came up, prompting for a four-number pass code. On a whim, I typed in "1-2-3-4." There was a buzz as the phone denied it.

Dwayne's heavy breathing was reassuring—he was still dead asleep.

I stared at the keypad, unable to turn away. I was still high from my night with Dwayne, and I was eager to try my luck. I was like a child who dared to hold her breath underwater—each time was a little longer, a little riskier.

Jayden said he hadn't seen Dwayne in a while, so it seemed that

Jayden's text was important. And if it involved the leak that we'd planned, then I needed to know.

I typed in two more obvious combinations (1-1-1-1; 9-9-9-9), slid my finger down the center column (2-5-8-0), and even pressed the numbers from the corners (1-3-7-9). Each time the phone buzzed, locked. I had one attempt left before Dwayne's phone would lock for an entire hour.

I closed my eyes, listening to Dwayne's breathing as he slept soundly. Dwayne was smart, but he seemed like someone who would prefer a familiar pass code, something so convenient that he wouldn't forget it.

After a few seconds, I finally typed it in: 1-9-9-3. Our birth year. The screen suddenly loaded Jayden's two recent texts:

69,000 days later . . . You good??? You still alive??

And youre dealing with shit . . . I get it, man, I do. It's a hard time right now with everything . . . But at least text back damn!!

I scrolled up and saw the long line of texts that had all come from Jayden recently. Dwayne hadn't replied to any of them. Jayden's non-stop texts had started a few days ago, around the same time that I'd met up with him and Charice.

$5 BURGER NIGHT @ SHIRLEYS DUDE LETS GO!!!

It's been like a week, man. You doing anything?? Bored AF

Jayden's texts soon became less playful:

What's going on?? Are you pissed or some shit??

Dude youre on FB now but you cant send me a text? If you want space just tell me but damn this shit's annoying

Jayden hadn't lied about the last time he'd seen Dwayne. He said it was because of the traumatic scene at the beach, but the texts said differently—Jayden seemed to think it was a personal issue between them.

A second later, I deleted the two newest texts. I didn't need Dwayne to find out that they'd already been opened. Jayden would send more later—I was sure of it. And his cousin had never replied back anyway.

Dwayne had a long list of texts from multiple people, nearly all of them from Goodhue Groceries. The snippets of conversations were about work—people texting in sick or taking over someone else's shift.

But Dwayne had very few texts outside of his coworkers. I saw no messages from old football teammates or high school friends or college buddies. He hadn't texted his parents in two weeks. His phone seemed inactive, like he rarely talked to anyone outside of work. But Dwayne wasn't someone cut out for loneliness.

I felt dirty, then, thinking about it. I was digging through Dwayne's personal life, seeing it naked in the open. No one liked to show that they were lonely.

I nearly shut off the phone, but then I stopped. There was a name peeking out at the bottom of the screen.

Olivia.

My stomach lurched.

My thumb grazed the screen.

The text message loaded.

I was looking at Olivia. She was naked and seductively staring into the screen, with only a purple bra on her body. It was the same picture that Dad, me, and everyone else at Littlewood Park Reserve had received.

Beneath it, Dwayne had sent a reply: That's hot babe . . . you're making it hard to focus at work right now. You're gonna get me fired haha

The message was dated October 18. The day Olivia had gone missing.

The phone slipped out of my hands, clattering onto the kitchen floor. I was struggling to breathe, my hands clamping themselves over my mouth. My heart was beating so fast that I could hear the blood pumping in my ears.

"Mary?" There was rustling from the bed.

I squatted down, grabbing the phone. I closed out of his text messages, my fingers slick. They were sweaty when I turned off the power button.

"What are you doing?"

I turned around just as the kitchen lights flickered on.

Dwayne stood a few feet away, shirtless in his boxer briefs. His eyes flickered from me to the jeans on the floor, the cell phone clumsily stowed away somewhere inside.

My heart was in my throat.

"What are you doing?" he asked faintly.

"I—I was looking at the time."

"On my phone?"

"I don't know where mine is," I said truthfully.

"Yours is on the counter," he said, pointing to my left. My stomach dropped when I saw it lying clearly in the open.

"Thanks," I stammered. "I—I just needed to peek at the time."

"Yeah?" Dwayne asked tersely, his gaze looking past me. "You find anything good while you're at it?"

I swallowed, shook my head no.

The studio suddenly seemed so small. And I realized that Dwayne was tall and large and muscular, taking up most of the space around me.

I was a speck compared to him.

And unlike my time with Kevin in the woods, I didn't have the safety of other people nearby to watch us. It was just Dwayne and me.

I was trapped.

The air was thin. My body was pulsing with dread, the panic not far away.

But Dwayne didn't move. He stayed put, staring at me.

"Mary, I think you should leave," Dwayne said stiffly. His voice was so measured that it put me on edge. "I don't think I feel comfortable with you here."

I nodded quickly.

When Dwayne said nothing else, I took my chance. I clawed at my clothes on the floor. In my other arm, I grappled for my phone and my purse. I kept my back to the wall, my eyes focused on Dwayne. I was afraid that he'd suddenly rush forward.

But Dwayne didn't move. He seemed glued to the floor, watching me carefully, as if he thought I was about to steal something.

I finally opened the front door. I swiveled back, made sure that Dwayne hadn't moved.

Half-naked, I walked faster down the hallway, my heart pounding in my ears. I turned around, expecting to be grabbed.

But the door to Dwayne's apartment closed. I heard the loud click of his lock, the rattle of the door handle as he checked it from inside.

I stopped just outside the elevators. I slipped on my pants and my jacket. There was no security guard downstairs. By the time I hurried to the car outside, I was shaking. And it wasn't from the cold.

26

I got home just after four in the morning. The streets were empty and quiet on the ride back. Most of the city was still asleep. But I heard the blood pumping in my ears.

In the shower, I turned on the water as hot as I could bear it. I let it drench me, a blanket of steam around my throat and my lungs. I was still shivering.

When I closed my eyes, I saw the picture of Olivia. She'd sent it to Dwayne. And she never imagined that it would fall into other hands, into other places. The image of her now burned forever on the Internet. Even when I scrubbed myself raw, I felt grimy, as if whatever malice at Dwayne's place had soaked itself inside of me.

Dwayne hadn't been at the Halloween search. He said he'd been with family, but I suspected that was a lie. From the texts, it was clear that even Jayden hadn't seen his own cousin since the morning at the beach. On Halloween, Dwayne had the perfect opportunity to leak the photo. I didn't know how he'd planned it nor how he'd gotten the contact information to do it. But he'd had Olivia's photo before the leak.

Things were sexual between the two of them—they'd still been talking to each other recently. Dwayne could have harbored feelings for her, the high school friend who had become Internet famous. But there was no reason to leak her photo. There was no reason to kill her.

Still, it only took a moment, a spark of rage.

Anger could push anyone too far—I knew that from experience.

After my shower, I sat on the toilet, my head in my hands. I was light-headed from the steam, but I preferred it that way, the images all hazy and blurry:

Dwayne and Olivia meeting up somewhere discreet. The two of them getting into a fight. Olivia dead in some spur-of-the-moment violence. Dwayne quickly disposing of her.

I could picture it all so easily.

But something else bothered me: DeMaria Jackson. She had to factor in somehow, but based on what I knew about Dwayne, she shouldn't have.

"You ever notice the kind of girls that Dwayne likes?" Madison once mused.

It was the day after the Patriots defeated Ondaasagaam High School. Liberty Lake was entering the state football championship, and Dwayne had appeared in the city newspaper, a hero standing proud in the rain, his fist held to the sky.

As soon as he entered the lunchroom, a group of his friends began to holler and cheer. Kevin was the loudest out of them. Everyone else quickly broke into applause. Dwayne grinned and took a long bow. Olivia patted his cheek before his friends ushered him away.

When the noise died down, Madison had a smirk on her face.

"Did you know Dwayne's hooking up with Penny Jones?" she asked.

"Really?" Penny was the co-captain of the color guard.

"Yeah," Madison said. "I was surprised, too. Penny's not that talkative outside of the guard. But then again, it kind of makes sense."

"Does it?"

"You ever notice the kind of girls that Dwayne likes?"

I shrugged, hoping that no one else had heard her. But even then I'd known she was right. Dwayne had dated Olivia Willand, who, at the time, had reached two thousand followers on Instagram. Before her, he'd dated Alyson Johnson, the student council president. Other sources confirmed that Dwayne had also slept with Alexis Vance, a star volleyball player, and Isabella Murphy, the runner-up to Miss Teen North Star.

The girls were all pretty and well-known. Their names appeared in the weekly announcements, their faces on the school's bulletin boards. Among the sea of students, they stood out. They were special, and Dwayne appreciated that. He was special, too. Number twenty-four of the Patriots had a type.

And it seemed like DeMaria Jackson was not it. In life, she drew neither attention nor praise. She was pretty but unremarkable. It seemed unlikely that Dwayne would have noticed her.

But then again, her arm had washed up outside his apartment . . .

When I opened the bathroom door, I watched as the steam floated out. The cold air crept in, mottling my arms with goose bumps. The cold air rattled me awake.

In my bedroom, I pulled up the office number for the Liberty Lake police on my phone.

They were only one click away.

But I couldn't do it.

I pictured Dwayne's grin, the one dimple on his cheek, the way his eyes crinkled up as he flirted with an old woman at work. I remembered the way Jim seemed to gush about him. Even if he had never finished college, Dwayne had still made something of himself. That was more than what a lot of people could say, including me.

Dwayne was too nice, too charming, too handsome, too normal to kill someone.

That's what I hoped.

But people had said the same things about other killers. And they had been proven wrong.

Before I knew it, an hour had passed as I sat in bed, paralyzed by my choices. I shut my eyes tight.

As a child, whenever I got overwhelmed about schoolwork, I would force myself to sleep on it. I hoped that I would wake up with a fresh mind.

And every single time, I would wake up as anxious and paralyzed as before.

There was a loud crash downstairs. The door from the garage had slammed open. I jerked awake, drool slipping down my lips.

The house was dark when I got downstairs. I could see the gloomy, brisk November day outside. But the light was turned on in the kitchen. Dad was brewing a pot of coffee. He hadn't taken off his work overalls or jacket. The light seemed to glow off the bald spot at the back of his head.

"Why aren't you at work?" I asked. It was only around lunchtime.

Dad turned around, startled. He looked so much older now, with his eyes sinking into his face, the crow's-feet now prominent at the corners of his eyes.

"Why are you home so early?" I asked.

"They found her."

27

The highway leading down to West End Park was packed. We never had midday traffic unless there was a snowstorm or a car accident along the highway. But the current situation was different.

As we sat in the car, creeping slowly behind a semitruck, Dad and I listened to the updates on public radio. The details so far were scant. The reports were focused on an ongoing crime scene at West End Park and the number of emergency vehicles and police force that were being sent in.

Earlier that day, Dad had worked on a client's roof. His cell phone kept vibrating, and Dad thought that I was calling him because of an emergency.

But it was Mr. Willand who called. He said that a group of teenagers had found something floating in the lake, just offshore from West End Park. The police had given him a heads-up. Mr. Willand had been crying on the phone—he was stuck in Atlanta for a brief business trip. He was asking folks from church to head over to the park on his behalf. Mr. Obermueller, Kevin, and John Stack were stuck at work, and he didn't think his wife was in the right mind to go.

"I couldn't exactly say no to him," Dad murmured.

I heard the pity in his voice. It could've easily been him making the phone call. And it could've been me at the lakeshore.

As we waited in traffic, Dad kept glancing at me. He seemed to be expecting tears or a show of histrionics. I didn't blame him—I would have expected that, too.

But my eyes were dry. I felt like I'd been cast in the wrong part, a comedian being forced to play the melancholy man. I knew what I was supposed to do—cry, pray, be openly distressed. But I only felt hollow.

Because in my mind, Olivia was too real to die. Her eyes had too much of a spark in them.

When we were kids, they lit up whenever we caught bugs together or tried climbing some of the trees in Littlewood Park Reserve. They burned when she told her nanny that we would be getting ice cream. And they glowed when she greeted her parents' friends by their first names—Chuck, Bob, Kelly—as if she, too, were an adult woman.

When she was older, Olivia looked people straight in the eye when she spoke to them. She knew her magnetism, the way others would fawn over her. And though she was cruel, Olivia never shied away from a challenge.

Olivia Willand, whose eyes said so much yet so little about her, was dead.

As we started inching forward on the highway, I noticed a little girl sitting in the minivan next to us. I knew she was staring at me, waiting for me to look back at her, but I couldn't. I couldn't play the part.

We took an exit and drove past the noise barriers that blocked off West End Park from the highway. The park had two massive brick pavilions and a view of the lake.

But the area was already blocked off by yellow police tape. We followed a line of cars down one road until a police officer told us to turn around. Eventually we parked the truck a few blocks away and hurried over.

There was a crowd gathered behind the yellow tape, competing with the news vans for a view. A police officer was making pushing motions, but no one moved. People whipped out their phones to record the scene. Others had brought binoculars. One person even used a selfie stick to film above the crowd.

Dad went to find a supervisor. But I doubted the police would tell him anything, even if he was there on behalf of Mr. Willand.

I entered the crowd, but no one moved. I began to push my way through it as if I were at a concert. The only ones who ever made it to the front were presumptuous, violent, unafraid. It didn't matter how hard anyone pushed back—those people believed that it was their goddamn *right* to be up front.

For once in my life, I was one of those people. I was shoving aside grown men and women. I deserved to be up there—I had seen De-Maria's arm in person, I had known Olivia in life, I was just trying to do something—

A man elbowed me. He hit me right in the stomach. I fell back a few steps, surprised. The man had a thick goatee. Furious, I shoved him right back, my energy propelled into my shoulder. I collided into the small of his back.

"Fucking cunt," he hissed.

But I was already pushing past him.

And then I felt my ponytail getting yanked back, pulling at my skull, and I started screaming at him, tears pooling in my eyes.

"Don't touch me! Don't you fucking touch me!"

People turned to look at us, and I strained even harder, pieces of hair already dislodged from my head. The man immediately let go. And just like that, people moved aside from me as if I were sick. I was in front of the crowd, right behind the yellow tape. The back of my head was throbbing, but I had an idea.

I waved down the nearest police officer, hoping that my hair looked awful.

"Sir, a man just attacked me," I told the cop, and I pointed back toward the crowd. "The guy in the green hat with the brown goatee. He was hurting me."

The cop surveyed the crowd. He suddenly ducked under the yellow tape, muttering into his walkie-talkie. If I was lucky, the man with the goatee would run, and the cops would chase him.

When another cop entered the crowd, I took my chance. I slipped under the yellow tape, running past the pavilion. I could feel eyes following me as I disappeared into the woods, but there were no footsteps behind me. The cops were most likely stationed near the news vans and the crime scene. If I cut through the trees, I would arrive at the beach undetected.

The trees at West End Park were dense and spiky, not like the ones at Littlewood Park Reserve. There were a few scattered flecks of light from above; the rest of the forest was soaked in shadow.

But I wasn't afraid. I knew where to go, even though I could hardly see ahead of me.

All those days with Olivia had paid off: our summers spent trekking inside Littlewood Park Reserve; those bouts of panic when she led us off-trail into a maze of trees; the time Olivia backhanded me across the forehead and told me that she'd killed a mosquito.

Perhaps it all led up to the present.

Or it was dumb coincidence, and I was giving meaning to nothing.

Eventually I saw the light past the trees. Peering out, I could see the beach ahead of me, the sand like brown sugar, the water looming just beyond it. Police officers roamed the beach. The ambulance and other vehicles were parked farther back. I could see two groups of people clumped together on the beach.

I pulled out my phone, turned on the camera, and zoomed in. The image was grainy, but I could see three teenagers sitting in the back of the ambulance, a blanket draped over them. None of them spoke to each other. One truant day at the beach had been turned upside down—the kids were now part of a murder investigation.

A few yards away, a group of people huddled at the crime scene.

They were two police officers and a woman. She looked to be an investigator of some sort. They peered down into the sand. A crime scene photographer hovered nearby, taking photos. They were blocking whatever the teenagers had found.

I snapped a few pictures of the scene, but I couldn't see what they were looking at.

After a minute, an officer finally walked away. I took another photo. There was an object on the ground. It glowed brighter than the sand around it. It was thin and fairly short.

It reminded me of DeMaria's forearm.

I tried to swallow, but my mouth was dry. I kept taking pictures.

Two new people entered the frame: a police officer being shoved aside by a man with brown hair and a deerskin jacket. The man gestured at the investigators to move, and surprisingly, they did. The man took one look and turned away, staring out into the lake. Then a bob of blond hair stepped in front of him. The woman wore a cream-colored trench coat.

I felt my stomach drop.

I was looking at Mrs. Willand and John Stack. She paused, staring at the sand. She crept forward, inch by inch, and then slowly lowered herself down onto her knees. I saw a speck of fluorescent pink on the object. I lingered on it, confused.

Then I realized: it was nail polish.

Mrs. Willand's hands fluttered over her face. I could hear her distant wail, the sound cutting through the wind. She'd recognized it.

The camera lost focus. My hands were shaking.

I felt my chest grow hot and tight, as if someone were squeezing my insides. I had to get away. I shoved my phone in my jacket pocket, and I stumbled back into the forest, past the trees and the flecks of light from above. In the dark, I focused on putting one foot in front of the other.

But Olivia seemed to follow me. I kept seeing her in the shadows:

Olivia at age eight in elementary school, finishing a word search at her desk instead of listening to the teacher.

Olivia walking ahead of me on the park trail, her ponytail swinging back and forth.

Olivia in our high school class, as our eyes randomly met from across the room, and I wondered if she ever thought about me at all.

She was nowhere and everywhere.

I stopped, my face wet. I was crying beneath a little crook of light. I looked up to see the clouds so white and opaque, it was hard to imagine any blue beyond them. It was as if God had bleached the sky entirely, washing out the sun, the moon, the stars, everything.

A sky wiped clean, spotless.

All of it bleached out.

And my mind suddenly began to race.

I remembered the sparkly sheen of a bathtub after a wash, the bathroom tiles a blinding white, the lingering scent of bleach near the toilet. It was as if the entire bathroom had been scrubbed recently to remove a large, ugly stain. Like blood.

And I remembered the security guard in the lobby who never watched us, the other security guard who wasn't there when I slipped by. *They're here for show. Cheaper than cameras, I guess.*

And the photo on the phone, received on the day she'd disappeared.

I felt dizzy. But my hand found my phone, pressing a number. The rings sounded faint and far away. The cellular reception was weak.

"Hello?"

My mouth felt gummy, the words already bloating into each other.

"Hello? Mary?"

"I know who killed Olivia Willand."

28

I planted myself in front of the living room TV that night. My personal vigil for Olivia.

All the news channels covered her. They discussed the body parts that had washed up on the western shore of Liberty Lake. While I flipped between channels, I kept seeing Olivia's senior-year portrait.

And I kept imagining the headlines that would appear:

SUSPECT DISCOVERED IN DISMEMBERED WOMAN CASE

ARREST MADE IN LIBERTY LAKE WOMAN'S MURDER

JUSTICE SERVED FOR OLIVIA WILLAND?

But then the news ended for the night, and I was stuck watching a late-night hospital drama.

The water was dirty. It was a hazy green with small particles that drifted along. Light filtered in from above, almost like a spotlight. I felt something tickling at my feet, and I realized that it was pondweed, rough, yet slimy. I realized that I was underwater, somewhere far below.

As I swam up for air, I noticed a glint of light. It glowed in the murky water. As my eyes adjusted to the dark, I could finally make out what it was.

A pale leg.

I opened my mouth, screaming, but no sound came out. Instead, water rushed in, filling my lungs. I struggled for breath, my arms moving wildly around me.

I began to notice more things in the water, all glowing.

Dismembered limbs, hundreds of them. Arms and legs and hands and feet and hair that seemed to swirl all around me. And I knew that they were meant for me. They were all slowly drifting toward me.

Something nudged the back of my head.

When I turned, I screamed. I wouldn't stop screaming as Olivia's head stared back at me, her gaze empty where her eyes should have been.

I was being shaken with callused hands. I opened my eyes, saw Dad looming over me. I was still screaming.

"Mary, stop it. Stop it, you're okay," said Dad, his hands letting go. He moved out of the way, and I could see that the living room was bright with sunlight. It was already Thursday morning. I put a hand over my mouth, trying to stop the noise.

"Jesus, what the hell happened?" he muttered.

I shook my head, forcing myself up on the couch. There was a fleece blanket on the floor along with my phone. I'd kicked them off in my sleep. Dad hovered nearby, a stain against the yellow walls. He handed me a glass of water and a prescription bottle. The escitalopram.

"I think you need these," he said, then retreated to the kitchen.

Slowly, I rattled the bottle, trying to guess the number of pills inside. I couldn't remember the last time I'd taken one before bed.

I chugged down the water and two pills—an extra one for good measure—and went into the kitchen.

Dad was brewing coffee—I could feel my head start to ache from the caffeine withdrawal. I was sticky with sweat, my T-shirt clinging to me like residue. I wanted to wipe the sweat, the dirt, and the faint scent of the park off me.

"The news said more FBI are getting called in," said Dad over the hiss of the coffee maker.

"I thought they were here already."

"After yesterday, I think things have escalated," Dad said. He didn't mention what we both knew. "They think there's a serial killer involved."

I sat down at the kitchen table, my head spinning.

I hadn't been crazy when I had told Madison my theory. I hadn't been crazy when I'd reached out to Leticia Jackson, Kevin, Mr. Nguyen, Charice. The authorities now believed that Olivia and De-Maria were connected. They shared the same killer.

We no longer needed to leak DeMaria's police file. I only hoped that Jayden or Charice was following the news. DeMaria's case was finally being examined, and her mother would get some peace of mind.

But it wasn't the news I'd been waiting for. It seemed like my phone call had done nothing.

In the shower, I washed my hair twice by accident. I let the water pelt over me even after the soap suds had long washed off. I watched as the water swirled down the drain in one endless motion.

When I came back downstairs, Dad was gone. He'd been running late to work because of me.

I poured myself another cup of coffee and sat down on the couch. I turned on the TV to a daytime talk show. I felt better having voices in the house, all talking and laughing. Their lives were frivolous and undisturbed.

Meanwhile, I had work the next day. I had to go to the grocery store and act normal, as if nothing horrific had taken place, as if I didn't know—

The TV screen flashed. The talk show was gone, replaced with a Breaking News banner. I jerked forward, the coffee sloshing onto my hands. I was trembling.

A reporter stood in the parking lot outside Goodhue Groceries. Behind her, police cars surrounded the loading dock. The reporter was frowning as she mumbled into an earpiece. But when she realized that she was live, her expression changed into one of concern.

"This is News Four's Macy Holmes, reporting live from Liberty Lake. I'm currently in front of the city's Goodhue Groceries location, where police have just made an arrest in the kidnapping and murder of Olivia Willand. Though authorities have not yet released a statement, we do have footage of the suspect being escorted out."

The scene cut to the loading dock. The screen suddenly became shaky and noisy—the cameraman, Macy Holmes, and everyone else nearby were rushing forward. A police officer was leaving, one arm trying to clear the news people out of the way.

But then Dwayne appeared. He stood like a giant over the chaos. He stared down at the ground. He was in his work uniform—the green polo shirt and the khaki pants. His arms were bound behind him. He was handcuffed and being pushed from behind.

As Dwayne moved forward, his head jerked up. He suddenly looked into the camera, his eyes wide with fear. And I knew why he was afraid:

He'd been caught.

He was going to pay for what he'd done.

As Dwayne passed the cameras, a blond crew cut peeked out from behind him. It was Kevin, who glanced briefly at the camera. His face was grim. Then he pushed Dwayne into a police car.

I remembered the mornings in the high school hallway as Kevin and Dwayne hung out; the lunch table where they congregated together; the prom photos where they sat in the back of a limo with Olivia and all their friends. Kevin and Dwayne had once smoked together, partied together, laughed together.

Now everything had changed.

Back at West End Park, I had stood still, staring into the darkness.

"Are you sure about this? Dwayne?" Kevin had asked. He'd been silent on the phone, listening as I fumbled through my words, trying to explain it all—the smell of bleach in Dwayne's bathroom; Olivia's nude photo that he'd received on the day of her disappearance; the lack of proper security guards and cameras at his apartment.

The more I talked, the more other things made sense. I told Kevin about Dwayne's sick days from work—he had been gone from Goodhue Groceries for three days after Olivia had been announced missing. I had trained with Jim because Dwayne was gone. Dwayne could have used his sick days to dispose of Olivia's body. He never even pretended to look for her, his old friend—he'd been more concerned with Jayden's birthday party.

And if the police were to investigate further, they would most likely discover that Dwayne hadn't been with his family on Halloween. If that was the case, then Dwayne had the opportunity to leak Olivia's nude photo during the Halloween search.

"Mary?" Kevin asked. "These are some serious allegations. You sure about this?"

I didn't want to believe that Dwayne was capable of murder. But at the same time, it all made sense.

He had never gotten over Olivia. If he discovered that she was seeing someone else, then the truth could have upset him. In an act of jealous rage, he had killed her, then cut her up and dumped her into Liberty Lake.

I knew Dwayne was capable of it. He had the strength to kill someone. He had the charisma to hide it.

And after my night with him, Dwayne knew that I was suspicious. He'd panicked, and he'd disposed of Olivia's body parts into the lake. Wherever he'd hidden her, he'd cleared it out. That was how she'd wound up at West End Park.

"As far as you're concerned, this is an anonymous phone call," I said quietly. "This is a tip. Please, Kevin, just look into him."

Less than twenty-four hours later, Kevin had done more than that. He'd arrested the killer, the man responsible for the murder of Olivia Willand, whose body had been ripped apart, her life and her dignity taken away.

The scene cut back to Macy Holmes.

"Though authorities have not yet released information, sources have verified that the suspect is twenty-two-year-old Dwayne Turner, an assistant manager here," she said. "Turner was an alum of Liberty Lake High School and former quarterback of the school's football team. In 2011, he was part of the school's championship team. It is believed that Turner and Olivia Willand had personally known each other. More updates to come. And now back to your regularly scheduled programming."

I turned off the TV. I looked through the glass doors of the patio. The sky was a clear, bright blue. Sunlight gleamed over the grass and the wooden fence in the backyard. It was too beautiful a day for November. But I went upstairs and changed anyway, putting on my jacket.

I took a long walk around the neighborhood, breathing in the crisp, cool air. I was steady again in what had seemed like forever.

29

The next day, I showed up for my night shift at Goodhue Groceries. Jim was especially sanguine—it was as if one of his employees had never been arrested for murder. Jim acted as if Dwayne had never existed at all. He had more important things to worry about, like the crush of Thanksgiving customers in the next three weeks. He had work to do.

"Look happy, Mary," said Jim as I put my jacket in my locker. "It's crucial that we all look relaxed and professional today."

"Is it because of—?"

Jim cleared his throat and nodded. Out in the hallway, the door to Dwayne's office was closed. The investigators would soon examine it.

"I'm sending out a store-wide email tonight with guidelines," said Jim, his voice oddly chipper. "Our policy is ensuring a good experience for our customers. No one here talks about you-know-who or thinks about him. No chitchatting with journalists or customers."

I nodded.

"And if anyone starts doing otherwise, I've been directed to fire them. And I trust you, Mary," said Jim as he pointed his index finger at me. "You're a smart girl. But some people here . . . not as smart. If I were you, I'd spread the word, all right?"

I nodded and watched as Jim flagged down someone else.

But work seemed normal. We were programmed for it, the routine. As daylight waned, I restocked the shelves and took over someone else's checkout lane. The other employees continued as usual, smiles plastered on their faces. Even Ron was calm. He walked past my lane without so much as a glare in my direction.

The customers, however, were shell-shocked. Their curiosity overwhelmed them. In their minds, a murderer had once lurked the shelves, touching their food, and thus indirectly impacting their lives.

"Did you know the man who worked here?" whispered a hockey mom. "The one from TV?"

"No comment," I said politely.

"Could you tell that he was a murderer?" asked a teenage girl a few hours later. "Did he seem off?"

"Your total is fifty-eight dollars and six cents," I replied.

"Have you ever felt unsafe here with that monster?" asked a concerned father.

I was so tired that I only shrugged.

It was a good question, though. In the past three weeks since I'd been home, I hadn't been afraid of Dwayne. I'd worked with him, talked with him, slept with him. Nothing had seemed strange. It was only afterward that I could piece everything together.

Olivia probably had felt safe with him, too, until she'd been killed. I could have been next. That was what should have frightened me. I could have been a mess of limbs floating in the water. I could have been hacked apart.

But the idea was alien, like an artifact on display—it was something to gawk at and then forget.

I was lucky because Olivia hadn't been.

Half an hour before close, a squat old woman came to my lane. As I scanned her items, she started searching through her small purse.

"I heard the news," said the old woman. "I know you're probably tired of talking about this, but what happened was horrible."

I said nothing as she dug out a handful of coins. She was planning to pay the exact amount down to the cent.

"Just awful," she said, shaking her head. "How does someone kill two women and then abandon their own son? That poor baby."

My stomach suddenly lurched.

"What are you talking about? What happened?" I asked loudly.

The old woman blinked.

"Haven't you followed the news?" she asked.

I was jittery when I got home. Dad was already asleep in his armchair. A late-night comedy show blasted on the TV. In my room, I beelined for the laptop. The woman had mentioned a press conference from earlier in the afternoon.

I quickly found the livestream. Someone had recorded the video footage of it.

The livestream showed Leticia Jackson standing outside of her house. She was surrounded by a crowd of somber people, reporters, and cameras. In one arm, she held baby Demetrius, who was bundled up in snow pants, a jacket, and a knit hat. Little dots of cell phone cameras glowed around them.

I unmuted the video.

"—gone for months now," said Leticia. Her voice was so soft that I had to raise the volume. "DeMaria died in horrible pain. She didn't deserve any of it. If I could've helped her, I would have in a heartbeat. But God knows I can't bring her back. I cannot change what happened. And yet . . . I feel *angry*."

Heads nodded around her. Leticia took a breath, staring at the camera. A tear streaked down her cheek.

"I feel angry that my child was taken away from me by a monster. I feel angry that DeMaria will never see her baby grow up. Never see him go to college, never be at his wedding." Demetrius sucked on his thumb, staring off camera. "I have so much anger for her, it's scary. But you know what I'm really angry about?"

The crowd was so quiet that I could hear the wind in the background.

"I'm angry about all the lies I've been fed."

Her eyes flashed at the camera, dark and bitter. I felt a shiver run through me, as if she had just seen me through the screen, hiding in the safety of my room. A coward.

"I've got reporters lying to me so they can get a good story," said Leticia. I flinched as if she'd just slapped me. "I've got others who didn't care. My story wasn't interesting enough, so they dropped De-Maria like trash. She was only mentioned in the news a few times. No one ever talked about her again.

"Then I've got the police lying to me that they *care* about the case. That they're 'working on it.' It's taken them *months* to work on it. But no progress. But when Olivia Willand goes missing, we've got the damn national news, cable news covering her. We've got search parties and the FBI. When Olivia is found dead, not even a week goes by before they make an arrest on her case."

Leticia paused, her head shaking slowly. She reminded me of Mr. Obermueller. She knew the impact of her words, and she was aware that people were paying attention.

"Olivia Willand died like my daughter did—cut apart like an animal. I wondered if it was the same killer. And I can't help but think that her death could have been prevented. If someone had paid attention to DeMaria's case, they could have caught her killer before he went after someone else. I blame this on the complete negligence of the Liberty Lake Police Department. Another girl had to die before they cared.

"And imagine my surprise when I learned about Olivia Willand's killer. He was the same monster who knocked up my daughter."

I felt like I'd been punched in the stomach.

A flurry of images began to flash in my mind: the morning after the party, the bottle of pills, the lake, the cream-colored Bible, the nude photo, the pale arms in the sand, me as I rocked myself hoarse in the apartment.

The camera now zoomed into Demetrius's face. He was unbothered by the news and the people around him. His big eyes were focused on his grandmother.

I had seen him before in person. I never saw the resemblance, but there was one feature that I recognized now: he had his father's dimples.

If I had noticed it earlier, could I have saved Olivia in time?

"DeMaria got pregnant about two years ago," continued Leticia, her voice bitter. "She'd just broken up with a boyfriend named Charles. But at a party in town, she met a handsome college football player. DeMaria showed me his picture and everything. Wouldn't stop gushing about him. 'He's so handsome, Mama. Like a movie star.' But when she told him she was pregnant, that boy said he had to finish school first. He said he'd finish his degree in Wisconsin and come back. 'But he's going to be a good father, Mama.'"

Leticia shook her head, as if she was reliving that conversation all over again.

"DeMaria was like fire. But when it came to this football player, she melted at his damn feet. And I knew his type," said Leticia darkly. "He was not interested in a pretty little girl from our part of town. Dwayne Turner was not interested in taking care of DeMaria or the baby. Hell, he never even went to Wisconsin. He was living in this very same town while she was pregnant.

"After she gave birth, DeMaria asked for Dwayne to add himself to their son's birth certificate. And you know what Dwayne did? He told her to leave him alone. He told her to focus on her ex-boyfriend instead. And he said that Demetrius wasn't his."

The camera angled itself down toward the baby. Demetrius was looking around silently.

I wanted the dark to swallow me whole. I had focused on the

wrong things: his charming smile at Goodhue Groceries; the customers and the boss who'd loved him; the scenic apartment next to the lake.

But this whole time, Dwayne had been a father. He had to have known that Demetrius was his. Though there was no proof, I knew deep down that DeMaria was right about her son's paternity. I understood why she had taken antidepressants—she was stuck raising a baby on her own. The man she loved had left her. And it hurt her to know that the man was right there, in town, making enough money to live comfortably without them.

If there was any part of me that had doubted Dwayne's guilt, it was gone now.

"I thought Dwayne Turner was just a coward. A stupid, selfish kid," said Leticia. "He didn't want to claim his own son because then he'd have to pay child support. But I gave him too much credit. It wasn't bad enough that he knocked up my daughter and abandoned her and the child. But the fact that he had to kidnap and murder my child . . . and then someone else's child, too? Well, that's something else. That takes a *monster*."

Leticia paused for one last time. She had all of us now, our strings looped around her fingers. And she wasn't quite ready to let go, now that she had gotten her time to speak.

"A murderer is a murderer is a murderer," said Leticia, her voice steady. "I want Dwayne Turner to pay, both in his assets and his life. And I am prepared for a paternity test, a court case, and whatever else comes. I will do what I said I would do—whatever it takes to get justice for my daughter, DeMaria Jackson."

The crowd started clapping, the sound thunderous over the laptop speakers. Leticia took in the faces around her, one arm wrapped around Demetrius, the other hand raised in thanks. She was stone-faced. I turned off the laptop, my stomach queasy.

I hurried to the bathroom and locked the door. I lifted up the toilet seat and dry-heaved, my face inches from the toilet water. I kept retching, harder than I had in my entire life. I didn't stop until my eyes were watering and there was spittle hanging from my mouth. I'd gotten nothing out.

But I couldn't stop.

I needed to cleanse myself of everything inside me—my expulsion from school, Carly, the food that I had binged in the past few weeks, the deaths of Olivia and DeMaria, the fact that Dwayne Turner could have killed me next.

And I had let him fuck me. The thought was clear in my mind like glass—I had let a murderer fuck me.

I couldn't stomach it. I gagged again, hoping the bile would start to come. I wanted the impurities gone, all of them. I needed to feel clean again. I was tired of being tainted.

When I finally heard Dad knocking on the bathroom door, I had gotten nothing out.

30

Before I knew it, a week had passed. We had our first snowfall on the ninth. The snow was so light that I wasn't sure if I'd even seen it. But then I blinked, and the snow was suddenly flying down in hard white flakes, like flecks of cereal. I was in my room when the snow fell, putting my old desk together.

A couple of people from college had texted me again. After weeks of silence, they asked me if I knew the victims or the killer from my hometown. The Liberty Lake murders were national news. No one asked me how I was doing—they just wanted details on the case.

I didn't respond. Those people only reminded me of Carly and campus, things that I'd pushed aside in the past few weeks. Everyone at school was stuck in the throes of midterms before Thanksgiving. A few weeks after that, it would be the end of the semester. For Carly, freshman year was almost half-over.

I missed the parties, the campus, and some of the people, but what I missed most was the opportunity—I'd only had a year left of school. The finish line was close, the diploma within reach. I had a future ahead of me, places to go and people to meet and things to do.

But that was gone.

The anger still burned inside of me—it would take a long, long time to die out. But by the time I'd finished assembling my desk, I was tired. I set the desk on its legs and pushed it next to the window. As the snow blew outside, I went online, looking at the nearby community colleges and state schools. I could still get a diploma. Ivy League Mary was not finished yet.

Time also slowed at the grocery store. It didn't matter how many smiles I gave or how many customers I helped—I hated the work. I was restless and bored all at once. And I was watching the clock more often now, counting down the hours and the minutes and the bathroom breaks until I could leave.

And when I wasn't thinking about school or work, I could only think of the murders: Olivia and DeMaria. Dwayne. I was ruminating over the past few weeks, retracing the conversations I'd had and the conversations I'd missed. The danger I'd narrowly dodged.

There was one hero to thank for solving the Liberty Lake murders. On Wednesday night, Kevin Obermueller appeared live on News Four. He was in his police uniform, his hands clasped firmly in front of him, his forehead gleaming with sweat. The news anchors asked him about his life in Liberty Lake, his job, what drew him to it. But when they finally asked how he'd gone after Dwayne Turner, Kevin stared at the camera, his mouth half-open.

"It was an anonymous tip," he said.

"But there must have been a reason why they reached out to you specifically," cooed a news anchor. "As a rookie, there must've been something about you that made someone trust you."

"Yeah. I mean, I guess," he said, looking away.

It helped that Kevin was related to a local celebrity: CITY COUNCIL PRESIDENT'S SON SOLVES LIBERTY LAKE MURDERS. An op-ed in the newspaper even drew comparisons between the Obermuellers and the Kennedys, of both families' stellar legacies in public service. For once, Mr. Obermueller said nothing to the press—he didn't have to. They were doing the work for him, sprucing him up for a future campaign.

Both Kevin and I knew that his fame was purely luck. He hadn't been particularly useful to Olivia's case, and he had downplayed DeMaria's death completely. He hadn't been the one stuck in Dwayne's apartment with him. He hadn't put his life on the line to find the truth. Each time I heard him mentioned on the news, I felt a bitterness in my stomach, hard as ice. All the attention they poured on him—and he deserved jack shit.

But Kevin was only a blip in the national news story. Some people were drawn to Olivia, the beautiful social media star from the Midwest. Others were drawn to DeMaria, the jilted young Black mother who'd been forgotten. Their names and their pictures flooded the news.

But Dwayne seemed to tower over all of them: the brutal, enigmatic killer from Liberty Lake. The news talked about Dwayne's troubled past in high school. He had performed poorly in a few of his classes; he drank underage and smoked marijuana in the school bathrooms; and he had briefly dated one murder victim in high school and impregnated the other. The news almost always included a clip of Dwayne violently shoving a lineman during a game.

Thanks to one article, I finally found out how Dwayne had ended up back in Liberty Lake—he'd been caught using steroids his freshman year of college. Dwayne was subsequently kicked off his school's football team, his full-ride scholarship taken away. After one semester of college, Dwayne dropped out and returned home. That was why he had never wanted to talk about school. He had blown his one chance, like me.

Then there were the think pieces about Dwayne. The more thoughtful ones discussed the toxic nature of rape culture in sports or domestic violence in the suburbs. Other pieces argued that Dwayne had been a psychopath. In response, others argued that Dwayne had multiple personalities, including a murderous one. There were conspiracy theories that Dwayne had been framed for the murders by the local police.

Then there were the more virulent articles that came out. One article suggested that Dwayne was hardwired for violence—it was in his *genetics*—and needed to be put to death. One commenter hoped that Dwayne would get thoroughly "ass-raped in prison." It seemed the case was growing uglier by the day.

The Liberty Lake Police Department discovered "explicit correspondence" on Dwayne's phone between him and Olivia. Correspondence had ended back on October 18, the day of Olivia's disappearance. People surmised online that Olivia's last message to Dwayne had been her nude photo. They didn't know how right they were.

Though there was no set trial date, the case against Dwayne was building.

People came forward to the police. An anonymous coworker claimed that Dwayne had once mentioned Olivia as the "girl he should've tied down back in high school." An anonymous resident at Dwayne's apartment reported a heavy black duffel bag that he often carried. Since the Jewel already had a gym inside, they thought it was strange that he left with a workout bag so often. Only now did they realize that it could have been used for more insidious purposes.

A gas station owner in the Sewers provided police with footage from the afternoon of Olivia's disappearance. Dwayne was shown filling up his tank at five thirty-four that night, only a couple of hours after Olivia had left her house for good.

I didn't know much about criminal law, but I knew enough to guess some of the charges against him: first-degree murder, kidnapping, the desecration of a body, the broken privacy laws around Olivia's nude photo, and whatever else the police had yet to uncover. Since Minnesota had no death penalty, Dwayne was most likely going to get life in prison with a bonus of solitary confinement.

Life was slowly turning upright again, like the hand of a clock climbing back to twelve. There was justice now for the victims and perhaps a little peace for me.

On the upcoming Saturday, the Willands were holding a private funeral service for Olivia at St. Rita's Catholic Church. Mrs. Willand had reached out directly to me and Dad.

"We consider you to be family friends. And, Mary, you were so close to Olivia way back when," said Mrs. Willand over voice mail. She sounded feeble and shaky. "We're not sure when we'll get a full confession—we could wait forever to get all of her back . . . but Martin and I thought it was right to give Olivia a proper goodbye as soon as possible."

The funeral sounded painful. I didn't belong there—we hadn't spoken since high school. I had resented her for years. I doubted that I ever really knew her.

But I wanted to go. It would be one moment in time, and it would be over. Even after everything, I needed to give Olivia a proper goodbye. Then I could finally let go.

31

The morning of the funeral, I woke up early—just a bit after five, when the sky was still dark. I sat up in bed. The room was chilly. Though my body was awake, the rest of me felt bleary, as if I hadn't slept at all.

I spent the next hour dumping out the garbage bags of clothes on the floor. I plucked out whatever was black, including a pair of dress pants, some leggings, some different tops, and a strapless dress meant for the summer. Without much thought, I settled on the dress, pairing it with a gray button-up sweater.

Within an hour, I finished putting on my makeup and curling my hair. That was how the women had looked at Mom's funeral—dolled up and proper in their fancy black dresses. It seemed the more effort you put in, the more you cared.

By the time I came downstairs for breakfast, I was already dressed for the funeral.

"We're not leaving for a while," said Dad, glancing over.

I shrugged, sipping my cup of coffee.

I spent the rest of my morning folding my clothes on the floor, sorting everything into piles: shirts, shorts, socks, underwear all separated neatly from each other. I hated organizing things, but I didn't know what else to do while I was waiting. I was restless.

We left the house at eleven twenty. Outside, the sky was a single sheet of white—there was no separation between the clouds. The street was dry, but a layer of snow covered the rest of the ground. From Dad's truck, it could've been any brisk November day.

But only a few blocks from St. Rita's, we saw the commotion unfolding: there were police cars, civilian cars, news vehicles lined down the street, and a couple of neon-vested traffic cops in the distance. They redirected drivers toward a detour instead of the street by the church. There were news teams and crowds of onlookers across the street, lined up behind a row of crowd control barriers. We could hear the low rumble of people outside.

"Not really private, is it?" Dad murmured, and I shook my head.

By the time we pulled up to the traffic cop, we only had fifteen minutes before the funeral Mass began.

"Names and IDs please," said the cop. After he crossed off our names from a clipboard, the cop directed us toward the church parking lot, where there were still open spots available.

The noise from outside seemed to only grow in volume inside St. Rita's. There were people everywhere, all dressed in black.

Everyone was packed tightly together, no room to flee. In the lobby, there was a group of people that I recognized from high school. They were Olivia's old friends. Kevin was among them, clad in his police uniform.

I immediately turned around. Even if Kevin and I were on good terms, I wasn't comfortable around the others. I began to feel like I was eighteen again, shy and ungainly and overweight.

Nearby, Mr. Willand and his friends had absorbed Dad into their midst.

I was alone.

I sped through the lobby. There was a sprawling group of college girls streaming in. Each of them had a gold scrunchie on her wrist—I realized that they were from Olivia's sorority. I hadn't seen any of them at the search. I moved faster and circled around a trio of altar servers and through a pair of glass doors.

I was suddenly in the nave of the church. It was quiet here and dim, except for the light that streamed in through the windows high above. Once again, I saw the large crucifix that hung in the air. Beneath it, there was a gleaming white casket. It sat at the end of the aisle, right before the altar.

To my right, there was a glowing figure. It was Father Greg. He sat at the end of the pew nearby, his cane propped in front of him. He wore a pale chasuble. It had a strip of lavender flowers that ran down the center. It was iridescent. It seemed so strange—the priest at Mom's funeral had worn black.

Father Greg glanced over. Our eyes met. He might have recognized me from confession, I wasn't sure.

But I fled instantly, my legs carrying me down the aisle to the white casket. On its left, there was a dazzling white funeral wreath; on its right, a large framed portrait of Olivia in her lacy white dress. It was the high school portrait that had been splattered all over the news.

Up close, the casket was seamless, smooth. But it was small, large enough to fit only a child's corpse. I realized that they didn't have much of Olivia to put in there. They only had the parts of her that had washed up. The rest of her was still missing.

It was all so pale and bland. The flowers, the casket, the altar servers, the guest list—all of it was for show. They had bleached her out completely. There was no color to her, no edges, no hardness, no depth. None of it was her.

I reached out, my fingers grazing the spot where Olivia's head would have been. The casket was cold to the touch.

I took a deep breath. Other people would have given a prayer or a silent message. They would have reflected on a shared memory. They would have thought of something meaningful.

But nothing came to me. I was frozen, my fingers stuck on the casket, my heart hammering in my chest.

"Sad, isn't it?"

I was startled. John Stack was next to me. He wore a dark suit, a white handkerchief peeking out of his chest pocket. John was staring at the casket. He slowly reached out and touched it.

"Just pitiful. None of it should have happened," he said, his voice low. "Every life is precious, every choice more so. It all counts—we can either love ourselves or sin against ourselves. Then we return to dust." John looked at me. The light glinted off his wire-rimmed glasses.

I slowly nodded—I didn't know how else to respond. John lightly patted the casket and walked away.

I heard a door clank from one side of the church, then another. The guests were streaming in now, seating themselves for Mass. Far down the aisle, Father Greg was slowly straightening up from his seat.

I suddenly felt everyone's eyes on me, lingering on the strange girl who hung out for too long near the casket.

As the organ began to play, I hurried past the pews to my right, moving against the current of people. I could barely breathe as I made my way through the lobby, past the front office, and down a hallway. I bolted into the women's restroom, beelining for the nearest stall.

I was gasping for air, gulping down swigs of it. I lowered my face toward the toilet bowl and stopped—there were drops of urine on the seat. I backed away, shuddering. I needed fresh air and space, to feel my legs pumping on the cold street, away from the crowds and the casket and the news cameras—

Someone was sniffling. The noise seemed to come from the other end of the restroom. It came from the handicapped stall.

"Hello?" I stammered.

Through the faint organ music, I could hear a wet hiccup.

"Hello? Are you okay?" I asked again.

I knocked on the stall door and accidentally pushed it open. Inside, Mrs. Willand was sitting on the ground, her back to the wall.

Her legs were splayed out beneath her black dress. Mrs. Willand's blond bob looked sharp as ever, as if she'd cut it recently.

But the rest of her looked disheveled—eye shadow and lipstick smeared on her face. A single line of mascara fell halfway down one cheek. She was wiping her face with a giant wad of toilet paper.

Her voice was so soft that I had to squat down on the floor to hear her.

"I don't want to go out there," murmured Mrs. Willand, her voice wet. She sounded like a pleading child.

"Are you sure?" I whispered back.

Mrs. Willand sighed.

"Can you shut the door, Mary?" she asked. "But don't go."

I closed the stall door behind me and joined Mrs. Willand on the floor. We stayed still, listening to the organ music through the walls. Beside me, Mrs. Willand's sniffling only seemed to grow louder. She yanked out more toilet paper from the roll, burying her face in the giant wad.

"Maybe we should go back," I said gently. "So you don't miss anything."

"What's there to miss?" she whispered. "I missed everything. Graduation, her wedding . . . her kids." Mrs. Willand's voice grew scratchy like sandpaper. "I won't have any grandchildren, Mary."

I looked into her watery eyes, unsure of what to say.

"Is there anyone I could get for you, Mrs. Willand? Your husband or a friend—"

"Martin can shove it up his ass," she croaked.

My jaw dropped.

"*Cremation is wrong, Heather. Why would we burn Olivia?!*" mimicked Mrs. Willand, a hand scrunched in her lap. "Good God, Martin . . . Unlike him, I actually think about the long term. Why the hell would we bury Olivia? There's almost nothing to bury."

I swallowed. There was so little of Olivia left. It seemed like a waste to bury her in a small grave. It seemed so final, as if they had no hopes of finding the rest of her.

"Why am I the bad guy?" muttered Mrs. Willand. She dumped the wad of paper into the toilet. "He's the one who never thinks ahead. He likes things to be easy and fast. He would've been gone by now if it weren't for Olivia."

I looked at her, surprised. But Mrs. Willand leaned toward me, her lips in a thin line.

"Martin and I are divorcing."

The words were stuck in my mouth. The Willands had always been a unit—both blond-headed and wealthy. At a glance, they fit each other like a puzzle. There was an order to them.

But Olivia had sensed it years ago, hadn't she? The comments she'd made about her mother cheating, the jokes she made about her father's magazines, the way Olivia preferred to be in the woods away from her parents. She had always known.

And I had seen it myself—the way John Stack had tenderly reached out to Mrs. Willand in times of pain. Her husband never would have done that for her.

Through the wall, I heard a woman's voice begin to sing. The melody was light and eerie against the organ music.

"Martin and I have been unhappy for a while," whispered Mrs. Willand. "But we stayed together for Olivia. I've seen enough divorces to know what happens to the kids. We made it past Olivia's high school years. We thought we could keep it going, we just needed to try. But Martin . . ."

"What about him?" I croaked.

"He's been having an affair," she sniffed, wiping her nose. "Maybe more, I'm not sure. But the damn credit card bills . . . Martin had all these hotel and restaurant charges on them. None of them could be accounted for. I didn't ask. I just watched him lie."

I pictured Mr. Willand at a bar with some model, the two of them giggling over drinks, his stomach bulging over his pants. Meanwhile his wife was at home, hundreds of miles away.

He'd called Dad from Atlanta on a business trip. He might have been lying to him. His daughter was missing, but Mr. Willand had still found time to travel. In a time of grief, he had found solace in someone else. The idea sickened me.

Mrs. Willand yanked out more toilet paper from the roll. It was a long, winding piece that she mashed together in her hands.

"I'm not even upset about it, Mary," she whispered. "My heart hasn't been in it for a long time. Martin knows it, too. But the money . . ."

"What money?"

Mrs. Willand shook her head, a drip of snot hanging off her nose.

"I don't know how it happened. Money was always Martin's job—he was good at his sales, we were doing fine, Olivia was starting high school. Then one day Martin tells me that the company's going bankrupt. I wasn't that mad—these things happen.

"But Martin . . . He'd been subsidizing it with our money. Never told me. And after the bankruptcy, all of these shareholders came out of nowhere, demanding their money. And guess who was stuck paying them back?"

Mrs. Willand was tearing up again, her voice growing watery.

"Olivia was used to a way of living, and suddenly we couldn't afford it anymore. We sold a car, our time share, some of his stocks. But Martin owed so much, Mary. And Olivia was heading off to college soon, but we were scrounging for money. We'd failed her." Mrs. Willand's voice was faltering now. "You know how upset she got when we couldn't go to Mexico anymore?"

My mind started to race. It didn't make sense—Olivia's Instagram had been plastered with vacation photos. She'd taken trips to Madrid, São Paulo, Dublin, Paris, the Great Wall of China. She'd been traveling since high school. I figured her parents had funded all of it.

"I thought Olivia went to France," I said stupidly.

"She did," said Mrs. Willand, wiping her nose. "But Martin and I didn't pay for it, that's for sure. Olivia paid for it all herself."

"Was she working?"

"If she did, I never saw it."

Her words pricked at me. Olivia was dead. We were putting her to rest. Her killer had been put away. Everything was finished.

But even now, Olivia still had things to hide. Like a child, I couldn't leave it alone—I would prick at it and peel it back until I saw the raw truth. I needed the explanation. I needed her to make sense.

"She could have made some money off Instagram," I offered. "She could have done a few paid ads."

Mrs. Willand scoffed. She shook her head.

"They paid her in *publicity* and free clothes. Half of it was trash," murmured Mrs. Willand. "Back then, her following was never good enough. The most Olivia made was a couple hundred bucks. She would've blown through it quickly."

"Then where was the money coming from?" I asked, my throat dry.

The restroom door suddenly opened. A woman walked in, stopping next to the sinks.

"Heather?" asked the woman.

Mrs. Willand didn't respond. She leaned in closer to me. I could smell the coffee on her breath as she whispered into my ear:

"I'm afraid she did something illegal."

"What?"

"I saw it . . . Her phone . . ." she murmured, her voice so quiet that I was straining to hear it. ". . . Doberman . . ."

I swallowed, unsure if I had misheard. The Willands didn't own a dog, but a Doberman seemed ominous. I imagined one sprinting toward the lake, its black coat a stain over the grass. It stopped short of the water and gnawed at a lump of flesh in the cold, hard ground, blood staining its teeth.

Before I could ask, Mrs. Willand suddenly backed away, her face discolored and messy, the grief clawing at her eyes.

"Heather?" asked the woman again. The door to the stall nudged slightly open. "Is that you? They've already started."

Mrs. Willand took a deep breath, one hand patting my leg. Mom used to tell me that a woman's hands showed her age, not her face or her body or her hair. Mrs. Willand's hands were small and brittle. She was gesturing at me to go.

A short woman entered the stall. She let out a gasp when she saw us.

"Hi, Val," said Mrs. Willand.

I left the two women in the bathroom, and I made my way down an empty hallway, listening to the hum of music.

Through the large windows, I could see a patrol officer waiting outside next to a motorcycle. He would lead the motorcade after Mass to the cemetery. It seemed like the Willands were putting themselves into more debt, paying for the cop, the casket, the service, the flowers, the funeral.

But to them, Olivia was worth it. She was their last shared expense.

My phone began to vibrate in my dress pocket. It was an unknown number. The phone kept vibrating, even after a minute.

"Hello?" I finally answered.

There was a pause and then a metallic voice: "Email."

It was the same voice from Littlewood Park Reserve.

I was trembling now as I fumbled through my email app, opening the most recent message. After a moment, a photo loaded.

Me.

32

I was looking at my mug shot.

I saw the numbers near my head, as black and oafish as the lines behind me. I saw my crinkly blue T-shirt, a long rip running from the top of my neckline. It was where Carly had yanked, trying to protect herself. I looked wild, my hair sprung around my face, the knotted ends clinging to my cheeks, my lips drawn into a thin line.

But mostly I saw my eyes, flat and grainy in the picture.

They were empty.

I had never seen myself like that before—and it scared me.

There were words around me, scattered like dots. I tried to read the article, connecting the words to my name, but each line seemed to slip right through me. I didn't need to read them to know what had happened.

Someone had sent me a clipping of a school news article with my mug shot. The email sender was E69Ch3aT896. It was the same person who had sent Olivia's nude.

But that had been Dwayne, and he was in prison. There was no way he could email me.

I spun around slowly, scanning the church hallway on both sides. My skin was crawling—someone was watching me. But there was no one else around. I walked away from the windows, planting my back against a wall.

I looked at the email again, my eyes landing on the recipient list. It was loaded with other email addresses and names. It could have been the same list of people from the Halloween search party. The email's subject heading simply read: "ivy league mary."

There was a headline that hung limp over my picture: CORNELL SENIOR EXPELLED AFTER ALLEGED ATTACK.

I had just been exposed.

I never meant to attack her.

Carly.

She was one of my freshman residents on the sixth floor. She was only eighteen, and she was pale and pretty with long red hair. A walking porcelain doll. Carly wanted to study art history, and she hoped to work in a museum one day. She wore a knapsack to class, a hand-me-down made of real worn leather. She was sharp and funny, and the other freshmen flocked to her during their first few days on campus. Carly had presence.

But the best thing about her: she admired me.

I met her during Welcome Week, when she knocked on my door.

I had a little bucket outside my room with free condoms. The RAs had to make sure that the freshmen weren't spreading chlamydia as they screwed about, untethered. But as liberated as they were, they were also shy—the freshmen were discreet about the condoms they took.

But that day, Carly sat on my floor with a large handful of candy-colored condoms in her lap. Carly asked me about my own life, where I was from, what I studied, what I wanted to do in the future. When she laughed, it sounded breathless and charming.

"I think I'm gonna bug you from now on," she said, grinning. "You actually know what the hell you're doing."

"I don't think anyone does," I said, but I was flattered.

Carly often stopped by my room to talk to me, no matter how late the time. She was an avid listener during her nightly visits, the two of us sitting on the floor in my room, talking about current events and books and pop culture and our everyday lives.

As laid-back as she was, Carly was shrewd. She was unbothered by the fact that I was a senior and an authority figure. I had none of the awkwardness toward Carly that I had with the other freshmen. I gave her advice, and she was my confidante at the dorm. I almost viewed her like a little sister. No one had ever tried to mentor me before, so I decided to do that for someone else.

By the time September ended, Carly had already accomplished so much. She'd slept with two boys from different frats and secured an internship at the college art museum. She'd found a reliable drug dealer on campus. She'd rushed during Greek Week and had five of the school's top sororities make a bid on her. Carly had dumped them all, saying she couldn't deal with the commitment. And somehow, she was studiously keeping up with her classes.

In the span of a month, Carly had done more than what I could've dreamt in my first year. She was going places. I told her that, too.

And she thought I was interesting, smart, funny. She loved to hear about my own experiences in high school, college, Liberty Lake. She empathized with me about my past. I was spellbound. My friendship with her was the equivalent of love at first sight. We weren't friends because we'd gone to the same church or school. We hadn't settled for each other. There was no unspoken distance or rivalry between us. I adored Carly, easy as that.

She looked up to me. I was flattered that someone like her was interested in someone like me. She was three years my junior with twice the life experience. I suppose deep inside, I was still the same fat Mary from Liberty Lake, who just wanted to be liked. And Carly did. She admired me.

I thought so, at least.

Then, late one Wednesday night, I was drying off in a shower stall in the dorm. I heard the bathroom door open, laughter spilling in, Carly's breathless voice among it. A pair of footsteps rushed past, heading for a toilet stall.

"God, you're such a lightweight," called Carly.

The person in the stall made no answer.

"Is it stupid that I'm worried about the RAs?" asked another girl, her voice scratchy. "I don't want my shit getting confiscated."

"You shouldn't," said Carly. "Fucking sucks, though. The RA system is so archaic. I didn't go to college to get babied by some prudes."

The other girl seemed to laugh in disbelief. I squeezed the towel in my hands, willing myself to stay still.

"Aren't you friends with one?" asked the girl.

"Yeah," said Carly. "Mary. She's nice. Super sheltered, though."

"She seems like a try-hard."

Carly giggled.

"You don't even know the half of it. She was like, *rough,* back in high school. Super rough."

There was suddenly silence from the two of them. I tried peering through the crack in the shower door, but the girls were out of view. After a moment, the two of them burst out laughing, their voices bouncing in the bathroom.

"Oh my God, who the hell calls themselves 'Ivy League Mary'?" said the girl breathlessly.

"They did her dirty with that picture."

"God, she was like twice your size, Carly. It's like she didn't even try."

I was cold standing naked in the shower, but my face was burning. Carly had showed the newspaper clipping of me back in high school, when Liberty Lake had announced my college acceptance. I only mentioned it once—Carly had gone out of her way to find it.

She was ripping me apart.

"Poor girl's overcompensating," said Carly, sighing. "I do feel really bad for her, though. First the weight, now this. If I was working as an RA, I'd be so depressed. Like if that was all my life had amounted to? God, I'd slit my wrists."

"Carly!" chided the other girl, but they broke out into a fit of laughter.

Their friend suddenly left the toilet stall, complaining about constipation. The girls cleaned up and left, talking about heading to Carly's room.

I was too afraid to move until they were gone. I felt the tears welling up in my eyes, livid and bitter. Carly had slashed me apart. Everything that I'd tried to abandon in Liberty Lake had come rushing back—I could never leave that place and that fat, boring girl behind. She followed me wherever I went.

I felt the fury well up inside me, the rage that a couple of eighteen-year-old brats had the nerve to look down on me.

Then, there was the shock. Carly had seen me for who I was. She hadn't liked me at all—she'd pitied me. That was what hurt the most.

I stayed in my dorm room all through Thursday morning. I skipped my thesis class. I had a couple of granola bars and a bit of water, and I texted some of the other RAs that I was locking myself up to work on some projects.

But I was afraid to leave my room. The floor and the rest of the building felt hostile, unsafe. I couldn't bear to run into Carly. Normally, she would want to stop and talk. But I couldn't face her anymore—I knew what she truly thought of me. It was humiliating, and I couldn't pretend otherwise.

By the time lunch came around, I was starving. I left my dorm room and smelled the pungent odor of weed in the air. The scent was only a few doors down the hallway. It came from Carly's room. There was laughter and loud trap music inside.

Looking back, I should have ignored them and walked away. Weed was a trivial matter in the dorms. It was more trouble than it was worth.

But that day, I was hungry and tired and bitter. A part of me snapped.

I knocked on the door. When nothing happened, I knocked on it harder, my fists pounding in quick succession. The music died down, and the door opened.

Carly was staring at me, her red hair falling down one shoulder. It was lovely hair, the kind that glowed even in poor lighting. Behind her, there were two other girls sitting on the floor, smoke wafting up behind their backs. I could see the glass of a bong peeking out behind one knee.

"What's up?" Carly said breezily.

"Where's the marijuana?" I asked. It sounded like someone else's voice, flat and robotic. "Dorm policy says I need to confiscate it."

Carly didn't move. She just stared at me, her face placid. Behind her the two girls started shuffling the contraband behind them.

"Chill, Mary, we're not doing anything," said Carly.

"I need to confiscate it. Now."

Carly frowned, immobile.

"Why are you acting like this? You don't have the right to be here," she said.

"Why not?" I asked, my voice cracking. "Is it because I'm a try-hard? Maybe I should slit my wrists?"

Carly only stared back at me. None of it had registered in her mind. I was getting heated, growing angrier by the second.

"We'll stop if you don't like the smell," said Carly. "Just stop being a cunt, Mary."

A second later, I slammed past her into the room. The two girls looked alarmed, their eyes bright pink.

Carly grabbed my shoulder. I spun around.

And I slapped her. I could hear the clap of skin echo down the hallway. The pain spurting in one palm as the other clenched shut, my fingernails digging into it.

Carly just looked at me, her pale cheek blazing bright red. She was seething.

When they later asked me what had happened, I said I couldn't remember the details. I wasn't lying. I just remembered my hands digging into her hair, pulling at her scalp. Her hands yanking on my shirt, scratching at my throat, my neck. Her friends screaming in the background. The sound of my shirt ripping near my neck. Her nails digging into my skin, my nails digging into hers. The ache in my fist as it flew toward her face.

Then there was a yank as an RA pulled me off of her. Carly's long hair was wild and knotted. Her dainty lips were split open, blood dripping down the middle. The skin around her eye was dark. I saw the rage in her face, white-hot, but instantly it disappeared. She was crying.

The RA, Vince, yanked me to one end of the hallway. Another RA took Carly and her friends down to the front office. I heard Vince mumble on his cell phone about what to do with me. And I only stood there, listening to the growl in my stomach. I was almost giddy. He took me down to the ground floor, but instead of stopping at the RAs' office, he walked me outside.

A police car was waiting for me. It was in there that I realized that my hands and my arms were bleeding with small cuts. My face had been spared.

By late afternoon, the police had taken my fingerprints and my mug shot. A police officer gave me some bandages and some ointment to clean up the cuts. They tried to interview me, too, but I could only blurt out short answers.

Yes, I slapped her.

Yes, she sort of threatened me.

No, I didn't feel like I was in danger.

Yes, she instigated the whole thing.

Afterward, they brought me to a cell in the police building. It was comically small, barely big enough to fit a small bed and a contraption that doubled as a toilet and sink. I was so exhausted that I collapsed on the bed. The sheet was dotted with suspect brown spots, but I didn't care.

The day seemed both faint and clear at the same time.

Before I closed my eyes, I felt something else simmering through me, as comforting as a blanket wrapped over my shoulders.

Satisfaction.

I later found out that Carly's father was a congressman.

I didn't even have the pleasure of speaking to him. I woke up the next morning and found a woman watching me on the other side of the bars. She was Carly's lawyer, most likely a friend of a friend of a friend of her father's. My lawyer, a bored public defender, showed up only a few minutes later.

In a meeting room, Carly's lawyer asked me how I would feel about being locked up for three years for fourth-degree assault against a helpless eighteen-year-old girl.

I tried to say something about how it wasn't my fault, she had touched me first, there was marijuana in her dorm room, she hadn't listened to me, I was sorry.

But I could tell that no one in the room was listening. Everything I said was futile.

Instead, I started to weep.

I hadn't bawled like that since I was a child.

Carly's lawyer read me a memo from her father. He was upset, but he believed in mercy. The congressman was willing to drop charges on two conditions: first, I had to recant my statement about the weed in Carly's room; second, I had to leave the university permanently, away from his daughter.

If I didn't follow through, they would take me to court.

I balked. There was only one clear choice.

But I could only think of campus and the brick buildings and the parties and the late nights I'd spent studying. The joy four years ago when I had gotten my acceptance. I thought of Ivy League Mary, who was thin and pretty and destined for bigger things in her life. I wasn't willing to give her up.

In the end, I didn't have to decide—the school did it for me. I was expelled within an hour of our conversation. Carly's father had clout with the administration, that much was clear.

My time at school was over.

Relieved, my lawyer told me that Carly's father was dropping any further legal action. He and Carly hoped that this would be a "proper learning experience" for me. They were praying for me to work out my behavioral issues.

I called Dad right after. I rambled through the events. He listened quietly until I told him about my expulsion. His first words were low and gruff: "I thought you were on medication, Mary."

I heard the disappointment, the disbelief, the anger. He thought my medication made everything okay. It held back the anxiety, the dread. But it didn't solve everything. It didn't account for my stupidity, my recklessness. It didn't account for Carly, her father, his influence. It didn't account for my mistakes.

Dad then told me to pack up. He said the car ride would take about seventeen hours.

When my lawyer left, I took a taxi service back to campus. I raced up to my room, staring at the ground. I knew that people were gawking at me, the RA with the bandages on her arms. Word was spreading.

I hid out in my room until Dad arrived Saturday morning. I ate the last of my granola bars and snuck out late at night to use the bathroom. And then Dad helped me move out of the dorm. I came back to Liberty Lake.

In the span of a day, I had lost it all. I was now the crazy bitch who had tried to attack a congressman's daughter. Carly had won.

▶ ▶ ▶

I deleted the email in the church hallway. My heart was pounding.

The email had been delivered to numerous people, and that could have included anyone at the funeral: our old classmates from high school, Kevin, the Willands.

I couldn't bear to face them. I didn't want to know what they thought of me after everything—the expulsion, the assault, the audacity I had to show up to a dead girl's funeral. I could already see the disgust on their faces and the humiliation on mine.

I walked out of church into the cold, and I kept walking until I found my thirteen-dollar Uber. When I was back at home, I sent Dad a text, telling him that I had gotten sick. He needed to attend the funeral procession without me.

Then I crawled under the bedsheets. I even half prayed that it was all a nightmare—Carly, the expulsion, the murders.

But I knew fully well it wasn't.

33

Dad woke me up early on Sunday morning. He tossed my work uniform onto my bed. He was already dressed for church.

"You're working today, Mary," he said. "You should be getting ready."

I was ushered into the bathroom. I felt filthy, my skin encased in a layer of sweat. In the mirror, my face looked puffy and sallow—after I'd left St. Rita's, I slept through the rest of Saturday afternoon. Dad checked on me after the funeral, but I told him I was skipping dinner. I never even asked about what happened. I took my medication and tripled the dosage. I wanted to be so drowsy that I could sleep in peace.

But my sleep was restless—I flickered between memory and nightmare:

I was back in a jail cell with Carly in front of me, my hand pulling at her hair, her hand clawing at my skin. And I was back in bed, listening to the TV downstairs. And I was looking at my mug shot, hundreds of copies of it scattered in front of me. And then I was drowning in the lake, my body back to its old, big shape. And my body began to burst apart, the limbs floating away from each other, into the darkness . . .

In the bathroom, I stayed on the toilet for a long time, my head in my hands. I was exhausted, as if my bones had doubled in mass. I only got up to shower when Dad started knocking on the door. He was listening in, making sure that I didn't try anything.

Dad waited for me to go before he left for Mass. I expected him to mention my mug shot—a comment from Mass, a question from the Willands—but he said nothing.

In the driveway, I saw him watching me from the living room. There was a light flurry of snow in the air, covering the house and the cul-de-sac. I imagined myself running into it, until I had gotten far away.

For once, the break room of Goodhue Groceries was comforting. I saw the jackets hung up on the coatrack, the employee locker bank, the empty lunch tables. Work was a repose. The customers were terrible, but I could depend on them. They would distract me.

After I opened my checkout lane, Jim came by. I could hear it in the way he walked, each step halting for a slight second too long.

I tried to smile so hard that my cheeks hurt.

"How's it going, Jim?"

"You have a criminal record?" he asked.

I froze midsmile.

Jim was frowning, his arms folded across his chest. He was wary, as if he were looking at a bomb instead of a person.

"So it's true?" Jim asked. "The fourth-degree assault charge?"

"It was dropped," I blurted out. My mind was focused on the email. Jim had received it. "It's not . . . it's not real."

"You lied, Mary. On the paperwork, you said you had no criminal record." Jim didn't blink. "And you've got a whole article. That's something you should've told us."

I was watching myself slip away, my hands slackening off the rope, gravity tugging me down. There was no stopping it.

"I quit," I croaked.

"You can't quit if you've been let go."

I shook my head. I could imagine the scene from a distance, from the other end of the store: Jim standing there, his arms crossed, and me too frozen to move. But the scene was too stilted, too flat, as if the volume had been turned off. I sensed no urgency, no panic.

I was still drowsy.

People were fired every day. They were let go because of budget issues or a lack of skills. Sometimes the boss was in a bad mood. Other times they deserved it.

But I wasn't like them. I was boring and smart and I had busted my ass off to get into Cornell. I was nice. I wasn't someone who got fired.

"I think you should go, Mary," Jim said, unsmiling. "You can return your uniform and employee card by the end of this week. I need your polo and pants to be cleaned. And as for other things . . ."

It was easy to block out Jim's voice. He talked too much for his own good.

Nearby, at the center of the self-checkout aisle, someone had decorated the pita chip display. It reminded me of a Christmas tree—the tall pyramid shape and the small pita chip bags that hung like baubles. But someone had recently put real ornaments on there, in glittery red and gold and silver.

We weren't even past Thanksgiving yet.

"Erin will fetch your things from your locker. You can wait by the bathrooms," Jim said, walking away. "Good luck."

It was my cue to leave. I left the aisle, trying not to look at the faces that watched me from self-checkout. Just like at the dorm, everyone was looking at me. This time, my cheeks were frozen in place, midsmile. I pretended I was fine.

But instead of walking to the back room, I looped around to the self-checkout aisle. My legs were moving on their own. I was watching myself from above.

It was only a nightmare, I was sure of it. None of it was real—it was too anticlimactic. Jim hadn't fired me. I had imagined the whole thing, just as I had imagined the Christmas tree of pita chips.

I reached out and touched a bag. I felt the sandiness of the paper. It was biodegradable.

And I shoved the whole display.

The little chip bags went flying everywhere. The rack crashed over. There was a scream from nearby. Then Jim shouted at me to get the hell out. I looked at the mess and walked away. If no one picked up the bags, then they would degrade into compost in the middle of the store. I wanted that, a little pile of dirt where I had once been.

I was buzzing in the car, my pulse racing. I saw the lake, a dark slab of gray beneath the sky. I pictured myself wading into the water, one foot in front of the other until I was completely submerged. It seemed like a lovely way to go.

But in reality, the lake was polluted with algae and zebra mussels and dead bodies.

At home, I slammed the door shut behind me.

In the gray morning light, the couches looked worn. Our coffee table was still chipped in a corner where I had once smashed into it with a toy. The carpet still had its ugly red design. And the walls still had the framed pictures of me and Mom and Dad throughout the years.

The living room had always looked like this, from my birth onward. It would stay the same even after I left.

And I was the same. Still fat, pathetic, and easy to ignore. Even easier to push around.

I thought I could make things different.

I wanted to be seen, so I excelled in school. I wanted to be remembered, so I aimed for an Ivy. I wanted to be treated well, so I lost the weight. And when Carly mocked me, I wanted to prove her wrong. I wanted to stand up for myself.

But none of it had worked.

No matter how hard I tried, I couldn't change.

The person I had tried to become in college—she was temporary, a mirage. She was never meant to last.

Ivy League Mary had never been real.

My throat was burning. My sight was blurry. And my chest felt tight.

I climbed up the stairs, my legs wobbly. I opened the door to my room, hobbling toward the nightstand. I grabbed my bottle of escitalopram and looked at the pills that were left inside.

I dumped the bottle out. Nine pills total.

I went downstairs into the kitchen and poured myself a glass of water. I rattled the pills in my fist.

I pictured Mom driving us to church, a knitted cap on her head, a box of canned goods in the back seat. Mom always loved to help people. She knew the end was coming. She'd been prepared.

I tilted my head back, my hands trembling. And I squeezed my eyes shut.

One second, two, on three . . .

My cell phone began to vibrate.

I waited for the caller to stop, my head throbbing.

But the phone kept buzzing for one minute, then another. Whoever was calling was insistent. I finally checked my cell phone.

It was an unknown number.

In my mind, I could hear the robotic voice again. I had gotten the call at Littlewood Park Reserve and Olivia's funeral Mass. The robotic voice always called before something was leaked.

But I had missed the implication yesterday:

The person who had murdered her was targeting me.

And Dwayne was in jail . . .

The panic was rising in me, like bile. I was being watched.

I looked out at the cul-de-sac through the living room window. And slowly, I put the phone to my ear, answering it.

"What is it? What do you want?" I stammered.

"Mary?"

"Mr. Nguyen?"

"Yes. It's me."

I heard the wind bellowing in the background. It sounded like Mr. Nguyen was out in the cold. Mass would have just ended at St. Rita's. He might have been standing in the church parking lot.

"What is it?" I asked, my voice growing softer.

It was silent on the other end, except for the wind. Then I heard Mr. Nguyen sigh.

"I saw the funeral on the news yesterday. For the Olivia girl. The church is hanging up her picture inside for a few weeks."

I said nothing. Olivia's parents had likely asked for it—St. Rita's was honoring its late parishioner.

Mr. Nguyen cleared his throat.

"You talked about a serial killer. You were right."

"I guess," I murmured.

"You asked about DeMaria before."

"I did." But then he had called the police on me.

"I don't want trouble," said Mr. Nguyen. "I stay out of it, you know?"

"I know."

Madison wasn't wrong about her father. All he did was work. Mr. Nguyen didn't want to get involved in anything outside of it. The rest of the world—particularly other people—just brought more problems. Madison said he'd dealt with enough in one lifetime.

"I don't think I did anything wrong," said Mr. Nguyen. "I didn't try to."

The pills felt sweaty in my hand.

"What happened?"

"I fired DeMaria. She kept coming into work late. First, it was ten minutes. Then fifteen, then a half hour. She had a kid, so I felt bad. But during the summer, she was skipping work shifts. I gave her two warnings.

"But July tenth, DeMaria was two hours late for her lunch shift.

I had another server come in. I was so angry—I fired her when she showed up. I told her to have fun at the job center," he said, his voice faint. He was growing uncomfortable as he retraced the events of that day.

"And you know what DeMaria did? She laughed. She said she was going to quit anyway, she was a model. She said one day I'd be cooking for her, then she'd fire me."

"I don't understand," I said. "What does that mean?"

"I don't know. That's the last thing she said to me." Mr. Nguyen paused. "But I watched her get into a car."

I felt goose bumps rise on my arms.

"A car?"

"DeMaria left the restaurant with one of my aprons. I went after her down the street, but she was walking into a black luxury car. It looked like a tank, like something from Germany or Switzerland."

"Did you see who the driver was?"

"The back windows were tinted from where I was."

I swallowed, my stomach now churning.

Mr. Nguyen could have possibly been one of the last people to see DeMaria alive. The driver of the black car might have been Dwayne, but he owned a tan car. Mrs. Jackson had also said that DeMaria had gotten a ride that day. Whoever the driver was, they had played a crucial role on the last day of her life.

Mr. Nguyen coughed.

"When the killer was arrested . . . I thought the police needed the extra information. I want you to know that I told the police."

"Well, that's good—"

"And it wasn't my fault," he continued, his voice cracking. "I didn't push her to die. I didn't want the other girl to die, either."

I heard the wind blowing from his cell phone. I could almost feel the chill from outside.

And I remembered what I had said to him last time—that there were other lives at stake, that if someone else died, part of it was his fault for not speaking up about DeMaria's last day. I had been overly harsh.

But Mr. Nguyen was afraid. He had known more than he'd let on. He was fearful of his own role—that in firing her, he had pushed her to walk into the black car that might have taken her to her death. He was afraid that by withholding that information, he had prevented the investigators from finding Olivia in time. And he was afraid that it had led to Olivia's death, and to her photo now hanging at St. Rita's.

I didn't know if it was true. None of us ever thought too much about our actions, our inaction—life was too fast, too complicated. We just kept moving forward. By the time we thought about it, it was too late. We kept moving forward anyway.

But there was a chance we could do better. We had to hope.

"Well, it's out of your hands now," I murmured. "You did what you could."

"I know."

"I shouldn't have bothered you at the restaurant."

"It's all done now," he said, sighing. He sounded tired. "It's over. They caught him."

"Right," I said.

But I thought of the black car. I thought of Dwayne, who was locked up in prison. I thought of the email that had exposed me. They didn't add up.

It seemed like there were other people involved in DeMaria's death. It even seemed like there was a small chance that Dwayne hadn't been the killer.

Uneasy, I looked at the pills in my hand. My palm was sweaty from clenching shut. My nails had left marks that now burned.

34

The email. The black car. Dwayne Turner.

It was my personal litany as I changed out of my work clothes and climbed into Mom's car. When I pulled out of the garage, Dad's truck was already parked in the driveway. He'd come home from church.

Dad rolled his window down.

"Why aren't you at work?" he called.

"I quit," I shouted back.

"What the hell," Dad said, the anger flashing in his eyes. But I continued out of the driveway.

He was losing patience with me. In one month, I had gone to jail, I had been expelled, and I was now out of a job. I seemed to run into one issue after another. Dad was growing tired of it—he seemed to think my problems were becoming his. I was a burden.

But I would fix things in time. I would prove it to him, somehow.

I just had one other priority first.

My head was spinning as I left the neighborhood, the litany repeating over and over again, as if I were afraid that I would forget it completely.

The email. The black car. Dwayne Turner.

I sat at a corner table in Espresso Haus. I had my laptop in front of me, my emails displayed. I kept my back to the wall and made sure no one was around. I opened the email with Olivia's nude photo in it, then the email with my mug shot.

I searched for the sender online: E69Ch3aT896. But not much came up. I only found news articles about the nude photo leak.

The email account was most likely a throwaway. The sender couldn't risk being tracked that easily. I had no other means to trace them online. They could have been anywhere.

I shivered, thinking about it. Dwayne was in the county jail, so the sender was somebody else. That person had doxed Olivia with her nude photo.

Now they were after me.

I scanned the coffee shop again. There was a church family sitting nearby, enjoying their Sunday coffees.

It seemed like Dwayne had an accomplice. There had been more than one killer.

My mind jumped to Jayden. He was close to Dwayne and one of the last friends he had left in the city. He could've helped his cousin cover up the murders. Through Charice, he could also monitor the police department. Jayden knew that I was trying to connect DeMaria and Olivia together, and maybe that was why his texts to Dwayne had been so persistent. And if he knew that I had reported his cousin to the police . . .

I felt a lump in my throat. I closed out of Olivia's email and looked at my own.

I was staring at my mug shot. The longer I looked at it, the less brutal it felt, as if I were applying pressure to a cut. The sender had tried to hurt me personally.

I checked the list of recipients. My email address was first. After mine, there was Jim's, and then those of dozens of Goodhue Groceries employees. The sender had targeted my employer. They had wanted me to get fired.

Only Dwayne had access to those email addresses, unless he'd sent them to someone else. The sender might have even worked at Goodhue Groceries. They might have gone to the search, unnoticed.

All those late nights that I had left work alone, somebody had watched me. I might have been followed home.

I didn't know how close I had come to disappearing like the others. My legs shook beneath the table, restless.

It was an eerie thought. But whoever had exposed me and Olivia, whoever had helped Dwayne with the murders, whoever had driven DeMaria in the black car—they were going to pay. I would make sure of it.

But there was one other confusing thread: DeMaria had called herself a "model." Her mother had never mentioned anything about it. Even Mr. Nguyen seemed confused.

I searched online for DeMaria's name with the terms "modeling" and "model," but I found nothing. I couldn't even find her Instagram account. She either didn't have one or she'd kept it hidden. But there was no evidence to back up DeMaria's words.

It was more surprising that Olivia hadn't said it. She wasn't on a runway or in a clothing catalog, but she had a presence on Instagram. She had nice photos, and she'd even made some money off them. It wasn't a reach to call Olivia an Instagram model.

I took out my cell phone and looked up her Instagram page.

Her followers had more than doubled in number. A month ago, she had nearly 50,000 followers. Her page now had over 120,000. In death, she had become more famous. No one found it strange that they were following a murder victim.

On her last post, with the slice of pizza, people were still adding new comments:

Rest in peace beautiful!

Hope your watching from above!! Praying your killer rots in hell

I feel bad about your nudes but you were pretty hot RIP

I began to tap through her photos, one by one. I didn't know what I was looking for. I had a rhythm going: tap a photo, tap away, repeat. I was skimming for *something* that tied back to modeling or Liberty Lake or DeMaria Jackson. I hoped I would recognize it.

There were images of Olivia at her college campus, at charity events with her sorority, on a beach in the Bahamas, in a park by the Eiffel Tower. But after finding the dozenth photo of her at a coffee shop, I grew frustrated. There was nothing useful.

I started scrolling past row after row of photos, my finger flicking impatiently. Then I reached the very end, back to Olivia's very first photo, from 2011. It was the same photo that now graced Liberty Lake and the rest of the country: Olivia in her white dress, smiling, with a glint in her eyes. The photo had garnered 117 Likes, a sign of more to come. She'd left a quirky caption: *Just me looking angelic I guess.*

I closed my eyes. The back of my head was starting to ache. Nothing made sense.

But with my eyes closed, I could only see two things clearly.

The black car. And Dwayne Turner.

I drove to the Jewel of Liberty Lake. I circled the ground-level parking lot. Mr. Nguyen said that DeMaria had walked into a black luxury car after she was fired. He said it looked like a tank.

Even if Dwayne hadn't owned a black luxury car, he could have borrowed one or rented it. He could have even used one near his apartment. But very few of the cars matched the description in the parking lot. An old woman passed me in her black Mercedes-Benz.

I parked at a guest spot and watched as a car slid down into the underground parking garage. If anyone had a nice imported car from Germany or Switzerland, they would've paid extra to protect it underground. But I had no way to access the garage on my own.

Through a glass window, I could see a white Christmas tree in the apartment lobby. It was lavish, with gold ornaments hanging off its branches. The rest of the lobby was decorated, too, with bright string lights and fake snow.

We had yet to celebrate Thanksgiving in two weeks. But the decorations were meant as a distraction. Otherwise, people would dwell on the fact that a murderer had just lived there.

I imagined Dwayne bringing DeMaria to the Jewel, her eyes widening as she took in the gorgeous view, the gaudy designs, the smell of money. The realization that she had met her Prince Charming.

But then again, Dwayne had lied about being away in Wisconsin. He might never have brought her to the apartment at all.

As I pulled out of the guest spot, a blur flashed by the passenger window.

Jayden was suddenly behind the car.

And I hit the brakes, screaming.

35

Jayden knocked on my back window, his face grim. He wore a dark gray winter jacket and a black hoodie underneath. He carried a small cardboard box in his hands.

I thought about honking. I thought about running him over. But Jayden kept knocking on the back window.

"We need to talk," he said, his voice muffled from the outside.

I lifted my foot just a little from the brake. The car rolled backward a bit. Jayden stepped back a few steps, but he wouldn't leave.

"Shit, are you really gonna run me over?" he jeered. "I just need to talk."

I was angry and jittery from the coffee. If I ran him over, I could argue self-defense. No one would bat an eye about it. And Jayden would pay for leaking my info at Goodhue Groceries.

But then again . . . what if he hadn't?

I remembered the way Jayden had held Charice at the apartment, the way she had talked about marrying him. Charice loved him.

I didn't want to run over the wrong person.

Jayden suddenly walked around the car. He hovered outside the passenger window, bending down so that we were at eye level.

"Mary, we need to talk about Dwayne."

I didn't move.

"Don't forget about the fun times we had," he jeered. "Remember last time at the mall? That shit was fun."

At the mall, we had talked about leaking a police file to the *New York Times*. It was a veiled threat.

I swallowed, glancing around the parking lot. There were other cars nearby. In the lobby, a girl sat at the front desk. A security guard stood alert nearby. It seemed that after the scrutiny with Dwayne's arrest, the Jewel had hired better security. I also had a cell phone with an emergency call screen under my thumb.

If anything happened, I wouldn't go down without a fight. Carly knew that firsthand.

I slowly pulled back into the spot.

And I unlocked the passenger door.

Jayden immediately slid into the seat, maneuvering the cardboard box on his lap. There were electronic wires sticking out of it.

"What do you want?" I asked.

"Chill, Mary. I'm not here to hurt you," said Jayden. Up close, his eyes looked sunken, as if he'd aged since I'd seen him two weeks ago. He looked tired.

"Why are you even here?"

Jayden rattled the box in his hands.

"I'm moving Dwayne's shit out of his apartment. They ended his lease since he's in jail now."

The box looked innocuous.

"And you put him in there, didn't you," continued Jayden, his voice low. It was more of a statement than a question. "You turned him in."

"I didn't do anything," I said. I sounded calm, even though my heart was pounding.

"I think it's damn interesting that you start hanging out with my cousin for a few weeks and then all of a sudden his ass gets handed to the police."

"It's a coincidence."

Jayden snorted.

"Some coincidence, Mary. You got Charice to give you the police file so you could use it on my cousin. She really thought you cared about justice and shit. But I knew you weren't like that, Ivy League. You've got something dark going on there."

The words stung, not because he'd hurt my feelings, but because they were true. The past month had proven it. Jim, Father Greg, Madison, now Jayden—it seemed like everyone seemed to know me better than I knew myself. They could sense something not right about me.

"I didn't snitch on Dwayne," I said, my throat tight.

"Sure you didn't. But Dwayne didn't kill anyone," said Jayden, his words measured and low. Jayden was restraining himself, trying not to snap in the car. It was too risky for him to be angry with a security guard nearby.

But I couldn't forget the scene back in the Sewers, how Jayden had knocked out Charice's assaulter in one swing.

"What do you want from me?" I asked, trying to keep my words steady.

"I want you to get Dwayne out of jail. Take back what you said to the police. Fix what you did to my cousin."

"I didn't rat him out."

Jayden shook his head. He wouldn't even look at me.

"How do you even know that Dwayne's innocent?"

"Because he's a dumbass," said Jayden. He was irritated, but I sensed it wasn't directed at me this time. "Dwayne had his whole life handed to him on a gold plate. Good college, football talent. But he just had to screw it up, didn't he? He got his ass kicked out of all of it. Then he knocked someone up. And look at this shit," said Jayden, gesturing at the glass tower in front of us. "You really think he could live here? Fuck that—Dwayne was burning through his student loans for this. He was living paycheck to paycheck. All so he wouldn't look like a giant fuckup."

I thought of the view from Dwayne's bed, the gray water below as opaque as concrete.

"When you fuck up that bad, that many times, you learn to be careful, Mary," Jayden continued. "And I know Dwayne—he's a dumbass who screws up, but he's not evil. He doesn't kill people. He wouldn't hurt DeMaria like that."

The anger was palpable, like smoke in the air. But there was something in the way that Jayden spoke, the steeliness when he mentioned DeMaria's name. The hint of familiarity.

"Did you always know about Dwayne and DeMaria?" I asked slowly.

Jayden said nothing.

That day at the mall with him and Charice—Jayden had acted like DeMaria was a complete stranger, another name in the news. But he'd known everything, hadn't he, about Dwayne and DeMaria, her pregnancy, and the way Dwayne had dumped them cold.

"You knew about her this whole time, and you said nothing?" I asked, outraged.

"Don't turn this shit on me," said Jayden, his voice suddenly rising. "I didn't kill DeMaria. I feel bad that she died. But Dwayne didn't kill her."

"He left her and his own son."

"I never said Dwayne was a saint," said Jayden. "But he's not a killer."

A silence had fallen over us. Jayden was looking at the window into the lobby. He was getting antsy, one knee bouncing the cardboard box on top of it.

"You know Dwayne's innocent," murmured Jayden. "You know shit doesn't add up. I need you to fix this."

A part of me understood his frustration—he was protecting his cousin. But the other part of me—the larger, uglier, more spiteful part—wanted him to get the hell out of the car. He could struggle on his own.

"Tell me Dwayne's innocent," said Jayden.

"I don't know."

"Don't lie to me."

"I said I don't know."

"How will you feel when an innocent man gets life in solitary because of you?"

And another part of me—the tired part—snapped. I hit the steering wheel with both hands. The car honked. And I was crying. Snot dripped down my nose, but I couldn't stop it—I was so tired.

"Damn, if I knew you'd be this emotional—"

"Fuck off," I blurted, but I buried my face in my hands.

Carly, the murders, the funeral, the firing—it was overwhelming. I wanted to be alone in the dark and left to rot.

But Jayden was right. There were certain things that didn't make sense even with Dwayne locked away. He wasn't the killer—I knew it. And now I was afraid.

I had screwed up again—and sent the wrong person to jail.

The real killer was after me.

My chest was heaving as I hiccuped for air, my eyes closed shut. After a while, I felt a hand awkwardly patting my shoulder.

"You need me to call Charice?" Jayden asked gruffly.

I shook my head.

A group of women walked by the car, staring at us. Jayden and I probably looked like a couple, and I was the girlfriend who'd just been dumped.

"Uh . . . you okay?" Jayden asked.

"I don't know, I've just been doxed—"

"Doxed?"

"Kind of," I stammered. My voice got quiet, as if I were afraid someone else would hear me. "I think it's the killer."

Jayden frowned. He peered behind us at the parking lot.

"How do you know?"

"The killer doxed Olivia Willand with her nude photo. Now they've leaked my private info at work. It's the same email address—"

"Dwayne sure as hell didn't do it," muttered Jayden.

I nodded, wiping my face with my sleeve.

"You know who it is? You got any enemies?"

"I don't know."

Carly hated me. After what I did to her, other people at school also hated me. But as far as I knew, none of them had links to Olivia Willand. They didn't even know where I worked . . .

I froze.

At Goodhue Groceries, there was one person who would have wanted me to get fired. Two weeks ago, he'd scared me after I left work. He once mentioned his background in computer science. And when I turned down the invitation to his Halloween party, he'd blown up at me. In his anger, he had brought up Olivia: *And you see what happened to her? That slut went missing.*

It was a threat.

I felt my stomach drop. I could picture his pale, scrawny face and his beady blue eyes. There was always a tension around him. He was hostile to me and Dwayne. Dwayne had intimidated him. I had rejected him. Then he'd leaked Dwayne's incriminating photo of Olivia. Now I was being punished.

I spent so much of my life being uncertain, but I wasn't uncertain about him. I knew exactly who he was.

Ron.

"You okay, Mary?" Jayden asked.

I shook my head.

"But I know what I need to do," I said softly.

36

After Jayden left, I sped home. I wasn't heading out until night, but I could already feel the anxiety building in my bones.

Dad was gone. I was relieved. I didn't want to lie to him about Goodhue Groceries, but it was easier that way. If he knew I'd been fired, he'd be furious. I just needed time to deal with Ron. Then I'd find a different job. Dad wouldn't need to worry.

In the living room, I wrapped myself in a blanket on the couch and turned on the TV to a reality show rerun. It was one of the *Real Housewives* spinoffs. I liked hearing the women's voices in the background, the excited peaks and lulls that filled the room. It made me feel safe. I stayed still on the couch, my eyes closed, slowly drifting off to sleep.

Among the voices that prattled, I suddenly heard Mrs. Willand's from the church bathroom:

I'm afraid she did something illegal.

I saw it . . . Her phone . . .

. . . Doberman . . .

I sat up slowly.

At the time, I'd been confused. The Doberman reference was random, but Mrs. Willand had seemed concerned. There had to be something more to it.

On my laptop, I searched for anything that mentioned both "Olivia Willand" and "Dobermans." No results. I looked for news stories of Dobermans in Liberty Lake, but there was only one article about a local Doberman attack on a child in the late 1980s. Nothing else.

I tried another search for "Dobermans" and "illegal." Instead, I found articles about laws that had banned the dog breed. But none of it was relevant to Olivia.

I sighed. Mrs. Willand had been distressed at her daughter's funeral—it seemed likely that she'd misspoken. Or I had misheard her completely.

It was all hearsay. She and Mr. Nguyen had both mentioned strange things about the girls. I wanted it to be useful information, but I was clinging onto nothing.

I nearly closed my laptop.

Then I stopped.

I was holding my breath.

At the bottom of the screen, there was one search result that looked different from the others.

It was a link to a website called Doberman Productions. Beneath it, there was a single snippet: "Porn videos so good they're almost illegal."

I pressed the link. My chest felt tight.

The loading screen featured a logo at center—a black silhouette of a Doberman howling in front of a mustard-yellow moon. The logo looked fitting for a dog rescue group. But as the site loaded, a grid of videos buffered at the center while the Doberman hung in the top-right corner.

I clicked out of the ads that began to appear: some promising penis growth, others offering sexy local singles. I got rid of them and hoped that the laptop's antivirus was turned on.

My cursor hovered over a video, and it began to silently play, like an X-rated gif. I saw a slim brunette girl grinding on top of a man, then in the next scene, her neck being choked by two large hands, then a full shot of the man's hairy backside. It was rough cuts of one sex scene after another.

I kept scrolling down the page as more videos buffered. The page seemed to go on forever. It seemed like a standard porn site offering a sample of its wares: lesbian sex, rough sex, group sex, toy sex.

But when I finally stopped, the cursor landed over a clip of a woman with long red hair. She wore a green Mardi Gras mask over her eyes. A group of masked men towered over her.

That was the common factor with Doberman Productions—the faces were hidden. Some videos used a blur effect; others used props, clothing, or strategic camera angles to block out identities.

I saw pale women, athletic women, thin women, curvy women, tattooed women, dark women. They were all different, anonymous.

I clicked around the site, exiting past more suspicious ads until I found the "About" page. It contained three sentences:

At Doberman Productions, we specialize in the production and distribution of anonymous amateur porn, featuring gorgeous women from the ages of 18 to 24. Yes, we might be ageist. Sue us.

Olivia and DeMaria fit the standard: they were both young, female, and attractive. The site promised anonymity—it would've appealed to a rising social media star and a young mother. If the site offered payment, then that was the incentive.

I turned off the TV. I suddenly needed the quiet.

I felt like I was creeping through someone's home, ransacking their drawers, dressers, shelves.

The two of them had died so brutally. Now it seemed cruel that I was dredging up something they'd buried. It was obvious why they hid it—porn had a stigma. Olivia's father was a conservative Catholic. DeMaria's mother was wary of her daughter's past. Neither of the women wanted to upset their families, so they kept it discreet.

But Mrs. Willand was aware of it. She'd somehow seen the site on Olivia's phone. She suspected something, especially since Olivia had brought in money out of nowhere.

And Mrs. Willand was afraid to talk about it. I doubted she would tell the police. It would be humiliating—people had already seen her daughter's nude photo. Some of the public had lost sympathy because of it. And if they thought a nude photo was distasteful, then a porn video would be repugnant. Olivia's image would be decimated. There would be assumptions about her that would never go away.

It would be the same situation for DeMaria's family. But she'd left behind a son. If her secret came out, it would follow Demetrius throughout his life—other people would make sure of it. Leticia Jackson would be broken.

I took a deep breath and rubbed my eyes.

I was assuming the worst, but I had no evidence.

On the site, there were thousands of videos—hundreds of them featured blondes and Black women. It was impossible to identify anyone.

On the "About" page, Doberman Productions offered an email address and a single phone number. Email was easy to ignore—the best option was to call.

But it seemed useless. No company would disclose their performers.

I cracked the joints in my neck. I could hear the tension that had built up in the past few weeks. Then I called the number on my cell phone and waited. I listened to one ring after another, my heart rate speeding up.

"Doberman Productions, how can I help you?" It was a motherly voice on the other end. She sounded like a saleslady at a candle shop.

I balked.

"Hi," I said. "I was—I was calling about—"

"Don't worry, honey. No judgment here," the voice said serenely.

"Okay . . . cool. I was just wondering—"

"Don't worry, hon. I'll redirect you to someone who can help you. Don't worry."

There was a pause on the line and then a click. After one ring, someone else picked up.

"Doberman Productions." It was a man's voice this time.

"Hi. I'm not sure who I'm—"

"A lot of our girls are never sure," the man said breezily. "But after they do it, they feel a lot better. It's like a bandage, you know? You just have to rip it off, and you'll feel better right after. With us, Mom and Dad will never have to know."

I felt the blood drain from my face. They thought I was a potential new performer.

"Does that make you feel better?"

"Sure. Yes."

"We don't talk about rates over the phone, but just know that you can build your way up," the man said. "We have two headquarters, in two major cities in the U.S.—"

"I—I don't think I can do it then," I said. I was eager to end the call.

"They're corporate headquarters. You can make your own amateur videos at home."

"I don't have the right equipment."

"You can use a phone camera or a laptop. But if you want more professional help, we got you covered."

"I don't think—"

"Where are you located?"

"Liberty Lake? It's the city in—"

"I got it, don't worry."

Doberman Productions knew how to deal with hesitant girls. They were friendly and coaxing, but they also kept things moving at rapid-fire speed. That way, no one had time to change their mind.

"Liberty Lake sounds like a real cute place," said the man. His computer keys rattled in the background. "Actually, you're in luck. We have an independent contractor there. The contractor specializes in solo videos. No partners around, so you don't have to be nervous."

I stiffened, the hair on my arms standing up.

"You want the contact information for them?" he asked.

"Yes."

He gave me the address and the phone number to reach the independent contractor, Lib3rty Inc., LLC. Aside from the misspelling, the name was generic—I could've mistaken it for an insurance company. I typed the address on my laptop, my cell phone cradled against my shoulder: 656 Ventura Way.

"Any questions?" the man asked.

I realized that neither of us had even exchanged names.

"Do you know who works at Lib3rty Inc., LLC?"

"I'm afraid that's private information. You'll have to ask them yourself. Ownership is under a man named Paul Bleeker."

I realized that my hands were trembling as I typed down the name. I was getting closer to it, the truth. And there was a very real chance that Paul Bleeker had played a role in the murders. Ron didn't work alone.

"Any other questions?"

"Is it safe?" I asked softly.

The man paused. He didn't seem to recognize Liberty Lake from the news. I wasn't sure if he even knew about the murders.

"We do our best," the man said finally. "Safety is important. But with our independent contractors, we only distribute the work. The contractors and performers do things their own way. We try to screen them all, though. No crazies on the loose."

I sighed.

"I guarantee you'll be fine," he said briskly. "Good luck on your video. You'll do great things."

After the phone call, I stayed put, my eyes unfocused on the screen.

There was no evidence that either of the women had performed on the site. I was relying on guesswork and assumptions, and those had been based off hearsay from other people. It was all so shaky.

But I had a lead.

A door opened from the garage. I slammed my laptop shut and

settled back into my seat. Dad entered the house. He carried plastic bags of groceries in both hands. He always bought them from Feed Farm. It was cheaper there, less fussy.

I followed Dad into the kitchen. He ignored me as he put away the groceries.

"Do you need help with that?"

"You really quit," he said, slamming the fridge shut. "Not even a month there and you quit."

"It wasn't a good fit."

"It doesn't need to be a good fit. It's a damn job."

"I just need a short break," I said. I sounded so sincere. "It's hard to work during the holidays. Especially after . . . you know."

I trailed off. Dad looked at me. I didn't know what he saw in my face, but he sighed and went back to his work.

"I'll find something else after New Year's," I said. "Don't worry."

Dad said nothing.

I helped him cook dinner in silence. After we ate, I joined him in the living room as he watched the news. There was a tense hum in the air. I kept waiting for Dad to say something, but he didn't.

At half past eight, I changed into a pair of black sports leggings, a black hoodie, and my dark winter jacket. When I came downstairs, Dad didn't even turn my way.

"I'm heading out," I said.

"On a Sunday night?" he asked.

"I'm going to a friend's place. She needs me to help with something before she turns it in tomorrow."

"Which friend?"

"Charice," I said as I quickly left the room.

In Mom's car, I waited for the heat to start.

On the passenger's seat next to me, I carefully laid out an old pillowcase, a red handkerchief, and one of Dad's old leather belts.

I was ready.

37

On the car ride over, the radio announced that there was a winter weather watch issued for the end of the week. We were
expected to get anywhere from eight to eleven inches of snow by
Saturday.

"Winter never makes a dull entrance here, does it," joked the me-
teorologist. I shut off the radio.

Instead of turning into the Goodhue Groceries parking lot, I continued past it and then turned right on Friedan Boulevard. There
was only one car parked on the curb of the street—an inconspicu-
ously black and compact one. Just as I'd been told.

I turned off the car at the curb just a few yards ahead of Jayden's,
so that a thicket of trees blocked me from the employee entrance.
From my vantage point, I got a glimpse of the light that spilled out
from Goodhue Groceries and the employees who left. I climbed to
the back seat of the car and moved the pillowcase, the handkerchief,
and the leather belt next to me.

Then I waited. The minutes seemed to fly by. I watched as a few
cars passed on the street. On Sunday night, the grocery store closed

just after nine. There were always at least two people who closed it together for safety reasons.

I kept checking my phone, waiting for a confirmation text. But none came.

At nine on the dot, I peered through the back window. I saw Jim walk out of the employees' door. I recognized his long legs as he strode over to his car, conveniently parked a few feet away. As Jim whipped out of the parking lot, the other employees started to trickle out, including a pair of female stock clerks.

Then there was Ron. His skin looked almost translucent under the parking lot lights.

He carried his skateboard under one arm. The top half of his body was buried beneath a puffy winter jacket. His headphones looked like ears protruding out of his skull.

While the others headed left, Ron turned right. He placed his skateboard on the asphalt and began to cruise toward the sidewalk. He was heading in my direction. I ducked down out of instinct, my hands clutching the belt and handkerchief.

My heart was pounding faster and faster. There were too many things that could go wrong, too many variables at play—

My phone suddenly lit up with a single text: GO GO GO.

I shoved open the back door and started running on the grass. It was slick with slush from the last snowfall, but I bolted for the sidewalk, sliding into place. In the dark, I could see Ron's silhouette. I heard the crunch of his wheels as he sped toward me.

I lifted both arms out from my sides, blocking the sidewalk.

Bracing myself in case of impact.

Ron suddenly saw me—a shadow out of nowhere—and he screamed, swerving off the sidewalk. As he crashed into the slush, his skateboard went flying beneath him. Within seconds, I saw another shadow fly right past me, clambering on top of Ron. There were grunts as the two struggled on the ground, but clearly one of them had the upper hand. Jayden was sitting on Ron's back, restraining both his arms.

As Ron started to scream, I raced over to them.

"You're slow," muttered Jayden to me, but I handed him the leather belt. As Ron squirmed, I wrapped the red handkerchief over his mouth and tied it. He was fidgeting so much that his saliva had gotten on my fingertips. As Jayden held him back, I looped the belt over Ron's wrists several times and fastened it.

Within seconds, Jayden shoved the black pillowcase over Ron's head.

Ron was all deadweight, but Jayden and I managed to drag him a few yards back to Mom's car. Ron was groaning, tied up, his back drenched in the slush. We managed to lift Ron onto the floor of the back seat.

I locked the back doors shut.

"You get the skateboard," I told Jayden as I rushed into the driver's seat.

As soon as I pulled back onto Friedan Boulevard, I could already see Jayden starting the ignition in his car. Ron was groaning as I turned onto a residential street.

I realized that in the span of a few minutes, Jayden and I had managed to abduct Ron. And during that time, no one else had passed by.

It had been easy. Too easy.

It only took fifteen minutes for Jayden and me to make it down to the Sewers. We stopped at a nondescript park tucked away in a neighborhood of single-story homes. Jayden said the neighborhood didn't see cops often and that the park was a popular spot for late-night hookups.

"Not that I'd know," he murmured.

I couldn't help but look behind us. We stood outside in the dark, our phone screens dimly glowing. Only a couple of feet away, Ron was still tied up in the back of my car.

"You ready?" Jayden asked, pulling up his handkerchief over his mouth.

"Yeah," I blurted, my stomach in knots.

Jayden shoved the back door open and climbed inside the car. I followed him.

As soon as I slammed the door shut, Ron started writhing around in terror, squawking. Jayden turned on his cell phone's flashlight to full brightness, shining it toward Ron's head. Ron squirmed, his face covered by the pillowcase.

"Here," said Jayden, handing me the phone. As I kept the light steady, Jayden finally yanked off the pillowcase. Ron's mouth was wide open as soon as the handkerchief was removed.

"Help! Help me—"

From his seat, Jayden stepped on Ron's back.

"Why you doxing people, huh?" asked Jayden as he yanked at Ron's hair. "Why are you such a creepy piece of shit?"

"I—I don't know what you're talking about," said Ron, gasping in pain.

"Then explain why my info was leaked," I said quietly.

"Mary?" Ron asked, his eyes squinting in my direction.

"You leaked my past to Jim. You got me fired, Ron."

"I don't know what you're talking about," he said, breathing hard. "I didn't do anything. But you are gonna be so fucked when I report this to the police."

"Not as fucked as you'll be when they find out you've been leaking a dead girl's nudes," said Jayden.

"You shut up, n—"

Jayden stomped on Ron so hard that the back of the car shook.

"You wanna say shit like that to me, you say it louder, okay?" said Jayden as he stamped down his foot again. Ron's screech quickly died into a whimper.

I had told Jayden that I didn't mind if things got violent, but in person, I could see all the factors that Jayden and I had missed, things like blood, hair, saliva. I could imagine a blue light shining on all of it. As Ron writhed on the car floor, he left more incriminating evidence behind. The police wouldn't need much to prosecute Jayden and me.

We couldn't afford to be wrong.

And it was too late—we had Ron in front of us. I needed to remember the evidence that pointed to him: the same email address that had targeted me and Olivia, the employee contact information from Goodhue Groceries, Ron's vendetta against me, and his strange outburst about Olivia.

In the car, it seemed obvious that Ron hadn't killed her—he didn't have the strength or the stomach for it. He had someone else do the work for him.

"Who's Paul Bleeker?" I asked suddenly.

"What?" Ron stammered.

"Paul Bleeker, the guy you're working with."

"I—I don't know who that is."

Jayden slapped him. Ron whimpered.

"You wanna explain why you killed Olivia Willand?"

"I—I haven't done anything. P-please—"

"We got your IP address, your email, everything," sneered Jayden. "We traced it all back to you, boy."

"P-please."

"Stop hiding it."

"I—I didn't do anything—"

"Man, I am so tired of your pasty ass."

Jayden bent over in his seat, shoving the black pillowcase over Ron's head. He wrapped his hands around the fabric around Ron's neck, trapping the air inside. I heard Ron's scream turn to muffled gargling—Jayden was strangling him.

Ron began to jerk, his pant legs rolling up past his ankles. I saw a flash of pale skin. I could almost imagine little flakes of it dusting onto the floor, a remnant of him.

"What are you doing?" I asked, frozen.

"He should've thought about that before he killed them."

I watched as Jayden squeezed his hands tighter around the pillowcase. The doubt crept in. I was so desperate to do something right—I was tired of being wrong. And I wanted someone to be the killer, I wanted someone to pay for what they'd done.

But the scene in front of me was grim. I had a scrawny, beaten teenager in front of me. And his hair and his drool and his flakes of skin were all over the place, waiting to be discovered.

"Why'd you kill her and DeMaria Jackson, huh?!" Jayden asked as Ron's breathing grew fainter. He was going to kill him.

I'd have a corpse in the car.

I tried to shove Jayden's arms away, panicking now.

Jayden abruptly let go. Ron gasped for breath, the pillowcase still on his head. I watched his back as it heaved up and down.

Jayden scooped the cell phone out of my hands and passed me a corner of the pillowcase.

I swallowed. I waited for Jayden to say something—anything—but the only sound in the car was Ron's heavy breathing.

My hands somehow traveled down the pillowcase. I felt the concavity of Ron's neck, the slight hill of his Adam's apple. My hands were small around the black fabric.

Ron suddenly began to struggle. He rocked his head back and forth, groaning, while he tried to wriggle his wrists free. I kept my hands steady on his throat. Jayden didn't move.

In that moment, I felt exhausted. It washed over me like rain. My limbs felt heavy. I was dead tired of the past month and the people who'd drifted in it:

Carly, for stripping me of my school, my dreams.

Jim, for firing me from a job I hated.

Ron, for exposing me, threatening me.

Olivia, for haunting me long after we'd ended our friendship.

It was one thing after another.

I squeezed both my hands around Ron's throat. He gasped again, and I felt the adrenaline moving in my fingers, and I clamped down harder and harder until my hands began to hurt.

Jayden leaned over, his mouth hovering close to the pillowcase.

"Why'd you do it, huh? What kind of piece of shit releases a dead girl's nudes?"

Ron's gasps grew quiet under my grip.

He fell silent.

I let go, suddenly afraid.

There was nothing, except for my own breathing.

And then Ron sputtered, gasping for air. Jayden yanked off the pillowcase. Ron's hair was messy, greasy with sweat. His entire body seemed to rattle as he took in one shallow gulp after another.

"You get one chance or I kill your ass."

"N-not me—" Ron sputtered.

"Yeah, course not," Jayden snorted.

"M-my c-cousin . . ."

"Sure, man, I believe you—"

"K-Kevin."

I froze.

"Kevin Obermueller?" I asked, my voice squeaky. Ron only hacked again.

I could picture Ron and Kevin both clearly—there was no resemblance between the two of them. One was tall and scrawny. The other was short and stocky. They seemed like inversions of each other: one pale with dark features, the other darker with light blond hair. Ron couldn't pass for an Obermueller, not compared to Kevin and his father.

Mr. Ronald Obermueller.

I felt the blood drain from my face.

Ronald Obermueller. Ron from the grocery store. One had been named after the other.

"You're Ronald Obermueller's nephew?" I asked, the alarm seeping into my voice.

Ron said nothing.

Everything became too sharp, as if a glass had been placed over my eyes. I could see Kevin again at Littlewood Park Reserve, when Olivia's picture had been leaked. The anguish in his eyes, the desperation when he'd yelled at the crowd to calm down. The conversations we'd had at Espresso Haus and in the woods.

And then our last phone call, when I told him about the picture on Dwayne's phone. On the other line, Kevin had taken a deep breath. Then he'd thanked me. He said that Olivia would've thanked me, too.

All of it had been a lie.

Jayden bent over, one hand in Ron's black hair. Jayden grabbed a handful of it, yanking Ron's head back as far as he could get. The latter was squealing.

"Ask him what you need," said Jayden to me.

"Did Kevin kill her?" I asked, my voice catching.

"P-please—"

Jayden yanked back harder.

"When I said I was gonna kill you, I wasn't joking," Jayden said slowly.

"N-no, please . . ."

Jayden pulled Ron's head back as far as he could. Then he let go. Ron's face immediately slammed onto the car floor.

"Talk."

Ron whimpered, then he began to murmur.

"K-Kevin and Olivia were dating since the s-summer. But he found out she'd been ch-cheating on him—s-sexting her ex. S-sleeping with her ex. Kevin found nudes on her phone that she'd sent to Dwayne T-Turner."

Neither Jayden nor I moved.

"K-Kevin was pissed off. He and Olivia got into a fight b-back in October. She told him to fuck off."

"When in October?" I asked.

Ron didn't answer.

Jayden reached down into Ron's hair.

"A c-couple days before she d-disappeared," Ron whimpered.

My skin grew cold. Kevin and Olivia had fought in the same weekend that she'd disappeared.

"And then what? You helped him chop up her body?" Jayden asked.

"No, no, no, we d-didn't kill her."

"Why wouldn't you guys kill her?" I asked. "He was angry that she cheated on him."

"He was p-pissed, but he thought they'd make up. He thought she'd feel b-bad and come back to him," Ron slurred, his mouth sloshed with saliva. "B-but then she disappeared."

Ron seemed adamant about their innocence. But to me, it seemed likely that Kevin had killed her on his own.

I felt the anger burn through me. I'd grown up with Kevin—I had seen him treat others like shit. I'd been treated like shit myself. Yet I had trusted him. I'd been gullible. Kevin had never really changed, had he? He just had a uniform this time.

"Let's say you're telling the truth," said Jayden, his words steady. "If Olivia magically disappeared, why would Kevin leak her nudes? Who the hell does that to their girlfriend?"

"Kevin thought she'd run away," said Ron, hacking again. "H-he thought she felt b-bad about cheating on him. And she w-was think-ing of d-dropping out of school for Instagram anyway. H-he thought it w-was a publicity stunt."

"That sounds paranoid," I said.

"I thought s-so, too, b-but look what happened. Olivia was all over the news. H-her Instagram exploded. People were talking about her. Kevin s-said she wanted the attention. H-he thought she took off—the t-timing was right. He wanted her to c-come back, but he wanted to teach her a lesson first. F-for cheating."

I shook my head—it was a reflex. But I believed Ron. Kevin was vindictive enough to get revenge, but he was also desperate to get Olivia back. In his mind, leaking her nude photo was an easy way to humiliate her. But he didn't seem to consider the aftermath for her.

On Olivia's end, I saw why she wanted to drop out of school. She was on the cusp of an Instagram career. She thought she could get further and make more money if she focused on it completely. She was ambitious, and if school didn't benefit her career, she would drop it.

But in the end, her disappearance hadn't been planned.

"K-Kevin was part of the s-search committee. H-he had access to everyone who was going," Ron murmured. "H-he had their email addresses and phone numbers."

"Why would you help him?" I asked, my voice squeaky. "Olivia didn't even do anything to you."

Ron said nothing.

Kevin could have threatened him, or Ron could've owed his cousin a favor. Or maybe he found some perverse pleasure in playing around with someone else's life, someone bigger than he would ever be.

But Kevin was still out there, walking freely in his police uniform. He was lauded as a hero. I wasn't certain that Kevin had killed Olivia, but I knew he was capable of it.

"What about DeMaria Jackson?" Jayden asked.

"What about her?" said Ron, his voice quiet. "W-we don't even know who she was."

Jayden turned in his seat toward me.

"You said DeMaria was connected to all this shit," he said slowly. "You said they had the same killer."

"I—I did," I sputtered. "The police think so, too. He's lying."

"N-no, I'm telling the truth!" screamed Ron from the floor. "I leaked Olivia's nude. But I didn't do anything else, I promise. W-we didn't kill Olivia. And w-we don't know who the hell D-DeMaria is."

"Goddammit."

Jayden kicked at Ron. The latter cried out. Before I knew what was happening, Jayden had already stormed out of the car.

I rushed out after him.

"You can't just leave," I said, grabbing Jayden by the arm. He shook me off.

"Lying bitch," he spat. "Olivia this, Olivia that. You don't give a flying fuck about DeMaria. You didn't ask a single thing about her."

"I do, okay? She and Olivia are linked, there's a connection between them—"

"Man, you think I'm dumb as hell, don't you?" Jayden stopped, turning to look at me, the whites of his eyes glowing in the dark. "I'm some meathead who does your dirty work."

"No! It's not like that, I—I don't— You're not—"

"Fuck you, Mary," he said. "You're on your own. You deal with your shit, I deal with mine."

I watched as Jayden walked back to his car. He dumped Ron's skateboard in the slush and drove away. I felt my blood boil, the fatigue and the rage rushing over me. I wanted to scream, and for a second, I imagined the satisfaction of hitting Ron in the face.

There was a faint thump coming from the car. I couldn't see anything. But as I drew closer, I saw a pale face knocking against one of the back windows. Ron had somehow inched his way up onto the seat, banging against the car window for help. I saw myself standing there, watching Ron. And I suddenly knew what to do.

I climbed into the back seat through the other door. Ron squirmed as I unclasped the belt from his wrists. It was moist with sweat. Ron turned around slowly. I couldn't see his expression, but I could hear his desperate, staggered breathing. And I knew the thought running in his head.

I leaned in.

"You do anything to me, and I'll charge you with assault," I said softly. "Your word against mine."

Ron didn't move.

"Now get the hell out of my car."

38

When I woke up, I felt like I'd barely just closed my eyes. The previous night didn't seem real. But as I rolled over, I felt my lower back start to throb, as if someone had left a permanent stamp there.

The back pain was from early in the morning. After I got home, I was bent over the car's back seat, frantically brushing off any hairs or scraps that had been left behind. When that was done, I took some laundry detergent and warm water and scrubbed the back seat and car floors. I worked myself into a sweat, imagining all the drool and bits of skin left over. With Ron, I wasn't taking any chances.

It had taken me around an hour and a half to clean everything up. It was nearly two in the morning when I finished, and I'd spent half that time glancing back at the door to the house, afraid that Dad would suddenly peer out.

In bed, I checked my phone. It was only at 40 percent battery—I was so tired that I hadn't charged it. The screen showed it was a little past eight in the morning.

I still felt like shit.

Through the windows, I watched as the snow pelted down, angry and violent. As if chips of plaster were crumbling from the sky.

When I came downstairs, I found Dad sitting at the breakfast table. His hands were held together as if in prayer, his eyes focused on the steaming coffee mug in front of him.

"Morning."

It took Dad an extra second before he stiffly looked up.

"You came home late," he said.

I shrugged, pouring myself a cup of coffee at the counter. I pictured Dad lying awake in bed, listening as his kid creaked around the house at two in the morning. He probably thought I was out late with a boy. And he was right in a way—I was out late with two boys, both of whom despised me.

"It looks pretty bad out there."

"We might get eleven inches," Dad said, his eyes following me. The bags under his eyes looked dark and purple.

"That sounds bad."

"It could be worse," he said.

I realized that there was something in the air, as subtle as a heat wave.

"I'll be careful on the road then."

"That's not what I meant."

Dad and I stared at each other. Passive silence was usually what we preferred. We could sit together and not talk for as long as we needed. We knew things would settle down on their own—they always did.

But today, the silence was loud. Hostile, as if the two of us were waiting for the right time to strike at each other.

"You've been hanging out with some people, Mary."

"I don't know what you're talking about."

"Thugs," he spat.

The word seemed to crash down in front of us, as heavy as a slur.

I could almost imagine the crater that it would leave through the table and the tiles on the kitchen floor. My mind raced back to the car with Dwayne, Jayden, Charice. They'd driven me home the day after the party, and Dad had noticed. He was talking about them, the contempt and the rage and the fear all threaded into one word.

And I didn't know what to do except squirm.

"You've been doing God knows what with them."

"I need to get ready," I said, fleeing for the stairs.

"What for?" Dad asked. "You don't have a damn job anymore."

I turned around.

"Your old supervisor called earlier. He wants you to return your uniform."

I felt my stomach drop. I couldn't focus on anything except the flash across Dad's face, the sheer anger in it.

"You lied to me, Mary," said Dad, his eyes dark. "You didn't quit that job, you were fired. And then you threw a goddamn tantrum in the store."

I said nothing. I could think of nothing.

"Jesus, you need to pull yourself together. Do you know how tired I am of this shit? The school thing—you assaulted a girl, for fuck's sake. That's the kind of thing that follows you forever. And now you can't even keep a nine-dollar job?" Dad asked, enraged. "What the hell happened to you?"

I felt my mouth drop open, but no sound came out.

"I know you have problems, Mary. But why the hell did you let things get this bad?"

I think I'd always known that Dad had been ashamed of me. Except he'd kept it unsaid. I preferred it that way—I liked being in denial. I liked pretending that I had at least one person who stuck by, regardless of what happened. That was family. But I'd known the truth.

And it hurt.

"Why can't you try to be normal, Mary?" Dad asked, his eyes looking through me. "None of this crazy bullshit."

I felt the tears welling in my eyes.

"Fuck you."

Dad blinked, his face turning red. I had never sworn at him before. We could do it to other people, but never to each other.

"Mary, you say that again and—"

"Fuck you."

Dad's face was bright red, but his hands stayed clasped on the kitchen table.

"You keep acting like this, and you can't stay here anymore," Dad said, his voice low.

I wanted to say something that cut. I wanted him to know that I would have turned out just fine had Mom not died, if only he had raised me better. I wished they would have traded places.

Instead, I said nothing. My body moved on its own, out of the kitchen and up the stairs into my room. I slipped into a ratty high school hoodie with a faded George Washington on the front and a pair of jeans.

I'd left my Goodhue Groceries uniform in a pile on the floor. I took both the shirt and the pants and dumped them in the wastebasket near my desk. I imagined the blood rushing out of Jim's face if he'd seen.

When I grabbed the car keys downstairs, Dad was still sitting at the kitchen table, his hands folded together, the coffee untouched. He didn't look at me.

In the car, I tried to put distance between me and the house. I wanted to clamp down on the gas pedal, winding through the streets until I was long past Providence Hill, Carver, the state border. But the snow continued to fall hard and thick, covering the view ahead on the roads. I felt Mom's car glide on the slush and the ice, even as my foot pressed on the brake.

I made it about as far as Espresso Haus before I got irritated. I pulled into the parking lot and hurried inside. I ordered a dark coffee and a breakfast sandwich. The barista asked me if I was okay, and I pretended not to notice that my eyes were teary.

As I waited, I saw a picture of the Willands on a newspaper rack nearby. The photo had been taken two days ago, after the funeral. It showed them walking out of St. Rita's, holding hands. Mrs. Willand had fixed her makeup.

Due to the blizzard, the coffee shop was empty. The table that Kevin and I had shared was free. I clambered into where he'd sat and scarfed down my sandwich, as if I hadn't eaten in days. Then I nursed my cup of coffee, watching as the snow wafted down outside.

I doubted that Dad had kicked me out for good, but I knew our relationship had changed. Things couldn't go back to how they'd been, the two of us passively coexisting. As family, we knew best how to hurt each other. Everything would now be tinged with bitterness.

I knew that Dad was ashamed of me. Dad knew that I no longer respected him.

We couldn't pretend anymore.

I was alone.

My friends at school no longer cared for me. I'd cut ties with Jayden, Charice, even Jim from the grocery store. I wasn't close enough with the Willands or Mr. Nguyen.

And Madison was gone. I'd crossed a boundary in attacking her father. A decade of friendship was over. I suppose that rivalry had always stirred between us. Her father just became the kindling. In the end, she knew the truth—she should've gone to an Ivy, not me.

I was a fluke.

I had spent my life trying to believe otherwise. I put so much stock into school. I wanted to succeed. I was willing to do anything to prove myself to the people who'd snubbed me, doubted me, abandoned me.

I was worth something.

In the past three years, I'd even believed it.

But the delusion couldn't last forever. I had to learn that eventually. And I had learned it, now that my life had crumbled around me.

And all for what?

The girl who had abandoned me all those years ago.

Olivia Willand.

I didn't know her beyond our childhood. But I remembered our summers in the woods together, Olivia trekking on her own while I lagged behind.

All these years later, I was still chasing after her.

I just wanted her to see me.

Outside, the snow continued to pelt onto the city. I wondered what it would feel like to walk out and scream into the stillness. After my lungs gave out, I would fall asleep in the cold, my eyes closed, snow dotting the tips of my lashes. It sounded nice.

I cradled my head in my hands, my eyes closed.

But in the dark, I saw only the arm at the lake.

Neither of the girls had a say in the end. Someone else had chosen it for them. The end had been violent, brutal. Now we said the case was over, and we'd chosen to end it at Dwayne Turner.

But it wasn't finished. There was more going on, and I was the only one aware of it.

I looked up slowly. The rest of me was frozen.

That was my way out.

No one else knew what I'd done. No one would hold me to it. I'd scared off Ron. He would leave me alone. And I could abandon the whole thing completely—everything with Dwayne, DeMaria, Olivia. I could move on with my life, just like she had done to me.

I could walk away.

My phone vibrated in my jacket. I thought it was Dad, but I nearly dropped the phone when I saw the text. It was a message from Kevin:

WHAT DID YOU DO?

39

My head was spinning.

Ron had contacted his cousin. Kevin knew what Jayden and I had done.

We were in danger. For all I knew, the police were already looking for us. But to Kevin, I posed a bigger threat. I knew what he'd done with Olivia's nude photo. I'd put his job, his reputation, his freedom at risk. And I had the power to make Kevin a suspect in Olivia's murder.

But he wouldn't let that happen. Kevin, armed with a Taser, baton, and gun, would be after me. He was either waiting at home with an arrest warrant, or he was planning something else. I suspected the latter would be violent.

I was afraid of him.

Ron was adamant that his cousin hadn't killed anyone. He only confirmed Kevin's role in the nude photo leak.

But I didn't believe him. Kevin had too much of a motive to kill Olivia. DeMaria could have factored in during a separate incident.

I looked out the window, half expecting to see a police car flashing through the snow.

My time was running out.

I needed proof against Kevin before he got to me first. There was the black car that Mr. Nguyen had seen and the independent porn contractor in the city—Lib3rty Inc., LLC. I had the name of the owner of the company, Paul Bleeker. Kevin was connected somehow. I just needed to find that link.

Outside, the snow was falling steadily. By the time the blizzard blew past, I would be in jail, if I was lucky.

I chugged the rest of my coffee, now cold, and sent Kevin a quick reply:

Why did you leak Olivia Willand's nude at the search? What kind of boyfriend does that, Kevin? Why would you kill her?

I would make him as scared as I was.

I left Espresso Haus in a hurry. I struggled against the wind to get to Mom's car. But I was more concerned about Kevin than the snow.

As I waited for the car to heat up, I looked up Paul Bleeker on my phone. There were over four hundred thousand hits on the Internet. But these Paul Bleekers were all in different parts of the country, like Florida, California, New Hampshire. A couple of them were dead World War II veterans.

One Paul Bleeker had gone to school in Minnesota, but his Facebook showed that he was currently living in South Korea with his family. The other one lived up north, and he was married to a man.

There were no other living Paul Bleekers in the state.

I tried narrowing the search to "Paul Bleeker Liberty Lake," but the search results became convoluted. It seemed that there was no Paul Bleeker currently in town. The other two from the state made little sense.

It was an alias, then. And it was either Kevin or somebody else behind the name.

The wind began to wail louder outside. It droned mournfully, like a woman's sad croon. I turned on the car radio to the classic rock station. I blasted the music until it drowned out the noise.

I tried searching online for "Lib3rty Inc., LLC," but I found only insurance companies, gun shops, a few accounting firms. These businesses had all used the proper spelling of "Liberty." But when I refined my search to the original spelling, I found no relevant results.

My leads on both Paul Bleeker and Lib3rty Inc., LLC, had been duds.

All I had left was the address for the company: 656 Ventura Way in Liberty Lake.

I looked up the address on an online map. It was located somewhere on the southeastern border of the city, deep in the Sewers. I entered the street view. After a minute, an image slowly loaded. It was a blurry snapshot of an auto shop. There was rust on the garage doors and wooden boards that blocked the windows.

The building looked as if it hadn't been used in years.

It looked foreboding, like a place where young women were killed all the time.

Neither Olivia nor DeMaria would've walked willingly inside. Nobody was that dense—an abandoned auto shop in the Sewers would have stopped anyone cold. They only would have entered if forced.

Or, they'd never gone there at all. The auto shop was located along a worn block of businesses, but across the street, there was a gas station. The location was too visible. It would have been hard to use the empty building without being noticed, even late at night.

It seemed likely that the shop was only a placeholder on the business paperwork. Doberman Productions wouldn't have noticed.

My head was starting to ache. The car was still running. I had already wasted a gallon of gas in the parking lot.

I pulled out from Espresso Haus, turning back onto the street.

Around me, it seemed that the cars on the road were inching along slowly, their headlights shining feebly ahead of them. It looked like the whole sky was crumbling above us, like ash curling down.

I had checked everything. And everything was a lie: a fake porn company owned by a fake person who'd used a fake address.

It all led to a derelict auto shop.

But why?

The address could have been random. But Paul Bleeker had put it on his business information with Doberman Productions— that would have involved other legal and financial documents. He couldn't have used a fake address on everything without getting flagged.

And he wasn't flagged because it was legal. Paul Bleeker really did own the auto shop. Only his identity was fake.

There was no Paul Bleeker in Liberty Lake. But there was a registered owner of the auto shop. His real name had to be tied to the property.

It was a tenuous lead, but the only thing I had.

The car behind me honked angrily as I made an illegal U-turn. But I crawled back east in the direction of the library, the despair closing in on me.

I'd forgotten the library. I hadn't been inside it since high school, but it remained unchanged: the white study rooms where Madison and I had locked ourselves for SAT prep; the slim floor-to-ceiling windows that striped the walls; the dark circular desk where the librarians worked; and the large skylight overhead that was now powdered with snow.

It was like I'd never left.

I brushed off my jacket and boots and quietly slipped toward the back of the library, where the archives lay. The hush around me was comforting.

After I passed the empty help desk, the bookshelves dipped down to my waist. There was a section of thick hardbound volumes that contained Liberty Lake property records by year and address. Some of them went back as far as the late 1800s. Most of the records were only available in person—I'd learned that during a high school project.

I crouched down and skimmed through the bindings, moving down the shelves until I reached the end. The most recent volumes sat in a bottom corner. They were dated 2011–2012. I yanked off the volume labeled "M–Z." When I reached the listings under "V," I trailed down the column with a finger, almost afraid that I would miss it.

Ventura Way was on the next page. I skimmed through the buildings and then stopped. Number 656 was labeled as "Private Property."

My blood ran cold.

Listed after the address was the property owner: "Stack, Jo." Shorthand for John Stack.

Dad's client.

40

At West End Park, John Stack had barely glanced at Olivia's remains. As her mother mourned at his feet, he'd been more enraptured by the lake. All those days that John Stack had watched Dad and his men as they worked on his roof—he was making sure that no one found anything suspicious. And the prayer that he'd led at the search had been a perverse lie.

I'd shaken his hand, too, not knowing that that same hand had butchered two women.

This whole time, we'd been friendly with a serial killer.

I sat back, my finger still glued to the page.

Oddly enough, I felt a strange calm.

I finally had something steady in front of me. It was certainty in the form of John Stack. He had lured two young women with promises of easy money. He might've even helped them for a bit. But when the time came, he'd gotten rid of them.

If he was friends with the Willands, then John Stack probably lived nearby in one of the wealthier suburbs. There would be security cameras and watchful neighbors. John Stack couldn't have brought the girls home without getting caught. It seemed likely that he'd used the auto shop for the killings.

As I checked the entry again for 656 Ventura Way, I saw another line beneath it: "Additional Properties: See 66th Ave.; Darling Rd."

I recognized 66th Avenue—that street was located in the suburbs, not far from Olivia's house. That was likely his home address.

I clawed for one of the other volumes on the floor. I shuffled through the pages so roughly that I heard paper rip. But I was so close. I leafed past the listings from "A" through "C." I found Darling Road hidden in the middle of a page. There was only one entry beneath it: "725 Darling Road Cabin, Darling Road." It was followed by a set of GPS coordinates and the name of the property owner, "Stack, Jo."

My hand was trembling as I typed in the address on my phone. As the screen loaded, each second felt like an eternity. I suddenly realized how sweaty I'd gotten in the library, hunched over on the floor in my jacket.

But there were no images of the cabin. The screen showed a single red pin on a map view of Liberty Lake. The pin was down south, just a little past the southern lakeshore. The forest blocked off the Sewers from the west. The area down there was packed with trees that served as a natural boundary line for the city. As far as I knew, no one used those woods recreationally.

The cabin was secluded from the suburbs, a perfect murder site to dispose of two women. It was close enough to the southern shore of the lake to dump a few body parts. During the fall, there would be days where the mist would gather over the water and the trees. John Stack would have no worries about being seen by anyone.

And when he was done, he would go back to his lovely house in the suburbs. There, he would take a warm bath and fall asleep in a soft bed. At peace.

I felt the anger rise up like bile.

He needed to be put away.

I took a picture of the property entry for 725 Darling Road Cabin and closed the volumes. Then I stacked them together and left them on the floor. I hurried past the librarian, who asked me if I had any questions.

Outside, the snow continued to fall. The wind nipped at my face.

But as I rushed to the car, I could already hear the doubt echoing around me. Everything that I knew was based off hunch and hearsay. I had no concrete evidence to point to John Stack. And I'd been wrong before, about Kevin and Dwayne. I had nothing but a convoluted trail of details, and part of that was information obtained illegally from Charice and her brother.

The police wouldn't take me seriously. If they interviewed John Stack, he would walk away free—I had no doubt.

Then there was Kevin, the son of the city council president and a member of the force. He would undermine my credibility. He would redirect everything back to me and what I had done to Ron.

No one would believe me.

I was cracked in too many places. My own past proved it: my expulsion from school, the altercation with Carly, my firing from Goodhue Groceries. It was easy for them to call me crazy—I had pills and a history to prove it.

And I was unreliable.

I had lied to Leticia Jackson. I'd conspired with Jayden and Charice. I'd gone after Ron.

Even Dad, if questioned, would take Kevin's side.

I watched the warm lights inside the library.

Then I checked my phone.

Kevin hadn't replied back. It was a bad sign. If he wasn't responding, then it meant that he was planning something. He was possibly at the house already.

Once I got arrested for Ron's assault, who would believe me?

I felt my insides squeeze together into a painful knot.

With Kevin after me, I was running out of time. I needed hard, direct evidence that John Stack had killed Olivia and DeMaria.

And most likely, I'd find it at the cabin.

41

My hands were taut on the steering wheel. In the winter, Mom's car sometimes lurched on the ice as the back wheels suddenly shifted left or right. Those brief seconds were terrifying.

But as the car slipped now, I only felt numb, watching as my hands straightened it out on the road.

I drove slowly, like the rest of the drivers on the highway, everyone crawling along at a speed of forty or less. I'd already passed by one wreck, a truck that had somehow slipped and smashed into the concrete barrier in the middle of the road. A police car was already at the crash site. The cop, a puffy shadow in the snow, stood near the driver's window. He shined a flashlight inside.

On the radio, I listened to a classic rock station. Each song was louder and gloomier than the last, an infinite loop. My head ached from the music, but I needed it. It kept me focused on the road.

As the snow continued to fall, I drove past the lake. It was big and gray and bleak beneath the white sky. In this type of weather, very few people would be outside.

The directions on my phone pointed down south in one straight shot, the same directions that would eventually lead to Ondaa-sagaam and Red Creek.

Before I knew it, I was climbing up the exit off the highway. Instead of taking a right turn toward the Sewers, I turned left and crossed the bridge over the highway. I continued past streets of worn homes and an abandoned church. I passed by a McDonald's, a lone swing set in an empty lot, and a used-car dealership. The latter was illuminated by a white billboard on the side of the road: STEVE'S BEST AUTO DEALS.

All of it was covered in white, devoid of people.

Soon, there was nothing but wilderness—large empty plains that separated the road from the forest. In the distance, the oak trees and elm trees and basswoods looked as if they would stretch on for miles. I was on the outskirts of the city, where no cars or people seemed to exist. Out here, the road was slick and bumpy, and I slowed the car to a crawl.

The GPS on my phone suddenly buzzed, once, twice, and then on and on. I pulled over to the side of the road. The GPS was malfunctioning, the blue arrow quivering left and right and back again. It seemed that John Stack's property was less than half a mile away in the woods. The GPS was confused about how to get there.

If John Stack's cabin was secluded, then I doubted there was a public road to reach it. Only those familiar with the area would have known how to get there, especially in the snow.

I had to continue by foot.

My heart was hammering in my chest.

I was out of my mind.

And I wished I were at school. I wanted it more than anything.

Olivia would have been a passing blip in the news. Liberty Lake would be a mere memory. And Ivy League Mary would feel bad, but she wouldn't dwell too long on the past. She had more important things to distract her: her friends, her thesis, her future.

Yet here I was.

I couldn't turn back. That dream was gone. At home, I had only Kevin waiting for me. And I would have nothing but shame if I went so far for Olivia and DeMaria, only to run at the last second because I was afraid. I was a coward.

I realized that I was shaking my head.

And I slowly straightened up. I forced myself to turn off the radio, the high beams, the ignition. I slipped on my gloves and tightened up the laces on my snow boots. Then I climbed out of the car.

The snow was falling in soft, airy pieces, like wisps of cotton candy. The wind was little more than a breeze, but my face was already freezing from the cold. I crossed the road quickly, but when I got to a field, the snow was higher and stiffer, caked together in one unbroken surface. It reached my ankles.

I was alone in a white field beneath a white sky, on the edge of nowhere. In an odd way, it felt peaceful.

But as soon as I reached the line of trees, my heart started pounding again, violent and desperate.

In my glove, the cell phone's GPS had calmed down. I was walking in the right direction. Once I entered the forest, I would head in a straight shot until I eventually reached John Stack's property.

I stopped about a yard from the woods. I couldn't see very far inside. The trees, towering from above, seemed to taper off into the distance, becoming nothing but shadow.

I could hear the blood pounding in my ears, my limbs aching to run back to the car, the house, the bed. And I would later wake up and realize that everything had been one awful dream.

But the cold was real. Everything was real. I tilted back my head, looking up at the empty sky. I let out a long breath, watching the cloud of warm air float up into nothingness. And then I walked in.

In the woods, the snow on the ground was pliant, as if the bulk of it had been filtered by the treetops. It was a little past noon, but the forest was dim. As my eyes adjusted to the light, I realized how quiet it was. Each crunch of the snow seemed to crackle for too long, each flap of a bird's wings swishing too close. I dimmed the brightness on my phone until it was barely visible, keeping it huddled against my chest.

My entire body was pulsing. I could make out the jagged edges of a large rock and the brambly little spikes of a bush. But there were other shadows that I couldn't quite place, menacing ones that seemed to crop up every few feet.

Any one of them could be John Stack.

My body seemed to move on its own, one reluctant step after the other.

My mind was racing, the thoughts colliding into each other like sparks: I had to go back, I had nowhere to go back to, there was only Kevin and jail, and I was a coward, and she was right, Olivia was right.

I continued on, my body shivering from the seeping cold air. The GPS showed that I was only a quarter of a mile away. And then I heard something in the wind—a soft twinkle of bells. As I got closer, I could make out a large husk in the distance, peeking over the white mounds of snow. Whereas the trees were gray and tall, the husk was pale and squat.

It was a cabin.

I stumbled behind the nearest tree, crouching down beneath it. With my phone, I zoomed in on the cabin, snapping feverishly. The photos appeared grainy and blurry. I was too far away.

I trampled through the snow with light steps, my body slightly hunched down. There was no sound or smoke or light coming from the cabin. On a Monday, John Stack had to be at work.

Up close, it was a delicate little cabin, darker than the snow but lighter than the trees. The cabin was a washed-out gray. The snow appeared unbroken on the ground, no car tracks or footsteps nearby. A firepit sat in the open, dusted with snow. There was a small shack next to it. The place looked innocuous, like any other cabin up north, where a family would visit each summer.

When I finally saw a door, I stopped and crouched down behind a brambly bush. I was a hundred feet away. With my phone, I zoomed in closer. The image was still grainy and dark, but I could make out more details. I was at the backside of John Stack's cabin, staring at a single screen door that led to the interior. There was a coppery red curtain behind it. A wind chime hung nearby, tinkling gently in the breeze. A rake and a shovel leaned outside against the wall.

There was an object sitting several feet away from the backyard, closer to me.

It was a tree stump with an ax lodged in its top.

I felt the hairs on my neck stand up. I rose from the bush, trying to take clear pictures of the ax with my phone. My hands were shaking.

But I noticed the window at the other end of the cabin. I zoomed in on it, trying to keep the cell phone steady. The camera view was pitch-black, nothing visible from the inside.

Until a pale face flashed in the window.

I froze, my heart pounding in my ears.

The door suddenly screeched. Someone was coming out of the cabin.

I turned, trying to run. My feet couldn't seem to move fast enough. I heard heavy footsteps behind me, bashing through the snow. I wanted to turn around, but I kept moving. I couldn't risk slowing down.

And somehow I was slipping.

I smashed into the snow face-first. I was blinded by the white flakes, the cold streaming under my jacket. There was a weight on top of my back, massive and heavy. I felt a pair of hands locking my arms on the ground.

I screamed.

And everything went black.

42

My head was pounding when I woke up. I felt unbearably hot and sticky. I wasn't even wearing my jacket, but it was so, so hot.

I was lying on a hard surface. A radiator hummed behind me. The room was dark except for a crack of light that slipped through a window. I tried to move, but I felt my wrists chafe against rope. I tasted fabric in my mouth and started to gag, the saliva pooling. But the fabric stayed put.

I was tied up on the floor, trapped inside the cabin.

As my eyes adjusted to the dark, I saw the outline of a couch, a coffee table, and a kitchen island far behind it.

I wasn't alone. There was a shadow standing behind the island. A cloud of steam floated up in front of him, drifting into the dark. John Stack was sipping from a mug, watching me.

I felt the tears start to drip from my eyes, hard and fast.

John Stack took a long slurp from his mug. His face was hidden.

"Hello, Mary," he said. His voice was lighter than usual. He sounded pleasant and warm, as if the two of us were catching up. "You were quite the surprise."

My heart was thrashing in my chest, my body trembling on the ground. I closed my eyes, trying not to think about the ax and the rope and the blood and the screams that flashed in my brain like a carousel that wouldn't stop.

"What you did was a crime, you know—invading someone else's privacy," he said, as if he was a tad bit disappointed. "It's rude."

I clamped my eyes shut so tightly that I saw sparks.

I heard footsteps pad over the floor. They drew closer, stopping near my head. My eyes spasmed open, looking up into John Stack's glasses. I screamed, the sound getting lost in the fabric.

John Stack continued to sip from his mug, one hand in his pocket. He was observing me the way a child would watch a zoo animal. Once I realized it, I froze.

"We spoke at Olivia's funeral," he said. "In case you don't remember."

I did remember. John Stack had reached out and touched Olivia's casket, and he'd said a few words:

Just pitiful. None of it should have happened.

He wasn't talking about Olivia's death. He was talking about the fact that he had to kill her.

After a long sip of coffee, John exhaled.

"It's strange that you showed up. Stranger that you took photos of my property. But I won't ask—I think I already know."

He stalked back to the kitchen. I immediately squirmed, trying to free my arms, my legs—anything. The fear pulsed through me.

"I have nothing against you," he said, turning on a faucet. "Your father's an honest worker. And the Willands said that you're a Cornellian. That's impressive."

I was sweating as I struggled. The rope stayed stiff on my body.

"I can tell you were raised properly. You seem modest, polite. A good woman in the making." He paused and turned off the faucet. "Can't say the same for the rest of your kind. You probably know this—we live in the time of the modern-day whore."

I felt a shiver run through me.

"It's sad. Womanhood has no value anymore. Women just spread their legs these days. No respect for the sanctity of marriage or one's body. It's a disease, Mary, an epidemic. They keep infecting our society . . .

"Some take it further. They whore themselves out for money—on the streets, online, in the movies. It's bad enough. But then they act like they *deserve* respect. Like they have value."

John Stack opened a drawer. There was a clank as he dug around inside, his hands pushing aside its contents—maybe a whisk, a wooden spoon, a knife . . .

"I can't stand it, the entitlement. If you act like a whore, you should be treated like one. No need to pretend otherwise. There are consequences."

He slammed the drawer shut.

"For example: 'When lust hath conceived, it bringeth forth sin: and sin, when it is finished, bringeth forth death.'"

I could hear my heart pounding in my ears. In the silence, John Stack was rustling around the kitchen, grabbing things out of his cabinets, his fridge. My limbs were growing sore.

"I was the consequence," he said, his voice soft. I stopped moving. "My mother dropped out of high school. She was poor. But instead of working for her money, she whored herself out. Then I came along, and she died during childbirth. I can't say she didn't deserve it."

He was padding back. I stayed frozen, the tears dried on my face. John Stack sat down on the couch nearby. He nibbled at a piece of toast on his plate. He'd smeared it with strawberry jam.

"When the DeMaria girl reached out to me, I gave her many chances. I warned her about the consequences. But she didn't care— she did the deed by herself. She had no shame when I filmed her. As long as she got paid.

"And the whole time, I thought to myself, What about your son? What will he think when he grows up and the other boys start taunting him? His mother's a whore. No matter how hard he cleans or how good he acts, he is still filthy because of her." John Stack's voice grew quiet. "It is an unfair burden on a child. DeMaria didn't understand this."

DeMaria's bedroom, her Bible, her son flashed by in a blur. But I was stuck watching John Stack as he finished his toast, deep in thought. He wasn't even looking at me.

"Olivia was fortunate to never get pregnant. Lord knows the filth that ran in that family. Martin was a sleaze in college—mediocre, could only think with his cock—but he was lucky. Beautiful wife, beautiful girl. He should've kept a better eye on them. Heather was so lonely she was throwing herself at me . . . And what was I supposed to do?" he asked, getting off the couch. John Stack headed for the kitchen again.

I closed my eyes, trying to calm myself.

"There are consequences. Imagine my surprise when Olivia reached out all those years ago . . ."

My eyes fluttered open, watching as John Stack returned. I was tearing up. He bent down, squatting beside me. I could smell the coffee on his breath.

He looked into my eyes, and I saw nothing crazy in his. John Stack saw no disconnect between his words and his actions. There was no hypocrisy around his affair with Mrs. Willand or the films that he'd made. The man was convinced he was right.

"Olivia was in high school," he murmured gently. "She was reaching out to a stranger to make some cash. When she found out that stranger was her father's friend, she was shocked. Most people would have backed out, but Olivia was *persistent*.

"So I filmed her. She got her money, she kept her mouth shut. And I prayed for her to walk away. I gave her so many chances—she was the Willands' little girl, after all.

"But like most modern-day women, she saw nothing wrong with her actions. She reaped the rewards. She was getting famous on the Internet. I saw her following—thousands of people looked up to her. Online, she was a sweet, worldly girl next door.

"But that was a lie, Mary. That wasn't the kind of woman she was. And I grew angry. She needed to be vilified, not celebrated."

John Stack reached out and touched my cheek gently, as if mesmerized. I winced, the tears falling harder, my nose dripping with snot.

"The modern-day woman is a disease," he murmured. "She's infectious. She needs to be treated as such. And how do you handle a disease?" he asked, leaning in toward me, his breath hot on my face. "You prevent it from spreading."

His fingers kept stroking my cheek. I wanted to grow limp, my body devoid of sensation.

"Now that I think about it . . . you are a college girl, Mary. You're educated. Sexually liberated."

I was trembling. His lips were next to my ear.

"A real modern-day woman," he whispered.

I flinched back, but I bumped into the radiator. I screamed, my vision blurring in pain. The radiator burned through my sweater, singed my hands as if they were paper. I tried to squirm away, but I couldn't move. My body was burning.

I was on fire.

He yanked me back. I could hear the disapproving click of his tongue. The heat was still attached to me like glue, the sweat dripping down my back, my face. John Stack's hands remained on my body.

"Your kind always want respect," he said. "But you don't behave like you do."

I could hear his thoughts drift back to Olivia, DeMaria, and whoever else he'd brought here. He was wistful about them, how malleable and soft and pretty they all were, like cherubs. But none ever seemed to behave, did they.

His thumb stopped moving, the nail perched on my cheek.

Then he pierced it into me.

I teared up again, my scream stuck in my throat. I blinked and saw his eyes come into focus. There was a gleam in them, little pinpricks of light that focused on my cheek.

In his eyes, I saw myself cut apart in the snow. I saw him scooping me up in his arms and dumping me into the lake—piece by piece. I saw him disappearing into the trees.

John Stack didn't blink.

I shut my eyes . . .

There was a buzz. The vibration of a cell phone.

My eyes spasmed open. John Stack pulled out his phone from his pocket. He stared at it, frowning.

"Shit," he muttered. He rushed into the kitchen, murmuring into his cell phone.

I instantly rolled on my side, stiffening up, forcing all my energy into the left side of my body. I wriggled my left arm, trying to pry my wrist out of the rope. I only needed one free arm to have a chance. Just one.

There was a heavy thud from far away. Then the footsteps rushed back.

John Stack was already at my side, scooping me up from the floor. He swung me over his right shoulder as if I weighed nothing. I tried to scream, to thrash out of his grasp. But John Stack carried me farther into the cabin.

I could only move my head. As we entered a bedroom, I rammed the side of my head into his. Our skulls cracked together, my head ringing, sparks in my eyes. John Stack grunted, but he kept moving.

Dazed, I saw a small crucifix on a white wall, a silver Jesus figurine glittering in the dark. St. Rita's occasionally sold those items after Mass. Mom loved to pore over them while Dad and I waited for her. Back then, I thought that Mom hadn't noticed us, our impatience to leave and have breakfast. But now I realized that she'd chosen to ignore us.

We were suddenly descending into darkness—John Stack was carrying me down a set of stairs. The little white bedroom grew smaller, distant. I realized we were entering a hatch. The wooden floorboards groaned; the air grew cold and brisk. There was an odor of bleach around us, so potent that I grew light-headed. It was as if John Stack had doused the entire basement in it.

He paused suddenly. His free hand disappeared into the darkness. A light switched on, blinding me. The basement slowly came into focus:

Concrete walls and floor. Wooden tables along the perimeter. A rusty red toolbox on the floor. A rack of saws on one wall and a display of axes on the other. And a large white chest freezer that hummed behind the staircase.

The room was pristine.

John Stack walked around the worktable at the center of the room. Past his head, I saw a table saw on one end. It was heavy-duty equipment.

For a moment, time seemed to stand still. The saw was glinting under the light. I could see how clean and spotless it was, how sharp it looked. John Stack had bleached it along with the rest of the room.

The blood drained out of me. I was frozen over his shoulder.

He suddenly stopped in a corner. I heard the crunch of plastic behind me. Then he lowered me onto the ground. I was lying sideways on a cold pile of blue plastic tarps. They smelled new.

John Stack stayed crouched for a second. He touched my cheek with his thumb.

"This could have been avoided," he said softly. "But there are consequences."

John Stack lumbered away, past the table saw and the side tables and the tools on the walls. He stopped at the base of the stairs, flipping off the light switch.

The basement went dark, except for a little square of light from the bedroom above. The floorboards barely creaked under his weight. At the top of the stairs, he stopped. Slowly, he looked back in my direction.

Then he disappeared.

When he closed the hatch, I was alone in the dark.

43

I couldn't tell if my eyes were open or closed anymore—it was all the same darkness. I could only hear my heartbeat in my chest, the panic swelling in my ears.

I was trapped where John Stack had murdered Olivia and DeMaria. This was the place where he had brought them, then butchered them. I didn't know what else he had done to them in the meantime.

But he would do the same to me. Once John Stack came back downstairs, it was all over.

My breath rattled. Tears leaked out of my eyes. Snot dripped down my nose, soaking the fabric in my mouth. My body was shivering— whether because of the cold or the panic, I didn't know. I closed my eyes, sinking into the dread that rushed through me. I heaved over from my side onto my stomach. My face was smashed against the plastic tarp. My tied wrists were raised behind my back.

I tightened the muscles in both arms. I pictured myself tearing the rope apart like it was paper. And then I pried. I kept moving my arms, trying to work up enough force to loosen the rope from my wrists.

But in a few seconds, the rope started to cut into my skin, the flesh turning raw where the rope had bitten into it. I was breathing heavily, my arms already sore. I kept struggling until I realized that the rope hadn't budged at all.

I stayed there on the plastic tarp, my face buried in the blue plastic. And I felt the tears pool under my cheeks.

I was bound up and left to rot on a piece of plastic, like meat left to thaw.

I was pathetic.

My mind kept darting from one thought to another:

I was close to graduating. I was doing well. If I had ignored Carly and my own bitterness, I would still be in school.

But school didn't last forever. And I didn't know what the hell I was supposed to do afterward. I just wanted to be successful and thin, and I wanted other people to see it. I wanted my success to make them feel small.

And Madison and I—we were supposed to do that together. We were unloved, but we worked hard. And if we worked hard, then we would get what we deserved.

But there was always that unspoken rivalry between us. As much as we loved each other, one of us had to come out on top. The other one had to lose. We knew it was inevitable.

And Dad—he was at home, sitting on his armchair in front of the TV. He wasn't worried about me. I'd told him to fuck off—that was the last thing I said to him.

I couldn't even remember the last time we'd hugged. Dad and I had never been that kind of people. But I wished I could remember.

And then there was my penance. After confession, Father Greg told me to pray the rosary twice. I drove away from St. Rita's without thinking about it. I hadn't purged those sins—I'd only added more.

And now I was going to die. And I was going to find out that God was real and Mom was in heaven. And she would tell me that I'd wasted my whole life not believing. Now, since I hadn't believed, there was no way to help me.

I was going to hell and I was going to suffer. And Mom would glow like an angel, and she would kiss me on the cheek and fly away.

The end.

But first I had to die.

My stomach lurched. The vomit suddenly projected up from my stomach. It lingered in my throat, the burn of acid slipping into my mouth. But I swallowed it back down.

I couldn't hear anything from upstairs. No footsteps above the ceiling or the murmur of a voice. No sound except my heartbeat.

The darkness made the silence more deafening. The more I stared into it, the more I felt it closing in on me. It would crush me completely.

And I realized how stupid I seemed—inevitably bound to die, but still afraid of the dark.

I was still the same person that I'd been at age five and twelve and now twenty-two.

I buried my face deep into the blue plastic. It was comforting. I tried to cry, harder than I ever had in my life, but nothing happened. My eyes were swollen and dry. My body was exhausted. I was a husk lying prone in the plastic.

I felt calm, empty. I wondered if it was normal to feel this way. When other people knew they were going to die, maybe they also stopped caring.

And I wondered how Olivia and DeMaria had fared. Maybe they had felt this way. They had learned to accept it. Maybe this was my way of accepting it, too.

I closed my eyes.

I let my body go lax.

I stopped thinking.

Everything else seemed to grow in clarity in the darkness. I noticed the bumpy, cool texture of the plastic beneath my cheek. The scratchiness of the denim against my legs. The hardness of my ankles as they rubbed together.

My hair was loose around my face. My arms were propped up behind me. My wrists were bound by a rough piece of rope.

I couldn't stop thinking about the pain in my wrists. The small fibers cut into me, making my skin raw and sore.

I couldn't think of anything else.

My wrists hurt.

I wanted it to stop. Just one thing to leave me alone.

I started twisting my left wrist around, back and forth against the rope, while I planted the other wrist against my lower back. The rope bit into my skin. It stung so badly that I chewed on the fabric in my mouth, stifling a moan.

The pain was sharp, unbearable.

Then it dulled.

My wrists were warm from the friction, as one wrist moved and the other stayed put. I only had to focus on the task. It was my one moment of peace until John Stack arrived.

I kept twisting, even as my left arm grew sore. I yanked even harder against the rope, egging myself on.

I wanted the pain to stop.

I wanted my wrists to breathe.

I wanted some peace.

I kept twisting, harder and harder. For every moment that my wrists burned in the dark, I was triumphant. If I kept twisting hard enough, the friction would start a fire. I was delirious enough to believe it.

And suddenly—relief. I felt the heat simmer down, as subtle as a breeze.

But I felt it. Cold air was seeping in between my wrists. I was loosening the rope.

I started yanking even harder. The pain grew again. It seared into my bones. Sparks flashed before my eyes. I was slowly sawing the skin off my wrist. I gnawed even harder on the fabric, trying to keep the scream from bursting out.

I was going to pass out from the pain, I could feel it.

I would wake up and find John Stack standing over me.

And he would walk away unscathed, unbothered, unrepentant.

I grunted, enraged.

And I unclenched my left fist, and I squished my fingers together, trying to make my hand as small as possible.

And I wrenched up my arm, full force, my wrist burning on the rope like fire.

44

My hand was free.

  I lay frozen, stunned. My left hand plopped in front of me. It stung all over, pulsing with pain. My right arm was lying on top of my back, heavy like deadweight.

Slowly, my left fingers twitched. I shook off the rope from my right wrist, bringing it in front of me. My hands were throbbing as if electricity shot through them, but they were free.

Just like that, I felt like I'd suddenly come up for air. My body was trembling from the shock.

With one hand, I ripped out the fabric from my mouth. Drool slid down my chin. I put both of my arms in front of me, trying to push myself up. I crashed back down instead, my ankles still bound together.

I scrunched smaller on the plastic, fumbling in the dark for the rope on my ankles.

I was shaking.

At any second, the hatch to the basement would open up. Light would come pouring in. And then John Stack would stagger down, finding me in a mangled mess on the plastic. He would finish the job sooner than he thought.

My fingers were slick as they found the knot in the rope. I tried to pry the knot apart, but I winced from the sharp pain in my left wrist. It was raw—the rope had ripped the skin off.

I kept prying at the knot until my legs suddenly crashed down on the plastic. They were spread far apart from each other. My feet prickled with pain, as if needles were jabbing into them—but it was the blood circulating back to my feet. After a moment, I forced myself up to my knees. I felt wobbly, kneeling up in the dark.

I suddenly pictured Olivia tied down on the plastic, then DeMaria. They were bound and gagged like I was, tearful and broken. The thoughts seemed to puncture my brain, and I couldn't stop them.

John Stack had experience.

No one was supposed to make it out.

I was shaking.

I finally heaved myself up from my knees. The plastic crunched under my weight, and I held my breath, waiting for footsteps.

But when the plastic settled, there was nothing but silence.

I wobbled forward, both arms outstretched in front of me. I needed to reach the light switch. I didn't know what I planned to do afterward, only that I needed to see.

My fear of the dark was back. Each step forward was more intimidating than the last. I was afraid that John Stack was hiding in the basement after all, watching me. Or that if I took a step too far, someone else would come crawling out of the dark.

I gasped, my hand jerking back from something hard and cold. I reached out again and realized it was wood against my fingertips—I was touching the worktable at the center of the room. If I followed it, I would end up right next to the stairway.

My right fingers traced the edge of the table, and I started picking up speed. Time was running out. I followed the long edge of the table, one hand blindly outstretched, hoping to grasp something solid.

My hand seemed to extend on and on into nothingness.

Until I brushed cold wood. My fingers wrapped themselves around a rail—I was at the foot of the stairs. I stepped toward it, my shin bumping against a step.

My hands started grasping everywhere in front of me, patting both the rail and the icy burn of the wall.

My body was desperate now, rejecting the cold and the darkness. My fingers kept patting around, faster and farther, until they somehow crashed against the light switch. There was a click.

Suddenly the lights flickered on.

After the sparks faded from my eyes, I could see my hands under the orange glow.

They looked small and feeble. My left wrist was raw and bloodied—it looked like I'd sliced off wide slabs of the skin. As soon as I looked at it, the pain kicked in. My wrist stung, red-hot and searing.

But it shook me awake.

And I realized the light was dangerous. If John Stack saw a glow from downstairs, he would know something had happened.

I needed to move quickly.

The easiest plan was to run upstairs and bolt.

But something stopped me.

I turned around slowly, my skin prickling. No one was there, except for the tables around the room. There was a gleam from the table saw.

If I sprinted out of the basement, John Stack would know. He would catch me, and he'd be armed with a knife or a gun. If I tried to sneak out, I ran into a similar risk.

I couldn't leave unprepared.

I hurried over to the display of axes on the right side of the room. There were six of them hung up in a neat row, their blades resting atop a wooden shelf. I picked up the one that looked lightest—its blade was small and its handle was red. I yanked it up. My wrist shot with pain as I lugged it toward the stairs. The ax was light, but my arms were trembling.

I had one chance to sneak out. If anything went wrong, I would put up a fight.

But on the bottom step, I stopped.

There was a gap between each step of the staircase. At eye level, I could see a flash of blue and white from behind the stairs. It looked sturdy and mostly white, and the lid was a darker blue than the plastic tarps.

The chest freezer.

My head spun. The panic seemed to rise like a wave. I saw too many possibilities, too many ways to die. And I was glued in place, stuck between each and every path. They all seemed scary, uncertain. But only one of them was blue.

My pulse quickened. I slowly peered around the stairs, almost afraid to find someone looking back at me.

But I found only a chest freezer tucked away.

I already knew what I would find inside. I knew it instantly, the way you'd know a familiar face in a crowd. I knew what I was going to find, and yet . . .

I put down the ax. And I opened the blue lid. A blast of cold air rushed up to my face, like a cloud of smoke.

Then I retched.

I leaned away from the freezer, gagging on the cold air that exploded from inside. Lines of drool dripped from my mouth onto the cement floor. I wanted to spill out my guts and everything else inside of me. But nothing came out except saliva.

Before I knew it, I found myself peering into the freezer again. As if I hadn't believed it the first time. I immediately doubled over, my gag reflex now screaming.

It wasn't the shock that was awful. It wasn't the fact that everything had been so neatly arranged over the ice, like artifacts on display. It was the expressions on their faces, empty and dismal. Their eyes were closed as if they'd just fallen asleep, on a bed of grocery-store ice. Their hair was neatly tied in place.

I shut the lid. And I gagged again, my heart nearly climbing out of my throat.

I needed to go.

Then I heard the hatch unlock.

45

The hatch door swung open.

Instinctively, I crouched down, leaning against the chest freezer as if I could melt into it. I tried to keep my breathing as still as possible. And I clamped my eyes shut.

The stairs creaked as John Stack climbed down quietly. I felt the weight of each creak over my head.

Then he stopped. It sounded as if he were standing right above me. If I looked up, would I find him looking back at me?

I kept my eyes shut. There was silence as he stayed still. I could hear my heart pounding in my chest, so loud that John Stack could likely hear it as well.

The two of us seemed to stay like that forever, the seconds creeping by. I could feel my legs starting to buckle under my weight, the rest of my joints ready to crack open. Ready to break.

And if I moved, then it would be over.

John Stack suddenly exhaled, the air tumbling out of his lungs like a car off a cliff. In that one breath, I could hear the frustration and the panic—John Stack looking over at the empty pile of plastic tarps and rope and soiled fabric. The rest of the room would be empty, as if a young woman hadn't been bound there earlier.

And after that . . . then what?

There was a loud creak over my head. John Stack was trundling back upstairs, his footsteps disappearing into the cabin.

I jolted out of my stupor, the seconds thumping in my ears.

One second.

Up.

Two seconds.

Ax.

Three seconds.

Go.

I stood beside the freezer, the ax burning in my hands, my head spinning. I could see the white walls of the bedroom upstairs. John Stack hadn't closed the hatch.

I saw myself racing up there, making a break for a door. Before John Stack could do anything, I would be flying into the woods. Free.

But I couldn't move. I kept staring up at the hatch, frozen.

The blood was pounding in my ears.

I was afraid.

And I could hear Olivia's laugh ringing in my head, twinkly, like ice falling into a glass. Mary had the chance to escape, and she couldn't even do that. Mary, eternally weak and pathetic.

A door slammed.

I backed up against the wall just as John Stack pounded down the steps. He beelined for the corner of the room, where the blue plastic lay. His back was turned as he flicked on a white flashlight.

He was piecing together how I'd gotten out.

And then I saw it slung over his shoulder, black and austere—a hunting rifle.

"Damn bitch," he muttered. John Stack bent down, his flashlight scanning the tarps.

My body was panicking, moving on its own toward him.

I knew what I had to do.

I crept closer, daring not to breathe, my hands shaking, and then—

John Stack turned around, the rifle slipping off his shoulder.

46

My body was burning, the fear and rage exploding in my veins. I imagined John Stack putting a bullet in me. Knocking me down and killing me. Just one more set of body parts to chop and dump into a lake. Another trophy for the freezer. He and I both thought the same thing.

And that made me absolutely, uncontrollably angry.

I rushed toward him, a guttural screech coming out of my mouth. John Stack was fumbling with the rifle, but I was too close. His face scrunched up as I came at him, my muscles screaming as I swung the ax.

The blade sliced into the upper half of his right arm, almost as if I'd sliced into a piece of meat. The rifle clattered to the ground.

I flinched.

But John Stack was frozen, the two of us watching the blade sink into his arm.

Then he snapped. He screamed, his voice hoarse, his body jerking backward. I clung onto the ax, getting dragged along with him.

The blade suddenly dislodged—and I stumbled backward, slamming into a worktable. The ax was still in my hands, the blade dipped in blood.

John Stack clutched his right arm, his breathing heavy. For a second, I could only see the pale of his hand over his plaid shirt. Then the blood began to leak through his fingers. We were facing each other, separated by a few feet.

I imagined that there was nothing else outside of the basement. No snow or trees or homes or city streets. No families sitting snug in front of their TVs. No warm meals to eat.

Nothing except for me and John Stack.

He wasn't even looking at me. John Stack looked off to the space beside me, his breathing ragged and heavy, as if I wasn't worth the look.

Then he lunged.

I backed up into the worktable. His shadow flew at me, his free hand falling over mine, the two of us wrestling for the ax. His hand was larger, coarser. The ax was slipping out of my grip. His warm coffee breath was near my face.

I kicked him, slamming my foot somewhere against his leg. John Stack recoiled. I swung my knee into him, harder, driving it into what felt like soft flesh. He suddenly let go, buckling backward.

And for once I didn't think.

I swung.

There was a dribble of blood. Dark red, like wine, and reeking of metal. I saw John Stack's eyes grow wide in shock, the blood dripping out across his chest. He seemed to inch back a little, his body heaving.

I dropped the ax. Heard the crash screeching in my ears. John Stack suddenly collapsed onto his knees.

I found myself staring at the empty patch of space where he'd been—staring but not quite seeing. I felt the seconds creep by, slow and painful.

I realized he was looking up at me, his eyes wide. The blood flowed down his body. It was mesmerizing, the way it seemed to crawl away from him, inch by inch.

Something inside of me shuddered.

I backed away, then bolted up the stairs into the blinding light. Before I slammed the hatch shut, I saw John Stack still staring at me from below.

He wasn't moving.

47

I hobbled out of the bedroom, slamming the door shut. I instinctively reached for my phone in my jacket, but neither of them was on me. John Stack had taken them.

I needed a phone, and I needed help.

I needed to get out.

I stumbled down the hallway and passed a bathroom.

When I reached the kitchen, I leaned against the counter for support. I noticed the blood on my hands. It was dark red and sticky. And it wasn't mine.

Dazed, I looked around the kitchen. The walls were eggshell yellow. The room was clean.

But I couldn't see a phone in sight. No landline on the walls or on the counter.

John Stack had planned it that way. He made sure the cabin stayed remote.

I yanked open a drawer, the pain shooting up my wrist. But my cell phone wasn't inside. There were just cooking utensils.

My pulse was racing, the panic swelling inside me.

The only other cell phone here was John Stack's. He'd gotten a call earlier. The phone was likely still on him. And to get it, I needed to climb back downstairs to his dead body.

But I couldn't do it. I couldn't force myself to be near him.

At the other end of the kitchen, there was a glass sliding door. Outside, it was growing dark. Within the hour, it would be nightfall. The earth was white, and the snow was higher than I remembered. But it wasn't snowing. It seemed as if the storm had flown by. I wasn't sure how much time had passed.

I was stuck. If I wandered in the woods at night, I wouldn't make it far. I would either get lost or I would freeze to death.

I needed my cell phone.

I bit down the panic and searched through the kitchen. I riffled through the cabinets, the drawers, the trash bin, the microwave. I pushed aside cans of soup and bags of cereal, lifted out the spoons and forks and knives and utensils and dumped them all on the counters.

I was so desperate I even checked through the refrigerator. In the freezer, he had stockpiled bags of frozen vegetables and microwaveable meals. On the bottom shelf, John Stack had stored bundles of meat. They were wrapped in plastic. I could see little spots of red and pink and the veins that ran through them. I closed the freezer, my stomach churning.

Frantic, I moved to the living room. There was a closet next to the hallway. Inside, he'd hung up an orange hunting vest, a dark green camo jacket, and his deerskin jacket. I found nothing in each pocket. My jacket was nowhere to be seen.

I slammed the closet shut.

Something creaked.

I froze, turning back toward the hallway.

I strained to hear it again.

But I could only hear my own haggard breathing and the wind outside.

I was growing agitated, hysterical.

I tried the rest of the living room. I shoved aside the cushions on the couch. I threw out the books on the shelves, including a black leather Bible and a set of prayer books. I checked the TV cabinets, dumping out the contents: CD cases, cables, DVDs.

But my cell phone was gone.

John Stack had put it either in the bedroom or the basement. Or he'd gotten rid of it completely—dumping it in the lake or smashing it to pieces. Or burning it. He'd had a firepit outside.

I stayed still, looking at the mess on the living room floor.

The situation became clear:

I couldn't find help until it was warmer and there was light outside.

I was stuck in the cabin for the night.

I wanted to scream.

The cabin was a hell. And I was trapped inside of it while a body was rotting in the basement and blood was on my—

Something creaked.

I stayed still.

I didn't dare breathe.

And I waited in the silence.

I heard another creak.

Then another.

They were coming from the bedroom.

John Stack was alive.

I backed away, my head spinning. I was in the foyer between the kitchen and the living room, next to the front door.

I tried turning the knob. It didn't budge. I rattled the doorknob, twisting it back and forth. I even tried yanking the door back with all the weight of my body. But it didn't move.

John Stack had dead-bolted the door. No one got out without the key.

As far as I knew, he'd done the same thing to the glass doors in the kitchen.

I was trapped inside.

A scream was stuck in my throat, the rest of me pulsing with fear. I thought about battering the door with my fists until they bled.

I wasn't thinking straight.

I needed a weapon. I noticed a set of wooden hooks on the wall beside me. John Stack had hung up a red baseball cap, a scarf, a black rosary. But the last hook caught my eye. I recognized the flimsy plastic keychain of a rose, the red mostly worn off, and the two small keys attached to it.

They were my keys—one for the house, one for the car. John Stack had kept them.

I grabbed them, my hands shaking. The metal was cold, but they felt more real and solid than anything else around me. If I could get back to Mom's car, I would be all right.

The thought made me gleeful, delirious.

But I heard another creak.

And the clank of a door handle.

48

I bolted for the kitchen island—it was the only hiding spot I could see. There were utensils splayed on top of it from earlier. I grabbed a small carving knife in one hand and kept my keys in the other. Then I crouched low.

The seconds stretched by, the silence growing heavy.

I waited for the door to slam open or a voice to boom—I was bracing for it.

But there was only a faint click. It was so soft that I almost thought I hadn't heard it.

The bedroom door squeaked open.

John Stack moved down the hallway. His footsteps were light.

"Dammit, Mary," he crooned, his voice low. "You're really somethin'."

Heart in my mouth, I crept even farther around the island, my back to the sink. I squeezed the keys in my hand, making sure that none of them jangled. John Stack was quietly padding into the kitchen.

"You come to my property and ruin my house. Disgusting."

He sounded like he was speaking directly into my ear. He was on the other side of the island.

I shut my eyes, holding my breath. I braced myself for it, that moment when I would turn around and find John Stack looming over me . . .

The floor creaked.

He was padding away, creeping into the living room.

When I opened my eyes, I saw the snow through the sliding door.

"Bad company ruins good morals," he said from a distance. "You've made me swear today, Mary. That's a problem."

I had only seconds left.

"You're making me very angry," he said calmly. He slammed open the living room closet. His back was to me.

I hurried toward the sliding door. I lifted up the black bar on the lock, trying to slide the door left.

But the door wasn't moving. It was frozen.

I tugged at it even harder, my heart pounding so loud that I thought he could hear it.

"You've been impolite, Mary," he called.

I panicked, yanking on the sliding door with both hands. It suddenly jerked a few inches left, screeching in the process. The cold air blasted in. I could hear John Stack entering the kitchen. I kept yanking at the door, but it didn't budge any farther. The gap was only a few inches wide.

He was close now.

I shoved my way through the gap, the door clawing into my stomach.

I thought I felt a hand on my arm.

But I was stumbling away from the cabin, the snow burying my shins. I lifted one foot after the other. The snow was drenching my pants, soaking my legs. I was already freezing. But I kept stumbling forward anyway.

When I finally passed a line of trees, I looked back. I expected John Stack to be behind me, only a few feet away.

But he hadn't left the house. He was standing behind the patio door, his glasses somehow intact, the front of him covered in blood. He had the rifle in one hand. But he didn't chase after me. He just stood there.

Watching.

49

I wasn't putting enough distance between us.

Night was falling quickly. The dark was now dripping over everything—the snow, the trees, me.

I kept putting one foot in front of the other, crushing through the unbroken snow. My legs and my feet were drenched. While the rest of me froze in the cold air, the bottom half of me was growing numb. But I kept moving.

My life depended on putting one foot in front of the other.

The trees were never ending. I kept moving away from the cabin. The car keys were frozen in one hand, the knife glued to the other. If I could make it out of the woods, then I could make it to Mom's car. If I could make it to the car, then I could leave. If I could unlock the door, if the car wasn't buried, if I hadn't died of the cold . . . There were too many ifs.

I passed tree after tree. There were no birds in the sky or animals scurrying about. No clearing in sight. I felt like I wasn't moving at all, like a hamster trapped in its wheel.

When I felt tired, I would look back. And I would see that I was right, that I hadn't moved at all. No matter how long I seemed to walk, I could still see the cabin behind me. I couldn't seem to shake off the large gray husk that brooded between the trees. I could even see a black tank of a car that had been hidden behind the shed.

I was making no progress. And I was leaving a trail of prints behind me. I was making it easy for him. If the cold didn't kill me first, then he would.

My head was pounding, as if I'd just woken up all over again. The cold seemed to intensify the pain, making it sharper, realer. I could feel each pulse in my head, a wave of throbbing pain like ripples in water. The cold air cut into my hands and my face. I could feel the skin start to split open, bit by bit. The frostbite had already crept over my fingers.

The longer I hiked, the faster my head spun. My mind was racing through the cabin, flipping past each scene. I could see the kitchen and living room, all trashed. I could see the freezer in the basement and the pool of blood and the ax in the air. I could see John Stack behind the glass, watching me.

I twisted around.

Nothing.

I tried to pick up speed, but my legs were stiff. I couldn't feel them anymore.

I imagined myself moving on like this forever—lost and half-frozen. There were cars and houses and people out there, but I would never reach them. They were all so far.

Purgatory was a wood full of snow.

It was nearly as dark as the basement had been. But I could see the shadows of trees just ahead of me. And on the horizon, the dark seemed to lessen.

My body was growing heavy, as if weighed down by stones. I hobbled over to a tree and leaned against it. The fatigue and the cold crashed over me in one swift wave. I needed to close my eyes for a bit. It was fine, I was getting my strength back.

When my eyes were closed, everything was warm. Safe. Peaceful.

I was drifting away into the darkness, the warmth. If I gave in, I would no longer have to worry anymore. I was at peace.

Then a car engine roared. The noise rumbled through the air like thunder.

Through a gap in the trees, I saw a flash of yellow light.

And I knew what had happened, deep in the pit of my stomach.

John Stack was coming for me.

50

I felt the panic spreading through me, warm as booze. I started hobbling through the snow again, one foot in front of the other. I didn't care where I was going, so long as it was away from him.

I was so cold. My hands were in pain, the knife and car keys frozen into my skin.

I was stumbling in almost complete darkness. And my mind was panicking. Every shadow near me seemed to become something else: a witch, a wolf, a demon. If I tripped, they would reach out and pull me under . . .

I felt the corner of my upper lip start to split. The cold was ripping me open. I was dying, and if it came suddenly, I wouldn't know.

My body shook.

And I realized I could beat the cold—I had a knife, I could end it all. Save myself from the misery of John Stack.

I didn't want to die like Olivia had, her body hacked open and torn apart. Olivia would have fought back until the very end. If she'd had a choice like me, she would've chosen to die at her own hands rather than at John Stack's. That was the way she was.

That was why I'd loved her as much as I'd hated her.

My eyes stung.

It was our last summer together, aged twelve, before the start of junior high school. We spent it at Littlewood Park Reserve.

But that summer, Olivia grew friendly with the junior high boys who passed by on the bike trails. They mostly spoke to her and ignored me. It was the same with the girls we met. They fawned over Olivia.

And I saw what separated the two of us: I was big. Olivia was small. She was beautiful. And I was dull.

I could already sense the end of us in the air, like storm clouds in the distance.

I spent that summer being ditched. Olivia often ran into people she knew, and the group of them would speed up, talking to each other. I didn't know what else to do, so I just clung on from behind, like a leech. Other times, Olivia drifted off on her own while I struggled to follow.

She once disappeared for two hours. I wasn't even concerned— just bitter. She'd begun running, and I gave up after the first few seconds of pain. I could only walk. I continued on the trail by myself, crossing a little wooden bridge. A small stream ran several feet below. I rounded the corner and saw Olivia.

She was standing at the edge of a cliff.

It was the one spot that I could remember in the park reserve.

She peered over the ledge at the drop below, her sneakers barely teetering on the earth. I stood several yards away, sweaty and uncomfortable.

"What are you doing?" I asked lightly.

Olivia said nothing. She only turned around and looked at me, unsmiling.

We stared at each other for a moment.

"I already know what you're thinking," she said. "You'd push me, right?"

I shook my head.

But I had thought about it, in that brief second—Olivia tumbling down and smashing into the stream below, her body punctured by the rocks. It was wrong to think that way, but I couldn't help it.

Something was changing between us—an imbalance. Next to her light, I was lackluster. My clothes seemed frumpy, my personality flat. And her words grew sharp. I hid my stomach when she complained about her weight. I asked her why no boys liked me, and she said I came off as gay. And when I said I was ugly, she told me I was fine—it never stopped anyone.

She was drifting away. I got used to it—being ditched, ignored.

But it hurt the most when we talked. Her eyes lit up around other people. They fascinated her. She listened to them. But when it was the two of us, she barely seemed to look my way. My words flew right past her.

I was no longer worth the attention.

With junior high on the horizon, she would make a clean break.

I would be left behind.

But if she tumbled off the cliff, Olivia couldn't abandon me. I could beat her to it.

For once, she could feel my pain.

"Can we please go back to your house?" I whimpered finally. "I don't like this."

Olivia sighed and took one final look at the drop.

That was the end of us. During the rest of the summer, I waited for Olivia to call. But she never invited me out again. We stopped talking entirely. At the start of junior high, I found Madison. Olivia found her people. Our lives diverged.

And we grew up away from each other. We learned how to wear makeup, how to kiss, how to pretend. We piled on the clothes and grades and accolades. And we learned that our lives revolved around other people—beating them, using them, winning them over.

We learned to be women.

And if we wanted to get far, we had to be cruel.

We hadn't changed that much, had we, Olivia?

Our bodies had become taller, curvier. We knew how to hide things better.

But we were still the same hungry, angry girls.

My throat burned. But I didn't have it in me to cry.

I kept moving.

Slowly I began to see it—a plain white field beyond the trees. I was nearly at the edge of the woods. If I could make it to the road, flag down a car—

I stumbled faster, closing the distance. Only a few dozen yards and I would be free. The road was somewhere just beyond that. I only had to keep going, one foot after the other.

A growl tore through the air.

I flinched, ducking down. The growl was angry, violent. It echoed through the trees, coming from everywhere at once. And it was coming closer.

Behind me, I could see two pinpricks of light in the distance. They seemed to glow brighter as the growling continued. John Stack's car was revving now, the engine roaring as the tires smashed through the snow.

John Stack was catching up to me, following my footprints.

I could feel my stomach starting to curl in on itself. There were no bushes in sight, no brush to hide in. I staggered forward, my brain starting to melt.

Only a few more yards, and I was passing a gap between two large elm trees. And I was out in the clearing, a blanket of pure white snow stretching out before me. The wind was whipping in my face. I was so close. I just needed to reach the road.

But the faster I moved, the faster John Stack seemed to follow. The car revved again, the growl bursting into a deafening roar. I suddenly saw my shadow in the snow, illuminated by the car's yellow lights. I could feel flecks of snow flying into my back from the tires. John Stack was right behind me.

I saw the basement all over again: the body, the blood, the ax, the table saw—

I slipped, crashing into the snow. There was a muffled, weak scream. I realized it was me, I was screaming, burying myself in the snow, waiting to be crushed—

Nothing happened. I saw the car's yellow lights around me. But the roaring had stopped. I could only hear the engine idling. Then a car door slammed.

I stayed frozen on the ground, watching as a shadow crept up on my right. Then it stopped.

I finally peered up.

John Stack was standing over me.

The hunting rifle in his hands.

51

I would splatter like a deer, my blood speckling the snow.

John Stack squatted down, his rifle propped up on his knees. He wore his brown deerskin jacket and a pair of black leather gloves. There was gauze near his collarbone—he'd cleaned and dressed his wounds. That was why he hadn't chased after me right away.

John Stack was only a few inches away from my face, his eyes dark and flat behind his glasses.

We'd been in this exact same position back at the cabin—me on the ground, John Stack leering over me.

Except this time, I would splatter.

"You lack manners," he said softly.

I pictured DeMaria's forearm washing up at Liberty Lake, all gray and chewed up by the fish. I saw a man kneeling in the pool of his own blood, his body split open by the ax. The blood now stained my hands.

I felt the bile rising in my throat, threatening to spill out in one go.

"You shouldn't have done what you did, Mary," said John Stack.

I shuddered at my name. I couldn't stop shaking, either, the cold and the terror mixing in my veins.

Mary, Mary, Mary.

I'd been so close.

"I'm sorry," I whimpered. My voice was high-pitched and squeaky. I sounded like a little girl again.

John Stack said nothing—he didn't even blink. Instead he seemed to sigh, as if he, too, were tired.

The wind picked up, wailing gently in my ear. The longer I looked up, the more John Stack and his rifle seemed to glow. Together, they looked real and clear and final. They were the last things I'd see.

"I'm afraid you did this to yourself, Mary," said John Stack, his eyes flat. "I'll be praying for you."

I shuddered again.

Mary, Mary, Mary.

Here one second, gone the next.

John Stack started to rise.

Here.

The gun was moving—

Gone.

I lunged.

I jammed the carving knife into him.

There was a scream and—

A crack exploded in the air.

A puff of smoke.

A ringing in my ears.

It was a gunshot, I realized.

But the bullet was gone.

And John Stack fell into the snow, screaming. The knife had frozen into me—it was a part of me. I could feel when the knife made impact, cutting into his flesh the way a knife would tear into a piece of meat. Whereas I was frozen, he was tender.

I rammed the knife in deeper and deeper, stabbing his thigh. John Stack was shifting around, trying to aim the rifle at me.

But we were too close to each other—the barrel was propped on my shoulder. It was aimed past my head.

And I slashed at one of his hands with the car keys frozen in my palm. They split the skin across his fingers.

He was screaming.

I hauled myself farther up his body, slipping beneath the rifle—

He slammed it against my head, like a baseball bat.

My skull was ringing, the world shaking. Everything was in agony as he swung, back and forth. He was battering me, shattering my skull—

I slashed at his neck with the key. I broke through the skin, slicing deep marks into the flesh. John Stack screamed, one hand flying over it. The rifle fell onto my shoulder.

I moved without thinking.

My other hand rammed into his throat. I rammed in the knife as deep as it would go, feeling the skin and the veins and the meat give way. His flesh was soft, and the blood was starting to stream out, warm and dark red. John Stack dropped the rifle, his hands fluttering over mine, trying to bat me away.

But I rammed the knife even harder.

John Stack was gasping, unable to breathe, blood flowing from his lips, his neck. His glasses had fallen off his face.

I realized his hands were on my neck.

He was choking me.

The two of us faced each other, our hands at each other's throat. I could see the scars where John Stack had cut himself shaving. I could smell the coffee on his breath beneath all the blood. He looked different without his glasses. He had two dark circles under his eyes, like caverns. His eyelashes were long and curved up toward the sky.

I couldn't look away. His eyes were alive. They were fearful.

John Stack suddenly sputtered, coughing up more blood from

his mouth. His hands slackened off my throat. I wheezed, unable to move away.

He began to convulse. His eyes started to dim.

In one second, they seemed to dart back and forth.

In the next, they were unblinking. They were flat.

I didn't move.

I stayed put, looking at him.

Slowly, I pulled out the knife. John Stack's head crumpled back onto the snow. His unblinking eyes looked up to the sky.

I stood up.

I stared at the blood on the snow and the blood that drenched my hands. I stared at the rifle near my feet. I was shaking uncontrollably.

Behind me, John Stack's car was idling. The headlights were still on.

I took the rifle and climbed into the driver's seat. I shut off the headlights. Then I turned up the heat, and I waited in the dark.

52

I pulled up into the driveway just after eight. I could only remember flecks of the drive home—the endless snowdrifts that now flanked the highway after the snowstorm; the many lights that appeared on the road; and the police car that trailed behind me in the Sewers. I waited for the siren to blare, for an officer to pull me over and ask me what the hell I was doing in a dead man's car. But after a few blocks, the police car turned into a gas station.

I couldn't remember driving at all. My hands had moved on their own.

The Castles of Cordoba were dark, silent. At the house, I could see a dim orange glow from the living room window and the white lights of a TV in the background.

I turned off the ignition. I stared at my hands, how pale and cracked and lifeless they were, the blood caked all over them. The feeling had come back into them—pricks of pain that seemed to pulse in my palms and my fingers.

Then I finally climbed out of John Stack's car and closed the door. I entered the code to the garage and slipped inside the house.

The TV was airing an old rerun of *Who's the Boss?* Amid the quiet and the soft lights, I felt myself thawing in the living room.

Dad was sitting in the armchair, his body turned away from me. He had fallen asleep, his head bent sideways on top of a sofa cushion. I could see the bald spot at the back of his head—it was prominent now, about the size of my fist. I wondered if he knew how big it had gotten.

I reached out and tapped him on the shoulder. I kept tapping, softly, until Dad began to stir.

He groaned, rubbing his eyes.

"Hi, Dad," I said faintly.

"You decide to come home?"

"Yeah."

"Next time, you need to answer your phone when I call you," he said, his voice icy. "I've been worried since yesterday."

"Sorry."

Dad finally glanced over. He sucked in his breath. His face was blank as he took in the blood and the bruises and the pale, flaky patches that covered my body. Then the horror ran across his eyes.

"Good God, Mary."

I found myself nodding along, my eyes starting to burn.

After we wiped off most of the blood, Dad disinfected the cuts with an old bottle of rubbing alcohol. I drifted in and out of sleep as he worked—I was exhausted, but the rubbing alcohol jolted me awake, as if my wounds were being seared open.

Afterward, I chugged down three aspirin and a glass of water. I changed into an old set of pajamas and climbed into bed. I kept a warm washcloth over my hands—they were hardened, but they still pulsed with pain.

I was drowsy until I heard car keys jingling in the hallway. I sat up, shivering.

But it was only Dad. He came into the room and shut the window blinds. Then he tucked me in, pushing the bedcovers up to my chest and smoothing out the wrinkles.

Dad seemed to linger, one hand awkwardly propped on my shoulder. I waited for him to say something. He seemed to be waiting for me. But neither of us knew what to say.

Instead Dad reached out and held my hand. His hand was large and coarse, almost apelike. But he held mine delicately, as if he were afraid of breaking it. I gave his hand a squeeze and then Dad left.

I heard the garage door open and close from downstairs, then the sound of a car door slamming shut in the driveway and the whir of the ignition. I kept vigil through the night until I couldn't anymore.

When I woke up, it was already midday. I could hear Dad cooking lunch downstairs. Through the window blinds, the world looked white. I knew that this was what the winter weather watch had promised. The snow from two days ago had been a precursor.

When I looked outside, I saw the fat flakes of snow that now tumbled down over the cul-de-sac, the neighborhood, and the rest of Liberty Lake.

John Stack's tank had disappeared.

And Mom's car was sitting in the driveway.

Epilogue

John Stack's car was found the day after Thanksgiving. It was about ten days after I came home. Two bird-watchers had found it while they were exploring the area. They saw a large black vehicle sitting outside the woods, its windows rolled down and the car doors left open. Snow had covered the interior.

"We thought somebody's car might've broken down on Thanksgiving," said one of the bird-watchers. Her eyes were small, and they blinked rapidly. "They might've tried searching for help in the snow and, you *know* . . . But then we saw all these extra tire tracks and footprints around the car and it was pretty obvious."

"Foul play," said her husband, nodding. A pair of ski goggles were bulging on his forehead.

The police were called in, who ran the license plate of the car. They discovered that it belonged to a resident named Johnathan Stack. They searched the area nearby.

Less than half a mile away, at the western edge of the woods, the police discovered the body. It was unclear why the body and the car had ended up in two different locations. But Johnathan Stack had been "brutalized" with "absolute savagery," his body left out in the snow.

"Never in my sixteen years on the force have I seen such evil done to a body," said Police Chief Todd Johnson. His mustache quivered. "John was a respected member of the community and someone I called a friend. He didn't deserve to die like this."

Dad and I watched the press conference on TV. We'd recently put up the Christmas tree, and the lights glowed in the background. But it felt as if the air had been sucked out of the room.

Dad grew paler as the news continued, but he said nothing. He polished off his Bailey's hot chocolate and poured two glasses of whiskey right after. He handed me one.

Within the first week of December, there was a media blitz.

When the police searched the woods near John Stack's body, they found the cabin. The news showed pictures of it, a gray husk in the middle of nowhere. When I looked at the photos online, I could retrace my steps inside of it. I pored over each photo, looking for a sign that I had been there.

Dad and I kept the blinds closed. I rested inside and never left the house. As the days passed, I felt like there were eyes on me. And I was afraid of Kevin waiting outside.

I had no plans to talk to the police. I didn't want to go through the hassle of an investigation. I didn't want to be charged for John Stack's murder. And I knew that Kevin would take the chance to incriminate me. I had a past, and I had no desire to be scrutinized by the police, the media, the public.

I preferred my distance.

Before leaving for work, Dad would lock the doors. He'd even test the door handles afterward to make sure. Neither of us needed to discuss what was happening.

The police then reported that human remains had been discovered at the cabin site. They didn't comment any further, but online, people could already guess what was happening:

I'm calling it now: Olivia Willand and DeMaria Jackson in the cabin.

They found the missing girls!!

Damn, I can't believe this stupid city has its own serial killer lol

why is it always a dude with a cabin

A day later, the police confirmed that several of the remains belonged to Olivia Willand and DeMaria Jackson. Their immediate relatives had verified the body parts. But the report suggested that there had been more. And I wondered who else had been hidden in the ice.

Within a week, there were two separate memorial events held in the city.

The Willands held a second funeral Mass at St. Rita's. The group of attendees was small, and Dad and I weren't invited. Neither of the Willands made a statement. Someone had snapped a picture of them rushing into the church, their coats pulled around them, their faces haggard. They'd grown tired of it all.

Leticia Jackson held a vigil and a funeral service at her own church, the Holy Winners Congregation of God. The entire church seemed to show up. They held candles and glowing cell phones. A few people gave speeches about justice and death. Leticia Jackson didn't speak until the end.

The crowd watched as she slowly made her way to the front. She was made up, her cheeks dewy and soft. She wore a baby-blue scarf around her neck. But Mrs. Jackson had a far-off look in her eyes— she seemed to look past the crowds and the cameras and the lights. At the podium, she pulled out a neat stack of index cards.

Mrs. Jackson took a deep breath, her eyes focused on the words. Her face went slack. And she wept.

I read the news coverage of the memorial events, and I watched the livestream of DeMaria's vigil. I was glad I didn't go to either of them—I couldn't stomach the spectacle or the questions that now haunted them.

The Willands and Mrs. Jackson wanted answers—why had their daughters been murdered by Johnathan Stack? Why their girls, of all people?

The answers I had, they didn't want.

The only person who might have known was Mrs. Willand. She had seen Doberman Productions on Olivia's phone. She was close enough to John Stack to sense that something had happened between him and her daughter. She could have pieced things together.

But I doubted that she would do anything. She didn't want to know. Olivia had been found and put to rest. In her mind, Olivia had a legacy that would transcend her death. And Mrs. Willand had her own memories of her daughter. She wouldn't tarnish all that with the truth.

A few days later, someone posted the text of Mrs. Jackson's proposed speech. Among her family and the supporters that she thanked, Mrs. Jackson apologized to Dwayne Turner:

My anger blinded me. But now I see. You made your mistakes and I made mine. But you are not a murderer, Dwayne Turner.

The Internet seemed to be in an uproar after that, demanding that he be released from prison. When I signed an online petition for him, there were already over forty-six thousand signatures.

In mid-January, Dwayne was released from the metropolitan corrections facility. News cameras followed him as he entered a tan car. Dwayne wore a dark suit, and he kept his eyes focused on the ground. Jayden was in the driver's seat, looking grimly at the cameras all around them. Before driving away, Jayden rolled down his window and flipped the middle finger.

After that, Dwayne seemed to disappear. His social media accounts were set to private. He'd unfriended me or blocked me completely.

I owed him an apology. I obsessed over it, thinking about the different things I needed to say, the different ways that I could say them. I had accused an innocent man of murder, and it had been my mistake. I was sorry.

But an apology wouldn't cut it—I had effectively ruined Dwayne's life. His name would be forever linked to the murders in Liberty Lake. His personal histories with Olivia and DeMaria—no matter how messy they were—had now been aired out for the whole world to see. He'd received death threats over the murders. Now he had an online conspiracy theory against him—people were convinced that he'd framed Johnathan Stack for the killings.

Dwayne needed a solution to all of this, not an apology. I could only give him the latter.

And distance.

In late January, the Liberty Lake Police Department held another press conference. Chief Todd Johnson was not in attendance. A female officer spoke instead and shared a few developments on the case.

City records showed that the cabin had been registered in 1997 by Johnathan Stack. Police were combing through his home and his additional properties in Liberty Lake. They were also investigating mutual connections between the girls and John Stack.

It meant that the police planned to reinterview the Willands. John Stack had been their family friend. But Olivia's mother was in a hard position—she'd had an affair with her daughter's killer. She had other information that she hadn't shared with law enforcement.

And Mrs. Willand would keep her silence. I knew it instinctively.

The police officer mentioned that John Stack had no criminal record in Liberty Lake. However, police from New Haven County, Connecticut, had dredged up a series of old police complaints from 1982 and 1983 for a college student named "Jonathan B. Stack." The student had been accused of assaulting two different women late at night: one at a bar and the other at a party. For some undisclosed reason, both victims had dropped the charges. Police suspected that after college, John Stack had tweaked his name and moved away from New England.

My throat was dry as I watched the press conference, my temple throbbing. I remembered the rifle that had battered into my head, the hands that had wrapped around my throat. I could smell the coffee on his breath.

And I could see the flatness in his eyes. The blood that leaked out of him. The way his body had split like butter.

"Finally, our investigation has found evidence of a struggle that took place the night of Johnathan Stack's death," said the officer. She seemed to stare right at me. "We ask the public to reach out to us with any tips or information into the matter. We believe that there is more to the story than meets the eye."

By the end of January, Dad was called in for a police interview. They were interested in his construction work for John Stack. When he came home afterward, he beelined for his bedroom, a beer in each hand.

I waited for my turn.

I waited for the police to find me, to tell me that my DNA had shown up on a dead man and his property.

I felt like I was holding my breath, waiting for the end.

February passed, then March. I spent my days doing chores, reading, and going out for walks in the bitter cold. I napped often—long and unrefreshing naps that covered most of the day. When that grew dull, I looked at classes at the state schools. I looked at jobs in town. I liked to imagine that I was going somewhere, anywhere.

One day, Dad brought me a new cell phone. He quietly ended our plan with our old carrier and said that my previous phone had been stolen. The new one had a nice camera, but that was it. I had no one to call or text. I had no social media to use. I had nothing to do.

Then spring seemed to come in the first week of April. The temperature suddenly entered the high forties—sweltering weather for the state. It was a false spring. The sky was gray, cloudy, but in the distance, you could see the faint trace of light.

After breakfast, I took the new phone and went for a drive to the lake. On the car ride over, I rolled down the windows, letting the wind blast in my face. I parked a few blocks away from Dwayne's old apartment and made my way over to the beach.

I crossed the sandbanks, icy and dusted with snow. Where the sand ended, the lake began—its surface was dark and glassy, stretching on into the horizon.

There was a handful of people around the lake, enjoying the warmer weather. An elderly couple clutched onto each other, giggling as they navigated the ice.

I snapped a few pictures of the lake. I tried to capture the horizon between the sky and the lake, as if two different worlds were melting into each other. But despite the nice camera, the photos looked cheap. They were nothing at all like real life.

I felt eyes on me.

On the other end of the beachfront, there was a blond man standing at the edge of the sand. He turned away as soon as I looked over. There was something familiar about the way he stood, his back tall, hands in the pockets of his military jacket.

I realized I was looking at Kevin Obermueller.

I felt the rage boiling in my veins, white-hot. Kevin looked quaint. He was a free man, enjoying a lovely lakeside view.

He was the same man who had scoffed at a woman's death. He'd leaked a private photo of his missing girlfriend. He'd avoided the consequences as other men were beaten or thrown into jail for things that he had also done.

Out of the mess of the past few months, Kevin had made it through unscathed. He deserved worse.

Without knowing why, I tramped across the beach toward him. The closer I got, the angrier I became. Whatever happened next was his own fault. He'd earned it.

I was a few feet away, nearly shaking with rage—

Kevin turned. He was looking right through me, a blank expression on his face. He didn't so much as blink. As I got closer, Kevin started walking past me. He seemed to glide over the ice toward the street. Up close, Kevin was pallid. He was thinner than I remembered, and his face was gaunt.

Before I knew it, Kevin was gone.

And my anger went with him.

I was just tired. That was all the feeling I could muster for Kevin Obermueller. The people he'd hurt were either dead or gone. I didn't want to be the only one left.

Maybe Kevin was always meant to be unscathed. There were other people like him. Nothing would happen to any of them. Maybe that was how the world worked.

And maybe that was why some people prayed so ardently. They hoped that God would take care of the things that they couldn't. They hoped that there was justice and righteousness out there. People prayed because they were tired.

I couldn't blame them.

After a moment, I scrolled through the contacts on my phone. It was one of the only things I had saved on my laptop from the previous one. I found Kevin's number and blocked it for the both of us.

I had sixty-three numbers left. My new phone had zero calls, zero texts.

I watched as a pair of geese flew overhead.

Then I drafted a message. My fingers moved so quickly that the words were scrambled, misspelled. The text message was one paragraph, then two, then three. I grew frustrated over the words—none of them were right.

After a while, I deleted the walls of text. I drafted a new one. I sent one text to Dwayne, one to Madison, one to Charice, and one to Jayden. Each text carried the same message.

I didn't expect to get a reply back. They owed me nothing. I only wanted a clean slate and a clean conscience. I wouldn't get that, but I liked the illusion that I could.

I put the phone back in my jacket pocket and slipped on my gloves. I wrapped my arms around myself as the wind picked up.

More clouds were setting in, blocking out the slivers of light. Several of the beachgoers had left.

But despite the weather, the lake was beautiful, the water dark and unending, the trees standing guard around it. The lake had outlived the first people who'd settled here and then the people after that. It would outlive everyone.

My phone vibrated in my jacket pocket, but I left it alone. I closed my eyes, breathing in the brisk air.

And I saw everything.

I saw myself getting arrested. I saw myself at school, working in a library. I saw myself in a cubicle, typing on a computer. I saw myself wandering the streets of Paris and Tokyo, a backpack across my shoulders. I saw myself in bed, neither asleep nor awake. I saw myself with a nice enough boy from town, the two of us settling down with a child of our own. I saw a million different things that could happen in a million different ways.

But for now, I was at the lake.

Acknowledgments

Writing is hard, but publishing is harder. I never would have had this book in my hands without the efforts of so many lovely people.

First thanks go to my agent, Eve Attermann, for her sharp insight, patience, and endless support. She saw something in this book, even when it was in its early, brambly mess. Thank you for believing in me! I also want to acknowledge the kind efforts of Sam Birmingham, Haley Heidemann, and everyone at William Morris Endeavor's literary department.

Equally big thanks go to my editor, Emily Krump. She's been lovely to work with, the perfect mix of cheerleader and drill sergeant. Thank you for encouraging me, putting up with my bouts of writerly neuroticism, and always challenging me to dig deeper, go farther. I couldn't have asked for a better editor. From one Minnesotan to another, thank you!

Much gratitude goes to my publisher, Liate Stehlik, and associate publisher, Jennifer Hart, for giving this book a chance. Additional thanks go to the lovely team at William Morrow: Julia Elliott, Kaitie

Leary, Brittani Hilles, Stephanie Vallejo, and Greg Villepique. I'd also like to thank Elsie Lyons for designing a beautifully grim cover.

Additional thanks go to Rawles Lumumba at Lucidity Editorial for her sharp, valuable insight into the world and its characters.

In my personal life, I'd like to thank Ana Rossi and Amelia Somlath, for the sheer chaos and laughter. You two are the best buds I could have asked for.

To my COVID season writing group, who keeps me accountable (sometimes) but mostly provides a lot of fun: Rtusha Kulkarni, Eden Palmer, and Annie Thompson. Big thanks to Julia Marshall for also reading the manuscript and providing feedback early on.

To Katie Gabrick, a dear friend who just "gets" it.

To Jim Cihlar, a friend who tried to help me out when I was down. I still remember.

Of course, I will always thank my mom and dad, Nhung Ho and Thinh Dang. Most Vietnamese parents would be uncomfortable if their kid wanted to write about suburban murder. But not mine! My dad is an endless well of jokes and optimism. My mom is a terrific cook, and she's equal parts sweet and snark. I get my terrible sense of humor from the both of them.

I could write an entire page on my sister Teresa, but I'll keep it short. She's an inspiration and my best friend. Thank you for always being there.

And finally, to Andrea Blatt. Thank you for pulling me out of the slush pile. You started it all.

About the author

About the book

Insights,
Interviews
& More . . .

Meet Catherine Dang

Joseph Dammel

CATHERINE DANG is a former legal assistant based in Minneapolis, Minnesota. She is a graduate of the University of Minnesota. This is her first novel. ◁

Behind the Book

When I was a kid, I used to write stories in the back of my parents' liquor store— sometimes there was nothing else to do after I'd finished my homework. Then on weekends at home, I'd watch the scariest things that I could find on local TV: *America's Most Wanted, 20/20, Law & Order: SVU*. Looking back, I'm not surprised that I fell in love with the suspense and thriller genres. I loved the grim ambience and that sense of mounting dread. There was something addictive about these stories, and the way they played with our hopes for a good ending and the bad guy to be put away. Fresh out of college, I wanted to write one of my own. I was drawn to the idea of a woman's disappearance in a place like my hometown. The real city is sprawling, where a single intersection can separate a middle-class suburb from a working-class neighborhood. People tend to rationalize that crimes only happen in certain areas, but I wanted to dash that assumption. I wanted to create a kind of fear that bled throughout a city, through every sidewalk and street. The familiar fear that no woman is safe. My protagonist, "Ivy League Mary," is supposed to be an underdog: an unpopular, self-conscious young woman who made it big and got into Cornell. She's changed her appearance and her life there. She's worked hard. She's not supposed to fail. But then . . . she does. When she's kicked out of Cornell, the narrative around her crumbles. She's no longer the successful underdog. Mary's ▶

3

Behind the Book *(continued)*

identity seems to transform overnight, from star student to pariah.
When she arrives back home, she discovers that a former best
friend, Olivia Willand, has gone missing. Since Mary has a long-held
grudge toward Olivia, her growing interest in the case is not driven
by good intentions. But the more she digs, the more ruthless and
Machiavellian she becomes. For Mary, there's a creeping fear that
she was never the person she thought she was. I was taught to admire
people like "Ivy League Mary"—those who kept their head down,
worked hard, and remained sweet. They never rocked the boat,
and they never showed anger. But I couldn't relate to them at all—
they seemed like such saints. As an adult, though, I learned that
people were generally good at faking it. Coworkers, classmates,
even teachers knew how to put on a certain face in public. It was
necessary to keep their jobs, their status. I learned to do the same,
but I could never shake off the sickly feeling that I was lying.
Just once, I wanted one of those saintly women to fall out of line.
I wanted to see how much cynicism and rage was buried under
that mask. And I suppose that's where Mary came from.

Q&A with Catherine Dang on Writing

First published on advicetowriters.com on July 13, 2021

Q: How did you become a writer?
A: My parents owned a liquor store when I was a kid, and occasionally my sister and I were stuck there. We did our homework and read books in the back room, but I'd get bored. That was when I started writing short stories in a notebook. They were often about shows that I wished I was watching instead.

I was a pragmatic kid. Writing never seemed like a "real" career. I figured I was supposed to do something more realistic, like law. Since my family never had much money, I wanted to change that in my own future.

I botched those plans in college, though. I told myself that I was only taking fiction and screenwriting classes for "fun." But I think a part of me just wanted to test the waters. I wanted to see how my writing stacked up to my peers. I wanted to see if I could commit to writing whole projects. I started with poems, then short stories. Then I finished an entire two-hour screenplay for my thesis. And I finally understood that I was a decent writer.

I knew I was going to regret it if I didn't take writing seriously. I wanted to give myself at least one chance to fail. So right after graduation, I started to work on the manuscript that would become *Nice Girls*. I also entered the workforce. I got a day job, I hated the day job, and I left the day job after ten months. But that experience changed my life. It made me desperate enough to finish *Nice Girls*. It kept me disciplined enough to edit the manuscript. And I began querying agents right after. Things began to slowly take off from there.

Q: Name your writing influences (writers, books, teachers, etc.).
A: I was a *Reading Rainbow* kid. LeVar Burton told stories in such a captivating way—he made me want to read everything. I also watched a lot of anime and true crime during my early childhood, then moved on to movies as a teenager. I think all those experiences taught me the mechanics of a good story.

Judy Blume and Sylvia Plath are probably the two biggest influences in my own fiction writing. Their novels felt so honest and confessional, and I happened to read them at the right times in my life. They resonated with me deeply. Blume gave me comfort, and Plath seemed to understand me. I've always wanted my own writing to have that ▶

Q&A with Catherine Dang on Writing (*continued*)

same undercurrent of honest emotion. It doesn't matter how light or brutal the feeling—it just has to feel real.

I also admire distinct prose. I love Sally Rooney, Ocean Vuong, and Haruki Murakami. Their prose is sparse and delves into the mundane (Murakami loves his food descriptions!), but they know how to pack an emotional punch. On the other hand, I've also been struck by Cormac McCarthy's and Ta-Nehisi Coates's prose. I read *The Road* and *Between the World and Me* in two entirely different summers. But the writing had the same kind of magic: just beautiful, elegant, winding prose about some of the most painful, brutal things. Their writing lingers.

I'm someone who gets influenced by a little of everything—music, articles, the way people talk. I even get impressed by memes.

Q: When and where do you write?
A: I usually write in the mornings at home. But when I'm in a slump, I like to go to a coffee shop and pretend that I'm as productive as the people around me.

Q: What are you working on now?
A: I'm working on my next novel. I told myself it would be lighter. So far, it's . . . *bloodier.*

Q: Have you ever suffered from writer's block?
A: It hits me fairly often. For me, writer's block can happen for a multitude of reasons: I'm bored, I'm not inspired, something in the book feels "off." If I'm feeling really stubborn, I'll keep chipping away at the writing. Sometimes a good run or exercise helps get rid of the block. Other times I get out of my funk by consuming other stories, whether it's reading a book or watching a movie. I like experiencing someone else's creation—it motivates me to get back into my own work. And honestly, some of my best writing comes after the writer's block.

Q: What's the best writing advice you've ever received?
A: The Nike ad: "Yesterday you said tomorrow."

Q: What's your advice to new writers?
A: Talent is good; resolve is better. 〜